KU-274-845

Picking up
the Pieces

ALSO BY AMANDA PROWSE

Novels

Novellas

The Game
Something Quite Beautiful
A Christmas Wish
Ten Pound Ticket
Imogen's Baby
Miss Potterton's Birthday Tea
Mr Portobello's Morning Paper
I Wish . . .

Memoirs

The Boy Between: A Mother and Son's Journey From a World Gone Grey
(with Josiah Hartley)
Women Like Us

Picking up the Pieces

AMANDA PROWSE

LAKE UNION
PUBLISHING

This is a work of fiction. Names, characters, organizations, places, events, and incidents are either products of the author's imagination or are used fictitiously. Any resemblance to actual persons, living or dead, or actual events is purely coincidental.

Text copyright © 2023 by Amanda Prowse
All rights reserved.

No part of this book may be reproduced, or stored in a retrieval system, or transmitted in any form or by any means, electronic, mechanical, photocopying, recording, or otherwise, without express written permission of the publisher.

Published by Lake Union Publishing, Seattle

www.apub.com

Amazon, the Amazon logo, and Lake Union Publishing are trademarks of Amazon.com, Inc., or its affiliates.

ISBN-13: 9781542024815
ISBN-10: 1542024811

Cover design by Emma Rogers

Printed in the United States of America

This book is dedicated to the memory of Robert Edward Bauer – 'Bob', you made us laugh with so many fantastic stories from your wonderful life. You will be very much missed.

PROLOGUE

Leonora's daddy once told her that no matter what fell from an aeroplane – a rock, an old apple, a car or a person – it would fall at the same speed. Wasn't that amazing? No matter how much something weighed or how much space it took up, when tumbling down to earth everything was the same. She wasn't sure she believed him. But then, they definitely all ended up the same way: squished.

She woke to the sound of a car door closing, the deep thrum of an engine and the crackle of stones under tyres as the vehicle travelled along the unfinished driveway, which threw up fire-coloured dust under even the steadiest of wheels.

Leonora's brain somersaulted with an unfounded yet familiar fear that she might have been left alone; her heart raced and her breath came in stuttered bursts. It was a hot, sticky night, much like any other, and she wondered where her parents had gone. The beach? The harbour? A bar? She strained to listen as the car rattled off into the distance, changing gear on the bend. She could hear the subtle pull of the engine and pictured it struggling up the hill. All cars struggled up that hill where the track grew narrow and rocks sometimes skittered down into the forest. She imagined them tumbling down and down before coming to rest on the valley floor – did they all fall at the same speed too? Her breath was now shallow, the pain in her chest real. 'La Fosca' – the grand, listing villa perched halfway up a mountain that she called home – was a big old place with creeping shadows, whining doors and creaky floorboards. The thought of being here without a grown-up was enough to make her tremble and fire a bolt of white-hot terror through her core. Images of the robbers and ne'er-do-wells that Luna liked to read to her about sprang unbidden into her mind.

Her fringe stuck to her forehead as she sat up in the middle of the vast double bed, where her small body left an anxious shadow on the once pristine white linen sheets. Blinking, she avoided the gloomy corners of the wide room and looked towards the window where plumes of the red dust cloud rumbled up towards the house. Pulling back the gossamer-like mosquito netting surrounding the groaning mahogany four-poster, she let her skinny legs dangle over the side of the deep feather mattress and looked at the floor. It seemed like quite a distance for a six-year-old who was, as her mother liked to remind her, 'no more than skin and bone'.

She would say as she drew on her cigarette, 'But I reckon you're stronger than you look and smarter than anyone will ever give you credit for, what with you being so very pretty.' The way she said it and her intense, lingering stare meant Leonora wasn't sure if it was a compliment or an insult, so she said nothing by way of response. This level of confusion was quite standard when being addressed by her mother, as was her own hesitant smile, which to the best of her knowledge was appropriate for either scenario.

She dropped to the tiled floor, landing with a flat-arched splat that sent a shooting pain up her ankles. Her cotton nightdress rucked around her middle and she pulled until it hung down, taking comfort from the way it softly tickled the back of her narrow calves. Bending low, she rubbed the dirty soles of her feet to ease the pain of the hard landing and in defiance of her parents' rules, tiptoed quietly and cautiously out of the bedroom. With the sound of her blood rushing in her ears and a thin film of sweat across her top lip and brow, she crept along the wide corridor where grand paintings of a family that wasn't hers stared down at her in their fancy ruffled shirts and red dresses, flat-coated dogs lying at their feet. She felt their eyes, captured in oil, follow her progress but paid no heed to their stares. The shutters were all closed although the windows behind them had been left open in the hope that a whiff of breeze might blow through.

Approaching the central courtyard, she pulled back the long muslin curtain that dragged on the tiled floor, the hem covered with a fringe of dust bunnies and cobwebs. It was a little dark and she had to squint to fully see as she peered through the intricately carved shutter panels that sat inside the wrought-iron scroll work of the doors, beyond which wide steps led to a tiled square with an Arabic fountain. She took in the big, soft, embroidered cushions that were dotted around. Brass lanterns with candles were scattered around the square; some had burned down, while others smouldered ominously and her heart flickered with concern; she might have been only six, but she hated the way the candles were left unattended.

Low rattan steamer chairs were strewn around the layered rugs and people seemed to be sleeping on them. The sight of grown-ups brought with it a degree of relief: she was not alone. One of the nudey girls who had arrived days ago with a friend of her father's was curled up in a little ball, like a dormouse in a teacup, which Leonora had a picture of in her reading book. Her mummy she recognised by the teal and gold caftan that was wrapped around her torso like a sheet as she lay with one arm over her face. Her head was tipped back and her legs were crossed at the ankle. Her gold shoes were on the floor. She was asleep.

Leonora felt her pulse settle. *They haven't left me alone . . . they have not left me alone . . .* It had been someone else leaving in a car. Her daddy, she could now see, was not far away, face down on the tiles with his arms by his sides and his face pushed into an orange silk cushion. By his head was an empty bottle and a pile of sick. She was glad the door was closed, knowing that if she got any closer, the smell of it might make her sick too.

It wasn't the first time she had stumbled across a scene like this – not that the fact made her tummy flip any less – and the relief at finding her parents home was short-lived. They might have been there bodily, but to see them sleeping so soundly, unaware and snoring, did little to make her feel any less afraid of what might be lurking in the dark.

'*Niña?*'

Startled, she held her breath, turning slowly at the sound of the male voice. Her chest fell and her muscles softened a little when she recognised the man who visited the house once a month. Señor Agostí. She could make out his shape in the half-light. He was a fat man with a small head and thin legs. He reminded her of an Easter egg, not that she had shared this with anyone.

'Why are you wandering around in the dead of night?' She liked the way his Catalan accent softened the English words.

'I came to find Mummy and Daddy . . .' She spoke quietly, pointing towards the closed shutter doors behind which they slept, aware that she was breaking the 'no roaming' rules. Her voice was small and her heart beat wildly in her chest. It felt like a little bird fluttering, trying to get out. She didn't want to be here, alone with the man in the corridor in the middle of the night. Again, she looked towards the courtyard, willing her parents to wake up; she might have called out were she not equally reluctant to invoke their wrath at discovering her up and wandering.

'It's very late. You should be sleeping.' He chuckled, as if this might have escaped her attention. 'Come.' He reached out, but instead of taking his hand, Leonora placed her thumbnail on her lip and looked down.

4

'Don't be afraid. I am your father's patron!' He beamed.

Patron . . . Mummy had explained that it was almost their duty to entertain other artists and creatives as this house was a gift from Daddy's patron for as long as he needed it, so it was almost an unwritten rule to open their doors to people like them. *People like them* . . . Leonora wasn't sure what a patron was, but she guessed that creatives were people who liked to sleep a lot on their holidays and who hung out with women who didn't mind showing their bottoms. This was an odd thought, as a holiday for her meant baking cakes in her Nana Dilly's kitchen in Yorkshire where she had seen snow, and where her nana would run her a hot bath to draw the chill from her bones when they returned from a long hike across the moors. Not that she had been back to England for a while now. Nana Dilly, her father's mother, was very different to Granny Magda. Nana Dilly wore jumpers and slippers and was soft like marshmallows, whereas Granny Magda looked like celery. Pale and thin and slightly bowed.

Again the man gestured, and she placed her small hand inside his, looking back over her shoulder, half hoping someone might appear. Someone like Luna who right now would be at home in the town with her own family, or her parents and their guests who were all sleeping. The man put his fingers to his lips and his eyes sparkled.

'It'll be our little secret. I shan't tell a soul I have found you up and about at this ungodly hour.' He nodded. '*Si?*'

'*Si.*' She nodded back, although she hadn't the first clue what she was agreeing to. They walked slowly hand in hand back along the corridor and into the wide, dark bedroom. Shaking her hand free of his, Leonora ran and jumped up on to the high four-poster, diving through a gap in the mosquito net. She pulled the top sheet up over her skinny body and settled back on to the soft pillows.

'A big room for such a little girl.' He let his eyes rove the walls.

'Uh-huh.' She agreed, wanting him to go now.

'It used to be my grandmother Elvera's room. She was a fierce old woman who I loved with my whole heart.'

Leonora stared at the man, not wanting to think about an old lady in this room. It made it creepy, but at the same time warmed him to her. She loved her Nana Dilly very much and wondered if his gran was similar.

'There's no need to be afraid of me or of this big old house. I grew up here. It's a kind house. A safe house.'

'It makes . . .' Her words came from lips still sticky with nerves as she whispered, 'It makes noises.'

'It does!' He clapped. 'It's saying hello! Welcoming you into each room! It likes having you and your mamá and papá here!'

His joviality was infectious, and she felt her breathing settle as her gut uncoiled.

'It's time for sleep for you and for me too.' He touched his chest. 'It's late.'

It seemed to her that the people who stayed here were very good at sleeping, and she was quite unable to understand the men who lounged by the side of the pool, slumbering, snoring even, though the sun was high in the sky. Friends of her father's, usually, who seemed to think a holiday meant sleep. There were lots of them who came and went. Men in linen suits and battered espadrilles, who sported narrow moustaches and paint-smeared denim tunics, and who were usually passing through. They laughed loudly, drank wine from the bottle and left quietly after staying for a month or so. Sometimes they brought girls with them, ladies who wore lots of lipstick and one or two who swam in the nudey and didn't seem to care that everyone could see their bottom. Her daddy had taken some of these women into his studio, a place she was absolutely forbidden to enter, and the fact that these random strangers got to go inside when she didn't smarted a little. Actually, no, it smarted a lot.

6

Señor Agostí smiled at her as he walked slowly to the heavy door; the soft tread of his shoes seemed to suck at the tiled floor. With his big fingers gripping the handle, he stopped and turned to face her. 'Sleep well, little one. And may all your dreams be of the sweetest kind . . . you never know when something wonderful might happen!'

She lay still long after he had gone, staring at the linen drape that hung overhead on the bed frame and wished, wished that it had been her daddy who had guided her back to bed, who had said those words, who had made her feel loved and safe.

But no, her daddy was asleep in the courtyard next to a pile of sick. This didn't trouble her as much as it might have, as happy thoughts gathered. Señor Agostí was right; you never knew when something wonderful might happen! And it had. She now knew that the big old house with its rather odd noises was simply saying hello, welcoming her into every room. She was no longer afraid of living here and that alone was something wonderful . . .

CHAPTER ONE

'If you would kindly be upstanding and raise a glass to Lieutenant Colonel Gordon Brightwell!' Benedict Leech, the Commanding Officer, led the toast as he stood with his arm crooked, holding up a small crystal glass of port.

There was the collective scrape of chair legs across the wooden floor as the officers who were gathered for the supper discarded their linen napkins on to the polished dark-wood table and rose.

Nora hesitated, thrown as ever by the formality, unsure, even after a couple of decades in her supporting role, whether she should stand or sit still by her husband's side, with the eyes of the assembled as much on her as on the man of the hour. Gordy reached out to gently and briefly touch her thigh under the table, the code for stay put. It was a gesture made in kindness, but always made her feel like a well-trained pet. *Staaaaaaay!* She knew it must bother him that she didn't have the seamless grace and understanding of the rules as, say, Benedict's wife Jasmine, who knew when to bow her head, close her eyes, stand, sit, applaud, smile and pray. It always made her feel a little like a novice line dancer who cluttered up the row. Misstepping her way through the routine, which quite frankly was not only humiliating for her, but also buggered up everyone else's enjoyment of what should have been a well-choreographed routine akin to man, woman and cowboy boot working in harmony. Not that her husband had said as much, and not that they had ever, or would ever, consider line dancing, but her faltering bewilderment was another failing that she suspected he quietly tolerated.

The assembled retook their seats. Leech took a deep breath and spoke slowly – he loved an audience. 'Gordy, these last two years have flown, but be under no illusion, the impact you have made during your time with the unit has been great.'

Someone called *Hear hear!* from the back of the room. She felt her husband sit up straight beside her, knowing this valida-tion from his team would mean the world to him. It always did. A quick thank you from a struggling soldier or a note left on his desk offering gratitude meant more to him than any honour or award coming from HQ. And there had been a few of those, several cita-tions, and one shiny MBE. He was well-liked and gave his charges more of his time than was customary. He learned their names, their history and was always on the end of a phone taking a personal interest in every aspect of their lives. He liked to remind her, when she moaned in semi-jest about another night sitting alone in front of a temperamental television or having to walk along the shore in the moonlight by herself, that these young people were in *his* care: men and women who were far away from home, and most did not have their families around them.

In truth she felt this to be a barely adequate rationale. Nora knew more than most what it felt like to grow up without your family around you, and while, unlike her husband's charges, she was not living a life of duty, her loneliness was no less felt.

It was not what she had envisioned when it came to married life: watching crackly episodes of *Midsomer Murders* on a static-filled screen, or sitting on the beach as dusk fell and the moon lit the surface of the sea, taking her back to her childhood when similar sights had been hers. And yet here they were. It wasn't as if she was going to ask Gordy to love her more, be with her more, prioritise her more – how could she? It was that old line dance thing again, coupled with an acute fear of humiliation.

'Your posting here might have been cut short' – Leech paused for effect, drawing her back into the moment – 'but with good reason; promotion is not to be sniffed at! We wish you every success in your new role and if ever you are passing through Akrotiri, then I know that there are a few of us in the mess who would welcome the chance to try and take that regimental golf award from you – a bloody hole in one!'

Laughter rippled around the room, accompanied by the banging of hands on the table for extra impact, which made the cutlery, crystal and regimental silverware jump. This was all part of the dine out: the ribbing, the joshing.

'Fluke!' someone shouted.

'Yes, bloody fluke!' The CO chuckled. 'But in all seriousness, Gordy, you leave the unit in better shape than you found it, and with our gratitude and very good wishes for all that comes next. Oh' – he took a sharp breath – 'and thank you too to Nora!'

Nora squirmed a little and felt her face colour. She was an afterthought.

'To Colonel Brightwell!' Leech boomed, and the thirty men and two women officers assembled echoed the phrase.

It was the first time she had heard his new rank used formally and it was a moment. He was good at what he did – soldiering – and she knew this promotion meant the world. Not that she was overly happy about giving up the warm Mediterranean heat of Cyprus for the cold climes of Westbury – a place she was yet to visit, but she knew it was in Wiltshire, a pretty county famed for its White Horse, Stonehenge and ham.

With the speeches out of the way, everyone stood, keen, it seemed, to shrug off the formality of the dinner and get to the bar with its wide sunny terrace, cheap beer and watered-down gin.

11

Gordy placed his palm on the small of her back, again that gentle guiding hand.

'I think I'd better get my round in.'

'Of course.' She smiled at him and looked towards the bar. 'Think I might leave you to it, if you don't mind?' She'd been glancing at the clock for the last hour and a half, counting down the minutes until she could leave. She now wondered what was on TV and pictured the half-tub of salted caramel ice cream lurking in the freezer that needed finishing.

'Why don't you stay for a bit? I think some of the wives and partners are getting together, it'll be a chance for you to say goodbye to everyone.'

I'm still waiting for most of them to say hello . . . She swallowed the thought.

'I'd really rather not. I'll only feel like a spare part, and I don't need you to walk me back to our quarter, I'll be fine! Please stay, have a lovely evening – I shan't lock the door.' She smiled again.

It was something she had found comforting at first: to live on a patch, wherever it might be, where armed soldiers manned the barriers and checked the ID of everyone coming in. A novelty to be able to leave the windows open and doors unlocked and a bit of a change from the small flat in Maida Vale that she owned jointly with her sister Kiki, which was currently rented out, where sturdy metal bars were affixed to the sash windows and an unforgiving spear-headed iron gate covered the front door. The appeal of the armed guard, however, had quickly waned, turning in her mind to something quite different. In her lonelier moments, she sometimes wondered if the barriers were manned to keep people out or keep people in – not that she shared this, of course.

'Nora?'

She turned at the sound of the overly energetic Jasmine Leech, wife of the CO. Her heart sank a little, having hoped to slink off unnoticed and slip into her PJs, which were always better on the second night of wear: a little softer, yielding and with the comforting scent of past sleep. Jasmine was, as usual, wearing a colourful tunic, which neither flattered nor disguised her shape, and snug Capri pants that Nora was sure the woman owned in every colour of the rainbow. Jasmine's ebullience and positivity only highlighted her own reticence and lack of confidence when it came to socialising in a group. It wasn't so much that Nora was shy, but more that she carried a fear of having nothing of worth to contribute. Gordy had warned her gently that seeming aloof and sometimes abrupt could come across as a bit stand-offish, but that was hardly her fault. It was a defence mechanism, no more or less, and surely Gordy with his shiny new rank could, if nothing else, understand defence.

'Hi Jasmine.' She waved.

'Evening Jasmine!' Gordy spoke with the enthusiasm befitting her husband's rank.

'Hello both! How was supper? Lovely, I bet? I think Agda and her team are marvellous, working in that hot, tiny kitchen without AC – I think I'd go nuts!' She opened her mouth wide, as she did when she laughed, showing all her teeth, which if you didn't know better and there was no sound to accompany the action, could be taken as a grimace or expression of aggression. 'I detest these formal events, especially when other halves are not invited – always find them such a chore, but for the love of God don't tell Benedict!' She spoke out of the side of her mouth, as if sharing a confidence, but her volume suggested otherwise. 'I do find, though, that Agda's food lifts even the dullest of occasion. And I guess you were doing your duty today.' Nora felt this to be a reminder that she had less than pulled her weight when it came to socialising on the patch. Not that she was about to explain to Jasmine how the thought of being in a group was her idea of hell. The woman continued, oblivious, 'I mean it wouldn't have been much of a 'farewell Gordy and Nora' dinner if you hadn't gone!' That laugh again.

'The food *was* good.' Nora nodded and smiled politely, deciding not to mention that her lamb had been chewy and cold, the potatoes hard as bullets and the sauce thin with globules of white fat floating in it. Nora knew this was what Jasmine did, overpraised the help, as if this somehow negated the guilt she must have felt at having help at all.

'Top job, as always,' Gordy affirmed.

Jasmine turned to face her. 'Thought I'd come and find you as a couple of the girls and I are going to have a cheeky snifter on our terrace – please do come. It might be the last chance before you ship off on Monday.'

Nora found it odd when a woman who was north of fifty referred to herself and her chums as girls.

'She'd love that, wouldn't you, Nora?' Gordy answered on her behalf, squeezing her elbow and speaking emphatically.

'Oh well, smashing!' Jasmine clapped loudly. 'I'll just go and have a word with Benedict, tell him not to come home pissed and fall in the bloody pool again! Sick of fishing him out at all hours – ruins my manicure. Wait here for me. Back in a mo!'

As Jasmine scuttled off, Nora turned to her husband, keeping her voice low. 'Why did you say I'd *love* that? I just want to go to bed! It's been a long enough day and an even longer evening, and now I've got to go and sit with Jasmine and her mates and hear them bitch about whoever isn't present. I was about to say I'd love to, *but . . .*'

'I know you were, and she knew it too. That's why I spoke up, it'll be nice to have some company.'

'Nice for who?' She shook her head. 'And why would I want company now I'm leaving?' He just didn't get it. It was as if he thought that by intervening, as he did on occasion, organising dates

14

and making suggestions, he could magic some confidence into her, or better still, turn her into a Jasmine Leech clone. The thought made her shudder.

'Do it for me.' He held her eyeline, his expression imploring. 'Please. I just want you to be happy.'

She opened her mouth to question how a drink on Jasmine's terrace might help achieve that, but he turned away.

'Gordy!' one of his colleagues called out and held up a tray on which sat a neat collection of shot glasses.

'I'd better—' He thumbed towards the bar.

She accepted the kiss he planted on her cheek and toyed with the clasp of her clutch bag, waiting for Jasmine to come and collect her. Like a child at the end of school or a dog tied up outside a shop.

◆　◆　◆

Nora lay on the soft bed and looked up at the ceiling where the wide bamboo blades of the fan whirred and made patterns in the dim early morning light. Pulling the green sprig-patterned cotton bedspread up by the corners, she covered her bare legs, which now felt the chill of the air-conditioned room. Her cheek met the pillow and she closed her eyes, hoping, praying there was a small window for more sleep. It wasn't like she had anything to get up for: no job to hurry to, no family that needed feeding. Her plants were either newly watered or packed up, waiting to be shipped to their new, cooler home. She felt a familiar flare of anxiety over their well-being.

It had been nudging 2 a.m. when she finally managed to extricate herself from Jasmine's gushing clutches and today, like any other when her routine had been so disturbed, Nora had woken and was tired. She disliked mornings like this; opening her eyes and

15

feeling less than perky set the tone, plunging her into a fug that she found hard to shake off. Before she'd even sat up, she was picturing an afternoon nap and an early night, delightful slumber on this soft bed, interspersed with good food and a walk on the beach. The perfect way to lock in lingering memories of the landscape, the heat, the light . . . These were the three things she would miss the most.

It might only have been four days until they moved back to the UK, but with army-supplied packers and movers on hand to do all the hard work there was literally nothing for her to do other than supervise the big clean that would start tomorrow. It was the rule: the quarter had to be given back in the condition she had received it. It was a procedure that always made Nora feel like a slattern, having resided in a house that had *dust* on the upper shelf of the airing cupboard – *dust! How could she bear it?* In moments like this she thought of La Fosca, the house in Spain – yet another place that had been temporary – and the grime that no one paid any attention to. La Fosca, where cooking smells and tobacco smoke clung to the curtains, anything made of wood was a little sticky and hair formed wispy nests on the bathroom floor. Her mother's philosophy, it seemed, was that with enough candles lit and enough wine drunk, the last thing anyone would notice was the dirty windows and grubby corners where mouse shit clustered. She was probably right. Nora wondered what her glamorous mother would make of the rigours of army life and the army's apparent obsession with cleaning.

Nora was an old hat at the march-in, march-out procedure having had at least six addresses in the last decade alone. Standard practice was for a woman with a clipboard to walk around her home with her Bic ballpoint poised, informing her with a deep sigh of the many, many things she would have to 'put right' before they could hand back the keys and move to an identical house, albeit across the sea and down a bit. A house that would then be inspected by the woman's doppelganger with a matching Bic and clipboard . . .

The one aspect of the move that excited her was the prospect of getting stuck into a new garden – always so much to do, to learn. It was certainly a frustration that they never stayed put long enough to see anything she planted grow. Containers and planters that offered colour or interest all year round were her forte. Her stomach rolled at the prospect of her beloved greenery being shipped overseas safely.

'You all right?' Gordy called from the terrace, jolting her from her musings and removing the last remote possibility of slumber. 'Are you napping – or rather trying to? I'll shut up if that's the case?'

She closed her eyes and breathed deeply through her nose. How on earth did he think she might be able to sleep if she was to engage in conversation?

'Okay, hint taken! Shutting up!' he chortled.

His loud voice made her insides shrink and her jaw tense; she was still smarting from being forced to socialise last night. What was it about a voice that could either make you want to listen to it for hours and hours, content to hear the interior monologue offered in a hum and never taking umbrage or offence at the topic because of your deep admiration, if not love, for the timbre and tone, the shape of the lips that offered the words? And then, conversely, there was a voice like Gordy's, who recently, in all honesty, could have been offering a gift, whispering words of love or reciting poetry, yet nothing he said was attractive. If a voice you loved in tone was like bathing in warm chocolate, his was like having a splinter picked out by a short-sighted arthritic: clumsy, ill-aimed and painful.

It hadn't always been this way – far from it. Many was the night when newly courting that they would lie on a rug as dawn broke, idly chatting, laughing at nothing, kissing with furious passion and making promises of a life that would be lived hand in hand.

17

Are you being unfair, Nora? Are you being mean? she asked herself and the answer to both questions was, '*Possibly.*' But she could no more help it than she could control it; it was visceral, instinctive, her dislike of her husband's volume, his accent, his bullish vowels and aggressive consonants. It wasn't only his voice; she did, on occasion, find herself irked by many aspects of him. His habit of combing his top lip with the tip of his index finger when he was thinking, the way he peeled off his socks, which he liked to pull from his pale feet at the end of the day, lobbing them at the wall by the laundry basket where they fell and nestled in a maroon woolly heap on the floor; how hard would it have been to actually put them in the basket? The way he chortled as he read a book or article he found amusing, laughing and tittering to himself like a madman when she had no hope of joining in; why could he not give her the gist? Invite her to join in if something was that funny?

Was it his fault? *Partly.* But it was hers too. Things to which she would have paid no heed in the summer of their marriage, when he seemed to have time for her, or rather *made* time for her, troubled her more with the passing years. Like a bloom of damp on a white wall that grew over time until it was all you could see.

She would on occasion remember those early days when supper wasn't eaten in silence, her with her nose in a book and him checking his phone. Those glory days when they would chew, pause, sip, giggle and recount, knowing that no written word or scrap of news was going to be nearly half as interesting as anything – anything at all – the other had to say. When moments of unrestrained hilarity bound them, united as tears coursed down their cheeks and they fought for breath at something so funny it tickled them pink! And there was their shared love of nature, of horticulture, hiking, good food, a well-mixed G&T. And their frequent sex that was a revelation – often powerful, all-consuming and somehow more intense because of the surprise of it.

She missed him. She missed 'them', the couple they had been. To open up, however, to reach out and confess this felt too hard. If, as she suspected, the ship had sailed, the train had left the station and the tether had reached its end, what was the point in exposing her fear, her sadness, her love, only for it to be rebuffed, rejected? It happened, she supposed, some couples just ran out of steam. Maybe they were no more than 'some couple', and her ideas, her hopes in the beginning that they had in some way been promised a cherished future were misplaced. It shouldn't have been a shock, yet it was. She had however reached an understanding that they would live this measured, often frustrating life and it would be enough.

'So, *are* you asleep?' Gordy called again through the open door of the terrace that ran along the length of their villa. She propped herself up on her elbows, staring at the back of his auburn head.

'Nope. I am very much awake,' she offered as she swung her long legs around and reached for the vintage silk kimono that hung on a hook on the back of the door. One of Granny Magda's cast-offs which she treasured.

'I have coffee!' He turned and smiled at her, knowing her weakness for caffeine at that time of the morning. 'And there might be some of Constantine's home-made yoghurt. Might help settle your tum if you had a Metaxa or two.'

'I think I might do just that.' It was undoubtedly one of the things she would miss when she left Cyprus. The offerings dropped on the step or at the gate by the toothless, smiley, ancient farmer who lived a little way up the valley were always a moment of joy. He spoke no English and she and Gordy only rudimentary Greek that could see them comfortably through the ordering of a light lunch or a couple of beers. But when, newly arrived, they had encountered the man on the lane during one of their treks, communicating with the aid of pointing, smiling, frowning and the lightest touch of his fingertips on her arm, they had formed a friendship of sorts.

19

He reminded her in many ways of her father's patron, Señor Agostí, someone who stood out brightly, as did any memory of her early years in Catalonia. The same deep wrinkles, the same twinkly kindness in his eyes. The man who had quelled her fear of living in that big old villa. Perhaps that was why she warmed to the farmer, the fact that he had a face similar to one that she remembered so fondly. Bowls of fat green olives; home-made, warm pitta wrapped in a checked tea towel; uber garlicky tzatziki; honey-doused, nut-stuffed baklava; and thick goat's milk yoghurt: all had found their way to the table on the terrace and were devoured greedily and gratefully by her and Gordy.

Nora took up the rickety wooden chair opposite her husband who was, she could see, freshly showered. His wet hair was combed back over his tanned forehead. It was when he looked most handsome, she thought. Out of his uniform, skin scented with lemony soap and his solid, muscular body, still in incredible shape at the age of forty-eight, on full view. His sweatpants gave him a casual air that meant he had relaxed and so in turn did she. It was a welcome hiatus.

Grabbing a shiny teaspoon, she removed the muslin lid from the glass jar and dipped the spoon into the thick yoghurt, which Constantine or his wife had topped with a generous swirl of fragrant honey and a crush of golden walnuts.

'Oh my God, that is so good!' She spoke with her mouth full, savouring the delicious treat with which she broke her fast for the day.

'Shall I ask the packers to pop Constantine in with the china and whatnot? Ship him out to Westbury so we can dine like this forever?'

Nora pictured just that and shook her head. 'I think the ingredients might be lacking if we ate them in the Wiltshire rain. I'm quite sure it's the warm sunshine, the backdrop of olive trees and the blue, blue sky that makes everything taste so good.' She held the jar under her chin and went back in with the spoon.

The weather had felt a little unbearable when she had first arrived. More accustomed to grey drizzle, the intense heat of the midday sun and the warm hum of night-time meant she found it hard to stay energised during the day and harder still to get to sleep at night. But two years in, she was acclimatised, loving the hot flex of the muscles on her bones and the way the heat softened everything. The thought of waking in a chilly Westbury where everything would go back to being cold and brittle didn't exactly fill her with joy. The beach, the heat and food like this were a distraction from the disintegrating fabric of her marriage, which had been slowly falling apart, fraying at the edges, and slipping through her fingers.

'Yes, you're probably right. Plus I think Constantine's wife might miss him. We should leave him here in his olive grove.' He chuckled.

'Doubt his wife'd miss him.' She looked at him through lowered lids. 'I've never seen the woman smile, don't think she seems that happy with her lot.'

He glanced at her briefly, knowingly, silently asking, she assumed, if she'd found a kindred spirit. She felt dots of colour rise on her cheeks.

'So' – Gordy lowered his paper and reached for his coffee mug, sipping the strong brew – 'what did Jasmine have to say last night?'

He always did this, insisted on a thorough debrief after each and any accidental contact, as if any snippet she might have gleaned about the CO might be useful to him either professionally or personally.

'Not much.' She licked the spoon and saw the vein on his temple rise; how he would hate this vague catch-all. She knew that if she were one of his staff, he would, about now, be raising his volume and explaining why specifics were necessary and important. '*I*

21

want that information in the ABC – Accurate. Brief. Concise. This can make a difference to your safety and my safety and the safety of those around us in a combat scenario!' At least that was what she thought he'd once said. They made her laugh, all these acronyms, mnemonics, codes, bywords, buzzwords, and sometimes it was just a good old-fashioned number. *'Tell Conrad to meet me in the stores, I want to go through the ten thirty-threes.'*

'Well, that's helpful.' He snorted.

'Oh, I didn't realise I was there to be helpful,' she lied. 'I thought it was for a friendly catch-up with the girls?'

'It was.' He glugged his coffee. 'But when the girl in question is the loose-lipped Jasmine Leech then one can always learn something that *might*, in the future, be helpful.'

'Well, lucky for you I recorded the whole evening on my phone.'

'Did you?' He leaned forward with something like delight shining in his pale-blue eyes.

'Of course I bloody didn't!' she tutted and then laughed. 'Honestly, Gordy! Can you imagine? And worse still, I can see that the idea doesn't horrify you!'

'Using your wits would not be horrifying.' He reached for the cafetière and topped up his mug.

'Using my wits?' His tone suggested this was something she didn't do often enough. 'We drank gin and then Metaxa and ate cheese-and-onion-flavoured crisps that had gone a little soft in the bowl, and Jennifer Wallace spent forty minutes talking about how horrible it was that her son Jack had been suspended from school. He and a boy named Gunther were caught taking drugs. And I felt really sad for Jack, and I mean *really sad*, because Jennifer's biggest issue was the fact that he was going to be coming home four weeks earlier than they had planned and she was, quote, "stuck with him", and not whatever the poor kid was going through at school – like why and how he was using drugs!' Jennifer's open irritation of her son's presence had more than struck a nerve.

'Oh dear.'

'Yes, Gordy, oh dear. And then, of course, everyone weighed in with similar school- or kid-related stories about how their kids are super-smart, love sport, and how their artwork is incredible, they are all such *special* kids! Sweet Lord! I sat there with zilch to contribute, didn't think it appropriate to mention that the one and only time I was left in charge of a toddler, I nearly killed her!'

'You always go there, yet you know it wasn't your fault! It's mental self-flagellation that serves nothing. The front door was left open, you were no more than a teen and your baby sister ran out of the front door – it happens. And she was fine!'

The sound . . . the sound of the brakes and the way she slapped against the side of the car! If he'd been going just a little faster or she'd run just a little quicker she'd be gone, squished like our parents, and I was supposed to be watching her, but I was reading, distracted and then Nana Dilly grabbed the tops of my arms and screamed in my face, 'YOU'RE JUST LIKE YOUR MOTHER! KIKI COULD HAVE BEEN KILLED! SHE'S ALL I HAVE LEFT!' And just like that I learned that, like my mother, I was not cut out to watch over a child, and equally devastating, I learned that I counted for nothing. Nana Dilly said Kiki was all she had left as if I was nothing . . . And what I couldn't say, what I can't say, is that Nana Dilly was all I had left and so it was the biggest blow, it changed me . . .

'You're right, she was fine, silly me!' she tutted, keen to get back to the conversation in hand. 'And then Sophie Cosworth actually turned to me and said, "I don't know how you make friends in a new place, Nora, it must be so hard when you don't have children – I mean that's how I make my friends, other women with little ones." As if choosing not to have kids made me a different species entirely! And no one said a word in my defence or

23

support! Not a bloody word, until Jasmine piped up with, "It's not too late – you might still get to hear the pitter-patter of tiny feet!" As if the reason I don't have kids is because I can't, or because I'm one of those women with a little piece missing in my life desperately yearning for them! As if my forty-six-year-old eggs are just quivering with the need to be fertilised. It's as humiliating as it is annoying.'

Nora felt it was a private matter and wasn't willing to share the fact with relative strangers that she was childless by choice, certain she did not have the requisite knowledge to raise happy, successful citizens of the planet. This supposition was based primarily on three factors: first, her own mother's lack of maternal skill and the fear that this failing might be genetic; second, she had, therefore, no example to follow; and third, when she had been left in charge of a child, and not just any child but her baby sister, it had nearly ended in tragedy.

'Ignore her.'

'Brilliant. Yes, Gordy, why didn't I think of that? I'll ignore her, and that would have been a whole lot easier if you hadn't made me go for drinks.'

'I didn't *make* you!' He sounded indignant.

'You absolutely did! You answered on my behalf, you told her I'd *love* it! How was I supposed to get out of that?' She let the spoon rattle in the jar as she placed it down hard on the table.

'Oh, I don't know, Nora, you are usually very good at getting out of things.'

'What's that supposed to mean?'

'Nothing.' He closed his eyes and rubbed his forehead and she understood, feeling too the physical tremble of their row that had, as ever, flared from the smallest of kindling.

'You mean sex, of course you do, and I've tried to explain that it's so much more than an act, Gordy – you can't expect us to be at

24

each other's throats during the day and then just cosy up for a shag at bedtime – it's not that simple.'

'It is for me.' He was trying for humour, but the glint in his eye was of pure sadness. It made her feel terrible.

There was a stretch of silence which, despite their eighteen years wed, made it feel like they were strangers. It was as uncomfortable as it was painful. Both stared at the sunny horizon, the prettiest of diversions from the topic in hand.

'Do you think we should maybe go and talk to someone, Gordy?' It was something she'd thought about before, but now more than ever it seemed pertinent, as the lulls between the moments of joy were getting longer, the rows more easily ignited, the tension more palpable and the joy, when it did arrive, was growing duller, like a failing light bulb that dimmed before it gave up for good.

'What about?' He stared at her with narrowed eyes.

'What do you think? About us! About this!' She pointed back and forth between them. 'About our lack of intimacy, our lack of . . .' She ran out of words, not knowing how to phrase all that raced around her head and struggling to define exactly what was wrong with them. 'This sadness. This feeling like we are standing on the edge of the end, waiting to see who jumps first.'

'The edge of the end . . .' he repeated, drawing breath sharply as if slapped. Her words had either wounded or awakened him, it was hard to tell which. 'Who in the world would you want us to talk to?' His words coasted on laughter that was insincere and riven with nerves.

'I don't know.' She shrugged. 'A therapist?'

Gordy stood and snorted laughter. 'A therapist? I'm a colonel in the British Army!' His tone made her wonder whose benefit he was saying this for. 'I don't go and talk to therapists – some nosey busybody who's done an online course and has a framed certificate above their desk that entitles them to listen in great detail to why my wife doesn't like sex and I don't like pretending it doesn't matter!'

'That's unfair!' She pulled her kimono closed; any talk of their lack of intimacy made her want to hide her body. 'I do like sex!'

'Oh, bloody marvellous, so what am I meant to take from that?' He pulled on the t-shirt that had been hanging on the back of his chair. 'That you do like sex but just not with me?'

'I . . .' She didn't know how to reply. It was complicated, but she knew that as a response that wouldn't wash.

'I'm going for a run.' He walked briskly past her and into the house, to grab his trainers no doubt, and she did what she always did in this situation: drank more coffee, stared at the Grecian-blue horizon and wished she wasn't so damn lonely. Maybe Sophie Cosworth was right: it was easier to make friends if you could join a mummy club, but if everyone in that club was as fixated with their kids as Jasmine and her crew were, Nora knew she wouldn't fit in anyway. Besides, how did that work? Choosing friends based on the fact that you'd all managed to reproduce? It really was as ludicrous as it sounded. She had friends from university whom she rarely saw but knew that if ever she were in Colorado or Milton Keynes, she could look up her old roommates and be assured of a friendly welcome and a bed for the night. But the kind of mate she could call up for a chat, meet for coffee, turn to for advice? They were a bit thin on the ground. She saw the fact that she was not quite one of the gang as further proof of her oddness, and it hurt.

In truth, Gordy had once been that person, the one she could turn to no matter what, and it had been enough. Criss-crossing the globe, trailing in his wake hadn't felt trepidatious because she was doing so with her best friend. That was until he spent all hours of the day and night grasping for the next rung on the career ladder and she had got fed up with holding the ladder steady and looking up at the view of his camo-clad arse. Loneliness was her enemy, and it was a well-tooled, motivated one that she found hard to defeat. The answer, of course, was simple: get out there, make friends! And oh, how she wished it were that easy, but when low self-esteem was holding the megaphone for her interior monologue, it made finding the courage to step out of her comfort zone harder than she could say.

Nora heard the loo flush and knew that it would only be a minute before he went running. She also knew it was rare to know the exact day, hour and minute that the gloss fell from a relationship, but she did, could see it in her mind's eye, frozen in time.

It was on a sunny June day and the clock on the wall read two forty-five. Light pooled on the block wood floor, and someone was playing a piano in the corner of the room, not well, but rather in that plink-plink manner that does a great disservice to both the noble instrument and any piece of music. She had, in the years since, often pondered the question: was it *possible* that a love affair so full of promise could curdle so completely? Wasn't it far more likely, more 'usual' that relationships were like old books whose glue had become weakened over time, the spine a little too soft and cracked, the bending cardboard and string too frail to support the weight of the story within, until it finally and suddenly gave way, fractured, spilling the contents of the story to the floor . . . leaving nothing but fragments of a thing once whole lying in sheets underfoot? Scattered words and sentiment, no more than clues as to what had once been quite magnificent when whole. That summed it up rather nicely, she thought. Gordy and her. Not that their story was that complicated or that weighty, come to think of it. They had been together, a couple, happy for over a decade when she felt the shine slide from her love like something rather dull being removed from a sleeve, the removal of which could only result in disappointment, having expected something so glossy.

As to what caused this change of heart at two forty-five on a sunny June day? The answer, disappointingly for those expecting or hoping for drama, was nothing loud or explosive or explicit or extreme or overt, but rather it was a small thing. But a big thing to Nora – deafening, in fact. It was a small, almost imperceptible sharp grunt of laughter that fled Gordy's nostrils in the manner of someone hearing a thing so disagreeable or amusing that the only way to respond to it was with this dismissive snort, accompanied by an equally short background hum.

She pictured him making this noise often.

Saw the way his head flicked back slightly as if the action, its magnitude known only to her, caused his head to ricochet. His lips, tightly pressed, had looked quite ghastly despite his fine clothes, pressed khaki shirt and the fancy leather Sam Browne belt sitting looped under his epaulette. He was dressed up, as one would expect for an occasion such as this, but no amount of finery could counteract that snort – aimed at her.

'So, you are now the wife of an MBE!' the Brigadier's wife had trilled.

'Yes, for my sins.' She had laughed, not knowing why – giddy possibly in light of the occasion and the three glasses of champagne she had consumed on an empty stomach since leaving the officers' mess.

'Well, you should be very proud!' The older woman patted her arm.

'Oh, I am.' She beamed.

'And how are you going to make your mark, dear?'

'I . . .' she floundered. *How was she going to make her mark?* 'I'm a gardener; plants are my passion.' This she stated with confidence in light of her voluntary or part-time roles that saw her rolling up her sleeves and getting her hands dirty whenever she arrived in a new place. She could currently be found three days a week pruning stock in a nursery in Chelsea where shrubs were bagged, tagged and sold at a farmers' market for an extortionate sum.

'I see.' The Brigadier's wife paused. 'But there's hardly a career to be found in that, is there?'

'I think there might be, kind of, if the army lets me stay in one place long enough to *make* a career out of it.' She had smiled, intent on winning the woman over.

'Oh, come now, Nora, I'm quite sure you could be somewhere for a decade and not reach any dizzy heights if your feet are always in wellies and you're raking leaves?'

Nora saw red. 'I'm sure you're right and that is very much what I do: wear wellies and rake leaves . . .' She decided not to elaborate on her years studying botany and horticulture, her ability to identify and care for plants, her keen eye for garden design . . . 'And not that it really matters, I can always dine out on my husband's rank or his shiny MBE. It seems like that's the done thing around here.' She couldn't help it, the woman had been rude and momentarily forgetting she was the wife of Gordy's boss's boss, her response felt justified.

Gordy had shot her a look that she couldn't quite read, which, again, could have been down to the fizz now sloshing in her veins.

'I suppose you can.' The woman's mouth now no more than a thin line of disapproval.

Turning to Gordy, Nora wanted to see the wink he liked to give her, the one designed to let her know that all was well, that she was making him proud, but the wink was missing. Instead, he stared at her and then at the Brigadier's wife and his cheeks coloured as his mouth moved, searching for the right words to reassure the older woman that his wife was not usually so sarcastic or dissenting, while not entirely pissing off said wife. An impossible task, even for an accomplished man like Major Gordon Brightwell, MBE.

Standing with the clock visible over his right shoulder, the clock that read two forty-five, he had snorted. His expression was almost embarrassed and in that second Nora, knowing herself to be the source of that embarrassment, had felt her stomach knot.

This was her husband's big day! And it should have been a glorious beginning, a celebration, but instead it was an ending of sorts for her. Not of the marriage, oh no, nothing so dramatic, resolving or freeing, but the end of loving him in the particular way she had. Prior to that moment he had seemed perfect and golden to her; the answer to every question that had dogged her for as long as she could remember. He was a steadfast thing, a rock in the fast-flowing river of life that had carried her along. It was only when he plucked her from the current, allowed her to draw breath, to rest, that she had realised how tired she was. He had pulled her ashore, held her tight and promised to evermore be her strength, her one. He had made her feel safe, promised to be her supporter, her champion, but that look and lack of verbal support revealed him to be human, flawed, and while this should not have been a surprise or a disappointment, it was. She hoped he might become glittery and shiny again, *prayed* it might be so. The prospect of being hitched to a man who would so openly side with her detractor was galling, ghastly.

Her mum and dad – Guy and Vanessa Brown – had been less than perfect when it came to parenting, but heavens above, even as a little girl she had been acutely aware of the unquestionable bond between them; a bond forged with unbreakable loyalty. What would her mother have done if someone had so openly belittled her husband? Nora remembered the sound of breaking glass and her mother running from the studio with a palette knife raised as she chased one of their guests from the property. Her dress tucked into her knickers and her bare feet racing over stones, as if her desperation to make contact with the man who now ran for his life was a higher priority than the blood that dripped from her cut soles.

'Mediocre!' she had screamed. 'How dare you? Mediocre is not a word you can use when discussing my husband's art! Never! Do you hear me!' she had yelled as the chap clutched his rather battered Panama and hightailed it down the driveway.

But Gordy had not chased the Brigadier's wife away nor had he defended Nora. It wasn't that she didn't love him – she did, she truly did – rather that she only loved him enough and no more, and that was *enough*, most of the time. Hardly the great romance she had hoped for and once thought they'd had, but then if life had taught her one thing, it was that it rarely delivered in the way you thought it might and there was no point squawking over it.

Gordy reappeared in his trainers with a water bottle in his hand and glanced at his watch. She knew he liked to record his running times. She also knew it irritated him that she was slender, rangy, could snack on half a tub of salted caramel ice cream, stay slim and had never run a step, if you discounted rushing for a bus. She had the build of her mother and Granny Magda – *celery* – and liked to emulate her grandmother's dress, favouring silk shirts, neat jeans, delicate strands of jewellery and minimal make-up.

'Do you think Westbury will be a new start for us?' Squinting, she placed her hand on her head, her fingers forming a visor to block the sun.

'I don't know, Nora.' He held her gaze, looking like a boy, hopeful and hopeless all at the same time. 'But I've been thinking.' His voice was low, gravelly.

'Go on,' she urged, aware that she held her breath, waiting to hear what he had been preoccupied with.

He rubbed his hand over his face and planted his feet, as if to steady himself. 'I've been thinking, I've been thinking . . .' – he took his time – '. . . that maybe, maybe Nora it might be best if we get a divorce.'

'Heh . . .' The noise escaped her mouth involuntarily in a small, nervous giggle. She didn't know why, the last thing she had meant to do was laugh. There was nothing remotely funny about it. His words had hit her like a punch in the throat and she placed her hand on her neck, as if she might ease the pain a little with the touch. Her pulse raced. 'Are you . . .' Again words failed her. 'What?'

'I just think it shouldn't be off the table.' He coughed. 'I think we need to talk, really talk, and that we should be aware that this might be the outcome. We need to accept that it might be for the best.' He swallowed. 'I do. I think it might be for the best.' It was obvious he had considered how to broach the topic kindly, gently, and yet this addition made it feel like a fait accompli.

'Shit.' She let her head fall forward and stared at her lap, anywhere other than into his face. 'Oh my God!' Her legs shook beneath the table. Fear and embarrassment helped her thoughts race ahead. *I can move back to the flat, ask Leah Richards to leave, end her tenancy, and go back. I can work in town, temp at first, do anything . . . I can retrain . . . take a class . . . He wants to leave me! Gordy! My Gordy! I will no longer be Gordy's wife . . . I can't imagine it. I can't believe it . . .*

'I'm exhausted, Nora, and I know you are too. Chasing the same row around and around in a draining spiral. It's no good for us. It's desperate.'

Desperate. It was quite the word. How had he arrived here without her fully realising? She squared her shoulders and tried to control the wobble to her voice. 'If that's . . . if that's what you want.'

'Jesus, Nora! Is it any wonder it's what I want when you react so coolly to the suggestion? How do you think that makes me feel? Look at you! Cool as a bloody cucumber. You're hardly fighting the idea, are you?'

'Is that what you want me to do? Fight the idea?' *I can't bear it! Yes, you drive me crazy, yes, I've been lonely, but I can't bear the idea of you not being mine. But if you don't want me, what's the point?* Again, she saw the shake of her mother's head in irritation at her very presence.

'I'm fed up of riding this Ferris wheel.' He rubbed his palms over his face. 'I just want—'

Her phone juddered on the table, an incoming call that robbed them of the moment. He stopped talking and handed her the phone, and after a second or two, with a shaking hand, she raised it to her ear.

'Yes, this is Leonora Brightwell.' She bit her lip, for how much longer would she be able to give that name? It was a thought too awful to consider. Formality of tone helped her retain her composure.

'And you are the next of kin for Kristina Morris?'

'Yes, yes, she's my sister.' She sat forward in the chair and placed one hand over her eyes to shield them from the sun and her husband's gaze.

'I understand you are not in the UK?'

'That's right, Akrotiri, Cyprus.' She gave the information to the man on the phone whose tone was pedestrian. 'Is everything all right? Who did you say you were?' Her mouth had gone a little dry with nerves.

'I'm Dr Hammond. I work at St Margaret's Hospital.' The words turned to fog in her mind. Why was he calling her?

'Has something happened?' she asked with growing urgency.

'I'm so sorry, Mrs Brightwell, but your sister has been admitted to hospital.'

'Oh no, is she okay?'

'I'm afraid not. She tried to take her life.'

His words were like glass that slid up and down her throat. 'She . . . she . . . I'm sorry, I thought you said . . . Can you please repeat that?'

The quiver to her voice encouraged Gordy to concentrate on her, his water bottle now abandoned on the terrace floor. He walked over and took the seat next to her, watching intently.

'She tried to take her life. Very nearly succeeded,' the doctor repeated.

'Oh my God! Oh my God, no! That's awful. When?' She listened and nodded, forgetting that the man feeding her the dismal information could not see. Lowering the phone she gripped it to her chest, her chin dipped, her hair falling forward over her face as the words ricocheted in her thoughts and she felt a little light-headed, convinced that had she not been seated she would have fallen to the floor.

'What's the matter?' Gordy placed a hand on her arm, the words of their conversation – his desire for divorce – giving this gesture a new awkwardness that under less urgent circumstances would have sent her reeling. 'Nora, what's happened?' His tone was pressing yet calm. His army training had kicked in. 'Talk to me!'

'It's . . . it's Kiki.' She struggled to catch a breath and talk at the same time; glancing briefly at the bed, she considered hiding in it. 'She . . . she . . . oh my God, Gordy!'

CASA PINO

'*Qué estás hacienda?* What are you doing, Papá?' Mateo Agostí trod softly as usual, holding his breath as the afternoon heat warmed the grand villa. Although in fairness he had been holding his breath for most of his life, with nerves lapping at his heels whenever he approached his papá, who was a great, great man. A man who could arrive at a fully booked restaurant and be offered the best table in the house, a man who caused people to nudge the ribs of the person next to them when they spotted him; a very rich man, and a famous son of Catalonia. Mateo had come to understand that for those without the same level of wealth, having that much money was a fascination.

The Agostí wealth had been made by Mateo's great-great-grandfather, Vicente Agostí, who with no more than a shovel and a pick had dug the earth and found coal. Pretty soon the shovel and pick were replaced by drills and diggers and his fortune was established. His great-grandfather, Esteban Agostí, diversified, planting olive and lemon groves on an industrial scale, increasing their wealth ten-fold. His grandfather, Francisco Agostí, with a passion for architecture, built and bought property and the land on which it sat. And his father, Santiago, invested in the arts. Mateo's heritage sat squarely on his shoulders with enough weight to make him aware of his responsibility but not so heavy he felt the burden of it.

As an only child, he knew his position was to serve, support and to quietly help the well-oiled wheels of his father's life keep turning, whether in matters of business or in the running of the household. Mateo took calls, organised meetings, put dates in the diary and did his very best, all with the scribbled signature of his father to rubber stamp and give approval. *A glorified PA* . . . Mateo swallowed the thought, knowing his life was, and would continue to be, one of extreme privilege and that he should be thankful. And he was, but whether he was happy or not was a whole other discussion altogether.

It wasn't easy walking in the ever-faltering footsteps of a man like Santiago Agostí who, even in his youth, was at best volatile. Today, with most of his contemporaries either dead or too old to put up the fight, age had become his papá's most fearless and relentless enemy.

Mateo approached cautiously, glad of the quiet tread of his loafer, not wanting to disturb the old man in case he was sleeping and, although he would never admit it, wary that he might not be, and of all that such a discovery would bring . . .

He made his way into the vast marble-floored ballroom where the walls were lined with the art his papá so loved. Most had companion pieces hanging in the greatest galleries of Europe and beyond, the artists' names such that even those uninterested in art would recognise them.

'*Solo mirando las pinturas* – just looking at the paintings,' Santiago whispered gruffly.

'I think you spend more time staring at these paintings than you do anything else!' Mateo, whose heart had slowed a little with relief, bent low and grazed his father's furrowed brow with a kiss.

'And does it matter? Is there somewhere else I have to be? Something else I need to do? I'm eighty-six, *hijo*. Your mamá is not calling me to dance to sweet music by candlelight, there is no wine I long to taste, I don't want any more sun on my skin and whatever morsels of rich food await me on a terrace tabletop sit in my old mouth like cold ashes. Isn't it the cruellest trick? Leaving me here on this earth to linger when I can't even enjoy *food*?' He huffed. 'I like it here in the cool, looking at this view that is only mine.'

'I guess so. Can I bring you some tea?'

'No, *gracias*.' He waved his fat, sausage-fingered hand, as he did whenever he dismissed an idea or a suggestion and, as ever, Mateo's stomach bunched a little to have got it so wrong. 'I've been thinking.' His papá took a slow breath. 'This painting, this particular painting' – he pointed – 'I would like it to go back to the rightful owners, to Guy Brown's children or grandchildren.'

'Guy Brown?' He had heard the name of course, but it had been a while.

'I took this from La Fosca after he died. Everything was abandoned, awash in sorrow, a mess. I had the place cleared out. Except this piece, which I salvaged to hang here, but I don't feel it's mine. It should go back to his children – his girls.'

'Are you in contact with them?' Mateo folded his arms and stared at the oil painting opposite him, the lines, streaks and shadows, which to his amateur eye looked no more than child's play, naive . . . That was until he took a step backwards and then one more, and suddenly the lines, streaks and shadows formed a beautiful scene: two young children on a beach he knew well. Their faces with an angled frailty to them. The older girl, with trousers unevenly rolled, holding a net and a jar as she waded barefoot in the rock pool. And a toddler sitting on the sand, her expression one of obvious delight as she watched her sister. Both wore straw hats and the sun warmed the composition, shading the sky with golden hues that suggested mid-morning. He would never, ever understand how it could be created by a hand and eye close up and with such a rough palette, only for it to come into focus as you moved further away.

Guy Brown had also painted his mother. That painting now hung in the master bedroom. She had been a great beauty, no clever artistry required. Mateo was glad that in looks he favoured her and didn't carry the rather bulbous, big-featured face of his papá and their aristocratic ancestors, nor did he sport his father's wide girth, supported by rather spindly legs. The thought of his mother was enough to bring a lump to his throat. How he missed her still. How they both did.

'No, I'm not in contact with them, but I will try. I have the name of Guy's mother and her last address. I have decided to write to her.'

'Surely she's not still alive?' Mateo didn't want to discourage his papá from his project, happy that in his ailing years something had sparked his enthusiasm. Since he had lost his wife, life for his papá had become more chore than pleasure.

'No.' He closed his eyes briefly as if to say, I'm old but I'm not stupid! 'But maybe the house went to a relative or a neighbour who might have some link, some information.'

'So Guy had children?' He didn't know this.

'Yes, two girls whose names were Leonora and Kiki. I remember them. Only very young when Guy and Nessa died – one no more than a tiny baby and the other in her teens, I think.'

'That's terrible.'

'It was terrible, it *is* terrible!' He hit the arm of the chair and coughed until he wheezed at the effort of it. 'But at least I can send this painting to them, and they will have part of their papá. Returned.'

'That's quite something!'

His papá shrugged as if it were of no consequence. 'I will of course keep Mamá. She is mine to keep, always.'

'Of course.' Mateo was relieved.

'It was my pleasure to host Guy and his wife at La Fosca for a number of years. He was such a talent and together they really were something, he and Nessa. Like a flint and a match' – he sparked his fingers together –'fire!'

Mateo watched the old man's face break into a smile, his discoloured teeth on display and a twinkle in his pale eye, as if a memory so glorious pulled him back to a place and time. It shook years from his face.

'Fire?'

'Yes! Beautiful and destructive in equal measure.'

Mateo nodded, used to his papá's rather eclectic group of friends and acquaintances who littered the memories of his childhood: the artists, the musicians, the poets, the writers, the muses, the gurus, the visionaries and the beautiful. People who drifted into their lives and took centre stage for a short while before the next person or starlit diversion came along and they faded away into the background from whence they had come.

'Help me up!' His father gripped the arm of the wicker chair in which he was propped. 'I need to get to my desk. I need to write that letter!' he called with urgency.

'Right now?'

'Yes! Yes, right now!' Santiago boomed and Mateo felt it reverberate in his chest. 'Time is of the essence!'

Bending low, he helped his papá to stand and with the other hand neatly hooked the catheter bag and its little stand over his arm in a practised motion. The two walked slowly and steadily along the corridor, the floor paved with antique mosaic tiles that made it seem as if you walked on a rainbow. The study door was open to reveal a large blond-wood desk sitting in front of the French doors, also thrown open to reveal the symmetry of the immaculate garden to the east. It had been his mother's favoured view in their vast, ornate, elaborate home. With the old man seated, drenched in sweat at the effort, Mateo put the sheaf of cream paper in front of him and removed the lid from his marble-patterned Mont Blanc, placing it in his left hand.

'I can go online if you wish and see what I can find out, Papá? See if there's any information on Guy Brown or his children?'

'You think I haven't done that already?' he tsked. 'It's a dead end! Nothing for Guy Brown – as if he never existed! How can that be? Such a talent! And nothing for Vanessa Farraday-Brown, her married name. It's the curse of existing before the digital age, nothing . . . they are truly ghosts. So, I will write and see where I can get.'

'Why now? Why do you want to return the painting after all these years?' Mateo was curious.

'Because' – his father paused and retrieved a linen handkerchief, on which the initials S&S were entwined in delicate embroidery, from his top pocket and wiped his watery eyes and sweat-dotted brow – 'I have finished looking at it and because it is time.' Santiago now looked his son in the eye, his expression one of love and one of knowing. 'It's time.'

CHAPTER TWO

'Are you quite sure about me rushing off like this? Feels like leaving you in the lurch, what with the move and everything,' Nora asked as she hurriedly shoved clothes into her wheeled suitcase and zipped up her bulging toiletry bag. Her tone, whether intentional or not, was a little more clipped, wary even, as self-preservation started to kick in. If this man no longer loved her, indeed wanted to end their marriage, then it was probably best a certain formality was established from now on. It was conflicting. Part of her wanted to get far away, to think, to clear her head, to be there for Kiki, and part of her wanted to stay close to him, to cling to him, to sob and try to understand how they had reached this point and whether there was any way forward.

'Yes of course I'm sure.' Gordy spoke calmly, and the reassurance of his words cut her, the reminder of what they were about to lose. 'Kiki needs you. Ted needs you more, and packing up here and shifting boxes is not something you need to be worrying about.' He spoke with a certain melancholy that was reflective and not unkind.

'Because pretty soon packing up and shifting boxes won't be anything to do with me?' she fired back as she pushed down on her suitcase, trying to encourage the zip to meet.

'Nora' – he closed his eyes briefly – 'I meant because you have much more important things to deal with. There's no large family to take over. We are the ones holding the reins.'

And he was right. They were both now without parents, and he was an only child, which just left a rather insubstantial safety net that appeared to have failed, considering Kiki had hit the floor.

Guilt pinged around in her veins. She and her sister weren't close. They spoke infrequently, had seen each other only once in the last three years. Nora had to admit that her assumption had always been that if she didn't hear from Kiki then all must be well. What was it they said? No news is good news! Their twelve-year age gap meant they had little in common. Nora had already been a fully fledged teen when Kiki played with building blocks. Plus, they'd never lived together, other than Nora's brief visits to Nana Dilly during her school holidays, before the day Kiki ran out and nearly got killed, all because of Nora . . .

'I guess so.' She sighed.

'You go,' he asserted. 'I can take care of everything here. I know you'll want to get over as soon as you can and be there for Ted.' He straightened, tapping into his phone, making arrangements, taking control, fixing things. 'What an awful business.'

'Yes. Poor Ted.'

Why would you do that, Kiki? Why would you do that to him? You know what it's like to be left and the gaping hole it leaves inside you! These thoughts felt at best unkind, and she swallowed them. But it was the truth; she found it hard to fathom how anyone could contemplate suicide when they knew what it felt like to grow up without parents providing a haven. Although at least Kiki, no more than a baby, didn't have to mourn all that Nora recalled and had lost. Her little sister was free to create the most perfect imaginary parents who were loving, engaged and devoted, whereas Nora's lived experience was somewhat different.

'Do whatever you need to, we can make anything work for Ted. We have spare rooms in our new quarter. He'd be most welcome for as long as is needed, poor little chap.'

Her husband's tone was commanding and reassuring; she could see how his recruits took comfort in it. *We have spare rooms . . . we* . . . it felt like a reprieve of sorts, and she fought the desire to howl her gratitude, in case he was just being kind.

'Not sure how far it is from Westbury to Stroudly Green, but we can figure something out. I think the routine of school would be best, but let's not overwhelm him. Nothing needs to be decided immediately. I think it's important he feels in control while we provide structure and safety.'

Nora stared at him, unsure how to feel at the suggestion that Ted come and live with them, even for a short while. It wasn't a case of not being fond of the boy, she was, nor was she tempted to shirk her duty, not at all. Ted was a child she saw infrequently, barely knew, in fact; how would it be having him come to live with them? What had he seen/heard of his mother's breakdown, and how was she to handle that little tornado spinning in his head? For she was certain it would be a tornado, and one she knew well. Remembering what it had felt like in the wake of her parents' death, as if the room – no, the world – was spinning and it was all she could do to hang on. Plus, was it fair to allow the little boy to get to know them as a couple when there was the very real chance that Gordy was going to divorce her?

Nora rubbed her brow and felt her jaw tense with the beginnings of a headache. So fearful was she of getting it wrong, of not 'parenting' him properly, and, she was not proud to admit, fearful of disrupting the life of predictable routine and habit that she had crafted. A life that felt safe. She bit her lip, unsure of exactly where Ted would be staying or the circumstances surrounding her sister's suicide attempt. How much responsibility had just fallen into her lap? The doctor said Kiki had cut herself and very little else. She assumed wrists, but until she knew the detail, she felt it best not to make hasty assumptions.

'Thank you, Gordy.' His kindness and practicality were both greatly appreciated.

'No thanks needed. We're family. No matter what happens between us, Nora. Right now, we are family.' He stared at her, looking up briefly from his screen, and she wanted him to hold her, but with the words of their earlier exchange still hanging in the air she felt awkward asking. *Family* . . . it was a curious word, so heavy with connotation and expectation and yet she knew more than most that the ties of blood were no guarantee of anything.

Just ask Ted.

The taxi stopped and started in the traffic. With nervous fingers, Nora smoothed her ponytail and pulled loose fine tendrils of hair free around her forehead, which she knew softened her rather sharp features. Sitting on the back seat, she stared up at the wide and ancient trees that lined the route, forming a canopy where the verdant crowns of oak and sycamore touched in places. She liked the smell of England, especially on a day like this after heavy rain. It reminded her of forest walks hand in hand with Gordy, of planting acorns and lying with her head on his chest among freshly bloomed bluebells that turned even the darkest, dullest patch of dirt into a magical, scented carpet of purple. Had circumstances been different she would have rejoiced at returning to the UK.

No matter her reservations about leaving the balmy climes of Cyprus, she was British and there was always something comforting about setting foot on home turf. It was where she belonged, regardless of how long she stayed away.

But there was very little joy in her today. Her heart and spirit were weary and her mind focused, still trying to fathom the unthinkable. The doctor's words rang inside her head: *Tried to take her life . . . she tried to take her life . . . Oh Kiki, why? Why didn't you call me? Why didn't I call you?* It was hard for her to comprehend; there were times when she had felt low, but suicide had never occurred to Nora as an option and the fact that her sister was a single mother . . .

'*I've been thinking that maybe it might be best if we get a divorce . . .*'

Gordy's words found gaps in the tangled worry of thoughts about her sister, exploding like fireworks in the most vibrant colours, meaning she had no choice but to give them her attention. It was sobering, horrifying and scary. *Divorce*, that's what happened to other people. Were she and Gordy 'other people'? She had never thought so. The idea of not being with him, not seeing him, not having him in her corner was too horrible to consider. *Desperate*. Yes, that was the word.

Pulling her cashmere cardigan around her shoulders, trying to ward off the chill that was nothing to do with temperature, she shook her head, his words still almost unbelievable. What would her life look like without Gordy in it? And wasn't that what she had wanted – freedom from all about him that irritated her? But *divorce*? It was a suggestion that had shocked her and sat like a spike in her chest. It felt akin to complaining of an ache in the arm and someone suggesting amputation – nought to one hundred in less than a second. Surely, surely, they were miles from divorce?

She felt hollowed out at the thought that it wasn't her decision to make. It was he who had said the word, woken the bear. Sometimes in life, despite your very best efforts and the most heartfelt of prayers, some things were simply beyond your control. If her husband was determined to relegate her to no more than a footnote along with the story of their marriage – *Colonel Gordy Brightwell off to write his next chapter* – there was very little she could do about it, no matter that she felt sick at the thought.

She took a deep breath.

The prospect of arriving in Stroudly Green to deal with goodness knows what was terrifying. She swallowed the bile of nausea every time she considered what might await her. This was based on three things: her fear of the unknown, concern over how to handle her young nephew, and the fact that she would rather hike alone up the highest mountain and howl her distress from the summit, waving her fresh family grief like a flag to flail in the wind – assuming she could do so anonymously. Public displays of emotion, along with the washing of one's dirty linen, were not and had never been her thing.

Paint on a happy face and soldier on, darling! She could hear Granny Magda saying that with regularity throughout her life, right up until she passed away when Nora was sixteen.

She was no stranger to disruption, upheaval and emergencies that left you feeling cleaved open at the heart, yet this new situation with Kiki felt precarious to say the least. What was she about to walk into?

Dragging her suitcase behind her and without time to reflect, her exit from Cyprus after two years of living there was hurried, anonymous and without ceremony. Jasmine Leech had tried to call her, but she had let it ring out, in no mood to hear whatever frivolity or sliver of gossip the over-excited woman was keen to share. And so she left quietly. There was no gaggle of friends with soggy tissues pressed under noses, weeping as they waved her off. She didn't and had never strived to be one of the 'girls', preferring a little distance and her own company and not caring a fig of what said gaggles might make of her preference for solitude. This was how she kept her thoughts in order, her emotions on an even keel. It was a method that had served her well – don't let too many people in, don't give them the chance to reject you. An image floated vividly into her mind of her father lunging for his wife, grabbing her wrist, and pulling her to his chest where he anchored her in a bear hug.

'Get off me, you big brute!' Her mother bared her teeth but her eyes sparkled with delight.

This had been part of their game: making out to bicker, quarrelling playfully over the smallest things before holding the other tight and kissing their mouths as if they were hungry. It always made Nora's tummy flip and left her coated with embarrassment, but at the same time it left her feeling inexplicably happy. Almost as if it was a comfort to know that there was love and touch in La Fosca, even if it wasn't directed at her . . .

'Poor Kiki.' She whispered the persistent refrain. Picturing her pretty younger sister the last time they had been together. When was that? Three years? Four? Kiki had grown her hair long and wore several strings of brightly coloured glass beads over her cheesecloth shirt. Her flared jeans were patched. Part hippy, part earth mother, she had that fresh-faced beauty of one who lived off greens and sunshine. Her teeth were very white, her eyes bright and Nora had noted with envy a flexibility in the way she moved, a languidness to her movements; whether that was down to a life of yoga or the fact that she was twelve years Nora's junior, it was hard to tell. One thing struck her then as now, her sister had looked healthy, so very, very healthy and happy. Relaxed, pretty and yes, happy, as if she had it all.

Cut herself . . . She tried and failed to imagine her sister in those minutes: that pretty face, thick hair, bright eyes. Had she been scared? Of course she had. Another wave of guilt washed over her. Why hadn't she seen more of Kiki? Called? Time passed so quickly. Too quickly. How had they grown so apart? Or, more specifically, why, when they were such a tiny family, had they not grown closer?

The answer was loud and obvious: because Kiki reminded Nora of all the bad things that had happened before she met Gordy. And to revisit that time was too painful.

Not long after she had spoken to Dr Hammond, came the email from Mr Rawlings, which had been perfunctory, asking her to get in touch. With the doctor's words still fresh in her ears, she had dialled the number with a shaking hand.

'Mr Rawlings?'

'Speaking.'

'It's Nora Brightwell.' She paused.

'Sorry, who's this?' His question jolted her. 'It's a rather crackly line.'

'Nora, Leonora Brightwell. I'm Kik— Kristina Morris's sister.'

'Oh, Mrs Brightwell, yes of course! First, may I say how terribly sorry I was to hear your sister is unwell.'

'Thank you.' Her voice sounded to her ears like she was under-water. She had eyed the bed through the French windows and wished she could crawl back on to it and hide, sleep, wake again to a day where this was no more than a bad, bad dream. It was a similar sensation to the day she had learned of her parents' deaths, when she had felt a little otherworldly, lost.

'It might seem of small consolation right now, and I'm sure you have a lot to consider, but Mrs Morris left a note, which I can only assume was intended to be found when . . . if . . . erm . . .' he struggled.

'She was no longer here.' She helped him out. Her steady voice belying the horror that filled her up. *A note . . . Kiki had left a note!* This made it real.

'Exactly, yes, very good, thank you. She had enclosed copies of your power of attorney and whatnot, and my telephone number, which is how I have become involved.'

'Yes.' She had no real idea what he was talking about, only half listening as a movie played on a loop in her mind, a snapshot of Kiki calling late at night some years before, crying, 'He's left me! He's bloody left me, and the hardest thing to understand is how he can walk away from Ted; he's not a year old, Nora, not a year, just a baby! And after one quick scroll through his phone, it seems he's already house-hunting with a leggy brunette in Wilmslow who, it would seem, is pregnant. I'm fuming! I'm hurt! I'm . . . I'm pissed off!'

'Kiki no! That's awful. You deserve better. Do you want me to come over? I could be there in a few hours?' It was an out-of-character offer and one she hoped her sister would not take her up on, unsure of how she could have helped and not relishing the thought of making the trip, the upheaval.

'No! No! I'll be okay . . . I'll calm down. Shit happens and life goes on, right?'

The words now resonated in their truth: her sister did deserve better, shit did happen, and life did indeed go on.

A wordy email from Ted's school informed her that he was waiting to be collected and that he had not been told of his mother's hospitalisation. Nora was surprised to read the words, 'As Ted's next of kin . . .' It shouldn't have been a surprise, she had after all agreed. Kiki had asked her on that rare, joyous evening when Nora had visited.

'*Well, who else am I going to ask, Leonoranoodle?*' Kiki had shrugged.

And Nora had felt a wave of something that felt a lot like love for this younger woman, a stranger in so many ways, one sent to live with Nana Dilly as a baby, while she was packed off to school, and yet the only person left on the planet to use this nickname. It was endearing, yet a painful hint of what life might have been like

49

had she had a normal upbringing with normal parents in a normal environment.

'*I'll email you the name of my lawyer and his address, blah blah blah . . . and I hope you never, ever need to call him and I hope he never, ever needs to call you.*' Kiki had rolled her hand as she spoke.

'*Me too!*' She had laughed as the chance of something happening that required her to jump up and take the reins had, on that light-filled, joy-infused night, felt slim.

And yet here they were.

'What day is it today?' she leaned forward and asked the taxi driver.

'Friday, love.'

'Friday, yes, thanks.' She'd momentarily lost track.

The taxi dropped her at the gates of the school, which was surrounded by a high green metal fence dotted with what looked to be strategically placed cameras. She was no stranger to this level of security but had not expected it at a primary school in a leafy market town just south of Cheltenham. Once again dragging her case, this time to the gate, she pressed the buzzer.

'How can I help you?' The woman's voice sounded harassed.

'My name's Leonora Brightwell. I'm here for Ted Morris, my sister—' She stopped, more than a little confused about what to say and unwilling to talk about something so personal to a tarnished intercom.

'Oh yes, Mrs Brightwell. I'll just buzz you in, lovely, we've been expecting you. Come straight through, I'll tell Mr Ormond.' The woman's tone was soft now, emotional and kind.

Nora had no idea who Mr Ormond was. She sucked in her cheeks and bit them as she walked through the gate, holding the pose until the desire to give in to tears had passed. Now was most definitely not the time.

Games like hopscotch and wiggly snake patterns were marked out in yellow paint on the playground, only making it seem smaller, she thought. The high fencing gave the whole place a slightly claustrophobic air. Her heart beat too quickly. She was nervous, unsure of what to say or what the protocol was for something like this. She headed for the double doors with large metal plates securing them closed.

Suddenly they swung open and a man in his late thirties walked down the steps. His pink collarless shirt was open at the neck, his jeans were red and his trainers brown, his shoulder-length hair was thick and stayed back from his face in fat curls. His colourful clothing drew her. She lived an army life where her husband's wardrobe was the colour of the forest and mud. He walked quickly with his hand outstretched and his eyes watery, his mouth sad, but a handsome, open face nonetheless.

'Mrs Brightwell.' He took her hand, not to shake it, but to hold it briefly in both of his. 'We are all so sad to hear that Kristina is poorly. The whole school, all the parents, the staff, everyone, we're just . . .' He shook his head.

'Thank you.' She didn't know how to respond. His sadness was genuine, and she was grateful. It eased her guilt a little; this man and the community clearly loved Kristina and that meant her sister was not alone, that Kiki was supported in her absence.

'I'm Jason.'

'Nora.'

'It's great you managed to get here so quickly, Nora. It's such a rotten time. Ted doesn't really know what's going on; we thought it best he hears it from you, but he's a smart boy and is obviously aware of something being amiss. He asked why his mum wasn't picking him up last night, as usually all changes to collection routine are written in the diary, discussed in advance.' He drew breath. 'But he's remarkable, stoic, going with the flow, quiet, as you'd imagine, typical of his little nature.' His eyes crinkled into a smile and she felt her cheeks flame. How many times had she met Ted? Twice? Three times? She didn't *know* his little nature and felt like an imposter and her mouth went a little dry. 'He stayed at Afsar's house last night and Afsar's mum said he was quiet but okay. He didn't eat much, but she says he slept, so . . .'

'Right. Afsar is his friend?' She again felt the wash of embarrassment that she didn't know these things.

'Not just a friend, his very best friend!' He smiled. 'They're pretty inseparable. As seven-year-old boys can be.'

She nodded and gripped the handle of her suitcase, looking back to the locked gate as the thought flickered in her mind that she could run . . .

'I expect you want to see Ted?'

'Erm.' She swallowed, nervously anticipating the very public reunion with this little boy, a stranger really, and trying to practise words in her head that slipped away from her thoughts like smoke. On the odd occasion, Kiki had forwarded photographs snapped on her phone, images of her and Ted on a beach and one in a park with a fat snail perched on the back of his hand, but would she recognise him? The thought made her feel a little nauseous. This was a huge event and yet she wasn't sure she could pick out her only nephew in a line-up.

'I don't want to disturb him,' she lied, not wanting to go through it at all, to placate a stranger, to face what was coming. How had she got into this situation where she was next of kin to this little boy?

'It is of course up to you, but we thought it may be best he stays in school for continuity and familiarity for the rest of the day. A distraction is sometimes good and then you can collect him at home time? Just to give a framework of normality over this very turbulent day. But it's good he knows you're around, it will no doubt help his mind settle, but if you'd rather take him home now, then that's fine too, of course. We completely understand. Whatever works.' He spoke with his palms upturned, open. 'And I'll help you in any way I can.'

'I . . .' She took her time, making it up as she went along. 'Have you been in this situation before? Had to deal with a child whose parent . . .'

'Yes.' His face fell. She respected the fact that he gave not one single detail.

'I think I'll talk to him after school, maybe go back to my sister's flat right now to get the lie of the land, tidy up or whatever.' She knew Kiki had been found at home and didn't want Ted to see anything untoward. Her stomach flipped, not sure *she* wanted to see anything untoward either. 'I can get groceries in.' She let the plan form in her head. 'I'll be here for the weekend as we don't officially move back to the UK until Monday, plus . . .' *What did she want to say?* 'I think maybe it's better I chat to Ted at home, just explain that his mum is unwell and then he's free to react and . . .' She ran out of words, remembering keenly when she had been told of her parents passing, thinking over and over of the day before that – the *last* day without the knowledge – the last good day, one where she lived without the bolt of grief lancing her gut and the fear of something unseen and indescribable that lurked in her peripheral vision still. She didn't know how to deal with this, what to do, what to say, what came next. But she did know that her parents' death had changed her, it had left her alone, unable to connect with the mum and dad who had hardly bothered with her, and she knew that when Ted was old enough to understand what Kiki had done, he would be changed too. The thought saddened her.

'That sounds good, but maybe just say hello to him now?' He pointed over his shoulder towards the school building. 'As I say, I think it might help him settle.'

It was almost a reflex, the way her palm shot up over her mouth. *I don't want to say hello; I want to run in the opposite direction. I want to be in Cyprus with my husband, trying to sort out our mess of a marriage. I'm not equipped for this . . .*

As if sensing her hesitancy, Jason Ormond took a step closer. 'I can't imagine what you're going through; *we* are all shocked and she is your *sister*. I think it's important to remember that you're not supposed to have it all figured out and that you need to look after yourself too.' He spoke with the quiet enthusiasm she was sure had a huge impact on his young pupils. 'Kristina is always smiling, always upbeat, always laughing, she is the very last person I would've expected—' He stopped short as if he might be overstepping a mark. 'Let's go get Ted from class. And if you want me to be there when you talk to him later . . .' He paused. 'I don't want to interfere, but the offer's there.'

'Thank you.' It was going to be hard enough to overcome her nerves and have the conversation she was dreading, but the thought of doing so with an audience was unthinkable.

They fell into step and made their way into the 1970s, flat-roofed building that smelled a little fusty with undernotes of cooked food and urine. The kind of place that could only have benefited from having all the windows and doors wedged open, allowing a cold breeze to clear out the stale air. She abandoned her bulky case in the reception, as directed by her host.

He stopped at a green-painted door along a corridor whose walls were a soft collage made up of coats and jackets in a rainbow of colours stuffed on to a row of crowded pegs. Vast works of art were tacked up, along with the words 'Welcome To Our School' formed by the sticking of scrunched-up tissue paper on to card, which was most effective.

'Ready?'

'Yes,' she lied. The corridor suddenly felt very narrow and airless. Her fingers coiled into her palms so tightly, her knuckles ached. *I can't do this. I can't do this . . .*

In a swift and practised movement, he knocked and entered before quietly acknowledging the young woman taking the class and walking over to a little boy with skinny legs and very dark hair who sat by the window. *Ted . . .*

Nora wasn't sure she would have recognised him. He had changed a lot. He was taller, skinnier, more of a boy and less of a baby than the last time she had seen him. He was quiet, seemed placid, for which she was grateful, and his eyes were huge with the dark-brown liquid centres of his grandfather and mother. This flicker of recognition in her kin made her pulse jump. It was an unexpected yet welcome physical hint of connection. Standing in the doorway she raised her hand in a wave as Mr Ormond, crouching beside him, pointed in her direction and spoke quietly to him before guiding him from the room with his hands on the boy's shoulders, and the stares of the little children all seated around at his back.

'*This way, Leonora, quick, quick! Don't keep Matron waiting . . .*' She remembered the older girl marching her along the corridor to Matron's office where Sister Edwina, head of school, a police officer, and the matron herself were indeed all waiting. She felt the usual flash of pain in her heart at the memory of the place – not that it was cruel or harsh, but more that the constant wishing to be back in Luna's kitchen was like a weight that yoked her. How she had longed to be in the villa, watching their housekeeper pluck and prep chickens for supper, rubbing the goose-bumped skin red with olive oil and pimenton before throwing the birds on to hot coals on which she blew to inflame their ire.

'*Sit down dear.*' Matron had spoken kindly and pulled out the leather club chair in front of her desk, which was odd in itself as everyone else was standing, and Leonora had known. Before a single word had been spoken, she had known.

Ted's fringe was long, almost hanging over his eyes, one of his front teeth was missing. There was a slight sheen to his skin, this sweat of anxiety the only clue to what might be going on inside his head, hinting at his awareness of the murmurs, the exchanged looks, the atmosphere of sorrow and concern. He stared at her, his surprise no doubt at this odd interruption to an ordinary day, following the one when his mum had failed to collect him from school, and where he'd had an unplanned sleepover with Afsar. These were the days that in the future, the older Ted would replay in his mind, a marker in his journey, and one in which she would have a reluctant starring role.

Mr Ormond thanked the teacher and closed the door behind him. Ted stood in front of her in the corridor. Her fingers now twitched by her sides; what was she supposed to do? Was it okay to hug him? Touch him? Was that allowed? She didn't know the rules. Taking her cue from Mr Ormond's behaviour she crouched low until they were eye to eye.

'Hi Ted.'

'Hi.' His voice was high, sweet and cute. She had expected the gruffness of a boy.

'This is a very strange day, isn't it? Me turning up during your lesson! Who's your teacher?' She looked toward the classroom.

'Mr Ormond.' He pointed at the man.

'Oh, I thought you were the head.' She looked up at him.

'No! That's Mrs Maitland, she's great. I'm Ted's class teacher and so pretty much have him for everything bar singing and swimming, that's right, Ted, isn't it?'

The little boy gave an exaggerated nod.

'Because you can't sing or swim?' The question burbled out, as things did when she was nervous.

'Something like that.'

With his thin arms dangling by his side, the little boy's nose twitched.

'Do you remember me? It's been a little while since I saw you last,' she asked, not sure of what she might say if he did not.

'Aunty Pickle,' he whispered.

'Aunty Pickle?' She smiled. 'You call me Aunty Pickle?'

Again, he nodded.

'I didn't know that. Why?'

'Mummy says you made her sandwiches and you always put a pickle in them.' He held her eyeline, his double blink at the mention of his mother making her heart swell.

'I did, that's true!' She pictured her teenage self catering for her little sister at their Nana Dilly's house during the holidays, sandwiches about the extent of her culinary know-how. And how awkward she had felt in the little house at 14 Midland Road that had once been her haven, until baby Kiki had moved there and Nana Dilly had become preoccupied. Instead of a haven, Nora began to dread the holidays, but dreading term time too meant she didn't quite know where she fitted, until she met Gordy Brightwell and knew she fitted right by his side.

I've been thinking that maybe, it might be best if we get a divorce . . .

She shook his words from her mind. 'Do you like pickles?'

'I don't know.' His honest reply.

'We'll have to get you one to try.'

Again, Mr Ormond bent down. 'So, Ted, Aunty Pickle wanted to say hello and to let you know that she will collect you at home time, is that okay?'

'Does Mummy know she's collecting me, because . . . because . . .' He faltered, fiddling with the hem of his navy school sweater. 'Because you have to write a note?' he asked with such clarity, such trust it was hard to hear. Emotion swelled in her throat.

'Everything has been arranged, you don't need to worry about a thing.'

She noted the way the teacher spoke to the little boy, in the same way he spoke to her: naturally, without any special voice or patronising tone. Ted nodded and turned to go back to class.

'See you later!' she called with as much positivity as the situation allowed.

'See you later,' he echoed flatly without looking back and disappeared inside the room.

She and the teacher watched him find his seat and she saw the way the little boy's gaze stayed fixed on his workbook, as if aware that all eyes were on him and not wanting to meet them.

'Sheila Henning has left a key for you in reception.'

'Who, sorry? A what?' She followed as he turned to walk along the corridor, trying to sort her fog of thoughts.

'Zac's mum? She has a key to Kristina's as they're often helping each out with childcare. She didn't know if you'd have your own but left hers in reception for you. She's in a terrible state. They're close. Good friends. Not that she saw this coming, none of us did. That's what makes it harder, the thought that Kristina didn't feel she could talk to us.'

'Yes.'

Nora ran her fingers over her mouth, feeling guilty that she, too, was not in a terrible state, ashamed of how disconnected she felt to her sister and nephew.

'It was Sheila who—' He stopped mid-sentence and faltered. 'It was Sheila who helped Kiki, helped her into the ambulance.'

'She found her?'

'Yes.' He winced.

'I'd like to thank her.'

58

'Oh, you'll see her soon enough.'

'Right and thank you, Jason, for . . .'

'No worries. I mean it. I'm here for whatever you or Ted might need.'

She thanked the teacher again and, towing her heavy suitcase, made her way along the street, thankful to be out in the cold, crisp air of the blue-sky morning, which on any ordinary day she would savour, but this was no ordinary day. Her thoughts turned to Kiki, poor, sweet Kiki . . . and that summer visit over three years ago when her sister, with her long locks and her cheesecloth shirt, had looked so very well. They had been drinking wine in her courtyard and both puffed on a slender joint; Kiki an expert, and Nora in a semi-sloshed state wanting to be as adventurous as her little sister, to not be seen as the old stick-in-the-mud she assumed was her reputation. The joint had been ghastly but holding it was really rather nice. Empowering and sexy somehow. She thought she might look cool and worldly, shaking off her sensible skin and imitating the fabulous, interesting girls at university, the ones she had admired from afar, eavesdropping on their conversations as they ranted with passion, her face always an inch from a textbook.

Later that night, however, after vomiting into the sink of the small bathroom, one quick glance in the mirror had revealed her to look more 'slept-in-a-skip' rough than cool. Joint-smoking was definitely not going to be her new hobby.

She had been to her sister's flat a couple of times, but wouldn't have been able to find it without the app on her phone guiding her along the streets lined with red-brick terraced cottages and white picket fences that all looked remarkably similar. Her suitcase kept getting caught on the uneven grey paving slabs or tufts of grass, yanking her arm backwards. She cursed the weight of it.

Suddenly, there she was with her hand on the gate that her sister had walked through thousands of times. She recognised it, of course, the ceramic house number, the overgrown dog rose climbing up a tethered trellis, and the wooden front door, once pillar-box red, now faded pink in places where sunlight had bleached it. In her mind's eye, Nora could see her sister walking up the path with friends, lovers, hand in hand with Ted, with books to read, groceries in bags, fragrant takeaways, the Sunday paper, charity shop objects d'art and rag rugs in a multitude of colours. She felt an ache in her chest as she pictured her sister's life. A smiling, colourful life, a happy and contented life, or so she had thought.

Taking a deep breath, she trod the path and put the key, mottled through age, into the dulled metal lock.

The flat was on the ground floor and comprised the lower half of the Edwardian terrace, with a Mr Appleton living above. She remembered Kiki describing him over the phone at Christmas as the perfect neighbour: in his eighties, he liked long naps, was hard of hearing and his only intrusion in her life was when he played his beloved ragtime music loudly on a Sunday morning, which Kiki loved, dancing along in the kitchen to the toe-tappers. How could it be that in a matter of months she had chosen suicide over dancing?

The first thing that hit Nora as she stepped into the hallway, which was narrower than she had remembered, was the odour. The place smelled of damp. It was pungent and sour and something else, a scent she couldn't readily identify, but one she didn't like. Her nose wrinkled as she made her way into the open-plan kitchen and sitting room, where two rooms had been knocked through with sliding doors at the back leading out into a small courtyard. The living areas were separated by a wide breakfast bar, which was cluttered with the paraphernalia of life. A mini compost bin, dog-eared magazines, a half-eaten packet of bourbons, a cluster of empty jam jars, two fat-headed dahlias in a delicate shade of peach, which sat in a vase of fetid water, and from a brown paper bag peered three curious lemons. It was this citrus fruit that bothered her the most. Such a deliberate purchase – for what? she wondered. A recipe? A large gin or two? And did this mean her sister's actions were unplanned? Who buys fresh lemons and then tries to end their life? What had been the straw that broke the camel's back, the grain of rice that tipped the scales, the thought that made her reach for the blade?

The flat, while not exactly putrid, was in the state one lived when not expecting visitors, making her presence feel even more invasive. As well as the cluttered breakfast bar, there were sticky honeypot rings littering the work surface. Discarded knickers, dirty socks, pillow slips and a pair of pyjamas sitting on the floor in a forlorn pile in front of the washing machine, which she could see was full of laundry. A small green light winked on the control panel.

A quick peek into the two small bedrooms off the front hallway revealed unmade beds, more laundry spilling from an overflowing basket and on her sister's bedside cabinet, three mugs with the remnants of tea in them, all in various stages of decay. This room smelled too of night breath, sheets that needed freshening, the dairy-like odour of grubby trainers and the tang of tobacco.

Kiki's teenage room at Nana Dilly's had been neat, if a little old-fashioned, and on the rare occasion she had visited here, the place had been magazine pristine. This state of disarray with hints of hedonism was how their parents had lived; not that Kiki would have memory of it. Nora drew the navy cotton curtains and opened the window to let the cold breeze whip around the walls.

'For the love of God, Kiki!' She gathered the dirty mugs and dumped them in the kitchen sink where two cereal dishes sat, each with splashes of milk sitting in the bowls of the abandoned spoons and with stray Frosties clinging to the outer rims of the china. Nora ran her fingers over the spoon handle. The last meal Kiki ate with

Ted, which could have been her last ever . . . it was as sobering as it was unthinkable.

Sliding open the wide metal-framed doors that overlooked the little courtyard, she took in the waterlogged plants, now no more than brown sticks in glazed pots where the soil appeared to be floating, all abandoned on the wet brick floor. In her mind the garden area had been well-tended, and she pictured how they had spent the evening sitting out there in the warmth of summer, when blousy-headed geraniums dotted the space with pockets of poker red, as they sipped cheap rosé wine, giggling as her sister rolled the joint and broke down barriers built from time apart and a lack of shared history, despite their blood connection. The conversation tilted as it always did to their parents, Kiki keen to glean as much as she could in the shortest space of time about the two people of whom she had no actual recollection. Nora had to remind herself that despite her own devastating loss as a pre-teen, at least she had some memories; she was still undecided if this was a plus.

Her phone buzzed in her pocket. A text from Gordy.

How's it going? Chilly I bet. Will call later – firefighting here as usual, not enough hours in the day. Gordy

His tone was a little formal, and yet she replied in the customary manner that was almost instinctive.

Love you X

Instantly she cursed the finger reflex and a mind that was clearly still catching up. *Love you* . . . These the easiest two words that would ordinarily require neither thought nor scrutiny from either party. She wondered if it were possible to unsend a text? This feeling of unease when it came to her husband was quite alien. She wished she could talk to him face to face, wanted to tell him how her head felt like it was full of glue. And how she felt like a fraud. *I never saw her, Gordy. We rarely spoke.* She wanted his advice on what she was supposed to do with a small boy, a child, Ted. They had as a couple shied away from getting dogs because of their lifestyle and now she had a child to care for? And not just any child, but one who was about to be traumatised.

Nora rested her head against the cool glass of the sliding door and spoke aloud.

'I know what's needed when your parents are unreliable, dangerous even, and it most definitely isn't me! And I could do it maybe, do it all, if I felt we were a team, Gordy. But you want a divorce, and my gut is hollowed out at the thought of it . . . I'm so lost . . . so alone and I thought feeling like this was behind me . . .'

'Hello?' a woman's voice called from the hallway.

'Hello?' she replied sternly, straightening as embarrassment flared, not only at the possibility that she had been overheard, but she also felt awkward, as if she had no right to be in this flat, opening windows and shifting cups. It felt intrusive and yet necessary and should surely fall on the shoulders of someone closer to Kiki than she.

'Oh! You must be Nora.' The woman, with a shock of red curls and glorious freckles on her pale skin, lowered her head as her tears fell.

'Yes.' She kept her voice low. Self-conscious on the woman's behalf.

'I'm Sheila, Zac's mum,' she managed, raising her head, eyes raw and her skin blotchy from crying. 'And I just wanted to pop in and say that we are all just devastated and feel hopeless. Kristina is . . .' Pulling a tissue from her sleeve she swiped her face and coughed to clear her throat, trying for composure. 'She's always there to help any one of us who comes unstuck, you know?'

Nora nodded, but she didn't know, not really.

'How're you doing?' Sheila stepped forward and ran her hand up and down the top of Nora's arm.

Nora took a step backward, keen to put distance between herself and the woman. She sat down on the low sofa where flattened embroidered cushions lined up to add a splash of colour to the grey twill. Sheila took a seat on the battered kilim-covered footstool opposite and stared at her.

'I'm . . . still trying to figure everything out.' Nora spoke the truth, looking into the middle distance and not wanting to open up to this stranger. 'I still don't fully know what happened. It's all such a shock. I've spoken to the hospital, and her lawyer got in touch.' She regretted mentioning the lawyer. It wasn't the time. 'But I know I owe you thanks – I believe you helped her?'

'Yes. It's just so . . .' Sheila shook her head. 'So hard to accept. It was an ordinary day. I saw her at the school gates at drop-off. She looked lovely, she always looks lovely. We were talking about Afsar's birthday party in a few weeks – they're going trampolining in Cheltenham. She . . . she kissed Ted, waved him into school and headed off, I thought to jump on the bus like she always did to head up to the hospice.'

'The hospice?' Nora felt her heart race, had Kiki been ill?

'Yes, she'd started working up at Longacre three days a week as well as doing her admin job from home; she fit that in around school hours and after his bedtime mostly, so she was always around for Ted. I know she loved it up at the hospice, giving hand and foot massages, helping style hair, paint nails, all kinds of beauty treatments. But that's her all over, isn't it, just wanting to help, be kind, give back?'

Nora nodded with relief.

'It was me that found her. By accident, totally by accident, had I been ten minutes later . . . I can't stand to think about it!' She hid her eyes and sobbed.

'But you did and thank God.' Nora folded her hands into her lap. 'And just . . . Thank you from us, from her family.' The words felt a little disingenuous; this woman probably knew Kiki and the workings of her life far better than she did.

'She was in the bath.' Sheila pointed tearfully towards the bathroom, the only room Nora had yet to venture into. 'She was in her undies and the water was cool, she'd drunk something, smelled like wine, and she was in this red, red pool and it was like it was a dream, a nightmare. I felt like everything was going in slow motion but at the same time happening really, really fast. It's hard to describe.' She looked up. 'I kept calling her name and I pulled the plug and managed to drag her out of the water on to the floor. I shouted for help – I'd left the front door open, and a man was walking past, I don't know who he was, a delivery guy maybe, and he called the ambulance, and they got here really quickly, but it felt like forever. I kept talking to her. I bound her wrists with pillowcases, and I kept . . . I kept telling her that everything was going to be all right and that Ted loved her, and I loved her, that we all did, and that we'd work everything out, and I kept asking her to stay with me . . .' She broke down, her tears clogging her mouth and nose as her body shook.

'Sheila, that must have been awful. I can't imagine.' The image of her sister in her underwear lying in a red pool as her life ebbed from her was more than she could stand. Nora felt the slow creep of tears. It was hard to hear and even harder to imagine. 'I can't thank you enough, and Ted will too one day.'

The woman shook her head and sat up straight. 'I went with her in the ambulance, grabbed the envelopes she'd left on the side, and as soon as we got up to St Margaret's everyone gathered around and they took over – the doctors went into overdrive, then they whisked her off . . .' Again she paused to wipe her eyes. 'I haven't seen her since, but honestly, Nora, I keep thinking about her at school that morning: she was smiling and seemed happy, we were chatting like we usually did, just talking rubbish, laughing, taking the mick out of our friend Fi, as we do, and then when I got home, I had my breakfast and I remembered that Ted is in goal for the first time this Saturday and he needs goalie gloves and I saw a pair in the window of the charity shop and I was going to ask Kristina if she wanted me to pick them up, so on my way to the shops, I knocked on the door . . . then I remembered it was her hospice day, but for some reason I peeped through the letterbox and I could just feel that something wasn't right. I called out, then used my key and then I found her.'

'There was clearly more going on than she let on.' Nora filled in the gaps with the obvious statement; her heart skipped at how close Kiki had come to losing her life, saved on no more than a whim. 'And I think if someone is mentally suffering, they're sometimes very good at hiding it, so don't feel bad about what you might have missed, feel glad that you found her, that you saved her.' Sheila's words had been moving, gut-wrenching! Kiki was her only sibling . . . but Nora couldn't cry, not in front of this woman whose grief seemed to run deeper than her own.

Sheila nodded. 'She'd mentioned to me once that she went through a phase when Ted's dad left when she felt low, but who wouldn't? I thought she meant normal down in the dumps, but something like this? Never. We spoke about everything. Or I thought we did. We're great mates. I can't believe it. I *saw* her, saw what she'd done, and I still can't believe it. I can't stand to think of little Ted without his mum right now. Thank God he's got you.' Sheila smiled.

Nora felt the spread of a red bloom over her neck and chest.

'I came back here when I left the hospital and tidied up, cleaned the bathroom and whatnot.'

'Thank you, Sheila.' She meant it, hating to think of what it must have been like if this current state was post clean-up.

'No, it's my pleasure. As I say, not only are we great mates, but I know Kiki would do the same for me.'

'There's a lot to think about.'

'Yes. I think someone has sent Richie an email, or called. Either way, Jason said he'd been told but as yet hasn't made contact. Typical!' Sheila snarled her dislike for Ted's father. She probably knew more than Nora did of the mechanics of her sister's relationship with him.

'I haven't seen him for a long time.' Nora thought about the loud, chirpy chap who her Nana Dilly would have described as 'a right flash Harry!' He and Gordy had verbally jousted on their one and only meeting, with Richie Morris mocking a military life and Gordy barely able to hide his contempt for the man who drove a top-of-the range Merc, rattled a gold Rolex on his tanned wrist and had paid cash for the flat that Kiki now called home. A man who had never given a day of service to others in his whole life and for whom little Kiki had fallen.

'Neither has Kristina.' Sheila paused. 'Ted's only seen him a handful of times. He pitched up about eighteen months ago, just turned up out of the blue and took Ted out for lunch, loaded him up with sugar and armfuls of plastic crap and then came back the next week, did the same again. Just enough for Ted to get excited, as if it might become a regular thing, but it didn't. Richie was just messing with them really. He'd had a row with his wife and was probably looking for something to make himself feel a bit better, and something that would piss off his wife, no doubt. So he came down from Cheshire, left his wife and kids up there, played at Dad for a couple of weekends and then buggered off again. Kristina was fuming! Not on her behalf, she knows the bloke's a dickhead, but she hated how Ted was messed around. So unfair. But I understand;

my kids' dad is similar. A waste of bloody space. Complete dickhead in fact.' Sheila folded her arms across her chest, suggesting self-protection.

'Does Zac have brothers and sisters?'

'One sister, Zoey, two years older physically, about twenty mentally. She's a serious little soul.'

Nora nodded, knowing this could have described her as a child.

'Do you have children, Nora? Can't remember if Kristina said?'

'No. No, I don't.' She held the younger woman's eyeline, waiting to see which response Sheila might choose.

'Ah, so I think I'm now supposed to say, "Oh, you have a career?" because we're told you have to have at least one of those things, right? It's bullshit, isn't it?'

Nora warmed to the woman. 'Yes, it is. It's bullshit. And no, I don't have a career. My husband's in the army and so lots of moving around. Feels hard to take on roles, get settled just to be moving again, but I get gardening jobs, volunteering, if necessary. That's my passion.'

'Gardening, eh?' Sheila smiled.

'Yes, it's my favourite way to waste time.'

There was a quiet moment, as if both she and Sheila remembered the reason for being there and that there was very little room for small talk when Kiki was currently lying in a hospital bed. Kiki who would not have given up her role as Ted's mum for any career, for anything in the world, in fact. At least that was what everyone, her included, had thought, until now. Nora was keen for the woman to leave so she could phone the hospital for an update.

'Would you like me to show you how the oven works and where things are?'

'What kind of things?' Her mouth felt a little dry with nerves; she was terrified at the prospect of the weekend.

'Things like Ted's clothes and toys, the Calpol in case he gets sick, his night-time snuggle blanket which he doesn't know I know about.' She gave a weak wink. 'His football boots and kit in case he feels up to football tomorrow morning. They train every Saturday at the playing field at the back of the supermarket.'

'I guess so, yes, please, show me where his things are.' She stood to grab her bag where her pad and pen lived. List-making was how she kept control, and this was no different. 'I don't know the first thing about looking after children, even if it's only for the weekend.' She caught the confused flash across Sheila's brow. 'But that's okay, I shall write everything down.' She raised the pad and pen in her hand.

'Think you might need a bigger pad.' Sheila smiled as Nora followed her into her nephew's bedroom.

SANTIAGO AGOSTÍ'S FIRST LETTER

My name is Santiago Agostí.

He paused and looked out of the window as the sun beat down on the lemon grove that edged the east garden. He used to be able to breathe deeply and inhale the citrus scent that floated on the air, which would transport him to that place where he and his beloved Sofia liked to wander. Old age had sadly robbed him of this olfactory clarity and now when he breathed in, he was met with a combination of scents that included sun-scorched grass, the amber-scented soap that the maid left in his bathroom and his own urine – inevitable when he carried it around outside of his body in a plastic bag. How he hated the darn thing. Concentrating, he again lowered his eyes to the task in hand.

> *It was my pleasure many years ago to be the patron of a promising young artist . . . His name was Guy Brown. I have a large room in my house, a gallery if you will, and in it hangs a piece of his magnificent work. It is entitled,* My Own Sweet Darlings. *I came across it quite by chance among the*

artefacts and detritus of life that was left behind after the sad death of the Browns. I made Guy's acquaintance accidentally, as is often the way when life or the universe puts you on the same but opposite path of another, and only when you collide do you realise there was a reason you took that route, made that choice . . .

Many years ago, Guy, his wife and young child were in my country looking for a property to rent, somewhere with enough space and good light for him to work. I offered them my villa, 'La Fosca', which is perched on a hill and blessed with red and gold sunsets that still take my breath away. Guy was a magician, nothing less! A rare skill and all the more incredible because he was not classically trained, nor from a line of artists; his father worked in a factory and his mother cleaned houses for the wealthy. To see him transform a canvas with a few deft strokes into a picture so perfect, so hypnotic, is something I've not seen before or since. Three strokes, four and you had a face, five strokes, six, an arm and so it went until you were captivated by the detail and the way his art made you feel. For that was his skill, he made you feel.

He made me feel.

Only today, I have looked upon the face of my wife captured some decades since by his brush and knife and I have wept with the need to run my fingers over the curve of her jawline, to inhale the scent of her, knowing that I could never, ever have captured her in the way he did, and I loved her, knew every facet of her!

I wish to return the painting to Guy's daughters, Leonora and Kiki. It feels only right that it finds a home with them.

This address is the last one I have for Guy's mother, Mrs Dilly Brown, and whilst I am aware that Mrs Brown will be deceased, I write in the vain hope that maybe you, the new occupant, might be a relative or have the address of a relative or maybe are in touch with a neighbour who might be in possession of such information? It's a long shot, I understand, and please forgive my urgency, but I am counting down the months, weeks, days until I once again get to hold the hand of my beloved wife . . .

And so, I seek help, and I await your reply.
Sinceramente
S Agostí.

Santiago sat back in his chair and reread the letter. He felt the almost forgotten stir of excitement in his blood. How he loved it when a thought or plan came to fruition.

CHAPTER THREE

The three hours since she'd visited Ted at school had flown. It had felt good to be industrious, distracted. The kitchen now gleamed, and the washing machine had been thrashed. Unused to this level of domesticity, she couldn't deny the reward of seeing the place shine. It alleviated a little of her guilt at not seeing Kiki more, doing more.

Retrieving her sister's knickers from the floor, she had held them in her hands as a wave of distress washed over her. The pants were marked, the smudge of life in the gusset so personal, so human, so real and so intimate. It was hard to picture Kiki at that moment in a hospital bed, medicated, bandaged. The nurse had informed Nora, when she had called, that Kiki had requested no visitors, and to call again in the morning, but she was sleeping and that really was the best thing for her. She also mentioned that her sister had been very lucky . . .

In that second she felt the reality of the situation like a kick in the gut. They owed Sheila a great deal, but lucky? Nora wasn't so sure.

It took courage for her to go into the bathroom, but was entirely necessary when she recognised the second underlying smell that had invaded her nose. Iron. It was the iron scent of blood. Sheila had done her best, returning to the flat when she left the hospital and scrubbing the bath out, mopping the floor, popping the towels and the used pillowcases into a black bin liner that she confessed to shoving in the wheelie bin at the end of the garden path. Disposing of them lest Ted should see. And to the naked eye, the place looked clean enough, but when Nora looked closely, there was a faint tinge of red about three quarters of the way up the bath. One or two crimson splashes on the white tiles that Sheila must have missed and one splat on the cold tap. But it was the scent that was the biggest giveaway.

Nora set to on her hands and knees, filling a mixing bowl, in lieu of a bucket, with bleach and water. She dipped the cloth into the potent mixture and wiped the floor in a circular motion, wringing the cloth under the hot tap into the sink before going back into the bowl, going over and over the tiled floor until the room smelled of bleach and the surfaces sparkled. Letting her fingers linger over the tiles, she found it hard to imagine the panic, the shock, as her sister's unconscious form, clad in her underwear, lay in a wet heap on this very spot as her life's blood seeped from her wrists.

It was sudden; Nora's tears came thick and fast without warning, making speech difficult and sending a hot cluster of distress that blocked her throat.

'I'm so sorry, Kiki,' she mouthed as fat tears snaked over her cheeks. What she was apologising for exactly would be hard to say, but still the need to make amends felt acute.

With the washing machine whirring away and the wet laundry drying on a rack in the bathroom, she now used her app to navigate her way back to the school, carefully studying the blue dot – the digital breadcrumb equivalent in this modern-day Hansel and Gretel method. She arrived ten minutes early. There was a clutch of parents and what looked to be grandparents at the school gate. Some in huddles, others in whispering twosomes, a couple of people standing alone, transfixed by the phones in their palms, and her. Pausing, she took her time in approaching, thinking of her last night in Akrotiri and the pointed questioning from the gaggle of women. The endless banal details about children, a topic on which she had no sage words of experience and no real opinions to offer.

Her stomach clenched at the prospect of a rerun with these strangers. She also dreaded having to discuss Kiki, not wanting to exchange pleasantries with these people who were nothing to do with her family. She didn't want her sister's situation to be fodder for gossip in a WhatsApp group.

She wondered who Kiki would stand with and knew she would probably greet everyone, find common ground, be sweet and generous and smiley, as was her nature. Nora's heart swelled, not only at the deceit of it, the mask that hid a situation so wretched that the solution had felt so very extreme, but also because it should be Kiki here to fetch her son, *sweet Kiki* . . . She bit the inside of her sucked-in cheeks; why did tears threaten at the most inconvenient of times?

'Hello.' A stout woman with a grass-green poncho around her sturdy shoulders blocked her path. 'You must be Kristina's sister? Sheila said you'd be here. I was hoping to see you and wanted to say that my thoughts are with Kristina, and whatever I can do to help you or her or Ted, please just shout.' The woman spoke with a lowered pitch as if in reverence.

'Thank you.'

'I bought you these.' Into Nora's hands, she placed a bunch of small-headed yellow roses, some still in tight bud. They were wrapped in brown paper and tied with string. 'I just wanted to tell you how sad I am. It's unbelievable. Such a shock for us all.'

Nora held the flowers and felt a little overwhelmed by such kindness.

'Thank you, they're beautiful. Yellow roses signify friendship.'

'I didn't know that. But I think they always brighten up a bad day.'

'They do,' she agreed, 'and today is a bad day.' She thought about the conversation she had to have with Ted and her gut bunched with nerves.

'I know, honey.' This woman too touched her arm and even though Nora took a step backwards, she understood a little more how Kiki was so self-reliant, capable. It must have been easier to navigate life's speedbumps surrounded by this love, this companionship. Again, the loss of her parents and distance from her sibling jumped into her throat. Ordinarily she kept this under tighter control, but very little was ordinary about this situation and with thoughts of her disintegrating marriage as the ultimate cherry on the cake, feeling flustered was, she felt, more than justified.

'I'm sorry, I don't know your name?' She cleared her throat.

'Oh.' The woman sniffed and wiped her nose and then her eyes with her fingers. 'I'm Fi, Fi Rowland. My son Rafe and Ted are mates. My daughter Millie is in the year above.'

Ted too seemed popular, no doubt because Kiki was so open, welcoming. She remembered that much about her own convent school: the mums who were willing to throw open their front doors during the holidays, offer lifts to hockey matches in the bawling rain and to pep up spirits over cups of tea to any other parent in need. Not that her mum had been such a mother. The thought of Vanessa Farraday-Brown inviting Nora's friends for sleepovers was ludicrous. Even if she had been in the same country as her daughter, it was hard to imagine her mother putting down her cigarillo, marguerita or wine long enough to bake cookies or pop on a pinny.

'Here's my number.' Fi handed her a folded notelet. 'I'm only around the corner; we live at the vicarage next to the church, and if you need anything at all or just want to chat, day or night, or if Kristina needs anything, call me. I'll keep my phone switched on.'

'Thank you, Fi. I really appreciate you and Sheila being so kind. Kiki's lucky to have friends like you two.'

'We're lucky to have her.' Her response was sincere and instant. 'Do you know when we can visit?'

'Not yet. I spoke to a nurse on the general ward she's on. Kiki's asked not to have visitors, for the time being at least. So I'm a bit in the dark about when we can go and see her or what the next steps are. The nurse suggested I call again in the morning.'

'In my experience, they'll keep her there for a while, assess her and put together a treatment plan. You should be able to visit her in a couple of days, but I'm not sure I'd take Ted, not yet.' Her eyes crinkled in concern.

'No.' She was slightly offended that the woman considered she might do so. 'Are you the vicar's wife, Fi? I always find vicarages quite daunting! Only really enter one to arrange funerals.' She shuddered, aware of how close they might have come to be discussing Kiki's funeral. 'Sorry, that sounded insensitive, I tend to babble when in want of something decent to say.'

'I think we all do that to an extent, and no, in matters of the church my husband won't be much use, but he's fabulous if you want a chaise longue reupholstered or a cabinet French polished. Lovely as he is, he isn't an authority on funerals, he restores antiques.'

'Oh, I'm sorry, I thought . . .' *What did she think?*

'I'm the vicar.' Fi smiled; clearly this was not the first time she had had this type of conversation.

'Fi, I'm so sorry, I hope I haven't offended you?' Nora straightened, embarrassed by her assumption that was as sexist as it was outdated.

'Goodness, no! It'd take more than that.'

'Hey guys.' Sheila joined them, a pink mohair jumper over her dungarees. 'How're we doing?'

'I was just telling Nora to call any time, for anything at all.'

'Yes, absolutely!' Sheila echoed. 'My number's on the fridge at Kristina's.' And just like that, at the mention of her name, Sheila's tears flowed. This emotional display was a sharp reminder of how Nora and her sister lived separate lives and the fact that these women, strangers, knew and loved her so, coated her with shame.

'Sheila, you are going to set me off.' Fi sniffed.

'Did you tell Nora about the chat we had with Kristina, about things . . .' She let this trail.

'No, I was just about to.' Fi took a breath. 'We were talking only a few weeks ago about our legacy, what we want to be remembered for, that kind of thing, as you do after a couple of glasses of plonk, and rather flippantly she said she wanted her legacy to be the fact that she survived long enough to guide Ted and be there for him for as long as she could.' The three stood quietly.

'We didn't think much of it at the time.' Sheila took up the story. 'It was just chat, but then we remembered last night that's what she said, as if she was hinting it was more than her desired legacy, but was in fact her struggle. "For as long as she could." Like she was giving us a clue to a puzzle we didn't know we had to figure out. I've tried to think about what we said next and what she said next, but it was all just chit-chat, laughter, nothing of significance.'

It was the first time Nora considered that Kiki might have been planning her exit for a while, and she could only think about the little toddler who had been left in her care at Nana Dilly's. Her sweet baby sister who liked to sit on her lap while they watched TV, a baby girl who liked to be read to. And yet no matter how sweet, Nana Dilly's words – *YOU'RE JUST LIKE YOUR MOTHER! KIKI COULD HAVE BEEN KILLED! SHE'S ALL I HAVE LEFT!* – were stronger than any familial sentiment. Stronger than the pull she felt to have Kiki in her life. Her nana's contorted face, screaming, her mouth twisted with flecks of spittle in the corners, the woman's evident distress at what could have happened to Kiki . . . for Nora, it was like being orphaned all over again. How could she have continued to visit? To see Kiki and hear about the cakes she'd made with her nana, the walks they'd had on the moors, when the little girl had stolen the life that was once hers? It had felt too difficult, too . . . desperate.

'I think you're right, Sheila.' She looked skyward. 'A puzzle we didn't know we had to figure out.'

'But how did we miss it, Fi?' Sheila's tone was searching. 'How did we spend every day with the girl, wave her off that morning after drop-off and then . . . ?'

'Because she hid it from us.' Fi sounded matter-of-fact. 'She hid it from us, everyone hides things. I do, I'm sure you do too?' She looked briefly at Nora who felt her face colour. 'And if we're being open, the fact is if Kristina wanted to end her life, she wouldn't have told us because we would have stopped her and that's why she kept it to herself, if I had to guess.'

'And you did stop her.' Nora voiced the positive.

'Yes,' Fi chimed. 'You did, darling, and so instead of focusing on how she got to that point, we should be bloody thankful for your intervention and now we need to look towards the future and building a safety net for her and Ted.'

Nora could only imagine a life where she had such a net, and just like that she was back to Gordy. Gordy who had held her tight and now wanted to cut her loose.

'Do you go to church? Or did you as a child?' Fi asked casually. 'Just that I find sometimes the quiet contemplation can help.'

'Careful how you answer, Nora, she's always trying to expand her flock.' Sheila pulled a face.

'No, no church as a child. My parents were . . .' She struggled to find the words.

'We've had the low-down on your parents.' Sheila spared her.

Nora swallowed, knowing that whatever Kiki had told them would only be a fraction of what Nora had witnessed. 'Chapel was compulsory at school and attending services comes with my husband's job – he's in the army. I quite like the singing and the architecture, just not too hot on the whole prayer thing. I prayed a lot as a child.'

She pictured the moment she saw the burro man and Luna holding each other tightly in the kitchen. The burro man usually came to sharpen the knives in the yard, but on that day he was standing by the stove with his back to her as she peered from behind the door. She had never seen him inside the house before. His leather boots creaked as he bent slightly to better grip their housekeeper's soft, doughy form, wrapping her in his arms. He was small and dark with a grey whiskery chin and a thick blanket around his shoulders, despite the heat. Leonora had looked around the kitchen, as if expecting to see the skinny burro close by as it always was, loaded up with baskets and with a box in which the man kept all he needed to earn his living tied to its bony back. Luna's face appeared over his narrow shoulder, bearing an expression of pure bliss. Her eyes were closed, her face smiling and her mouth emitted a gentle murmur that spoke of complete satisfaction. Not that Leonora had wanted to be this close to the burro man, of course not! But she would have loved to have been held in this way by her parents, to know what it felt like, to be held in such a way that the rest of the world seemed to disappear, and your face melted into happiness . . . yes, she would have liked that very much.

Before Señor Agostí had come to her rescue, Nora had prayed for Luna to take her with her to her home in the city so she would feel safe at night. She prayed for her mum and dad to come and tuck her in. She prayed not to be sent away to school. And later she prayed for it to be a mistake and that her parents weren't in fact dead. None of it came to fruition. 'I'm not sure anyone was listening.' Nora felt awkward expressing the view in front of a woman of God. 'So I go to church but let's just say my expectations are low.'

'Kristina definitely feels the same; church is for Christmas carol concerts, the odd christening and harvest festival. She certainly doesn't believe.' Fi spoke plainly and Nora was glad of it. 'Are you' – Fi lowered her tone – 'are you going to talk to Ted this evening? Do you want support with that? It's not easy.'

This was the second offer of help with what would surely be a horrible task. 'Yes, I'm going to tell him tonight; it feels a little off that we know and he doesn't, but at the same time I like the fact he doesn't have to deal with it yet.'

'Children are very intuitive, he'll already know something's up, and he will guide you. I'd say respond to his reaction, go at his pace . . .' Fi sounded wise in her instruction.

'I will.' She felt the flutter of nerves at the prospect.

'I can't stand to think of little Ted having that chat.' Sheila's mouth contorted in sadness, and she understood.

'Ah, the kids are coming out, let's catch up for coffee over the weekend? How about after football?' Fi turned to the gate where little children, younger than Ted if she had to guess, were marched out by their teacher, who patiently waited to see the waving hand of each parent or grown-up, who was then allowed to take their child from her care. This went on, clearly a well-practised system, where parents stepped forward to raise their arm, make the teacher aware and hug their child to them before turning and walking away.

The thought of gathering in a coffee shop with these women to catch up was not something she relished. 'I can't this weekend but thank you.'

'Oh right, well, if you change your mind . . .' Fi let this hang.

Sheila stepped forward. 'We all head to the Grumble Tum Cafe to let our toes thaw out, consume coffee and share cakes. The kids have a second breakfast, they're always ravenous after a kick about. It might be nice for Ted to have that routine.'

These were the women she'd seen in so many towns over the years. Grouped together around a table, budging up to make room, stowing buggies along the wall. A mothering collective, laughing, sighing, whispering, drinking coffee and making plans . . .

'Maybe next time.' Nora shut the conversation down.

'Am I late?' A woman came racing over in a tailored dark suit and impossibly towering heels that showed off her slender legs, but which were, in Nora's opinion, far too high to be running in.

'You're always late!' Fi tutted.

'Some of us work, Fi.' She rolled her eyes.

'I work!' Fi tapped her own chest. 'I work hard!'

The women tittered softly with affectionate laughter. Even Sheila stopped crying and smiled. Gordy always told her that this type of person was invaluable in the army – the morale-lifter, the joker, the one who could alter the atmosphere with a few carefully chosen words and, more importantly, the confidence to lead the change.

'Sure you do, bit of vicaring here and there, dusting that big old free house of yours.' She smiled broadly and briefly at her friend before turning to Nora. 'Nora?' Her eyes fell in a desolate expression.

'Yes.' She gripped the flowers.

'I'm Mina, Afsar's mum, he and Ted are great mates.'

'Yes, Mr Ormond said. Thank you for taking him home with you.'

'Oh love' – she shook her head and fished in her large leather tote for a plastic shopping bag, which she pulled out and handed to her – 'of course! Kristina would do the same for me, for anyone. She's bloody brilliant. I just wish she knew that.'

'She is and when I speak to her, I'll tell her.' Nora jostled the flowers into the crook of her arm and peered into the bag.

'It's only Ted's pants, socks and polo shirt from yesterday, all washed and ready to wear. Thought it'd save you a job for Monday.'

'Thank you. It feels like that's all I say, "thank you", but honestly, you're all so kind.'

'That's what mates do, right?' Mina held her gaze steadily. 'Are you speaking to Ted tonight?'

She nodded. 'Yes, we were just talking about it.'

'It won't be as bad as you are imagining.' Mina sounded certain and Nora knew she must be right because she was imagining the very worst, recalling how it felt to receive bad news and how it felt as if the bottom had dropped out of her stomach. 'Kids are resilient, far more resilient than grown-ups sometimes.'

'Here they come.' Sheila painted on a wider smile, no doubt not to alarm Zoey and Zac with her lingering distress.

Nora felt the knot of anxiety in her gut tighten at the prospect of having to go forward and claim Ted; the boy she didn't really know, the boy who had been a chubby toddler on her last visit and for whom she was about to place a fault line in his little life. Jason Ormond walked out with his class following in pairs behind him like little ducklings.

And suddenly there was Ted in a little blue padded coat, looking lost, and she knew it was time to step up in every sense. With no small amount of embarrassment, she raised her arm. Jason smiled and acknowledged her before bending low to whisper to Ted, ruffle his hair and squeeze his shoulder. It was with a rising sense of panic that she realised she was going to be alone, solely responsible for the child. Her legs trembled and she felt a little lightheaded, a reminder that she hadn't eaten since she'd grabbed a sandwich at the airport that morning, which now felt like days ago . . . He walked towards her.

'Hey Ted, how are you?'

He shrugged and held out his book bag which she took, jostling her flowers to hold both in the one hand.

'Do you know the way home?' She reached for her phone, preparing to open her app and feeling ridiculously self-conscious at the thought of doing so in front of the other parents.

He nodded. 'Yes.'

'Well, in that case, lead on. Thank goodness you're smart enough to navigate.' She waved briefly to Sheila, Fi and Mina whose eyes she felt on her back, assessing her suitability, no doubt, weighing up how successful she might be and whether they should intervene. It did nothing to aid her confidence.

'Do you have any prep?' she asked, more to make small talk than anything else.

'I don't know what that is.' He stopped walking and stared up at her.

'Prep, schoolwork to do at home?'

'We call it homework and I've got some reading. I've got a new book.'

'Oh, okay, homework, I wasn't sure. What book is it?'

'It's about a clever snail called Cyril. I have to read a chapter and you have to mark it in my notebook to say how I read. Mummy usually does it.' He blinked.

'A clever snail? Well, that sounds interesting. I can mark your notebook. We'll figure it out, Ted.'

He carried on walking, running his hand over the neat hedging and low brick walls of front gardens. She wasn't sure if she should stop him or remind him that sharp objects might be lurking in the hedge like twigs or broken bottles. The thought of him damaging himself while in her care made her heart lurch.

The entrance to the park called to her from the other side of the road. 'Shall we have a wander in here, Ted?' She pointed, something telling her that actually to give him a chance to digest things before they reached the haven of his home might let his sanctuary remain, in some small way, untainted. At school, whenever she'd had to walk the corridor between her classroom and the matron's office where she'd heard the news about her own parents, every step made her tremble, like returning to the scene of a crime every single day.

He loped around and skipped back to her and without saying a word, slipped his hand inside hers, waiting to cross the road. Clearly Kiki had trained him well. Nora felt the pull of tears, which she coughed to clear, knowing that to reach for her hand, to trust her, was misplaced, because not only was she about to be the bearer of confusing news, but also, she was no sanctuary.

'Okay, all clear.' They tripped across the road and Ted ran ahead into the park, which was clearly familiar.

On the other side of a wide stretch of close-cut lawn, dotted with two ancient oaks whose boughs spread in a reaching canopy, she spied a bench and headed for it.

'Come on!' she called in a sing-song voice that was new to her, trying again to maintain the façade of normality until the last possible second, knowing as a child what it felt like to have a hammer brought down on the kernel of happiness that sat in your stomach, and how it could lie fragmented inside you for years – forever in fact.

'Let's sit here for a bit.' She plonked down on the end of the bench, hating the calculated nature of the act, getting him in position. The yellow roses lay in her lap.

He sidled on to the bench while looking longingly at the play area where shouting children, also in school uniform, jumped, swung and leapt.

'Can I go on the swings?' He looked directly at her, making her look away.

'Maybe in a little while.' She kept her eyes fixed on one of the mighty oaks, planted as a most selfless act by someone who knew they could only toil to ensure its safety but not enjoy any of its full-grown benefits: the absolute wonder and joy of planting a garden. A gift. She figured parenting was a bit like that. 'The thing is, Ted, I wanted to have a chat with you.'

He wrinkled his nose, and she made herself hold his eyeline.

'And it's not an easy chat, it's a hard one, and I am a bit nervous, because you and I don't really know each other very well, do we? Although I'd like to get to know you, what do you think?'

'Sure.' He scratched his nose.

'Do you ever get nervous about things you have to do, and you aren't sure how you are going to do it and it makes you feel a bit . . .' She paused. 'A bit fizzy in your tummy?'

'I'm going to be goalie tomorrow at football and' – he kicked his legs against the bench – 'and that makes my tummy fizzy because I've never done it before, and Jonah said he was going to kick the ball hard at me and Mummy is getting me goalie gloves.'

'Yes, a bit like that, Ted.'

He stopped kicking his legs.

'The reason I'm here to look after you . . .' The words sounded sticky in her mouth. 'Is because your mum is poorly.' *What else to say? How should I phrase it?*

He stared at her, and she would in the coming days and months remember his stillness, while her leg jumped with nerves.

'Is she in the hospital right now?' he whispered.

'Yes, she is, and she will have to stay there for a little while—'

'How long will she stay there?' he interrupted.

'I'm not sure, it might be a few days, or it might be a few weeks. I will know more tomorrow when I call them again.' Nora suspected he hated the inadequacy of her response as much as she did.

'A few weeks?' His voice caught.

'Yes. Or maybe not. Maybe less.' She didn't remember much about being seven but knew that weeks could feel like a lifetime.

'Who's taking me to football tomorrow?' He gazed up at her.

'I will!' There it was again, that sing-song voice of a stranger.

'Do you know where it is?'

'I think I do, and I have my app.' She lifted her phone.

'Can't they let her out of hospital so she can come to my match? I know she wants to see me in goal. Milo's mum came to see him once at football and she was in a wheelchair. His dad pushed her to the edge of the pitch. She had a blanket on her.'

'No.' She sat still, waiting to take her cue from him. 'No, she can't. Not tomorrow. But she'll be mad to be missing it, that much I do know.'

'Milo's mum came.'

'I don't know the circumstances surrounding Milo's mum, maybe she just came out of hospital, or broke her leg. Could have been her final wish I suppose, but—'

'What's a final wish?' He faced her now.

Shit!

'It's when someone's dying and, erm, they want to do one thing.' Her arms flailed. 'I don't know, like, "I've been shot, take me to see my dog!"'

'Can she . . . can she . . .' He hiccupped, as if forming all the questions about things he was figuring out that she would not – could not – be doing, or attending, and her heart broke a little. 'Did someone shoot her?' His eyes now wide and his bottom lip trembled.

'What? No! No one shot her.' She blamed herself for conveying the situation so poorly. 'She's just feeling a bit down in the dumps and she's in hospital for a rest and a good old sleep. But she's fine. She will be fine.'

'Is she down in the dumps because she's not well?'

'Yes.' She spoke softly, feeling the stir of sadness at his tender and unwitting accuracy.

He nodded and looked again at the children on the swings who squealed their delight as they were pushed higher and higher.

'Are you going to take me to school instead of her?'

'Yes. I'll even learn the way so I can do it without looking at my app.' She tried for humour.

'I only like Mummy taking me to school,' he managed.

She had thought he might become upset, unruly, charging around, unravelled and spikey, and was thankful that he wasn't, not quite sure how she would have handled that. If anything, he was stoic, calm and somehow it tore her heart even more to see such fortitude and control in such a little one, guessing that maybe he was contained because he didn't know her well enough to open up.

'I know you do, but I promise we'll figure it all out, Ted. We will. Everything is going to be okay.' She hoped this was not a false oath.

'Do you know about my cereal?'

'No,' she confessed; Sheila had not covered cereal.

'I don't like it to go soggy and so she puts it in the bowl and then calls me and she doesn't put the milk on until I am sat up and holding my spoon and then I eat it very quickly while it's still crunchy.' His level of detail told her this was important.

'I can do that.' It was a kind and tender thing Kiki did for her son. She was a good mum. Nora shuffled her feet, again feeling the full weight of her own inadequacy, knowing her sister's were big shoes to fill.

Minutes passed with Ted staring at the floor, fidgeting with the zip of his coat, but silent bar the slight stutter to his breath and the hiccup of sadness and uncertainty that lassoed his heart and throat. She figured a mum, or someone used to kids, would know what to do, what to say. Instead, she sat by his side, a guppy gasping on the bank, and it didn't feel good.

'I . . .' Finally he swallowed and drew breath to speak. 'I don't . . . I don't think I want to go on the swings today, Aunty Pickle.'

'That's okay, Ted. Shall we just go home?'

He nodded and hopped down from the bench, putting his little feet on to the earth, his first steps on a planet where his world was changed, a world where his mum, instead of taking him to and collecting him from school was in a hospital and he didn't know for how long. He stumbled twice, his gait shaky as if relearning how to walk, how to be in a world where his safety net had been temporarily removed. His footfall was solid, his movements slow. Her stomach folded, remembering that lumbering sense of loss that had sat in her gut, dragging her down and down in a situation that felt precarious and unwelcome.

'*You'll be staying with Nana Dilly now during the school holidays and that'll be wonderful because little Kiki will be there too . . .*'

'*But . . . but . . .*'

'*But what, child?* Granny Magda had snapped.

Her thoughts had raged: I don't want Kiki to be there! Nana Dilly's house is my place! It's always been my place! I want to stay at La Fosca, it's my home and I want to be with Luna, and I'd like to stay close to where Mummy and Daddy have been so I can smell her pillow and sit in the chair he sat in and I feel scared, very scared and like the whole world is spinning and I'm worried I might fall off!

'*Nothing,*' she had whispered and Granny Magda had looked relieved.

Ted walked with a slouch, as if some of the life had gone from him and this, too, she more than understood. In no particular hurry, both seemingly reluctant to arrive at the place where Kiki was not, they ambled in the direction of home.

Suddenly he stopped in the middle of the path and looked upward to the sound of birdcall.

'Is that an eagle?' he asked, pointing with more enthusiasm than she had seen in him up until that point. His eyes wide, his legs jumping in anticipation.

'An eagle?' She followed his gaze. 'Where?'

'Yes! Yes, there! Is that an eagle?' He danced on the spot, his eagerness and energy as surprising as it was sudden.

'No, Ted. That's a seagull.' She watched the squawking, chip-seeking menace soar higher and circle out of sight.

'Are you sure?' He glanced at her before turning his attention back to the skies.

'Yes. It's a seagull, definitely.'

His arms fell to his sides as if he was suddenly exhausted and once again his shoulders slumped. He looked so weary it tore at her heart.

Pushing open the door of the flat, she watched him walk forward into the open-plan living space and scan the room. As surreptitiously as she was able, she inhaled through her nose, trying to detect the faintest whiff of Kiki's blood loss, and was relieved that she could only smell bleach. At least she had spared him that. One small thing she had got right. She looked at the closed bathroom door; the unwelcome image of Kiki being hauled from the bath by her friend and lying prone on the bathroom floor was one that sat behind her eyelids.

'I had a bit of a tidy. Hope that was okay.' She spoke as she ran the cold tap at the kitchen sink and placed the roses in an earthenware jug, positioning it on the end of the counter. They were pretty, buds of the palest lemon. She ran her fingers over the delicate stems, which sat elegantly, uniformly. A little miracle of nature to brighten the gloom.

'Huh?' He whipped around to look at her, as if he had been lost in thought.

'I . . . I was just saying that I had a tidy, washed the dishes and things.' She swallowed, unsure if he thought this was overstepping the mark.

'Oh.' He dropped his coat on the floor behind him and she realised that he hadn't been taking in the dust-free surfaces or admiring the shiny countertops, he had been looking for his mum.

'What's for tea, Aunty Pickle?' Ted's question drew her from the memory.

'What would you like?' She retrieved his coat from the floor and hung it on the hook by the door in the hallway, glad that he was hungry and relieved she could cook – something to occupy her mind and hands for the next twenty minutes or so.

'I don't mind. Not spinach.'

'You don't like spinach?' She pictured the mouth-watering, warm spanakopita that she had devoured for lunch thrice weekly, accompanied by a thick dollop of Constantine's home-made tzatziki. Her stomach growled at the thought of the salty tang of feta on her tongue, the soft, wilted spinach encased in sesame-sprinkled, buttery filo that flaked and littered the front of whatever she was wearing. It was another reminder she needed to eat.

'No, it's yucky!'

Ted stuck out his tongue and screwed his eyes shut before picking up the remote control and settling back on the sofa as a cartoon filled the air with all manner of ridiculous hoots, squeals and noises. She found it loud and unpleasant, invasively so. Ted, however, curled his legs on to the cushion and smiled, the programme clearly familiar as he mouthed some of the sayings and laughed quietly. She studied him, unsure whether to mention their conversation, ask how he was feeling. Was it a case of least said soonest mended? It was akin to walking on eggshells and she felt useless.

The contents of the cupboard didn't exactly invite inspiration. There was a Kilner jar of quinoa, a couple of packets of macaroni, some tinned peaches and on the counter sat the three fat lemons she had placed in a glass bowl. The fridge was similarly sparse, she knew from having emptied and cleaned it earlier, disposing of squished, liquified green vegetables that might have once been courgettes or cucumbers, it was hard to tell. A quick look in the freezer in the top of the fridge revealed half a packet of peas and some ice pops in shades of blue she was certain should not be ingested.

She closed the cupboard door. 'Okay, Ted,' – she clapped – 'slight change of plan, we are going out. You can choose. We can either go to the supermarket and I'll cook us supper or we can go and grab a pizza.'

He scooted off the sofa and switched the TV off. 'Pizza! Yes!' He ran to grab his coat. His enthusiasm both delightful and surprising.

'Pizza it is.' Her mouth watered at the prospect.

As she closed the door and was about to put the key in her bag, overly worried about its safety because it wasn't hers, a man jumped out of a van and trundled up the path, a large bouquet in his arms.

'Mrs Morris?' He read the card.

'Erm, no. but I can take them. Thank you.' She looked over at Ted who kicked at the path, eyes down. 'Come on, Ted, let's go pop these in water and then we can go out. It won't take a minute.'

They traipsed back into the flat. Nora breathed in the heady scent of stocks, roses, gypsophila and irises. It was a stunning display. She pulled the little card from its envelope.

> *With love to you Kristina, wishing you a speedy recovery and keeping you in our thoughts and prayers, from all at Longacre.*

'Are they for Mummy?'

She turned to see Ted standing on the rug. He picked at the zip of his coat and blinked up at her with those big brown eyes.

'Yes. From the place she works.'

'Where people die.'

'Yes. Sometimes.' She wondered how much he knew of hospice care, how much a seven-year-old should know.

'Aunty Pickle?'

'Yes, Ted?' She laid the bouquet on the side and went over to him, dropping down, the way Jason Ormond had done.

'I don't want to go outside. I don't want pizza. I'm not hungry any more.' Shrugging his arms free from his coat, he let it drop on the floor behind him. Making his way back to the sofa, he again curled against the cushions and put his cartoon back on.

'That's okay.' She spoke softly and retrieved his coat from the floor, hanging it once again on the peg in the hallway. How had they managed to get on to the topic of death again? Her stomach dropped into her boots and again she felt bloody useless.

One quick search on her phone for a pizzeria that delivered, an order punched in (NO SPINACH) and voila! A mere forty minutes later, a large, flat, greasy-lidded box arrived. Sitting next to her nephew on the sofa, and despite his earlier protestation to the contrary, the two demolished the piping hot, fat doughy base smothered in melted cheese and a piquant tomato sauce. It was delicious. More than delicious, it was just what she fancied. Nora tried to remember the last time she had consumed so much junk and couldn't – before Cyprus, certainly.

With full stomachs, the two sat on the sofa. The cartoon was seemingly on a loop as another episode popped up and then another, not that she could make head nor tail of the cacophony. Darkness began to pull its blind on the day, and it came fast and hard, a sharp reminder that she was in the UK and winter was a-knockin'.

The wide, sun-soaked terrace, soft lamb with apricots that was her go-to supper, fresh figs plucked from the tree and the rhythmic chirp of cicadas all felt like a world away. She wondered how Gordy was, missing his presence and his knack of shouldering whatever life threw at him and simply getting on with it. She tried and failed to imagine a life where he was not on the end of a phone or climbing into bed next to her.

Divorce . . . we need to accept that it might be for the best . . .

She shivered, deciding to call him later. Check in. *Was that allowed? Should she stop calling?* It was a shock how quickly the boundary lines and normal behaviours had become blurred.

'Shall we do your reading?' she asked, ripping up the pizza box so it fitted in the bin and washing the pizza residue from her fingers.

'I don't feel like reading.' His voice was low.

'That's okay.' Nora wiped her hands on the tea towel and pulling the footstool in front of the sofa, she sat down and faced Ted. 'Can we turn the TV down for a bit?'

No stranger to the orientation of the confusing array of buttons, he deftly muted the cartoon. The flashes, bright colours and fast action was still a distraction that drew the eye, but she didn't want to nag or instruct, not today when everything was frail and new and temporary.

'How are you . . .' What did she want to ask – *faring* with me at the helm? *Coping* with the fact that your mum is unwell? 'How are you *feeling*?'

'I don't know.'

She remembered what it had felt like to feel out of sorts, in shock, with a boulder of grief sliding up and down her throat that threatened to suffocate her, and not having the first idea of how to express all that weighed so heavily on her mind.

'Did you know that my parents, your grandparents, died when I was young?'

'Yes. Mummy's parents too.'

'Yes. She was only little, a baby, really. But I was almost a teenager and I remember it didn't feel real.' She glanced at the little boy who stared at her. 'I was at boarding school.'

'What's boarding school?'

'Oh, it's a school where you sleep and live during term time.'

'You slept there?'

She noticed how he wrinkled his nose when he asked a question, just like his mum.

'I did.' *Reluctantly. They sent me when I was nearly nine and it felt like punishment . . .*

'Where did they put the beds?' He narrowed his gaze as if unable to conceive of such a thing.

'We had dorm rooms, bedrooms with four beds in each room and I shared with three other girls.'

'Like a sleepover?' He was clearly intrigued.

'Kind of, but without midnight feasts and natty toiletries.' She smiled. He looked a little nonplussed.

'Where did you keep your toys?'

'I don't think I had many toys there, possibly a couple of books and a little furry elephant on my bed, I seem to remember, but that was about it.'

The image of her beloved Luna floated into her mind on the day, aged eight, that Nora had left for boarding school. Luna collapsing in a heap at the bottom of the driveway, inconsolable, loud and distressed, while her mother rested her head on her husband's shoulder and they waved slowly from the open front door, getting smaller and smaller as the car rattled along the red, dusty track. It would be four more years until Kiki was born, and Luna got to mother a little one all over again.

'Just one elephant?' He looked concerned, as if the prospect of choosing just one of his furry toys might be too much. His collection was large and had, she noted earlier, taken up the top of his wardrobe.

'Yes. He was a gift when I lost a tooth. Our housekeeper bought him for me.'

'Didn't the tooth fairy give you money?'

'No.' She noticed his look of horror. 'It was a week when they were very busy tooth-fairying and, erm, I think they ran out of money and so I got an elephant, which was better than money.'

'I've got a wobbly tooth.' He opened his mouth and moved the little white thing on his lower gum back and forth with the tip of his tongue. It was quite revolting.

'I'm not too good with teeth.' She looked away. 'Had a wisdom tooth out a few years ago and the dentist practically knelt on my chest and butchered me. I was in agony. Lost a lot of blood and then walked around for a week looking like I had golf balls in my mouth.' She shuddered at the memory.

'I don't want to go to the dentist!' His tone now one of fear.

Shit! Again, she'd forgotten who she was talking to.

'Oh, most dentists are gentle and kind, this one was a bad dentist. He got struck off. So now all dentists are great!'

He stared at her with a look that told her even he didn't quite believe this. She needed to change topic.

'I went to boarding school because my parents lived in Spain and they were . . .' *drunks, recreational drug users, louche, hedonists, selfish, disinterested in me . . .* 'very busy. My father was an artist, a very good artist.'

'Mummy told me that. She told me about his pictures.'

'Yes, well he was, and so I came to school in England, which my Granny Magda organised – she was your great-gran who was my mother's mother. Very strict – she would never have eaten pizza straight out of a box with her fingers. And that's a shame because she had no idea what she was missing.'

He didn't smile or laugh or agree. She felt the pressure to fill the silence.

'And then when I had been at school for a few years, I found out my mother was going to have a baby and I was going to be a big sister.'

'And that was my mummy.'

'Yes, it was. I remember the first time I met her.' How to sanitise what followed? The fact that, aged twelve, Nora had walked into the villa, still in her school uniform, fresh off the plane as an unaccompanied minor. Her dad had met her at the airport and she'd dragged her suitcase behind her up the driveway. And there she was, Luna, holding the baby, cradling her with a look of adoration, and to see her beloved housekeeper with a new child, a replacement, was like a knife in her gut. Her dad cooed over the little one and called Nora 'Sport', while her mother was aloof, gazing at her husband as though he was sunshine and gripping her cigarette like it was oxygen. Nora couldn't understand it – they'd sent her away and had another daughter, a little girl like her, but prettier, cuter, smaller. She felt replaced and uncomfortable and wished she'd gone to Nana Dilly's like she usually did in the holidays . . .

'She was very pretty and tiny, and if I held her, she stopped crying and that felt marvellous. It was a skill. I went back to school at the end of the summer, and it was just before Christmas that they died.'

'In a car.'

'Yes, that's right.'

Drunk. They skidded off the road and skittered down the mountainside, just as she had known they would. And she recalled her dad telling her that no matter what fell from an aeroplane – a rock, an old apple, a car or a person – they would fall at the same speed. No matter how much the thing itself weighed or the space it took up, when tumbling down to earth they were all the same. They were certainly all the same when considering how they would all end up: squished. And weirdly, when she was marched to the matron's office and told, in the first instance she had felt nothing but relief, as if she'd been waiting her whole life for the axe to fall, and the waiting was exhausting. Yes, it had almost been a relief to get it over and done with. It meant she had to get on with life, and her head was clearer, not so anxious, wondering how it would happen or when it would happen, as if it had only ever been a matter of time . . .

'And I would see your mum during my holidays from school, and when I was fourteen and she was nearly three, I started making her sandwiches.'

And then I stopped going, preferring to stay at school after that terrible, terrible day when I nearly lost Kiki too, and Nana Dilly screamed at me that I was just like my mother. And she was right, I could never, should never be in charge of a child . . . and yet here I am.

'Sandwiches with pickles.'

'That's right.' She smiled at the one shared memory of that time, hoping, praying that the day Kiki got hit by the car might not have lodged in her sister's thoughts, as it had hers. 'So even though it's not the same, I know a little bit about how you are feeling right now, Ted. About having things turned upside down and how rotten it can feel. And of course, this isn't the same, because Mummy is coming home,' she stressed.

There was a second or two of pure awkwardness as the two stared at each other.

'Shall I have my bath now?' He hopped off the sofa.

'Oh right, yes, if you like. I'll run it for you.'

She entered the bathroom cautiously and scanned the tiles and floor, trying to spot any splashes she might have missed. The thought of Ted seeing them, enquiring after them, or worse, sitting in the bath oblivious of their presence, left her cold. She ran the bath and added a hefty capful of bubble bath from her toiletry bag, filling the room with the scent of gardenias and trying not to picture the drama that had unfolded right there; Kiki, lying in a pool of her own blood . . .

Nora felt the breath catch in her throat. Looking up, she saw Ted standing in the doorway.

'Do you . . . can you . . . do you get yourself undressed?' She hated the blush on her face, unaware of what was allowed, expected. Should she undress the child? Should she stay while he bathed? A thin film of sweat covered her. It was uncomfortable, awkward and embarrassing all at the same time and she wasn't sure who she could ask about it. Gordy was the person she could talk to about anything, or used to be, but she was pretty sure even he would be wanting in the 'how to raise a boy' topic.

'I can do it all myself, if you put my pyjamas on the loo. That's what Mummy does.'

'Right, okay.' She breathed with relief. 'I'll go find your pyjamas.' She tested the water temperature by running her fingers through the suds and went in search of nightwear. With his Ninja Turtle PJs folded on top of the loo seat, she left him to it and pulled the door to, taking up a spot on the sofa in case of emergency or if she was called. Closing her eyes she took a deep breath, as her phone buzzed.

'Gordy.'

'Hello. First chance I've had to call today, been chasing my tail. How's Ted doing?'

Nora cradled the phone to her face; to hear his familiar voice in this unfamiliar environment, to be reminded of his kindness that was about to disappear from her life was enough to encourage her tears to pool.

'Erm,' she whispered, 'quiet, you know. Thoughtful, but calm, brave really; it's heartbreaking. We had a chat and he seems to drift in and out of thoughtfulness and has eaten pizza, watched TV, but right now he's splashing in the bath as if nothing is amiss.'

'No doubt he'll handle things in his own way. The hardest thing will be that he doesn't really know what's going on, unless he has more of an idea than we realise of what *is* going on and that must be unnerving for him. I'm assuming you kept things vague?'

'I did, I hope. I'm so nervous about getting it wrong, about doing or saying the wrong thing. It feels like a huge responsibility and I'm not sure I'm getting it right.'

'I think for Ted it'll be enough that you're there. Don't over-think it.'

'Easy to say,' she sniffed.

'Yup.'

There was a silent pause while she considered how to continue, holding back the desperate words of sorrow that lined up on her tongue – like how the thought of getting divorced petrified her, and the thought of being divorced horrified her.

'I feel so sorry for him and so sorry for Kiki.' She glanced at the beautiful yellow roses signifying friendship.

'Any update on her?'

'Not really. I spoke to a nurse earlier who told me Kiki doesn't want visitors. She suggested I call back in the morning. But I'm thinking of trying again when Ted's asleep. I wonder if it might be quieter at night – the nurse sounded harried.' She pictured the piece of paper in her bag, printed off from the email with the details of the ward Kiki was on and the number to call. 'She said I could ring any time if I was anxious, but not during mealtimes. But I didn't feel like she meant it.'

'I wish I could help in some way.'

Her tears burst their banks and slid down her cheeks at his words of support, his kindness.

'You help just by checking in, more than you know.' She wiped her eyes. 'I'm tired, haven't done anything really, but the mental exhaustion . . . I can't wait to go to bed. And even that feels odd, sleeping in Kiki's bed. And I keep forgetting that you and I are mid-conversation about something so ghastly, the end of our marriage, and when I remember, it's like a knife . . .' She stopped talking and concentrated on her breathing, on keeping it together; there was a little boy who was relying on her.

'Don't think about it. One thing at a time. It's a lot to shoulder and you're meeting this head on, but I'm worried about you, Nora.'

'Oh, don't worry about me, I'm okay.' Sitting up straight, she took a breath, trying to sound in control and tougher than she felt. 'I'm figuring it out as I go along. I don't know . . .' She paused.

'Don't know what?'

'I don't know what I'm supposed to do or say. To Ted, to you, to anyone.' She bit her bottom lip, knowing he was the only person she could confess this to. 'Kiki's friends are lovely, the school supportive, which is great, but I keep getting this feeling like . . .' Again she took her time, drew on her thoughts. 'Like I shouldn't be here, like this is nothing to do with me, like I'm an interloper who shouldn't be involved. I mean, yes, she's my sister, but we aren't close, are we? I feel like I don't really know her, I certainly had no idea she was suffering or in danger and yet here I am in her flat, with her child, looking through her cupboards and sorting out her laundry.' She rubbed her forehead. 'And if I weren't here, where would I go? Home? To you? That's not an option.' She bit her lip, upset and angry at this truth.

'That's not true, you have a—'

'But it is true! That's what divorce means!' She hadn't meant to raise her voice and looked towards the bathroom door, knowing the last thing Ted needed was to hear a row in his own home.

'What can I do?' he asked, and she wished he hadn't. His soft tone and offer of help only made the prospect of splitting up even harder.

'Nothing, thank you. It's not about me needing support so much as trying to figure out my place in this, you know?'

'I do.'

She heard him breathe through his nose.

'Besides, I think you have enough on your plate organising the move and your handover. How's it all going?' She returned to the clipped tone that was all about self-preservation.

'Fine, you know, the usual last-minute cock-ups and panics, and a mountain of paperwork, but it'll all be fine, it always is.'

'Yes.'

'Don't worry about the move, about anything. I don't expect you to make it over to Westbury on Monday, there's nothing I can't handle. It's not as if anything is desperate to be unpacked or sorted. I'll do what I can, but as I say, don't worry, no timescale, no rush, you do what you have to.'

She felt a rush of urgency that verged on panic, aware of all she was about to lose, as Gordy seemed to already be calmly living a life without her. 'Please, please make sure the moment my plants arrive you take them out, water them well, don't let them stand in water, but make sure they are given light and space. Let them breathe and get used to their new environment.'

'I will.' She could picture him rolling his eyes. 'Remember, Nora, the only thing that really matters right now is doing the right thing for that little chap who can't be with his mum.'

'Gordy,' she cut him short. 'I never forget that.'

'You sound angry.'

'Do I? Not sure how I'm supposed to sound. You want a divorce; it hardly puts me in the mood for chit-chat and jokes.'

'I know that, but . . .'

'But what?' she fired.

'But I hope we can be civil, and I hope we can, as a *family*, get through this difficult time.'

'Family. It's just a word, isn't it?'

She pictured growing up in her 'family', fractured by a bohemian lifestyle, her parents' untimely death and the fact that she had been sequestered in a convent for much of her adolescence. And with little idea of what family life could be, had waltzed into the arms of Gordy Brightwell at an army soiree where she had accompanied her roommate whose father was a retiring officer. Gordy . . . an army brat with a twinkle in his eye and as little idea about living in a regular, nuclear environment as she. Two odd socks – paired with relief if not unbridled joy. But not for much longer.

'I think family can be anything you want it to be.' He again poured balm on her despair. This was what he did. And what she would miss the most.

'Yes, I used to think so too.' *Happy that it was just you and me. Nomads drifting around the world until we could settle somewhere pretty and get a dog.*

The two sat in silence that echoed down the line and time seemed to slow as they changed tack.

'Don't suppose you've heard from that idiot of a father of his, have you?'

She closed her eyes, unwilling to talk about Richie as she knew it would only rile them both again.

'Aunty Pickle?' Ted called from the bathroom.

'Gordy, I've got to go, Ted's calling.'

'Righty-ho, yes of course. Night.'

'Night.'

She ended the call and ran to the bathroom door. 'Everything all right, Ted?' she called through the space where the door was ajar.

'I . . . I need goalie gloves! Mummy was going to get me some. I'm in goal tomorrow and I don't have any gloves.'

'Oh yes, that's right.' *Dammit! What on earth was she supposed to do at this late hour?* 'Leave it with me. I'm on the case. I'll call Sheila or Fi and I'm sure we can borrow some and then tomorrow we'll go and buy you some, so you have them for next week, how about that?'

'Okay.'

Shit . . . With her mobile in hand, she lifted a bus timetable to look for the telephone number tacked up and voila, there was a piece of paper, stuck to the fridge with number magnets. Carefully, she dialled the number.

'0774 . . .' Holding the phone to her ear, she waited, rehearsing what she might say and feeling ridiculously self-conscious as she called Sheila's number. As soon as the call was answered she began to babble, 'Oh hi, it's Nora, gosh I'm so sorry to disturb you! My first emergency, well not emergency exactly, but first test, I suppose.' She hated how flustered she sounded, entirely thrown by this simple task. She was a capable woman, why was the prospect of caring for this little human so very daunting? 'As you know, Ted's in goal tomorrow, and we don't have goalie gloves, not even sure I know what goalie gloves are . . .'

'Ah, no worries!' The man's voice threw her.

'Oh! Is this . . .' She couldn't remember the name of Sheila's ex, what had she called him? *Complete dickhead . . .*

'You've called me, Nora. It's Jason, Jason Ormond from school.'

She closed her eyes and let her head drop, mortified to be disturbing the teacher in his downtime, while wondering if all teachers shared their mobile numbers with parents these days.

'Jason, I'm so sorry!' She kept her eyes closed and rubbed her embarrassed brow, as if this made it somehow easier to deal with her faux pas.

'No, don't be sorry! And yes, I have goalie gloves. I'll drop them off in about an hour? I'm going out anyway and you're only a couple of streets away from me, so no bother at all.'

'No, really, I can't let you do that. I feel awful.' She sighed.

'Listen, Nora, we are a tight community here and we all look out for each other. You are going through something right now, and if I can make things even a little bit better for you or Ted then I'm more than happy to do it. See you in a bit. Must dash, Wilf needs the loo.'

And just like that he was gone. She wondered who Wilf was and why he needed help with a bathroom visit – a baby maybe? A little one of his own? Nora could only imagine how Wilf's mother would feel at having her evening disturbed. Jason was probably sharing the tale of her ineptitude right now. She cringed at the thought.

'Did you get me some?'

She turned to see Ted in his PJs, his hair wet and stuck to his head, his bare feet looking little against the rug. *Just a baby . . .*

'I did. We are going to borrow some from Mr Ormond.'

'That's good.' He took his place on the sofa. 'Can I have a drink?'

'Yes, what do you have? Tea? Coffee?' She winked, and he shook his head.

'Water please.'

'Coming right up.'

He took the slippery glass from her hands and downed the liquid, and she understood – the pizza had left her a little dry too.

'I'm not sure . . .' He licked his lips and handed her the empty glass.

'Not sure what?' she asked gently as she put the glass in the sink.

'When I can go and see Mummy.'

'Ah, I'm not actually sure either, but as soon as she is up for visitors, we will be there. Absolutely. At the very first instant.'

'When Mr Appleton upstairs had his foot operation we went and visited him, and I did him a picture and Mummy bought him grapes and chocolate and we sat on his bed and the nurse shouted at us that we might have dirty bottoms. Mummy laughed and we kept saying "*bottoms*" all the way home on the bus!' He chuckled, and his laughter was pure delight in the way that a private joke could sometimes lift you like no other. And then just like that his laughter faded and she saw the wobble to his bottom lip, and it was terrible, the worst moment and one that shredded her.

'Oh Ted, what can I do?' It would only be laughable in hindsight that she was asking the child how to help, how to make things better! What had made *her* feel better when her world felt like it was falling apart? Nothing. That was the truth: absolutely nothing. This realisation only added to her feeling of helplessness. Nora slid her arm across the back of the sofa and cautiously let her hand rest on his narrow back. He leaned forward and arched his shoulders, so her fingers sat awkwardly on the nobbles of his spine. Embarrassed, she slowly removed them and placed her hands in her lap.

'I want my mum!' he howled, his open-mouthed cry allowing dribble to fall on to his pyjama bottoms. 'I want my mum!' He spoke louder now, as his sadness echoed around the walls.

'I know, Ted, I know.' Nora felt her tears pool, and there they sat, joined in sadness, both helpless, distraught and floundering for different reasons. Inadequacy wrapped her in a tight hold and her breath quickened as she stared at the little boy.

'I want my mum!' He turned and punched the back of the sofa. His face contorted, teeth bared, pain etched on his baby face.

She watched as he punched and punched, first one fist then the other, pummelling the cushion until his breath came in stuttering gulps and he seemed to slump.

Fuck! She wondered if she should call someone. But who? Never had she felt so inept.

'I don't know why she's not here.' He looked up at her finally with old eyes, his hurt manifest in the expression of loss that was bound to neither age nor circumstance, and one she had seen in her own young face when tragedy or upset had rendered her similarly powerless.

'I know one thing for sure.' She turned her body so they were face to face. 'Your mummy loves you very much and she would never, ever in a million years choose not to be here. Never. She only wants to be with you, to help you get ready for your bath, to get your goalie gloves, she only ever wants to be with you, Ted. Never forget that.' She pictured Kiki going through the cereal rigmarole, the sunny mum who always had time at the school gates, and her heart ached for the effort it must have taken.

His breath slowed and eventually found a natural rhythm. They sat in silence that wasn't forced or unpleasant but necessary for them to mentally regroup. Nora was thankful, unsure of the next step if his frustration had escalated. It was another reminder of how she was woefully undertrained for this role. When he eventually spoke, his words were soul-shredding.

'Can I please go to bed now?' he almost whispered.

'Of course you can.' She reached out and ruffled his hair. He drew his head back, again leaving her feeling a little embarrassed. 'Would you like me to read to you or sit with you for a bit?'

'No, thank you.' His politeness cut her to the quick. She could only imagine what it must feel like to be in his home, but with everything changed and in the company of a stranger. He hopped off the sofa and padded across the rug.

'I've put your blankie on your pillow.' She remembered Sheila's instruction.

'Okay,' he whispered without looking back. She heard his mattress creak as he clambered into bed and her gut bunched in sadness for the boy.

It was mere minutes later that she listened to the sound of her nephew's dulcet snores and retrieving the sheet of paper from her handbag, she dialled the number for the general ward at St Margaret's.

'Can I help you?' The man's voice sounded breathless, busy.

'Yes please, my name is Nora Brightwell and I've been given this number to call for information on my sister, Kristina Morris? I spoke to a nurse earlier who suggested I call back in the morning, but I'm worried about her and, erm . . .'

'Just one sec.' She heard a kerfuffle, as if drawers were opening, metal jangling and chairs moving, before the voice spoke loudly in her ear. 'Kristina Morris, yes, and you are?'

'Nora Brightwell, her sister.' She tried to stem her impatience. Swallowed the string of questions that bubbled on her lips.

'I've got a different name here as her main contact.'

He paused and she stated her name clearly. 'Leonora?' She closed her eyes and pinched the top of her nose, frustration building. 'Is it Leonora?'

'Yes, that's it. Right, hang on, let's have a look. Morris.' He exhaled loudly and it was some seconds before he spoke, and when he did, it made her jump. 'She's still heavily sedated and is awaiting a full psych evaluation so we can determine next steps and treatment, but she's comfortable.'

'What does comfortable mean? Is she in pain or—'

'She's comfortable,' he repeated tersely. 'Sorry not to have more to report. My colleague was right, there might be more to tell you in the morning.'

'No, I understand, and thank you,' she said, even though she didn't. 'And is it still a case of no visitors?'

The man gave a short laugh. 'No visitors yet, as per her request, and in situations like this it's best to respect the patient's wishes, give them time. We'll keep you informed and if anything changes, we'll contact you.'

How she hated the thought of Kiki all alone, recuperating, distressed.

'Does . . . does she need toiletries or a nightdress, something to read or . . .' She wanted to do something, anything to ease her sister's burden. What did Ted say they'd taken Mr Appleton, grapes and chocolate?

'No.' Again he was abrupt. 'I think she has everything she needs. She's sleeping, Mrs Brightwell, and that's the best thing for her, so please rest assured, she's quite peaceful.'

'Can you give her a message?' She cursed the crack to her voice. 'Sure.'

'Can you tell her . . .' It felt exposing, speaking the words to a stranger. Ye Gods it was hard enough for her to speak freely to the man she loved. 'Can you tell her that we love her and that we just want her home.'

'Will do.' His hurried manner gave her no confidence that this was going to be passed on. She felt the knot of frustration in her stomach.

'So, I . . . I should call again tomorrow morning?'

'Absolutely.' And with that he was gone.

'Fucking hell!' She closed her eyes and covered her face with her hands, half hoping that when she removed them, she'd be staring at the whirring fan above the wicker bed and the terrace door would be open, a warm breeze would be blowing up from the valley and a candle would be burning on the outside table, a large gin would be waiting for her and the whole thing would be no more than a bloody awful nightmare . . .

14 MIDLAND ROAD

Maggie Yates squeezed the tea bag against the side of the cup and opened the fridge, only to see that they were out of milk. It bemused her how her teenage sons could put an empty carton back on the shelf. How hard was it to nip three doors down to the shop and spend mere pence on a pint to ensure that when she got in from her shift there was milk for her much-awaited cup of tea. She heard the heavy footsteps on the stairs and Jordan's familiar whistle.

'Who finished off the milk?' She poked her head around the fridge door and stared at him, feeling instantly guilty that this was his morning greeting, knowing tiredness was to blame.

'Not me! Robbie got in late and I bet he had cereal – he'll be your milk thief!' He gave her the wide smile that made her forgive her kids anything and in turn showed that she was forgiven. He was a good kid.

'Suppose I'd better run up to the shop.' Her feet throbbed at the thought, only recently freed from the sturdy, sensible shoes in which she clopped around the floors, rich with the scent of disinfectant. It had been a long night. The residents of the sheltered housing complex, whose needs were varied and paid no heed to the position of the hands on the clock, had been busy.

'I'll go.'

'Thank you, Jordan, I'm so proud of you.' She smiled at the truth, watching as he tied the laces of his trainers, grabbed his navy puffer jacket and closed the front door behind him. Mere seconds later, she heard the metal flap of the letterbox close against the wood and reluctantly went to fetch whatever the postie had shoved through the door. Catching her reflection in the glass panel of the door, she laughed at the halo of wild hair that had escaped her ponytail as she worked, her thick, blonde hair now a wiry mane around her face. Even in the hazy reflection she could see tiredness. Two shadows of fatigue sat beneath her eyes. Her heart lifted at the thought of bed in half an hour or so. Smiling at the prospect, she felt the happy flutter of recognition that she was still pretty. Older yes, with her forties knocking loudly, but still pretty despite the challenges of a life with too little time and money to ease her path.

She turned her attention to the mail. Not that she was expecting much bar the usual: pizza vouchers, taxi flyers or the gas and leccy bill. How she hated that they all seemed to arrive at the same time. As she bent low, her back aching in protest, she spied the fat cream envelope covered in a beautiful spidery script.

'What on earth?' The weight of it was intriguing, it felt like a communique of value, standing out with the luxury touch of the paper, the unusual stamp and the fact that it was handwritten. She pulled it close to her face under the light to properly see.

'Correas. España.' She read from the ornate red stamp, before studying the address. '"Mrs Dilly Brown or to whom it may concern at this address, 14 Midland Road." Well, that's my house, but I've never heard of Mrs Dilly Brown.' She spoke aloud, as she was wont to do. It was an odd arrival that filled her with anticipation and trepidation in equal measure.

With the letter propped up against her handbag on the kitchen table, she eyed it from across the room while she waited for Jordan and the milk. Mere minutes later, he plonked the plastic carton in front of her. 'There you go.'

'Thank you, love. Look what arrived when you were out.' She nodded towards the letter. 'It's from a place called Correas, Spain. Do you know where that is?'

'No. Never heard of it.' He grabbed the envelope. 'Who's Mrs Dilly Brown?'

'I've no idea!' She felt a ripple of excitement as Jordan got involved. 'Shall I open it?' She splashed so little milk into her tea it hardly felt worth his effort.

'Or to whom it may concern!' he read aloud in a deep and menacing baritone reminiscent of Hammer House narration. 'It's a bit creepy!'

'And a bit wonderful!' She liked the arrival of something so intriguing, a lift to her very predictable mornings in this grey, wet Yorkshire market town where they lived. 'So, should I open it?' She put her mug down and took the envelope from her son's hands.

'Yes, open it! Of course!' He watched as she lifted the back of the well-stuck flap.

Carefully extracting the two sheets of paper over which a hand had danced, paying no real heed to lines or order, she read the whole letter aloud.

'. . . It's a long shot, I understand, and please forgive my urgency, but I am counting down the months, weeks, days until I once again get to hold the hand of my beloved wife . . . And so, I seek help, and I await your reply. *Sinceramente*. S Agostí.' She lowered the paper and looked at her son. 'Jordan! What do you make of that?'

'Scam.' He filled his water bottle for the day, before putting two slices of white bread into the toaster. 'Definitely a scam.'

'What do you mean? Why are you saying that?' Her tone was a little sharper than she had intended because she did not want this to be the case. She put the letter back into the envelope and reached for her cooling tea, turning the chip on the edge of the mug away from her mouth.

'There are loads of them, Mum. You know like, "*We have your long-lost paintings, and they are worth three million quid so send us a hundred for postage and we'll send them straight to you!*" And they send it to a thousand people and get a tidy sum. I see things like this all the time online.'

'Yes, but this feels different. It's a lot of effort for a scammer to go to: a handwritten letter and the paper is lovely and he's not asking for anything, just information.'

'But we don't know who Dilly Brown is or the other bloke he mentions. We've been here nine years and the people before us – do we even know where they are now?'

'I don't think I do. But they were Mr and Mrs Choudhary. I think they went south to live near their daughter.'

'Well, there we go, you can't help him even if you wanted to.' Jordan put his bottle in his sports bag and when the toast popped, grabbed the spreadable butter from the fridge.

'So what shall I do? Return the letter, put a reply in? There's a return address on the back of the envelope?' It felt like the least she could do.

'If you want.' Jordan bit into his thickly buttered toast.

Robbie came down the stairs, walked straight to the fridge and pulled out the carton of milk.

'It's like magic, lad,' Jordan addressed his little brother. 'You put an empty carton in and pull a full one out!'

'Great!' Robbie smiled. 'I'll put my wallet in and leave it for a bit.'

'Or you could just get a job?' Jordan chided.

'Now why didn't I think of that?' His brother shook his head; jobs that he could fit around college were not exactly easy to come by and having no transport apart from the unreliable bus made things doubly tricky. 'What's that?' He nodded at the envelope on the table.

'A scam and Mum's about to send off the catalogue money so we can receive our heirloom.'

'Ignore your brother. I don't think it is a scam and I'm going to reply!' She had decided as she responded.

'Well, I'm out of here.' Jordan kissed his mum on the forehead and her heart soared. 'Don't forget to give him your account details, PIN, date of birth and the name of your first pet.'

'Cheeky beggar, I can't remember the name of my first pet, and he'd be lucky if he could get anything out of my overdraft.' She sipped the tea as the boys rushed to get out of the house. This was always how it was, the chaos, bustle and laughter, and then the quiet after the front door shut, her boys gone for the day. The peace was simultaneously welcome and terrifying. The quiet calmed her, readied her for sleep, but was also a reminder that in less than two years when they had finished school and college, the door would close and the quiet would be long and she would be in this little house all alone while they went in search of life and adventure. She wanted this for them, of course she did, but didn't relish the price she would have to pay for watching them soar: loneliness.

'See you later!' Robbie called as he followed his brother down the front steps.

'Tiddles!' Maggie yelled. 'That's it! My first pet was a cat called Tiddles!'

CHAPTER FOUR

The quiet knocking on the front door roused her. Nora had forgotten all about goalie gloves, and Jason for that matter, her thoughts far more self-centred, wondering how this situation had fallen into her lap and trying to shake off the desolate feeling that she could only fail and how this in turn would let Kiki and Ted down even more.

Her hands shook as she opened the door, and it was nice to see the smiling, pleasant face of Jason. She put her finger on her lips to warn the kindly teacher to keep the noise down. 'He's asleep.'

'Well, that's good.' He reached out and handed her a pair of odd-looking gloves, white with grey grippy palms.

'I can't thank you enough. I feel terrible about disturbing you, I thought I was calling Sheila. I must have got the numbers on the fridge mixed up.'

'As I said, I was coming out anyway. It's honestly no bother. Wilf likes an evening stroll.'

It was then that she looked down at the smooth-coated Staffie by his side.

'Hello you.' She dropped to her haunches and ran her palm over the flat of the Staffie's head. She was a dog-lover – all dogs, any dogs, and it had always been that way. Gordy had promised that when their lives were more settled, they could get one, but with a move every couple of years, and the prospect of being posted abroad, feeling the soft body of a canine companion coiled against her on a cold winter's night still felt quite a way off. *More settled . . .* the phrase was almost comical now! She felt the sharp end of realisation prod her; there might not be 'more settled'. There might not be a shared and beloved dog. Wilf was a glorious blue colour with kind and knowing amber eyes. 'You're a poppet.'

'He really is.' Jason spoke with obvious pride. 'I have a big old house that I'm in the middle of renovating and he keeps me company. My neighbour looks after him during the day and he is thoroughly spoiled. She makes him chicken for lunch and when I try to give him his supper out of a tin, he turns his nose up as if to say, "Where's my chicken?"' They both smiled. 'How's Ted doing? Have you . . .' He paused. 'Have you had a chat?'

She straightened, one arm clamped across her stomach, and cursed the wave of anxiety that threatened. Having to explain the dire situation felt almost as bad as living it.

'Yes. In the park on the way home. I told him his mum was in hospital and he asked me if she'd been shot. Which was kind of my fault, the whole evening's been a bit . . .' She shook her head. How had the evening been? *Shit? Horrific? Draining?* All of the above.

'Their minds run riot and the conclusions they come to are not always logical.'

She shook her head again, embarrassed by the tears that sprang; this was not how she liked to conduct herself, but in that moment, everything felt a little overwhelming and she was glad of the company. What she wanted was to feel Gordy's arms around her, but in his absence it felt nice to have a grown-up to talk to.

'Nora, can I make you a cup of tea?'

'I can make my own.' She sniffed.

'I know that but take a breather. Let me get you some tea.'

She nodded, thinking that a cup of tea might be just the thing right now, and stood back against the wall of the narrow hallway as he passed. Instantly she regretted letting him inside, wanting him to go. She didn't know him, and as a visitor in Kiki's home it felt uncomfortable to have invited another stranger in. She followed him and Wilf into the living area. The stocky dog, now off his lead, took the opportunity to sniff every furniture leg, every toy, every bookshelf and every square inch of the laminate flooring. His claws tip-tapping on the floor as he roamed.

'Talking to Ted about what's happened is the hardest thing to do. But you did it,' he encouraged, his words a reminder that he was close to Ted, not a stranger at all.

'He had a bit of a meltdown; he was quite calm in the park, but then after supper he started crying so hard, I shan't ever forget it. He punched the cushions and shouted, and I honestly didn't know what to do,' she admitted.

'I think it's a good thing he can get it out. And remember there's no blueprint for what he's going through. We just have to ride with him and keep him safe.'

'My husband reminded me that we don't really know what Ted knows or what he's seen. I mean, I know Kiki adores him and he's lovely, but when you're as unwell as my sister . . .' She let this hang in the air. 'I had no idea she was unwell . . .' This admission laced with guilt that weighted her shoulders.

'None of us did.' He shook his head before asking gently, 'Shall I fill the kettle?'

'It's fine, Jason, thank you, I can do it.' She wanted to show she was back in control. 'Sorry about that, I'm not usually a crier, but it's all a bit too much and sadness comes over me quicker than I can rein it in sometimes. Can I get you a cup? Or do you have supper waiting?' she asked, more out of obligation than interest; it felt rude not to offer.

'No supper, just a cold beer or two and whatever is on the TV on Friday night, which I will watch half of and then fall asleep, as is my MO. I'm always knackered at the end of the school week. Cup of tea would be great, thank you. Lovely flowers.' He ran his hand over the firm stems of the bouquet.

'Yes, I don't think people know what to do or say and flowers seem to say it better than any words.'

She looked at him then, his long hair sitting about his collar, his bright colours now traded for a soft denim shirt and a pair of canvas slacks and trainers, and wondered whether it was the done thing for her, a married woman, effectively babysitting her nephew, to be here with this man; she wouldn't like anyone to get the wrong impression. He leaned on the countertop as if the place was familiar.

'So, how well do you know Kiki?'

'We're mates, yes. We chat, drink wine, go for walks.'

'I see. So are you . . .' She took a long breath, figuring out how best to proceed without causing offence or appearing too nosy. An image of Jasmine Leech popped into her mind.

'Oh! Oh no!' Jason shook his head vigorously, catching up with her thought process.

'Right, sorry, I just . . .'

'No no, it's fine, I'm a pretty open book.' He swallowed. 'But no, we're just mates, good mates. I'm very fond of her.'

Nora was a little saddened by his response, thinking it could only be a good thing for her sister to have someone nice like Jason to lean on. She preferred to fill the air with chat, knowing it was the way to stave off potential sadness, to keep her mind distracted. 'It's all new to me, the whole family/teacher relationship. If I think about the staff at my school, mostly nuns, there's no way I can imagine them chit-chatting to my parents or having their mobile number tacked to the fridge – had such things been invented.'

'How old *are* you, Nora, if there were no such thing as fridges?'

She liked his humour. 'Actually today I feel very old.'

She filled the kettle, deciding tomorrow to scrub the ring of limescale around the rim of the lid and spout. 'Ted was so upset earlier, I wasn't sure how to make it better. I just didn't know what to do.'

'The truth is, sometimes you can't make things better.' He held her eyeline and gave a sympathetic smile. 'Sometimes you have to let them lead. *You* know, and *I* know that he'll be okay, because this will pass, as everything does, and his life will take on a slightly new shape and everything will carry on, and his mum will come back eventually, but it's how to convey that to him. Not only will he find it hard to understand, but probably won't believe a word of it either.'

'I can see that and I know a little bit about what he's going through. I mean, it's not the same, but I lost my parents. *We* lost *our* parents,' she corrected.

'Yes, Kristina told me that. You've been through it.'

'I suppose so.' There it was again, that clipped tone, aloof, ensuring any unwelcome sympathy or intrusion would ricochet off her protective forcefield.

She recalled the way the matron had sat her down and in a kindly soft tone that poured warm caramel over her worries, given her the terrible, terrible news, and she remembered thinking, as she often did, that these women, cloistered away in the service of God, might be older than her, ancient even, but by the age of twelve, she had probably seen more of life than they had . . . She pondered it still on some days.

Ted was only seven years old. Nora tried to imagine his little feet, like hers, tripping over bodies passed out flat drunk as his pyjamas flapped around his ankles in the intense summer heat of the Mediterranean, alone in the dark, stopping to run his fingers over the necks of empty champagne bottles, to feel the slip of a silky stocking across his palm or to pick up and sniff a small brown stub of cigar that smouldered in a heavy glass ashtray on the floor. And outside, needles on the terrace floor, lying like brittle worms dried out in the hot sun, but with sharp ends that would make her tummy flip at the thought of them sticking into her soft foot, as her instinct told her that whatever had once been contained within *should* make her tummy flip – scary stuff.

Hindsight and the passing of time had taught her that no good parents who loved and cherished their child would behave in such a way. She had been an encumbrance, so no wonder they had shipped her off to school at the first opportunity, no matter that she was not yet fully formed emotionally, not versed in how to be the 'open book' that Jason had confessed to being, unschooled in how to hang on to those she loved or how to stop those who loved her leaving . . . She thought of Gordy.

Nora handed Jason a mug of tea.

'Thanks. Did you look after Kristina? I mean, you were only young yourself, but she was tiny. What happened to you both, if you don't mind me asking?' He stood up straight, as if aware that this might be too personal a question, overstepping the mark. And it was, a little.

She took a restorative sip of hot tea, as the day's events caught up with her and tiredness pawed at her. 'Not really. Kiki went to live permanently with my nana in Yorkshire, and I pretty much stayed at school, only going back for the odd holiday or to stay with my other gran in London.' Her thoughts were a little foggy, her words carried the slight slur of exhaustion, and she shrugged, as if that was that. *And then, just like when I saw Luna with the baby, I saw my Nana Dilly with chubby Kiki on her hip and she replaced me in that house too, and it hurt because Nana Dilly's house was where I found peace, my little slice of normal in a rigid, confusing world of school and hopping over to Spain to see my parents and their mess of a life close up . . .*

'Mummy!' Ted called from the bedroom. She placed the mug on the countertop and sped to his side.

'Hey, Ted, it's Aunty Pickle. Did you have a dream?' She bent down and sat by the side of his bed, noticing the soft worn blanket, the corner of which he had wrapped around his fingers and ran over his nose, as he rested his thumb in his mouth. His forehead looked a little clammy.

'I want my mummy!' he cried, as he turned on to his side and curled against the wall. His back looked narrow, his spine frail and she reached out, hesitating, unsure about touching the child who she knew needed something but didn't know what.

'I know, Ted. I know.' Drawing on all her confidence, she tentatively palmed circles on his back, and he didn't shrug her away. Going on no more than instinct and without time to second-guess herself, she lay on the rug by the side of his bed with a fat blue dinosaur as a pillow. Nora closed her eyes, just for a second . . . and that was where she was when her buzzing phone woke her in the morning.

She came to and wandered around the flat.

'How embarrassing!' She realised she had abandoned Jason, who had very kindly washed up the mugs and upturned them on the drainer. With no idea of how long he'd stayed, she wondered if he had seen them asleep and cringed at the thought.

'You slept on the floor!' Ted called as he appeared in the kitchen, his tone suggesting the idea was not distasteful. 'I woke up in the night and saw you!'

'I did and now my back is as stiff as an old board.' She rubbed her lower spine.

'I'll get the blow-up mattress that's in the airing cupboard for you tonight.' He spoke matter-of-factly as he jumped on to the sofa to switch on the damned cartoon.

'Thanks.' She smiled, not at the fact that it seemed his narrow bedroom floor was her new bed, but rather at how happy he seemed about it.

◆ ◆ ◆

Around the edge of the football pitch, parents clustered. She spied Sheila and Fi, who waved. What was it about these women who waved even though you were approaching? It was like piling friendship on top of friendship, an overt display, and she was mistrustful of it. These women, the very type she had over the years done her best to avoid, yet here she was about to join them.

'Morning, Nora.' Fi patted her arms under her armpits, trying to warm her fingers.

'Morning.' She stood on the touchline a little sheepishly with her hands in her coat pockets, unsure of what her role here was exactly, but knowing she needed to try. Not only was she expected to look after Ted during this hiatus, but also to protect and tend to all Kiki had built, including these friendships. It felt like too big an ask and she made the decision to definitely avoid the cosy post-match coffee at the Grumble Tum.

'How is he?' Fi nodded towards Ted.

'Well, better than I would have guessed. We had a chat last night and I told him that his mum wasn't coming home for a little while . . .' She kept her voice low.

'My heart breaks for him.' Fi sighed.

Mine too . . .

'Hi lovelies, how did he sleep?' Sheila asked as she stomped on the spot in her yellow and blue striped wellington boots that looked a little childlike.

'Well, actually, he had a dream and woke up, calling out, but then settled and went right through, so . . .'

'Nora told him last night that his mum's not coming home for a bit, so he knows,' Fi whispered. It made her feel uncomfortable to be the topic of gossip even though she was standing right here.

'Bless him. Every time I see him, I want to scoop him up and hug him so tight!' Sheila sighed.

Nora licked her lips, a little nervous to admit that she didn't scoop him up and hug him, not sure of the boundaries or the norm. She recalled the way he had pulled away from her and how it had taken all of her courage to touch his back as he went off to sleep.

'How did he react? Did he say anything?' Fi's tone was kindly.

'He wanted to know if his mum had been shot.'

'Oh Ted!' Sheila sniffed. 'The way their little minds work.'

'It's wonderful he's got you, Nora.' Fi spoke with such certainty that Nora gave a brief smile of unease.

'Right!' a man shouted, and a whistle blew. She turned to see Jason in a tracksuit holding a football and organising the boys and girls into groups.

'Jason takes them for football?'

'Yep, there wasn't a football team until he joined the school. The kids love him; we all do.' Sheila spoke with obvious admiration.

'Shit!' Mina yelled.

They all turned to watch her arrival with Afsar, who was eating a slice of toast and running towards the pitch.

'Am I late?' Mina asked, pulling her long, thick hair into a high ponytail that showed off her pretty face, her complexion flawless.

'Of course you are!' Fi tutted. 'I give up.'

'I can't help it.' Mina looped a large, hot-pink scarf around her neck. 'I hate getting up on a Saturday. I bloody hate it! Don't you ever wish you were sixteen again when you could lie in bed all day and go out on Saturday night and then lie in bed all day on Sunday?'

'I've never done that!'

'Oh well, I might have known, Fi. Were you vicaring then too?'

'No, but I've never seen the attraction of lying in bed all day.'

'That, my love, is because you've never done it!' Mina pulled a face at Nora, conspiratorially.

Nora could imagine Kiki liking Mina, her direct manner with that effortless humour; they shared exuberant personalities and Kiki, too, loved a laugh. Although she doubted her sister would be laughing much today and wished again that she could visit her.

'Come on, Rafe!' Fi bellowed as the little boy ran across the pitch, as if to take up a position.

'Come on, Zac!' Sheila echoed.

'Nora, you look petrified. Don't worry, you don't have to yell, that's just these two posturing, trying to intimidate the other seven-year-olds and make Rafe and Zac winners!'

'It's not about him being a winner, it's about him feeling supported,' Fi explained.

'Exactly,' Sheila echoed, as was her tendency when Fi spoke.

'You shouldn't put pressure on the kids, they might be crap at football, but with you hollering instructions they physically have no hope of following, it can only make them feel like rubbish. Anyway, if that's your logic, Afsar doesn't stand a chance. He knows I would have given my left tit to stay under that duvet for another hour or two . . .'

'He'll never make the Premier League,' Fi pointed out.

'Thank goodness, he's going to be a doctor.'

'And you talk about us pressuring the kids?' Sheila sighed.

'I'm not serious!' Mina tutted. 'It's a family joke. All my parents ever wanted was for one of us to be a doctor. My cousin is a doctor and oh the shame for my poor parents that I work in HR and my brother is a sparky.'

'That's it, Brad! Keep it in play!' one of the dads on the other side of the touchline called as Brad hurtled down the pitch.

And just like that Nora felt the sinking feeling of fraudulence, here among all this shouting – pretending. This was Kiki's life, not hers. That, and it was hard to drum up enthusiasm for the game in play while her mind was with Gordy and her sister was in a hospital bed and, to the best of her knowledge, was no more than 'comfortable'.

Brad hurtled forward and Nora watched as Ted made his arms wide, the goalie gloves looking large on his small hands, his expression one of grim determination. Brad, still being coached by his enthusiastic father, took a moment to pause, to position himself, before kicking the ball towards the goal. Ted lunged to the left and the ball hit his chest before rolling away.

'Good one, Ted!' Jason blew his whistle.

His teammates ran over and ruffled Ted's hair and high fived him. His grin was wide, and he did his best to tame it, but it was a smile of victory.

I wish Kiki was here to see this . . . Her thoughts pulled tears from her well of despair. There was the sound of sniffing and she turned to the women with whom she stood, Kiki's friends, her sister's support network.

'Oh God, she should be here!' Sheila made no attempt to stem her ugly crying.

Fi closed her eyes as if in prayer and Mina held her hand over her eyes as her shoulders shook.

'It's so fucking unfair!' she growled. 'I hate that she got to that point but couldn't talk to us. I can't stop thinking about it. Where were we when she was falling apart?'

This Nora understood. Where had *she* been while Kiki fell apart? She watched her nephew give a thumbs up to his teacher and scan the touchline. She waved, and he waved back. This little boy whose immediate well-being rested on her unqualified shoulders. Her gut folded with the opposing pulls of duty and freedom, which when it came to Ted meant two very different things. What on earth was she to do if Kiki was unable to look after him long-term, what then? And all of this as she and Gordy rode an uncertain rollercoaster. She closed her eyes briefly, wishing she were somewhere else, anywhere else, knowing she was the last person equipped for the job.

'Yes.' She nodded, Mina was right. 'So fucking unfair.'

MAGGIE'S LETTER

It was three in the afternoon; Maggie had an hour before she had to leave for work and hoped the boys might get in before she ran for the bus. It buoyed her up, seeing them briefly before she trundled off to work. It wasn't so much that they needed mothering, but more it settled her worries if she could at least say hi, ask about their day, gauge their expressions, try to placate any concerns or resolve any issues, no matter how minor. She liked to remind them that there were fishfingers in the freezer for tea or eggs for an omelette or beans on toast, not that they didn't already know this and were dab hands at rudimentary cooking. It was a case of having to be when, aged fifteen and sixteen, she had taken this new job.

Eighteen months on and they had survived. She had switched to the night shift on Jordan's eighteenth birthday, a horrible shock to her body, but a positive shock to her bank account as it was a third extra in pay. Not that the extra cash didn't come without its own price. To not see them before she left, knowing it wouldn't be until the following morning that she got to catch up with them, made the night shift feel overly long and left her feeling a little unsettled. But it wasn't like she had a whole host of options.

Sitting at the kitchen table, she laid the two pages of Santiago Agostí's letter out and reread it for the umpteenth time. And just like the first time, it intrigued and captivated her, delighted her, in fact!

Slowly and with purpose, she folded back the dog-eared cover of the spiral-bound notebook and took the lid off her blue Bic ballpoint. Conscious of the thin nature of the writing paper, her less than fabulous penmanship and concerned over her lack of grammar, she took her time.

> *Dear Mr Agostí,*
>
> *My name is Maggie Yates and I live at 14 Midland Road with my two boys. I received your letter addressed to Mrs Dilly Brown or to whom it may concern, and I guess it concerns me as it's now my address! It was actually lovely to open your letter, you have beautiful writing and your words have been running through my head since I first read it. I wish I did know Mrs Dilly Brown as I would love to help your painting find its way to Leonora and Kiki, but sadly, I don't.*
>
> *My ex and I bought the house from Mr and Mrs Choudhary nearly a decade ago. The Choudharys were lovely and went to live near their daughter who I think is in Essex. They might have been able to help you better, but sadly I have no address for them.*
>
> *I asked Mrs Deveraux's son who lives at the top end of the street as his family have been here for as long as anyone can remember, and he said the name Dilly vaguely rang a bell but that was it*

and that his nana might have been the best person to ask, but she's been dead for over twenty years, so that's tricky! Plus, he might have been drunk, it was a Wednesday night and I know he plays darts in the pub of a Wednesday afternoon and my boy said he's seen him more than once, a little sozzled on the bench halfway home. Anyway, I'm babbling, which probably means I should finish off this letter and pop it in the post.

I am truly sorry that I can't be of more help, but I would like to say this, Mr Agostí – and please don't think I'm being rude or nosy – but I wanted to say, how lovely it was to hear how you describe your wife. I have the letter in front of me right now.

'I have wept with the need to run my fingers over the curve of her jawline, to inhale the scent of her, knowing that I could never, ever have captured her in the way he did, and I loved her, knew every facet of her!'

I don't mind telling you that this made me weep. My son's dad and I split up when the boys were small. He's a good man and a great dad, we're mates, see each other in the town for coffee and it's nice, but I know I have never been loved like that and I know I have never loved like that, and even though it's so sad that your wife is no longer with you, how wonderful it is to have experienced such a thing. I think you are very lucky. I think you were both very lucky.

Anyway, I am returning your original letter and popping mine in with it.

Best of luck to you, Mr Agostí – I hope Mr Brown's painting finds its way home and I hope you do too.

Maggie Yates.

CHAPTER FIVE

Nora sipped her morning coffee and decided to FaceTime Gordy. There was so much she wanted to ask him: What did next steps look like? Did he have a timescale for ending their marriage? And exactly how did you dissolve something that had been a way of life, a union for so long? When her parents were killed, it was a neat and clean ending. They exited the world as they had lived it, as one. Their possessions were disposed of. Mail forwarded no doubt to their mothers, and she and Kiki were packaged up and sent off. Divorce was different. Still a death of sorts, or certainly an ending, but without the sharp and clear edges of severance. It was instead ragged with decisions and actions steered by emotion and possessions sticky with rejection. She hated the thought of it. The questions in her mind were easy because it didn't feel real, how could it?

'Ah, I see you're caffeinated too.' He raised his mug towards the screen. His jovial air and ease of greeting threw her, sharply at odds with her internal monologue and 3 a.m. musings, where they snarled and were defensive. If anything, this made the subject of divorce even harder to broach.

'Getting there.' She sipped. 'How's the great unpack going?'

'It's rather stalled, I'm afraid.' He pulled a face. 'Had to go straight into the office so digging through the box mountain has been relegated. Some of your plants arrived and they're watered and look quite sprightly.'

'Oh, that's good news. Thank you.' This was a relief.

'And I've managed to find the coffee machine, but sadly no plates, so last night I ate a rather fabulous Indian chicken dish straight out of the foil takeaway box. I think it tasted all the better for it.'

'We had pizza the day I arrived, eaten straight out of the box with our fingers.'

'Nora! What's happened to you? Straight out of the box with your fingers? What next? Paper napkins instead of linen? Builders' tea instead of that herbal muck you drink?'

It warmed her to hear his ribbing, the kind of chat they used to have before recrimination and resentment bookended every conversation.

'What's happened to me is that I'm having to live without planning; figuring it out as I go along seems to be the phrase.'

'Improvise, adapt and overcome – I've never been prouder,' he boomed.

She bit her lip. 'So, four days in the new house, how's bachelor life suiting you?' The words slipped out without consideration and her heart twisted at the turn of phrase.

His expression turned suddenly serious. 'I'm . . .' He paused. '. . . feeling my way, I guess.'

Tears slipped down her face.

'Don't cry.' He spoke quietly with an undercurrent of concern, holding the screen closer to his face.

'I can't help it, there's so much going on, Gordy, and I keep it together the best I can, but I don't know what the bloody hell I'm doing! I'm so far out of my comfort zone and to see you so, so *fine* and so *smiley* and knowing this is what it'll be like. And already I don't know if I'm allowed to call or what's appropriate . . .'

'Nora.' He breathed deeply. 'I am far from fine. And you must call whenever you need to and whenever you want to, just like always. I'm here for you right now – family, I told you that.'

'Yes.' She sniffed and wiped her eyes. 'But only for as long as Kiki and Ted and I are in crisis and then what?'

'That's not what I said.'

'No, but it's the way it is, isn't it? And I'm quite sure that if I hadn't got the call about Kiki, we would be further down the line with the whole thing. But there we are.' She sat up straight, tucked the loose tendrils of hair behind her ears and coughed to clear her throat.

He looked into the middle distance, almost as if he forgot he was visible, and her heart lurched with the desire to reach out and hold him and to be held. '*We* have reached crisis point, Nora, you and I, and when that happens things have to change. They have to. One of us needed to say it.'

'One of us did,' she fired.

He took his time in responding, her stomach tensed in readiness to hear what he had to say.

'We need to do this face to face. Arguing in snatches on the phone is about as galling as it can be. I don't have the energy for it and I'm certain you don't either.'

'I don't,' she conceded.

'Why don't you and Ted come this weekend? There must be things you want to pick up and it'll do Ted good to have a run around and we can talk. Properly talk.'

'Okay.' Her stomach flipped in anticipation of seeing him, edged with dread that it might be one step closer to not seeing him at all . . .

'Good.' He changed tack. 'This is the kitchen, it's a decent size. All the rooms are spacious.' He panned around to give her the view of what would have been hers. Pulling the screen closer, she took in the wide, bright kitchen, noticing how the sun flooded the windowsill and imagined the plants that might have graced the surface; a cluster of colour year-round if she planned it right. Once more, she felt the watery rise of tears and was embarrassed to again show herself falling apart. She swallowed the emotion. Where was she to go?

'Lovely,' she managed.

'How's the little chap this morning?'

'Haven't seen him yet.' A glance at the clock told her it was time she rattled him awake for breakfast. Which she'd do once the cereal was in place on the breakfast bar with the milk and spoon on standby . . . 'Well, haven't seen him awake, but as I'm his roommate . . .'

'His roommate?'

'Yes, I sleep on a blow-up mattress on his floor. My back's killing me, but he seems to settle better if I'm there.'

'It sounds like you are doing a great job,' he encouraged.

This compliment she tucked beneath her thoughts for easy retrieval in the low moments. It was amazing how quickly she had established a routine and how the hours flew without time to dawdle, to pause on the shoreline, to browse the local market, to drink strong coffee in the sunshine, to sit on a sunny harbourside and make detailed drawings of the garden she would one day like to have: a terraced affair with stone walls and hanging ferns, pots of exotic grasses and benches secreted in sunny corners . . . Entries she made in her notebook, while capturing the sights and smells of fishermen and their early morning catch, which had largely been her life in Cyprus. And now an image, a dreamscape she had to reimagine without Gordy in it.

'And Kiki?' His interest in and concern for her sister was welcome. 'Have you heard from her?'

'I've spoken to the hospital a few times.' She recalled the fourth drawn-out, uninformative, laboured conversation in as many days. 'She's seeing a new doctor today that specialises in her illness.' She chose her words carefully, more than aware of how little ears were close by. 'And so that should be helpful, I hope. It was pretty much the same conversation as I've had before. I asked to speak to her directly, but she wasn't feeling up to it. I shan't settle until I hear her voice. It fills me with dread – I mean, if she can't speak to me and won't see me, when and how is she ever going to feel well enough to come home?'

'Fingers crossed things start to move forward.' Gordy voiced her thoughts. 'But in her own time, Nora. She's been through something that isn't only life-changing but carries a lot of shame and remorse. She needs to come to terms with that on top of whatever might be going on physically.'

His insight was a reminder that the army was a microcosm of society and that he would have dealt with similar many times over.

'Yes.' Out of the corner of her eye she spied her nephew standing in the doorway, 'Morning, Ted.' There it was again, that singsong voice that was alien to her ears.

'Morning.' He was quiet.

'I'm just chatting to Gordy, do you want to say hello?' She held the phone up for the two to communicate easily.

Ted shook his head and she and her husband laughed. 'Fair enough!' Gordy called down the line. 'Well, have a good day anyway, buddy, and looking forward to seeing you this weekend. I thought you could help me explore the woods?'

Ted nodded.

'Thanks, Gordy.' She sipped her coffee. What she was thanking him for she wasn't quite sure, his knack of making everything feel a bit better maybe.

'Yes, looking forward to seeing you both,' Gordy called out, whether to reassure her or the boy she was unsure.

As she ended the call Nora noticed the two high spots of colour on her nephew's cheeks. Her first thought was that he might be sickening for something, and her pulse sped up accordingly; what was the MO if a child was sick? Calpol, yes, she remembered Sheila pointing out the Calpol in the bathroom cupboard. How much should she give him? Was it possible to give him an overdose? She decided to call Sheila before reaching for the bottle.

'How are you feeling today?'

Ted shrugged and unusually stood in the doorway instead of racing to the sofa to flick on his ghastly cartoon.

'Are you hot? Do you have a tummy ache or anything? Or maybe you just feel a bit sad and that's made you feel—' She searched for the word, *made him feel how?*

'Can I have a bath?' He cut her short.

'A bath? I guess so. Although I'm sure you're still squeaky clean from your bedtime bath, but if that's what you want.'

She tipped the capful of bubbles under the running water and inhaled the scent of gardenias as she heard the thunder of his little feet on the laminate flooring. Peering from behind the bathroom door, she watched as he hauled his duvet, sheet, and blankie into the kitchen and tried his best to stuff the overly large load into the washing machine. The opening was obviously too small, and the bedding hung out over the floor.

'What are you doing?' She felt the flicker of irritation at this mess, this upheaval at this early hour. Didn't she have enough to think about? The bath was already throwing their routine.

'I . . .' He looked from her to the washing machine and back again.

'Not sure what's going on this morning.' She felt the beginnings of a headache, and it was as she formed the words that she noted the large wet patch on the front of his pyjama bottoms. *Oh Ted . . .* She paused, thinking back to a night in La Fosca before Señor Agostí had shown her how to live in peace with the noises and creaks of the old house. She couldn't have been more than five and had woken in the early hours with the need to pee all she could think about.

'Mummy!' she had called from the door, staring into the dark corridor that, unlit, looked eternal. 'Mumma!'

Nothing. No reply, no flicker of light making its way toward her in the night. Just darkness. The thought of walking alone to the bathroom was more than she could stand, even if she had been able to hold her pee for that long. Instead, she had crept back into the bedroom, opened the closet door and climbed in, crouching down to pee on the spare bed linen that lived there. Hoping no one would discover her action. Nora thought she'd got away with it until the very next day she heard her mother shouting and her father laughing and Luna gabbling quickly in a foreign tongue. Nora had paused from her colouring book at the kitchen table and looked up as her mother, her dressing gown flapping behind her, came running into the kitchen. 'Disgusting little mouse! Disgusting!' she spat and Nora, with her cheeks aflame, knew her crime had been discovered. She had never forgotten the way those words made her feel. *Disgusting . . .*

'And now, here you are helping me out!' She beamed. Gone were the harsh undertones that she bitterly regretted and hoped he might not have noticed. His obvious embarrassment and attempt at secrecy were like a dagger to her chest. 'Bath's run! Thank you so much. How did you know I was going to wash all the bedding today? That's such a marvellous help that you brought it into the kitchen for me. Right, go hop in the bath and I'll get your uniform ready and leave it on your chair, okay?'

'Okay!' His wide smile and manner spoke of pure relief.

The smell of ammonia was overwhelming, offending her nose and stinging her throat. Not that there was an ounce of reproach in her blood; she could only guess at the level of upset that might cause this reaction and it killed her. With the washing machine whirring and the rest of the bed linen waiting to be washed, she listened now to Ted splashing in the bubbles, and thought again of smiley, serene Kiki and understood that you really could never tell anyone's story by looking. She couldn't wait until she could talk to her sister. The radio silence and uncertainty were a frustrating preoccupation that only added layer upon layer to her worry at how bad the situation must be. She made a plan to scrub his mattress as soon as she returned from the school run and to deploy the phrase, *least said, soonest mended* . . .

It was eight fifteen. The wind whistled around the courtyard, whipping up leaves and battering the abandoned pots and detritus that littered the floor. Guilt washed over her, knowing how she might have judged her sister's less than savoury domestic skills had she turned up unannounced, when all the while, Kiki was wrestling with something so much bigger than whether her aspidistra might need watering and did the hydrangea have enough acidity in its soil. How long was she suffering? Had she thought about taking her life before? Nora paused and shook her head.

'Oh Kiki. I need to talk to you, need to see you!' She liked to say her name and close her eyes as if the silent call might reach her sister, make her feel loved. It wasn't only guilt at her judgement that swam in her veins, but also the terrible feeling that she had let her sister down. Stepping in now like a pillar of support when what she should have done was be there for her over the last few months, the last few years. When this perfect storm was rising, where had Nora been then? Wandering the shoreline at sunset and feeling resentful at having to appreciate the view alone. What would have been the harm in calling Kiki as she sat on the damp sand, for five minutes, ten? What difference might that small act of connection have made for them both? Would it now mean she had a friend and not just a distant sister? How she longed to talk to someone about her marriage, her overwhelming sorrow that it was coming to an end, her fears for the coming weekend and all that came after.

'I'm lonely.' She spoke into the courtyard and wondered if her sister had stood in the same spot and said the same thing. Maybe they had more in common than she thought.

When he was ready to leave, Ted raced ahead on the pavement, and as she walked towards the playground she was struck by the noise. Children chattered and parents at first spoke softly to the little ones whose hands they held or who were wrapped in their arms.

'Love you, have a great day! See you later!'

And then as the children moved away, heading towards the school gate with their little nylon bookcases in their hands and more often than not a water bottle, they called a little louder. 'Bye darling! Have a good day! I'll be here at pick-up!'

Then came the reply from their little one. 'Love you, Mummy/Daddy/Nan/Laura/Katie' . . . whoever.

And then one final shout before they disappeared inside the building. 'Love you!'

And the reply. 'Love you too! See you later!'

And this for the hundred or so children and the hundred or so parents/guardians/carers. It was a cacophony and yet each word was to her distinct. It was a public outpouring of love and promise she had never experienced. And with it came the distinct pull of something inside her – what was that? Longing? Regret? Bitterness?

She wasn't sure if it was all too much, a performance of sorts, but the expressions on the faces of the children and their grown-ups told her this was real, it was passionate and she found it strangely moving, noting the often crestfallen look of despondency on the faces of the adults who walked quietly away to carry on with their day, as if to be separated from their child was not something they relished. Nora knew she could not imagine feeling like this about a child, about anyone. *What was wrong with her?* The answer came sharply into focus: *it's hard to love when you have grown up without being loved* . . . Not in the mood to loiter and chat to Fi who stood in the crowd, Nora looked down, averted her gaze and walked back to the flat, feeling a little empty and a little awkward in a way that had been familiar to her since she was a little girl.

The day had passed in a blaze as it did when domestic chores needed tending to, and with Ted now slumbering on his freshly laundered bed, a supper of baked, cheesy pasta served, the dishes washed and the floors swept, she sat back on the sofa and thought about the planned weekend that loomed.

It was bizarre to feel such a level of nerves at the prospect of seeing the man she was married to, and without children or pets to discuss, and assets that would be easily split, what would be the need to further converse or meet up at all? The thought left her with an empty feeling in her gut, hollowed out at the prospect of not hearing his key in the door at the end of the day. What would happen to all the memories, the in-jokes, the shared experiences known only to the two of them? The answer came quickly, lodging in her brain like a sharp thing: it would be the same as any good memories she had of her mother and father, of Granny Magda or of her and Luna, they would be lost, spare, without value, swept up and dumped somewhere, fragments of something that used to be whole. Because without the other party to endorse or reflect, what would be the point?

She agreed that to see Gordy, talk to him face to face was entirely necessary. But the prospect of setting foot in another army house and the ugly, predictable uniformity of the decoration and furnishings: magnolia walls, magnolia kitchen units and hated magnolia curtains lifted by a small diamond pattern in pink and green, filled her with dread. But for different reasons this time; it was a home that might not be hers. A house similar to ones she had scoffed at but now longed for. Funny how your view could change depending which side of the fence you stood.

Yes, what she felt was unmistakable apprehension, but Gordy was right, the lingering bickering, the weighted silences and meaningful stares, the sheer frustration – it had to stop. It was damaging and regressive and not what either of them needed or deserved at this juncture in their lives. It was as if neither had the strength or confidence to make the changes necessary, or worse, couldn't be bothered to go through the rigmarole and distress of addressing their issues. And so they had limped on, distracted by work and life, walking the beach and picking flowers, eating meals on the terrace as the sun sank, the flavours of which were so exquisite they grinned as they did so, distracted in that moment by something that masqueraded as joy. These rituals, these habits reminding them that what they shared was, for most of the time, enough. Until it wasn't. And just the mention of divorce had focused her like nothing else. She did not want to give up on her marriage, she didn't want to lose Gordy, but this was not only her decision to make. Curling her legs beneath her, she tried to imagine this silence every evening; it left her confused, bereft and scared beyond belief. Was this what it had felt like for Kiki?

Lonely . . .

Who knew what the weekend would bring? The two of them locking horns, raising their voices, using words as weapons with one eye on the door and the weight of car keys in her palm, ready to bolt, and all with Ted in tow. She felt the beads of perspiration on her top lip. What would it be like for Ted? How much did little ones take in and recall?

A memory came sharply now.

Nora pictured her six-year-old self, standing with the muslin curtain wrapped around her as she loitered in the doorway of the inner courtyard. Her mother reclined on one of the old steamer chairs with a cigarette and glass of wine in the same hand. Her nails were painted scarlet. Her father sat on the floor by his wife's chair bent low to kiss her bare foot. Granny Magda jumped up from her chair opposite as if scalded and her parents laughed. Her mother caught sight of her.

'Hello, little mouse, hiding in the shadows. Don't mind Granny Magda, she thinks artists and louche behaviour go hand in hand and maybe they do.' Her words carried a fuzziness around the edges that happened when she drank too much wine. 'That and she's still smarting over the fact I could have married Simon de Villier-Brown and would now have a title!' She laughed again and her father cradled her feet in his big hands.

'You know he's bald and broke!' he cut in.

'I do. At least you've got hair.' She reached out and ran her fingers through his curly mop. 'Although I guess he could always sell the country estate to raise funds . . .'

Her father laid his cheek on her mother's instep and not for the first time, Leonora felt as if she were intruding. But with no one to play with and more than a little bored of watching Luna salt anchovies, she was in search of company.

'What's louche behaviour?' she asked quietly, ever aware of intruding.

Her father tittered and she felt her face flush red.

'It's something you don't need to concern yourself with. All you need to know' – her mother sipped her wine – 'is that Daddy and I love each other very, very much. And just because we don't live the most conventional life, because Daddy doesn't put on a shirt and tie and go off to slowly die in a nine-to-five that would rob him of all spark, while stockpiling cash, then some people – Granny Magda included – might see us living a life that's a little off-centre. But it's the life we were *born* to live. He is a wonderful artist, Leonora, and a wonderful man, and the fact that he makes next to no money is only because the world is yet to catch up with his extraordinary talent. But they will, one day.'

'I don't . . .'

'What?' Her mother turned sharply; her impatient tone made the words get stuck in Leonora's throat.

'I don't . . .'

'Speak up, little mouse, you don't what?'

'I . . .'

'For fuck's sake, why don't you go and help Luna with supper?'

'Language, Nessa!' her father boomed mockingly.

'She won't remember!' Her mother giggled.

She saw her mother's subtle head-shake of irritation and felt her insides shrink with something that straddled embarrassment and shame. Dismissed, she let the curtain fall, and crept back along the dark corridor. What was it she had wanted to say?

'I don't want Daddy to slowly die in a nine-to-five.' Leonora didn't know what a nine-to-five was but didn't want her daddy to die in any way.

Her mother was wrong. It might have been over four decades ago, but Nora did remember. She remembered what was said, and even more the sensation, the feeling that her voice, her view, nay her very presence was probably unwelcome.

This thought made her determined to keep things civilised this weekend with Gordy. She wondered what the new neighbours in Westbury might be like, picturing another military community that offered very little chance to hide from the gossip. How much might Gordy have told his new team? The idea alone was as exposing as it was upsetting; the more people knew of their imploding marriage, the more real it became. Jasmine Leech had left her a message asking her to get in touch and Nora figured she'd call her at some point, but really was in no mood to hear the woman's clichéd wailings of how she was missed in Cyprus and how terrible it had been to hear her 'news'.

The thought struck her that she was now married to 'Colonel'. The one-word moniker garnering admiration from others and befitting of the high esteem in which they held her husband; the single-word rank that put him on a level pegging with Madonna, Pelé and Elvis. All that work to attain this new rank, all those hours in the office, showing willing, putting in the hard yards as he would call it, during which she had felt abandoned, and all for what? A shiny new badge on his lapel. She knew that once her arrival had been heralded, she'd retrieve a couple of skilfully guillotined and prettily adorned strips of paper from the doormat inviting her for coffee. Her name would, she knew, be mud, or at least muddier, if she didn't accept. It irked her, the lumping together of the spouses.

As if she'd been born a colonel's wife and hadn't for many years had a life as a normal person until she was dragged to an event by her roommate, drank enough port to sink a battleship and ended up in bed with Gordy before quickly, some months later, agreeing to become the other half of the military. It was different for Gordy; as the son of a military man he had had a fair idea of what he was signing up for; she had not.

She had had to learn to navigate the choppy waters of army wifery using the smiles, frowns, tuts and hugs of the community as navigational aids. Gordy's progress from Captain to Colonel had been smooth and assisted. Her journey from horticulture enthusiast to Colonel's wife, rather less so. She had given up her job, packed a bag for Münster, Germany, and grabbed his hand to board the plane. Where was her manual? She had considered writing one, keeping it positive so as not to scare all newcomers, but she'd realised that by the time she'd omitted the chapter that dealt with being left alone while your other half was away 'getting the baddies', and the chapter that detailed the period of adjustment/anger/conflict/angst leading up to them going on tour, and the chapter on the period of adjustment/anger/conflict/angst when they came home from tour . . . it would be less of a book, more of a pamphlet. Her resentment was, she knew, a little unfounded; she had hardly gone out of her way to join in, she was no Jasmine Leech.

The front doorbell pulled her from her thoughts. She wasn't expecting anyone, but guessed that Fi, Sheila or Mina might be checking in. She felt a little aggrieved at having to stand up and interact when the blow-up mattress was calling to her.

'Jason.' It was a surprise to see Ted's teacher at the door. She wondered if he thought that because she had invited him in for tea on one previous occasion this gave him carte blanche to tip up whenever. It bothered her.

'The very same, not interrupting, am I?' He smiled and she noticed Wilf ambling on the path, both, it seemed, waiting for an invitation.

'Not really. I was just having a little think about my new house in Westbury, that kind of thing.'

'Are you excited about the move?'

'Not sure.' This felt safest.

Wilf surged past her legs to repeat his reconnaissance of the previous visit, sniffing and pausing at every object.

'Wilf, come here! Sorry, Nora!' He followed the dog along the hallway, and they all ended up in the kitchen.

'How's Ted doing?' He leaned on the countertop as if he had done so a thousand times before, and this bothered her too.

'He's okay. I think that's the best I can say. Still thoughtful, missing his mum, of course.' She kept her manner terse, hoping to speed the chat and hasten his departure.

'I expect Kristina's missing him more.' He spoke softly, a reminder that he and her sister were friends. She tried to soften her stance, too, not be . . . aloof.

'I never called her Kristina, always Kiki. That's what my parents and I called her and I never think of her as Kristina.'

'Kiki's a nice name,' he mused.

There was an awkward silence, which she found irritating. 'So, here we are, Jason, you'll have to put your head under a blanket when you leave or people will talk!' The words that had been cued up on her tongue tumbled out.

'People have been talking for years, think I'm just about immune to it now.' He rolled his eyes.

'What do they say?'

'Just what you'd expect: why is he single? Is he divorced? Does he play the field? Who is he shagging? Is he gay? I wish I had his hair . . .' He shook his locks and they both laughed. Had she known

147

him better or for longer she would have pushed for responses to all of the above, but at that moment to do so felt rude. Besides, after pondering this, too much time had passed to revisit his words and they both took a deep breath to fill the quiet.

'Does it bother you? That they talk?' She knew it would her.

'Only because there's someone I like and the thought of them getting the wrong idea about me would be less than ideal.' He looked at the floor and swallowed. 'I can't believe I told you that! I've only told Kristina. It's probably because I'm in her kitchen and it's like I'm chatting to her.'

She was flattered. 'Someone you like? Who?' She felt the rise in her pulse, feeling the long-forgotten thrill of sharing such an exchange and the joy of friendship. She could certainly see the attraction in it and knew that if she had more confidence in being able to make a contribution, it wouldn't be the worst thing in the world to have a friend.

'If I tell you, you can't say a word.' He held her eyeline.

'Cross my heart.' She drew her finger in a cross over her chest.

'Sheila Henning.' He pulled a face.

'You like Sheila?' This was a surprise, but not ridiculous. Both were sweet.

He shook his head. 'No, I don't like Sheila, I'm absolutely head over heels in love with her, like completely, one hundred per cent, hook, line and sinker.'

'Wowsers!' She painted an image of the two of them together and they looked good.

'Yes, wowsers.' He sighed.

'Does she know?'

'No! God no!' His response was a little panicked. 'As I said, Kristina knows, she told me to be brave, to go for it, but I'm not like her.'

They both paused in silence for a moment or two, realising that her sister's bravery was only a masquerade. Smiling Kiki who had run the bath, written a note, selected a blade. Again, she wished she could speak to her sister.

'So, what are you going to do about it? Love her from afar and never say a word? That doesn't seem right.' The irony was not lost on her that she had been married to Gordy for nearly eighteen years and was still unable to fully express her fear at losing him. Too afraid of admitting the horror she felt at the prospect of not climbing into bed with him each and every night.

'It's not. Trouble is, I get tongue-tied. She's . . . she's amazing!'

'Yes.' Nora again gave silent thanks to the woman who had pulled Kiki from the bath, saved her life, realising that to her, Sheila would always be a little more than amazing. She had saved her sister. She had saved Ted's mum. 'She really is.'

'I guess I'm waiting for the right moment.' He grimaced.

'And how long have you felt like this?'

'Three years.' He kicked at the floor.

'And the right moment hasn't arisen in three years?'

'You sound just like Kristina!' He smiled and her heart swelled to know this: a link, a similarity that meant they shared . . . something. It was comforting.

'Have you spoken to her?' His expression was one of pure concern. Nora was beginning to understand that Sheila, Jason, all of them, they were Kiki's family.

'No, not yet. I call the hospital and it's always the same platitudes and I want to push, but I'm aware they're busy and when they say no change or whatever, and that she's not up to having visitors and doesn't want to take my call, I have no choice but to accept it.' She sighed. 'But I've decided that if this is still the case after the weekend, I'm going to turn up and try to encourage her to see me, to talk.'

'That sounds like a plan. I can't get her out of my mind, Nora. I keep thinking about the last time I saw her before it all blew up. I thought she looked lovely, you know, really lovely. She was beaming as she always is and I'm so mad at myself for not digging deeper, not talking to her more or letting her know that if she needed to talk, I was there for her.' He blinked. 'I thought she knew it. I thought it was a given as I always felt I could talk to her.'

'Mina said something similar, and I think it's how we're all feeling. But I guess that's the hard bit. If you think someone has everything under control, then why would you intervene?' This sounded plausible, but actually did nothing to assuage her guilt. She avoided his gaze.

'I suppose so.'

'And trust me, I feel the same; she's always on my mind.'

'I guess all we can do now is be there for her when she comes home and work together to make sure her safety net is strong. There's so much love for her, and she needs to feel that.'

'Yes, she does.' Nora liked his intentions, feeling a misplaced and ugly flare of envy. Who was going to provide her safety net when Gordy cut her loose? 'She's in a battle and yet I'm sure her main worry will be for Ted. I just want to speak to her to reassure her, let her know he's good.'

'She's a great mum.' He enunciated the word 'great' as if keen to press the point.

'I'm sure that would mean a lot coming from you.' This much she could guess. 'I suppose the issue is how we protect him from the fact that one day, he might very well understand that she, even in some small way, made an attempt to leave him. Wasn't there for him. That's a hard one to navigate.'

'It is, but I guess as he gets older, he'll learn about depression and how mental illness means you sometimes have no control over your thoughts and that it's not really you but the illness talking or making you act.'

It was hard to hear her sister labelled with mental illness; no matter the truth, it was, no less, a stark and sobering fact.

'Long before my parents died, I must have been about ten, or younger even, I don't think Kiki was born, my mother told me to remember that when my world fell apart, I had two choices: I could either collapse and sink into the ground, as if I were never really here at all, too broken to be, disintegrated, back to the earth. Or I could pick up all the little pieces and rebuild myself.' She wasn't sure why she had shared this with Jason, maybe because he had confessed his love for Sheila, a secret for a secret.

'I think they're wise words.'

'Yes, but she was drunk and kind of looked through me.' The words leapt from her mouth. 'I know how these things, these happenings, can scar you and I hate to think of Ted similarly scarred.'

'They can, but not always. Not with the right communication, the right support. I see that in action every day. And maybe your mother was right. I mean you are strong, you did rebuild.'

Nora shook her head, he just didn't get it. 'It wasn't her words that were the problem because you're right, it's good advice. That's not what upsets me.' She took a stuttered breath. 'It's the fact that she knew I would *need* them, felt the need to say them at all.' She remembered the discussion about Kiki's legacy, suggesting that she too was aware she might not be sticking around, and her heart flexed. 'I was only young. It just confirms to me what I felt was true, what I figured out as I got older: that I didn't have a safety net, a nest, a haven. I just happened to live in my parents' house, eat some meals with them, sit by their side for the odd bedtime story at dusk, but essentially, I was on my own. They were far more interested in each other and their crazy life, and they cared so little about what the consequences of that life might mean to me that they felt the need to warn me, give me advice as to how to behave when the whole ship sank. Or more specifically when the whole car skidded down the mountainside. But to know even when I was young that my world *would* one day fall apart was actually one of the scariest things ever, scarier than when they died and I was physically alone.'

'Do you think . . .' He paused, and his mouth moved but no words came, as if he might be deciding how best to proceed. '. . . do you think Kristina felt the same, feels the same . . . ? Do you think that's maybe why?'

She held his stare; she'd already dismissed the idea. 'Could be. We've never really talked about it. She was only a baby when they died, won't remember it at all, but that feeling of being left, abandoned . . . I don't know.'

'You've never talked about it?' He sounded incredulous.

'No.' She folded her arms across her chest.

'Why not? That feels fundamental for you both, I think. If you don't mind me saying.'

How to respond? The truth was embarrassing, thin and none of his business, but it felt harder to stop talking once they had started, like trying to put an egg back into its shell or a genie back into the bottle. 'I guess it's one of those situations where it feels like a subject is too big to swallow and so we leave it to one side and talk about the weather, drink wine, giggle in the courtyard.' She looked towards the window and saw her sister throw her head back on that summer's eve, laughing, her long tawny hair about her shoulders. 'We're like the band playing on the *Titanic*.'

'Iceberg? What iceberg?' He looked around sharply.

'Exactly.' She rolled her eyes at the absurdity of it. 'Our upbringing was odd, uncomfortable at times, with pockets of utter joy!' She thought of swimming in the sea with Luna and baking with her Nana Dilly, all pre Kiki. 'Or at least that's how it was for me. Kiki and I have only ever known each other as sisters set apart, different lives, different experiences. Different generations. The only thing that binds us, the glue if you like, is our shared heritage; our sad tale, almost of neglect, or if not neglect then of extreme distraction. Our parents were far too busy living their lives to care for us and so it feels shitty to raise it, to rake over it. What would be the point?'

'To put it to bed maybe?'

'Maybe.' She wondered if there was truth in this.

Wilf did a loud fart.

'Wilf!' he called out, giggling. 'Jeez, sorry, Nora. He really is the very worst houseguest.'

'I've had worse. My husband's old school chums once got so sloshed they vomited in my chest freezer. I didn't find it for days.' She shuddered at the memory. 'Thought a bag of mixed veg had split, but no . . .'

'That's disgusting. I think I prefer Wilf's farts.'

'Oh, me too! And for the record it wasn't my husband, Gordy, but his mates. They haven't been to stay since. One now runs the Treasury, the other's a high-ranking diplomat trying to keep spirits up in a war-torn corner of the world.' She remembered who she was speaking to and that this was the kind of loose-lipped gossip that Gordy would have frowned upon.

'It must be hard for him, you being here and having to do the move on his own; the thought alone gives me hives. I can't even unpack after a holiday!'

She laughed and felt the unwelcome threat of tears at how unprepared she was when it came to discussing their divorce. It felt easier to say nothing, to allow the mirage.

'It's true! I have a real thing about it and once left damp, sand-filled trunks and a grotty towel in my case for weeks. Oh, the smell!'

'That's terrible!' At the mention of a smell, she ran her finger under her nose to stop the lingering scent of the bathroom, of Kiki's blood snaking back into her nostrils, the memory of it enough to make it real.

'It *is* terrible, what can I say?' He twisted his mouth. 'Just hope your husband fares better or you'll have some stinky laundry to come home to.'

'He's used to it; we both are. Shifting plans at a moment's notice, living at the beck and call of a wider strategy in which you have no say, it's been a bit like that on and off for years. But I married a military man and this kind of comes with the territory.' She straightened. Her tone, she was aware, was a little clipped, but it was that or break down, so she chose the former.

'An exciting life though, getting to live in Cyprus and other places. I think that sounds wonderful.'

'Yes, wonderful.' Her sigh was audible.

'I should probably . . .' Clearly sensing the shift in her demeanour, he pointed towards the front door.

She nodded in agreement, wanting nothing more than to be alone.

'Thanks for popping by, Jason.'

'No worries, it was nice to talk.'

'It was, but it's not me you need to be talking to, is it? It's Sheila.'

'I know and I will . . .'

'When the time is right.' She finished his sentence and he smiled.

Jason clicked his tongue and Wilf rose, following him along the corridor. He opened the front door before stopping and turning back. 'Sometimes,' he began and looked towards the sky, as if that might be where inspiration lurked, 'sometimes things that happen in our childhood can shape us in ways we don't even realise, good and bad, and I think you and Kiki should probably talk about your childhoods, about the way you were raised, about all of that stuff. It might help her.'

And it might help me . . . she read between the lines.

'You might be right.' She took a step backwards, trying inadvertently to put a physical barrier between her and the man she had opened up to.

'Kiki was right though, you are lovely and there's something you should know about Stroudly Green: once it throws its arms around you, shows you love and friendship, it's very hard to wiggle free. I should know, I was only supposed to be a temp and here I am seven years later!'

Jason shrugged and turned and she watched his shadow make its way along the path and disappear with his beloved hound into the cool night air. She wondered where she would be in seven years and her head filled with images of Gordy.

With Ted sleeping soundly and Jason long gone, she lay on the sofa and thought again of her mother's words. The truth was, until Gordy had given her a home by his side, everything in her life had had an air of transience.

Even here, hanging out with her sister's friends and her sister's son in her sister's home, it was a borrowed life and one that she would hand back soon enough. The thought filled her with dread and relief in equal measure.

Her buzzing phone roused her from her thoughts. She didn't recognise the number but answered it anyway. Her brain jumped from foggy to alert the moment she heard the voice say one word.

'Nora.'

It was Kiki. *It was Kiki! Kiki!* Her relief at hearing that one word was sweet and instant.

'Oh! Oh my God! My darling!' She placed her hand over her mouth, aware of just how much she had been longing to hear her sister's voice and understanding how very close she had come to never hearing it again. But there was no time for overwhelmed silence, she didn't know how long the call might last and had questions.

'Kiki, oh my goodness! Is it really you?'

'It's me,' she croaked.

'It's . . . it's so lovely to hear your voice and that's an understatement.' It was! It erased some of the horrible images that she had conjured. If Kiki was on the phone, talking coherently, she wasn't restrained, drugged and a million other scenarios, gleaned largely from movies, that had filled her head. She sat up and squinted at the clock on the kitchen wall, trying to decipher the time. 'H-how are you?' It was, she knew, ordinarily the easiest of questions, but for her sister it seemed almost impossible to answer. Nora only asked it out of habit and regretted it the moment the words rolled from her tongue.

Kiki took her time in forming an inadequate pained response. 'Not great, Nora.' Her voice cracked as the sound of her crying whistled down the line. 'They're transferring me to a psychiatric ward, and I'm scared.'

It was an admission so frank, so raw and yet so relatable it was at once both heartbreaking and hopeful, in that if Kiki was scared, that meant her mind was focused and able to understand that this was indeed scary.

She gripped the phone, wishing she could reach into it and wrap Kiki in her arms. 'Don't cry. Don't cry, darling. Please don't cry.'

'I don't—' She cut away in a great gulping sob. 'I don't know what my mum sounded like, but I think she'd sound like you right now.'

Nora could only speak with her eyes closed, battling to control her own emotions, which threatened to spill from her, that bubbling sadness over her loneliness, all that was wrong with her childhood and all that she and Kiki needed to resolve.

'I . . . don't know what she'd say, but I can tell you this: you're going to be okay, you're doing really well and all the people who love you are waiting to tell you just how much.' She licked the tears that coated her top lip and swiped at her runny nose with her fingertips. 'This transfer will be the best thing, they will know how to treat you, they will help you feel better.'

'Everything. Is. Such. A. Mess.' Kiki spoke the words slowly and forcefully as if to get them out at all took more effort than she possessed.

'It might feel like that right now, but it really isn't. The greatest thing you can do, the greatest thing anyone can do when they feel like they've had enough, is hold on. And that's what you have to do, Kiki, you have to hold on! Take it one second at a time, then one minute, then an hour and before you know it you will be home.'

At the sound of the word home her sister let out a noise that was part wail.

'Don't cry, darling,' she cooed again. 'I've been trying to get hold of you, trying to see you and I appreciate it needs to be on your terms, but how I have longed to hear your voice, Kiki.'

'I didn't want to talk to anyone, didn't want to think,' her sister managed, sounding at once childlike and distressed. It was hard to hear. 'But now, now I want to come home.'

This was progress! Huge progress!

'And you will. You will. Soon.'

'How can I hold him, how can I look him in the eye when I nearly . . . ?'

Kiki didn't have to use his name, Nora knew her sister referred to Ted, the little boy sleeping soundly across the hallway with his secret blankie.

'Because you're his mum and he adores you and nothing will matter to him other than having you home, nothing.'

'I miss him.' Her voice again high-pitched as each word coasted on distress. 'I miss him so much.'

'And he misses you too.' Was that the right thing to say or a pressure Kiki could do without? It felt like a minefield. 'But he's happy! And doing great at school this week and he saved a goal at football, and—'

'I have to go, Nora.'

'Oh, oh okay, darling. Sleep, rest and try not to worry about a thing.' Again the words sounded hollow and misplaced, and fear flashed that she might have inadvertently said or done the wrong thing. 'And know that everything here is fine and when you come home you will receive the warmest welcome!' she added brightly, thinking that if these words were the last thing Kiki heard of their conversation, it might be something she mentally replayed and had the potential, in some way, to lift her.

'Tell Ted.' Her sister took a slow, deep breath, her tone nervous. 'Tell Ted.'

Then the phone went dead.

Nora let her head fall forward and gave in to her tears, crying long, lingering sobs that left her breathless. There was something so intrinsically sad about the call. She wasn't sure if it was the sound of Kiki's voice with its rasp and the echo of tension, her vocal cords pulled taut with fatigue and distress, or her actual words. It had been hard to hear.

'Why are you crying?'

It was a surprise to hear Ted's young voice calling from the doorway. She toyed with the idea of denying that she was crying, but remembered what it had felt like when adults had lied to her.

'*Things will be different, my little one, but they will be fine. Just you wait and see . . .*' Nana Dilly had no doubt meant well, but Nora knew in the base of her gut that things were not going to be fine. Not when she was packed off to school and Kiki got to live at Midland Road. And she had been proved right, because at forty-six, she was still 'waiting to see . . .'

'I was crying because I was feeling a little bit sad. And a little bit thoughtful.' It was conflicting, whether to tell Ted she had spoken to his mum or whether to keep quiet. It didn't feel that she had much news and Kiki's distress was not something she would share.

'What are you thinking about?' He took a step closer.

'About things I wish I could fix. Things I wish I could wave a magic wand over and make everything good.'

'Would you wave a magic wand over Mummy?'

'Uh-huh.' She managed as more tears fell down her cheeks and clogged her nose and throat.

'Aunty Pickle?'

'Yes, Ted?'

'I think it might be laundry day again.' He chewed his lip as his hands fidgeted by his sides.

'Is it?' she asked with a wide smile to mask her own concern and any embarrassment that he might be cocooned in, trying not to let her eyes linger on the large damp patch on his pyjama bottoms.

'Yes.' He blushed.

She jumped off the sofa. 'Do you know what the time is, Ted?' She beamed.

He shook his head.

'It's midnight! And do you know the rules about midnight laundry?'

Again he shook his head.

'The rule is this' – she bent towards him conspiratorially, her voice no more than a whisper – 'when you do midnight laundry you can only do it with a midnight snack!' Going on no more than instinct, she did her best and hoped her actions, the fun, might in some small way temporarily make up for the fact that his mum was going into the psych ward and he had wet the bed.

He jumped up and down on the spot, his expression one of joy. And the unexpected wave of happiness that washed over her mirrored his. It felt good to be getting it right and even better to trust the feeling that she *was* getting it right.

'So, you go change your PJs, I'll shove the laundry in the machine, and I'll meet you by the fridge in two minutes. Go! Go! Go!' She clapped, watching him run across the laminate floor towards his room. 'It'll be okay, Ted, we'll figure it all out,' she whispered. 'We'll figure it all out.'

With the washing machine whirring in a ball of suds, and bowls of cereal eaten quickly at the breakfast bar, her nephew once again went quiet.

'Aunty Pickle?'

'Yes, Ted?'

'I like you being here.'

His words lifted her spirit and filled her with something close to joy. 'Well, that's jolly good because you're stuck with me!'

'I used to cry when Mummy was sad in the night. She woke me up with her noisy crying and I didn't know what to do. I think when she comes home, if she cries again, I'm going to make her a midnight feast.'

Nora felt his words land like daggers. Was this their world? Kiki crying in the night? It was about as far from the sunny image she had carried of her sister as possible and one that tore at her heart. For the second time she thought of all the lonely nights in Akrotiri when she could have called her sister, checked in . . .

'Ted, I don't think there's anything in the world that doesn't feel better after a midnight feast!'

Her words were flippant, but her spirit sank at this new insight into their lives; she was determined to do better, to be better for her sister.

'Right, I don't know about you but I'm feeling a little sleepy. I'll pop clean bed linen on your mattress, you go clean your teeth, and we can turn in our toes. Okay?'

'Okay.' He hopped down from the bar stool and his bare feet slapped on the kitchen floor. It was a small sound but one that took her back to a warm night in La Fosca, the night the kindly Señor Agostí had taken her back to bed and wished for her sweet dreams . . . His words had made all the difference to a scared little girl. It was rare for her to think of him. Someone she had not seen in decades, part of her life that had died along with her parents. It occurred to her then that she had never mentioned the incident to her parents, never told them how he had made her feel better – not that it mattered now of course, not that any of it mattered. What was it he had said? 'You never know when something wonderful might happen . . .'

She listened to Ted humming as he reached for his toothbrush. How she hoped Señor Agostí was right.

CASA PINO

'*Esto vino Papá!* This came Dad!' Mateo crept into the study and walked around the desk.

'*Qué es?* What is it?'

'A letter, from England. Looks like it's from the woman you wrote to about Guy's painting.' He watched as his papá's face lit up as if wakening, despite it being mid-afternoon.

'Let me see!' Sitting up poker straight in the chair, Santiago reached for the round, gold-rimmed glasses that lived in the top pocket of his linen shirt and, fumbling to open them, popped them on to his nose. He scanned the jiffy bag and ripped open the top to find his original letter in the envelope and two folded sheets of cheap, lined paper that, judging by his expression, were a little disappointing in their flimsiness, as he stroked them between his fingertips. 'You read it, Mateo, your English is better than mine when reading. I prefer to write it, take my time. You're quicker. Go ahead!' he urged with impatience.

Mateo took the sheets from his papá and noted the rather clumsy handwriting. 'Okay.' He coughed to clear his throat and translated as he went, reading aloud while Santiago stared, rapt. As he neared the end, from the corner of his eye he saw his papá slump a little with disappointment and once again the air of joyous expectancy was replaced with the rather tense weight of frustration, like someone had blocked out the sun and they were again in this limbering shadow where his father waited, waited for the tap on the shoulder that would see him travel to the place he had described as home. It was conflicting for Mateo; he wanted his papá to find peace, but at the same time didn't relish being left all alone.

The old man slumped forward and with his head resting on his chest, started to snore. Mateo left him to snooze and took Maggie's letter to the kitchen, where he popped the kettle back on the range to boil, keen to replace the coffee he had so hurriedly discarded, before studying her words closely.

> *I know I have never been loved like that and I know I have never loved like that, and even though it's so sad that your wife is no longer with you, how wonderful it is to have experienced such a thing. I think you are very lucky. I think you were both very lucky . . .*

'*Esto es tan triste*, Maggie Yates. So very sad.' He stared at his reflection in the silver wine coolers, buckets and teapots, the crystal vases and glassware that lined the shelves of the little kitchen, once known as *la habitación de las flores*, where his mamá would cut stems and arrange blooms while she hummed the hymns she so loved. Maggie's words had moved him so because he understood – more than understood. He understood because it was his story too: he too had never known a love like his parents shared. And was resigned to the fact that he never would . . .

CHAPTER SIX

Nora was happy to be leaving the flat, which for all its sparkling surfaces, folded laundry, plumped cushions and freshly watered plants was beginning to feel somewhat claustrophobic. She could see how Kiki might have felt a little hemmed in and how this would do nothing good to someone whose mental state was suffering. The memory of her sister's broken voice still haunted her thoughts.

'You're off for the weekend, aren't you?' Sheila asked with a note of envy as they clustered around the school gates at pick-up time.

'Yes, I've got a hire car and we're heading down to Westbury.' She was doing so with trepidation and fear in equal measure, but knew she had to do her best to shield Ted from it, aware of how nerves like that could be infectious. Sheila and the others were, of course, unaware of how her marriage teetered on a crumbling cliff edge while she waited for her husband to take her hand and jump. 'I've told the hospital that if Kiki needs anything or the situation changes, I can be back here in just over an hour with good traffic.'

'Try to relax, Nora, try to rest. And remember if you need me to go and see her, be with her, whatever, I can get there and hold the fort until you arrive. Whatever you need, just call.'

Sheila was a sweet woman – what was it Jason had said about Stroudly Green? *Once it throws its arms around you, shows you love and friendship, it's very hard to wiggle free . . .* Was that what was happening here? She allowed a smile in Sheila's direction, understanding that she cared and maybe Nora, like Kiki, could do with more love like that.

'I will, and thank you. I'm hoping she'll say yes to visitors soon.' Looking around, she felt the blush of an imposter spread over her neck; it should be Kiki here, collecting her son, living this life.

'Sames.' Sheila sighed.

Jason walked to the gate with Ted. 'Nora, hi, Ted tells me he is going on holiday this weekend so don't worry too much about homework. If he gets a chance to read that'd be great, but I think a lovely weekend running around and having fun is more valuable.'

Ted looked predictably chuffed.

'Oh, I'd love a weekend away.' Sheila sighed again, letting her shoulders droop.

'Where do you want to go?' Jason asked.

'Oh, Mr Ormond, how lovely! I thought you'd never ask.'

Nora noted the instant expression of joy on the man's face and did her best to keep schtum. Had these people still not been relative strangers, the temptation to intervene, to drop a not-so-subtle hint that might bolster the woman's joke, was strong. But a promise was a promise.

Sheila stared at him. 'Anywhere,' she continued, 'absolutely anywhere.'

And there was a moment, just a moment, when he looked a little overwhelmed and Nora considered making some brusque comment to defuse his obvious awkwardness in the way that Jasmine Leech might, but that, too, felt like interfering.

'I'd better . . .' He thumbed in the direction of the children waiting to be dispatched, but his smile was fixed and there was, she would say, a definite spring in his step.

Nora smiled at Sheila.

'What?' the woman who had saved Kiki and to whom Nora owed the greatest debt asked playfully.

'Nothing.' She smiled. 'Nothing at all.'

◆ ◆ ◆

It felt odd and yet familiar to be driving in England. The fact that in Cyprus cars drove on the left-hand side meant that while she wasn't out of practice, the volume of traffic made it a different experience. That and the lack of blue, blue sky with glimpses of sea to cheer her along the journey. The roomy silver hire car had that new, clean smell and the brakes were sharp. It had felt strange, taking time to blow-dry her hair, apply a little blusher and to spritz her décolletage with scent as if she were heading on a date, wanting desperately to, if not appeal to Gordy, then at least to leave him with the memory of good times and what they had once shared. Her stomach felt hollow at the prospect of not receiving a warm welcome from him, quite unable to imagine a time when she would see him and he would not be hers and she would not be his – a couple, a twosome, a bickering, loving pair who might have wrinkles in their relationship that needed ironing out, but a pair nonetheless. Nerves raced around her stomach at the prospect of seeing him and everything being different.

She gripped the steering wheel, driving steadily, cautiously, checking her speed and feeling the responsibility of driving with a little one for the first time. Still with the barely disguised fear of what it might feel like if something bad were to happen to Ted on her watch. It was a challenge not to peer at him every five minutes in the rear-view mirror to check how he was doing. The snacks she had carefully packed – a cheese sandwich cut into squares, a bag of stinky puffed crisps and a quartered red apple – had been devoured before they hit the motorway.

'You made quick work of that, Ted.'

He ignored her and stared out of the window, looking up at the sky. She wondered how much he and Kiki had travelled and whether they had had day trips or holidays? It was another reminder of the gaps in their relationship, the shared knowledge that she was certain was often commonplace among other siblings. Something she wanted to fix in their future, all part of her plan to grow closer to Kiki, to help more, to get to know her and to be there if she fell.

Ted discarded his empty lunchbox on the seat beside him. There had been a distinct increase in his appetite, which pleased her, his face now somewhat more rounded, less gaunt, as if the bubble of anxiety that had previously filled him up had deflated a little and his nerves had settled. It made her far happier than she would have imagined. This was a new sensation that was both a revelation and a surprise: how quickly she felt connected to the boy, how much she cared about such things like his diet, his happiness, his well-being. Did she love him? No! No, of course she didn't; the reality was she barely knew him. But did she care for him? Yes! Yes, she most certainly did.

'Look!' the little boy shouted, pointing upwards over a field.

'I can't, Ted, I have to keep my eyes on the road. What is it?'

'I think that might be an eagle!' His voice was high and keen.

She glanced in the mirror to see him craning his neck to study whatever bird hovered and held him fascinated. His skinny legs jumped against the seat in excitement.

'It might be, but it might not. First, I can't see it from here and second it might be another bird of prey which would be just as cool, wouldn't it?'

'No.' His answer was resolute, accompanied by a definitive shake of his head.

'Oh, well that told me.' Leonora smiled warmly. 'I mean, it could be. I'm not great on birds, but I tell you who is – Uncle Gordy. He knows a lot about them, so remember what it looks like, and you can describe it to him. How about that?' She wanted to recommend her husband to the boy, for him not to feel anxious about the weekend ahead, and this felt as good a way as any.

Ted remained silent, as he did when he was thoughtful or a little overwhelmed, before emitting a deep, low sigh of the weariness that belied his tender years.

'But I promise, if I see an eagle, I will point it out to you, okay?'

He nodded. 'Where do eagles make their nests?'

'That's a good question. I *think* in the tops of very tall trees.' She wasn't sure where she had got this information or whether it was true, but it sprang to mind, nevertheless. 'And I bet not that many live in the middle of cities, maybe a few,' she added, keen not to pour cold water on the flames of interest that flickered around the feather-covered topic. 'And I think they like coastlines and islands, don't they?' He didn't answer. 'I read an article once about an eagle that took a puppy, grabbed it in its claws and went off into the sky, can you believe that?'

One quick look in the rear-view mirror at his widened eyes told her this had his interest.

'Really? A puppy?'

'Yes, the bird swooped down while the dog's owner was walking it in a field in America somewhere. It was a sweet little thing with a flattish face, can't remember the breed, but I do happen to know it was called Norman, as that was my mother's great-uncle's name and it stuck with me. Can you imagine? It's a sunny day, you take Norman out for a lovely stroll and whoosh! He gets taken by an eagle! I bet Norman's mum felt terrible.'

He ignored her as if deep in thought.

As a child, she'd wanted a dog more than anything, pleaded for one with boring regularity. On the odd occasion, she smuggled flea-infested, snaggle-toothed strays into the kitchen, luring them with a nub of sausage and the kindest tone of affection imaginable, laced with false promises of a forever home . . . All to no avail, of course. Her daddy had explained that this was not their forever home, they were instead only living here for a bit, and it would be disastrous to make a dog part of their family, only to have to leave it behind when they travelled back to England from Spain.

'But why couldn't we take it with us?' she'd pushed, while her tears gathered and her heart simultaneously ached at the prospect of abandoning the much-loved hound, her acquaintance with whom had been brief.

'Because,' her mother had drawled, 'we live in a flat in central London that was only ever intended to be your grandpa's pied-à-terre, an escape from Granny Magda, and not a home for a family.' She sucked on her cigarette before cupping Leonora's chin and looking into her eyes, as if studying something unfamiliar. She could smell the scent on her mother's narrow wrist; it was strong and reminded her of black pepper. 'You're an odd little mouse. There's barely enough room to swing a cat in the flat, a tiny cat at that, a kitten.' She'd laughed then with her head back and her long platinum hair shivering down her back and over her bare, sun-kissed shoulders.

'So does that mean we can get a kitten?' she asked, brightening. This, she had decided, would be the next best thing.

'No!' Her mother jumped up. 'For fuck's sake . . .'

'Language, Nessa!' Her father had chuckled.

Nora remembered this too . . .

Again, she looked at Ted in the rear-view mirror, trying to imagine speaking to him in that way. He looked thoughtful and stared up at the sky.

'I feel sorry for Norman. Do you think the eagle ate him?' he asked softly.

She realised the topic may have slightly backfired, yet another poor choice of anecdote, which she silently cursed, choosing her words carefully.

'Possibly, or maybe right now they're living together in a lovely nest and Norman and the eagle are very good friends and they drink tea and eat biscuits together, what do you think?'

'I think it ate him.' He stared at her.

Nora popped the radio on, giving them both a break from the conversation.

With the satnav heralding their arrival, she turned into the unfinished road where approximately ten houses sat in a wide loop of cul-de-sac, each with high laurel hedging and a metal garden gate that led up a paved path to a wooden front door. The houses were rendered and painted in magnolia, which in certain lights showed an alarming hint of peach. Not that she would expect anything less from a design perspective; no doubt the colour had been chosen at random and in haste by a staff member working for the Defence Infrastructure Organisation who had been charged with the chore.

She parked the hire car behind her husband's, knowing he would be pleased to have it out of storage – his beloved forest-toned, short-wheelbase Landy, of which she had so many fond memories. Picnics, thunderstorms, camping out under the stars, trips to the beach; and in each one they were laughing, with no clue that the word divorce would be uttered in just a matter of years, turning her whole world upside down. She took a deep breath and coiled her fingers to try and stop their shake, before beeping the horn.

The sky bore the mauve bruise of dusk, the ground was damp with fallen leaves and mushroomy odours, and the air smouldered with the aroma of real fires. It was the scent and sight of autumn and one that made her feel nostalgic for a life that was never hers but was more a memory borrowed during childhood from Agatha Christie novels and the Famous Five. It made her long for crumpets toasted on a fork over a dancing flame, soft socks on warm feet curled under a cashmere blanket, a good cup of tea in a cup and saucer and slow jazz playing from a crackly record that lulled her muscles and eased her worries . . . But this was real life and the best she could hope for was that her husband had remembered to put the central heating on and any animosity could be held off until Ted was snoring.

'Hey Ted.' Gordy, alerted by her beep, waved from the front door. Her heart jumped at the sight of him. It felt odd to see him in his uniform with the sleeves up past the elbow, hands on hips, so comfortable in front of a house, his home and somewhere she had never set foot.

This is what it will be like, she thought, *him here and me elsewhere, him carrying on as if we had never been: going for his run, eating supper with any old sport on the TV filling the silence, and heading off to his office each and every day. His new normal. How will I live? And where will I be? The flat in London? Possibly, or further afield – India, Italy, Mexico* . . . She briefly pictured all the places lined up on her mental to-do list and imagined travelling there alone, travelling light. A chill crept over her bones at the prospect.

Ted climbed out of the car and stood still. The reasons for his hesitancy she could only guess at: a strange house, Gordy, the man Ted had last seen as a toddler, of whom she doubted he had any real recollection, and the fact that he wasn't with his mum, but had been bundled into a car with his Aunty Pickle. And who knew what the weekend held? Gordy was right, though, not only did the two of them need to talk face to face, but a bit of fresh air and a gambol through the forest would be the best distraction for a little boy in turmoil.

'You remember Gordy?'

He nodded and took a faltering step forward. She and her husband exchanged a knowing look, the one that under any other circumstances would be familiar and comforting, the one that said, 'We are on the same page'. But it was false, and she knew it, designed to comfort Ted, and any solace she took from it was misplaced.

'Jolly glad you're here, Ted, I could do with the help.' Gordy clapped his hands together. 'I need to chop some kindling and build a fire in the sitting room. Are you a wood-chopping man?' he boomed. She'd forgotten his easy manner, the way he could make anyone, even a small boy, feel comfortable, valued. It was a skill she envied, feeling the cloak of inadequacy about her shoulders, thinking of her mentioning death to the child and putting him off dentists for life . . .

'I don't know.' The little boy's standard response.

'Well, it's a good idea we find out. Now, do you have wellingtons? It's muddy at the back of the garden where the log store lurks.' Ted ran to the trunk and once she'd opened it, he leaned in and hoicked out his wellington boots. Then, sitting on the damp ground in his jeans, he kicked off his trainers and pulled them on. 'And you won't need that thick coat; kindling-chopping is hard work, shirtsleeves will do just fine!'

It amazed her how willing the child was to go with Gordy. Clearly the thought of wielding an axe and setting fire to stuff was too tempting a prospect. Shrugging his arms from his anorak, Ted let it drop to the floor behind him and she retrieved it from the moss-covered driveway, laying her hand in the warmth where his little form had been. Gordy held her eyeline and seemed to study her face, and it took all her strength not to burst into tears. But as ever, she reminded herself that public displays of emotion weren't and never had been her thing – whatever next, line dancing?

173

'Hey.' His eye twitched and for the first time she saw the hint of nerves.

'Hey.'

'We'll be back in a bit, and we can chat later?'

'Sounds good.' She nodded. 'I'll go make supper – if I can find the kitchen.'

'It's at the end of the hallway – turn left,' Gordy called as the two trotted along the path that ran down the side of the house and disappeared from sight.

'Righty-ho.'

Her mind danced back to some of their old houses, army quarters in all shapes and sizes, where he would greet her with a grand gesture and tour, even on one occasion a bouquet of flowers to welcome her – but not tonight. This lack of fanfare an acknowledgement that this was not her future home, it was his. Cursing the tears that stung the back of her nose, she headed inside.

Same curtains, same wallpaper, same colour palette. What would be the convention? Unpack a box. Make supper. Get oriented. Learn the lie of the land: the best coffee shop, the local baker, the quickest route to the supermarket. Acquaint herself with the neighbours. Spend a Christmas or two making memories that would fuse with all others as the festive celebrations merged into one in her mind. Receive notice. Pack up the boxes. Move. New house. Same curtains . . . but not this time. This time the story would continue without her, and her stomach folded with loss at the prospect. This realisation enough to make her feel overly aware of every action that would ordinarily be second nature.

The hallway was nice and spacious. The house, Edwardian. Some of the windows were sash, the staircase comfortably wide and the rooms uniformly square. A quick glance into the sitting room revealed a fireplace that had been butchered in the 1980s, if she'd had to guess, and was ugly with a tiled surround, but at least it worked. Automatically, she figured out how best to disguise it, settling mentally on an embroidered screen or a large display of dried grasses and flora. She imagined making a display of white ruscus, pampas grass, bunny tails and statice, thinking it would be kitsch and in keeping with the fireplace. This was what she did, made the houses they were allocated into homes. Or at least she had. Gordy had made an attempt at positioning the standard army-issue sofa and two chairs, which she would ask if it was okay to rearrange after she'd given the kitchen the once-over and organised bedding. Even the idea of asking permission wrapped her in sadness, but still she wanted the place to be nice for Gordy. Because she loved him. This thought hit her like smacking her head on glass: she loved him, she loved him, she loved him! This realisation made the thought of losing him even harder to bear.

The house had a peculiar smell. Not unpleasant or offensive, but simply the collective scent of the previous family – their food, cologne, household products, the odd pet or two – and one that she knew would disappear, replaced by her husband's, no doubt just before he got the order to pack up and ship out, which he would do alone. Or maybe not, maybe he would remarry quickly, find a girlfriend, shack up. It was a concept too ghastly to consider, and one that caused her throat to constrict. Wrapping her arms around her torso, she did her best to soothe away the images of another woman with her hand in his; it was enough to make her shiver.

Finally, she found her plants dotted on the wide windowsill and all over the floor in a long conservatory that had been tacked on to the back of the building. Gordy had watered them, freed them from the packing crates and she was grateful.

'There you are!' She beamed as though greeting old friends. 'Hello, lovelies!' Moving the pots so they had adequate space, she poked her finger into the soil to check moisture levels and some she watered from her trusty long-spouted watering can that Gordy had left filled on the floor. It was a relief that he remembered her plants preferred their drink to be at room temperature. An act of kindness that suggested he was still considerate of her, which boded well for all that might follow where civility had to be the goal.

It gave her immense satisfaction to be close to her flora. One or two of her aspidistras drooped rather and she gently touched their floppy leaves. 'It's okay. You'll soon get used to it here. Not too light, shady, just the way you like it.' She administered drops of plant food where necessary. The spider plants had grown and while she knew the roots liked a close-fitting pot, she decided to upgrade their living quarters to allow for expansion. She'd keep her eye out for her favoured vintage terracotta, although where she might be shifting them to, God only knew.

Ted's burbling chatter drifted from the back of the long garden and through the open window. It was the first time she had heard a child's voice in their home and she wondered what it might have been like to live a life like Jasmine Leech: one where days were punctuated by the school run and the organising of homework and bedtimes, the year strewn with the markers of birthdays, Christmas and Halloween. They were holidays and celebrations that she and Gordy gave a small nod to, but without kids to stoke the excitement, hold parties and make costumes for, attend the nativity and all else that she saw – Easter egg hunts, tooth fairy collections, sports days – they passed with no more than cursory consideration. She realised the list of all that had passed her by was long and in truth she had never felt the loss of them – of any of them, until now, maybe, just a little. She wondered if children would have made the difference, whether they might have been the glue that stopped him wanting more than she was able to give. They had discussed it, of course, but always with the compass firmly in her hand, choosing the direction, leading the way, making her views on motherhood known, and Gordy following, kissing her gently and telling her she was enough.

'Too late, Leonora, all too late,' she whispered as she made her way to the kitchen.

◆ ◆ ◆

Gordy and Ted ambled in via the back door to the kitchen where she was jostling frying pans on the range, listening to the sizzle and pop of the ingredients in the hot pan, and trying to quieten the growl of hunger in her stomach that the smell had awakened.

'How did you get on?' she asked, putting the warmed plates, which waited to receive the standard weekend supper of bacon, egg and beans, all polished off with a healthy stack of hot, buttered toast, on to the counter. 'Hope it's okay, I . . .' She gestured to the mess she had created.

'Of course it's okay!' he reassured her. 'Ted is a natural woodsman.' Gordy stepped out of his muddy wellingtons and placed them by the back door, Ted followed suit and she found it strangely moving to see the little boots sitting next to the big ones. It was jarring how these small things, snapshots of another life, moved her so. 'He wielded the axe like a pro!'

'Wielded the axe? For goodness' sake don't tell Kiki, she'll have my guts for garters!' She found a smile.

'Is she here?' Ted yelled, misunderstanding her comment as he ran from the kitchen. 'Is Mummy here?' He rushed around the downstairs of the property, flinging open doors, and navigating the strange house for the first time, each room echoing with the heartbreaking call of '*Mum! Mum!*'

'Ted!' she shouted, abandoning the task of serving supper as she chased after him. 'Ted, she's not here! I didn't mean to give you the impression she was. I'm so sorry. I just meant when she gets to hear about your weekend.' Her gut folded at the fact that she'd screwed up again.

The boy stared at her with his chest heaving and his eyes searching hers. Nora's veins ran thick with the syrup of loss that she not only recalled, but which his expression conjured.

'Where is she?' he whispered as his mouth contorted with the effort of containing his tears.

'She's still in hospital, but I'm pretty sure you can see her very soon. How about that?' She bent low, mimicking Jason.

'I want to go home. I don't want to be here. I want to go home! I want my mum!' He began to cry, great gulping sobs that made further speech impossible.

'I know.' She spoke calmly, quietly, damning herself for having upset the status quo, albeit inadvertently, and struggling to contain her own distress at the sight of his. 'It's only for two sleeps and on Sunday we'll head back to the flat and you can sleep in your own bed. And I'll go back to the floor!' She pulled a face. 'I promise we'll try and do fun things; you can help Gordy with the fire after supper and tomorrow you can build a den or we can play board games, or—'

'I want to be at home in case Mummy comes home.' His words pitiful and brave for one so little. Nora cursed making the trip; it would have been wiser if they'd stayed in the flat, opted for routine.

'I understand that, Ted, but I promise you she is not coming home today. I checked so you don't have to worry.'

Gordy walked into the living room slowly. 'I tell you what, Ted, me old mate, I've just stolen a piece of bacon, don't tell Aunty Pickle. It tasted really good – how about we go and eat while it's hot and if you really want to go home after supper, then I shall drive you and Pickle back, how about that?'

She knew that her husband was a man of his word and felt the pull of tiredness at the prospect of packing up and heading back to Stroudly Green having only recently departed. But if that was what it took to make the little boy settle, so be it. There was also no escaping the fact that her heart soared to hear Gordy being so sweet, so patient with their nephew when he needed it the most. She smiled at him, thankful, remembering that most wonderful thing about him: his kindness.

Ted nodded and wiped his eyes on his sleeve. 'Okay.'

'That's the spirit! Come on, Pickle!'

It made her smile that her husband had adopted her nickname.

'I've never had a pickle,' the little boy stated, perking up a little and making his way into the kitchen. Gordy followed him and plonked him on a high stool at the breakfast bar, before grabbing a fork to tuck into the rapidly cooling supper. Her husband displayed none of her reticence in picking him up, handling him, and she could see Ted took confidence from it. Nora rummaged in her handbag for the ketchup she'd picked up at the supermarket that day, knowing that for Ted it was a prerequisite for most meals. She placed it in front of him.

'Never had a pickle?' Gordy boomed.

Ted shook his head.

'For the love of God, Pickle! Get the pickles!' he shouted, and Ted laughed. The diversion seemed to do the trick. A light moment that helped her heart forget for a second that they were only playing happy families.

She rummaged among the jars and tins in the larder, which Gordy had thoughtfully stocked up. All the necessities were there: wine, tonic, gin, beer, rum, port, more wine, more tonic, some cornflakes, a large tin of coffee and two jars of pickles. She held the jar of gherkins aloft.

'Eeuw!' Ted wrinkled his nose at the jar. 'Is it the same as the little slice of frog you get in your burger?'

Both she and Gordy laughed, unified in the joy. 'Yes!' She smiled. 'I personally think the little slice of frog is the best bit!'

'I don't want to eat one of those.' He was adamant, shaking his head.

'Well, lucky for you we have a frog-free supper.' Gordy winked.

'Do you know where eagles live, Gordy?' he asked suddenly.

'Eagles, you say? Now, let me think.' Gordy looked towards the ceiling. 'I always picture the bald eagles of North America and Mexico, but I think eagles live in every country, and I'm not terribly sure about habitat but at a guess, I'd say cliffs, coastal areas, forests maybe? I'll investigate further and get back to you. Do you like eagles?'

'Yes.'

'Me too, the most majestic of birds!'

'Did you know that there was a puppy called Norman who got taken by an eagle? It just swooped right down and took him off.' He mimed the action with his fork.

'I can't believe it!' Gordy looked aghast. 'I simply can't believe it!'

'It's true!' Ted nodded furiously. 'It did, it took Norman, and his owner, who was a lady in a field, never saw him again.'

'No no, I mean I can believe the story, I'm sure an eagle *did* take the puppy, but what I can't believe is that anyone of sound mind would call their puppy Norman!'

She and Ted both laughed; seemingly his earlier anxiety and tears had melted away as quickly as they had bloomed. It was a lovely moment and one that if circumstances had been different, she would be folding away in her memory, there for recall whenever she needed it. It was a surprise, the joyous addition of a child over supper, and again she wondered what this would feel like if it had been their life and not a slice of Kiki's that she was merely minding.

'He was!' the little boy shouted, as if volume might help prove his point. 'He was called Norman.'

'Ted has asked a couple of times if there was an eagle overhead, but the one in the park turned out to be nothing more than a chip-seeking seagull.' She tutted her forced laughter and forked a fried egg on to a slice of toast before grinding a generous slick of salt over the top. 'And I couldn't see the one he spotted today as I had my eyes on the road, but I told him that you know much more about birds than I.'

'So, we have a budding ornithologist in our midst, is that right?' Gordy addressed the little boy who gave his standard response of, 'I don't know.'

'You like birds?' she clarified.

Ted shook his head. 'Not really.' He toyed with his fork.

'So why the fascination with eagles?' Gordy asked gently.

'Because . . . because . . .' – the child's breathing increased – 'because Mummy told me that if ever she couldn't be with me any more she'd become an eagle and I'd only have to look up to see her. She said she'd find me.' His voice was small. 'She said that no matter where I was or what I was doing or how old I was, she'd find me and so I thought if I found an eagle, I might find her.'

It was as beautiful as it was heartbreaking, and the biggest clue that Kiki might have been planning, preparing her son for the consequences of her leaving him. The realisation went through her like a lance. Gordy held her eyeline, similarly aware of just what this meant.

'I promise you, Ted, you are going to see your mum very soon. She *can* be with you, she *will* be with you, and she is most definitely not an eagle; she is right now in the hospital, taking medicine and talking to the doctors and nurses and very soon she will be home with you. And when she's home, I'll come back here to chop wood with Gordy and make him bacon sandwiches!' She tried her best to laugh, to make light of the direst of situations, to not worry his little head. Her husband blinked and gave her a tight-lipped smile.

'Can I go and watch TV? I don't want any more supper.'

'Yes, of course.' Gordy abandoned his plate momentarily. 'Let's get you tuned in, my bacon can wait.' He looked over at Nora, addressing her directly and pointing towards her. 'And don't think about stealing my bacon, I have counted the rashers!'

She was grateful for her husband's wonderful handling of the boy in need, he made it look easy. With her mouth full, she made a strong pot of tea from which she filled a large mug. Gordy came back and folded a slice of bacon into his mouth before reaching for another.

'Poor little chap.'

'Yep.' She sipped the dark brew greedily, liking the way it washed her supper down.

'I'd say he is quite aware of the severity of the situation, and that must be unnerving.' His summary.

'Hard for him not to know, really, with everyone rallying around, me popping up like a bad penny and Kiki's friends openly breaking down in tears in front of him – not that I blame them, it's hard for everyone and the collective guilt is enormous. I feel terrible, Gordy, that I wasn't more clued-in, didn't reach out to her. I guess I thought because I didn't hear from her everything must be okay.' She rubbed her face.

'What do you make of it, Nora? Was it a cry for help? Did she really want to end her life?' He mouthed the last bit.

Falling back against the countertop, she bit her bottom lip. 'I don't know is the truthful answer, but I get the impression from her friends that it's not the first time she's had a mental slip-up, which was news to me. I always pictured her laughing, drinking wine, easy-going . . .'

'Poor Kiki.' Gordy sighed.

182

'Yes, poor Kiki.' Again she thought about the recent phone call. 'When she called the other night, she sounded . . .' Nora took her time, trying to find the words that best summed up how her sister had presented. 'Exhausted, broken. It was awful. Scary.'

Gordy stared at her, as if at a loss. 'I guess we don't know how much the little chap has seen or heard.'

'She would have done her best to keep things away from him, I'm sure. She's a great mum, you can see it in him, and I hear it from everyone who saw her daily.' Any suggestion that Kiki was not the very best mum hit a nerve. Nora had only been in her shoes for the shortest time and was aware of the effort it took to parent right, and this without the failing mental health her sister had to contend with.

'There's no need to sound so defensive.' He sounded stern. 'I don't doubt she is. We are on the same team, Nora.'

'For now,' she interjected. He ignored the comment.

'But I also know that mental illness often robs you of all reason, even momentarily, and that means your judgement, your priorities, routine, everything is skewed by it and so while not intentional, I think it's inevitable that Ted will have experienced more than maybe he should for one so young. And more than most of us would be happy to experience.'

'I guess so.' She knew frustration had made her snap at him and instantly regretted it. 'He told me he would wake up to her crying at night sometimes. And there have been one or two little accidents – he's wet the bed and is mortified by it.' It was at these moments that she felt the responsibility keenly.

'How did you handle it?' He kept his voice low.

'I . . . I made light of it, went along with his suggestion that he was just helping with laundry, that kind of thing.' She pictured the kerfuffle when her pee was discovered in the closet. 'I didn't want him to feel shame in any way. It can stay with you, that kind of thing.'

'Sounds like you handled it well, your awareness, he's lucky to have an aunty like you.'

Her smile was automatic, although his words invoked joy, validation that she was doing okay – and from someone who seemed a natural when it came to childcare, it meant the world.

'Thank you.' She meant it.

'He's a smart kid who's going through a lot. He'll be aware. I think our eagle conversation proves that.'

'Yes. It's heartbreaking, the fact that Kiki has had that chat with him at all; it must worry him. It's worried me, it's as if she knows that one day she won't be around – a pre-emptive strike almost, to ease his pain, a plan . . .' She shuddered at the thought, remembering how her mother had done something similar, warning her that strength would be needed to rebuild, to pick up all the little pieces . . .

'Maybe. Or maybe she said it in response to something he asked or has seen on TV, or a million other things. "Don't worry about losing me, I'll come back as an eagle!" She might even have been joking!'

'But his little face.' She locked eyes with her husband who was eating the last of his toast. 'It didn't sound like a joke.'

'I know.' He dislodged food from his gum with his tongue. 'I guess that was *me* trying to placate you, put your mind at ease.'

His words were another reminder of how he looked out for her, showed her love. Was he showing her love? She really hoped so. Because in that moment she wasn't sure she had the strength to face the separation that loomed.

'What do we do, Gordy? I mean what am I supposed to do?'

'The simple answer is we do whatever's necessary. We keep him safe; we keep him distracted. We work as a team, answer his questions as truthfully as we are able, and we provide a safe place. And when we can, we return him to his mum with one eye open so that if and when we are ever needed, we step in again and we keep repeating it until we don't need to keep one eye open . . . and we deal with whatever comes up as it comes up. That's it.'

We . . . we . . . we . . .

'Do you have any guns?'

'Guns?' Gordy turned to face the little boy in the doorway. 'No, but I can take you to see a tank tomorrow, if you like, which has an almighty gun on the front. Would you like that?'

'A real tank?' His eyes lit up.

'Yep, a real tank, but we'll have to put you in some camo, face paint, a helmet, that kind of thing, are you up for this, soldier?'

Ted actually jumped on the spot. 'Yes! Yes, I am!'

'Then that sounds like a plan! But first we need to go gather the kindling. I'll grab the torch and then we can make a fire in the hearth.' Gordy stopped suddenly and turned to face Ted who came to a fast halt behind him. 'But remember, going to see the tank tomorrow is a secret mission, okay, soldier?'

'Okay!' Ted breathed deeply, his eyes wide.

Gordy winked at her as the two swept from the room. She admired the ease with which he chatted to Ted. How she wished she were not so overly conscious of contact and wanting to get it right, or rather, more accurately, not wanting to get it wrong. She wished she could relax more with the boy.

With the house to herself, Nora took the opportunity to wander from room to room, familiarising herself with the layout of the floors, the size of the bedrooms, the cupboards and handy storage spots that would no doubt be filled in the coming weeks. Gordy had made a sound attempt to put all the boxes in the correct rooms, and ordinarily she would start unpacking and fussing in an effort to turn the quarter into a home, in the quickest possible time, but this

185

was not ordinarily, and she was no more than a visitor. It bothered her, adding to her sense of redundancy, how the house seemed to be functioning perfectly well without the addition of ornaments, framed photographs, or her shoe collection tipped into the base of a wardrobe.

Having located the bed linen, she made up the bed in the big square bedroom at the rear of the house, which had its own sink and a glorious view over the garden.

Ted's room . . . She wondered if he might like a nameplate on the door or was that too much? Was that suggesting this might be more than just a place to come at weekends while he was in her temporary care? She didn't want to unnerve him and didn't know who she could ask – certainly not Kiki, and Gordy would, she knew, go with whatever she suggested. Maybe she'd pitch it to Fi, Mina and Sheila. She smiled at the thought of their input, looking forward in a strange way to seeing them, as if they were . . . as if they were *her* friends. It warmed her to know these women were in her corner. Jason was right, they were showing her love and friendship and she was finding it hard to wiggle free. And as it seemed she was about to lose Gordy's support, this felt like no bad thing.

Picturing the comforting clutter of Ted's small room at the flat and the collections of plastic tat that lined his shelves, this room looked rather bland in comparison. Maybe she'd look out some books to add a splash of colour when and if they came again. Her thoughts turned to Kiki, wondering how much longer she would be in hospital and if there was anything she could do for her sister to aid her recovery. She decided to call again on Monday to possibly arrange a visit during school hours; all she wanted to do was look her sister in the eye and get the lie of the land. The phone call had been as inadequate as it was distressing, and her heart twisted each time she recalled the rasping tone of despair that had echoed down the line.

With a chill to her bones, she made up the bed in a single room and wondered about getting a nameplate for this door too, *Nora's room*, lest her presence gave anyone the wrong idea that they were a happy couple.

◆ ◆ ◆

With Ted bathed and sleeping soundly in the room at the back, Nora pulled the sofa into a better position, and she and Gordy sat in front of the roaring fire, which had been masterfully constructed.

'That's better, I can see the TV and feel the warmth of the flames; you have the knack of making anywhere feel cosy.'

'I've certainly had enough practice over the years.'

'You have.'

'It's a nice house.' She spoke quietly, matching his air of formality and looking up over the wide cornice.

'It is.'

The air crackled with the snap of kindling, the pop of logs and the weight of the silence. Nora knew open conversation was needed, further discussion about their future and the large holes in their marriage, which she had to admit, as they sat there on the sofa, seemed to have grown a little smaller. This she could put down to the separation that allowed for reflection and the kindness and support Gordy had shown her. Plus, she'd be lying if she didn't admit to feeling a certain warmth when witnessing his skilful handling of Ted – his *parenting* of Ted. It stoked fires of affection that were closely aligned with regret. She dreaded the thought of the topic of divorce, wanting to put it off for as long as she was able, wanting to pretend. Unsure of how she would respond and fearful of letting Gordy see her utter distress at the thought of it.

'Cyprus feels like an age ago already.' She spoke the truth, curling her cold toes inside her socks.

'Tell me about it. Straight into the new job, learning as I go, and my bloody tan has already faded,' he jested.

'Mine too.' She held out her pale arm and studied the freckles.

There was a further second or two of silence.

'I must admit, I've been rehearsing in my head how I thought this conversation might go, all the things I should say, but now you're here, I'm feeling a bit . . .' He paused.

'Nervous?' she suggested.

'Yes.' He gave a faltering smile that was endearing. 'Nervous.'

'Me too.'

'I feel very guilty about the fact we were rowing and that I said what I did about divorce when you learned about Kiki.'

'You didn't know, how could you?'

'No, but I curse the timing of it.' He swallowed.

'I doubt there's ever a good time to announce the end of a marriage.' She stared at the flames.

'I don't think I announced it Nora, more acknowledged it, or at least suggested that it might be a possibility, something I'd been thinking about.'

'Mm,' she hummed, keeping her eyes on the fire and trying to tamp down the rising need to howl her impending loss for the whole county to hear – this was not and never had been how she behaved. Yes, it felt easier to hum.

'Although I must admit, things seem a little softer since we've been back. I've missed you and strangely that's been nice.'

His words, hinting that all was not lost, caused a flicker of joy in her gut, one that she was careful to manage in case it was not the reprieve she wished for.

'I get that.' She nodded. 'Plus of course you've been here living a life of Indian takeaways and no doubt rereading Dick Francis until you fall asleep . . . no room for rowing with me.'

'I love Dick Francis.'

'I know you do. And yes, despite all that's going on with Kiki, it has been nice. I can't remember much about the early detail of that row, but I know it was about sex, or rather the lack of.'

'Partly,' he clarified. 'I don't know how to feel, Nora. I'm a little lost.'

'You and me both. But I do know you can't lob a grenade into a marriage in the way you did and not have a plan. You must have thought about the next steps, about what you want and the mechanics and so forth. That's what I'm here for, isn't it? Although it should all be fairly straightforward – we have no shared property, I won't go near your pension or whatever.'

Gordy shook his head. 'I hate it when you do that.'

'Do what?' She turned to face him.

'Talk to me like I'm a stranger, put up a barrier! Close off, become clipped and reserved and play the part of someone hardened and indifferent. It cuts me!'

'I . . .' His admission was difficult to hear, knowing it was rooted in truth. 'I guess it's a defence mechanism.' This too was not easy to say, it took courage. 'There have been many times in my life when I had to sound tough, to be tough, just to get through.'

'And I get that, I know that.' His tone was a little kinder. 'But I'm your husband. We were a team.'

'Yes, we were, but not in recent years. There have been times when I've been so lonely, Gordy, so lonely.' She spoke earnestly, knowing this was the time and she had nothing to lose – they were talking divorce and that was about as bad as it got.

'Me too, if that's any consolation.'

'It's not.' She shook her head. 'It just makes it sadder. You've dragged me around for all these years from place to place, and that was fine when you and I were having fun, making the most of it, but when you were at the office all hours of the day and night and

189

I was on my own . . . I wondered what the point of it all was. What was my role?'

'You were hardly dragged. You're my wife, we got posted.' He stiffened.

'You know what I mean. And this isn't about me stamping my foot for attention, it's about the fact that I find, *found*, it hard to find my place with the mummy gaggle and yet you stopped being there, I had no one. You know this.'

'I suppose I do.' He took his time. 'And I've been thinking about that, you feeling lonely. You're right, I've been more focused at work, putting more hours in. I wanted that promotion.'

'And you got it, Colonel.'

He nodded. 'I wanted it, but not at the expense of us. I guess I took my eye off the ball, took you, our situation, for granted. Not that I'm entirely to blame, if blame is the right word.'

'It takes two,' she agreed. 'Takes two to mess up what could have been so wonderful, what used to be so wonderful.' Her breath stuttered as she fought to control her emotions. 'Truth is, the lonelier I felt, the more you irritated me and the more I fantasised about a single life, and it made me happy in those moments to imagine adventure and freedom, but then when you said the word divorce, it was like . . . it was like . . .' She struggled to relay her horror. 'It was like I'd been fired into space. On my own. And it was cold. And I still can't . . .' – she swiped at the tears that fell – 'I still can't believe that you and I . . .'

His fingers twitched, as if unsure how to comfort her, this a new and torturous development. 'I don't think you were fantasising about a single life. I think it more likely you were imagining jumping before you were pushed, because you always expect me to let you down – you expect everyone to let you down, to abandon you and that's why you don't trust friends.'

190

'I . . .' His accurate summation took her breath away, his perception as startling as it was uncomfortable to hear.

He continued, denying her the opportunity to further respond, as thoughts of Fi, Mina and Sheila ran through her head, women who had touched her arm in welcome, who had gifted her yellow roses. 'It's odd for me, Nora, because if I think about a single life, I remember the dissatisfaction of it, the baseline worry that I might never meet someone and how when I met you, I felt' – he stared at the fire – 'I felt like I could relax, as if I didn't have to worry or feel lonely any more.'

'And I did too, I did.' She spoke with conviction as if she might be trying to convince one or both of them. 'But I did wonder why I sometimes felt so itchy footed, intolerant, which I know I can be, and I wonder if it's because I don't love you enough.'

'Wowsers.' He gave a sarcastic laugh. 'That's quite the statement.'

'I mean I did love you! I do!' She leaned forward on the sofa, matching his stance. Her admission had sprung without preamble, but it was the truth, she did love him. 'But knowing you're unhappy, that you want out, makes me want to run – not that it's what I want, because it isn't. But I've spent too much of my life being somewhere I wasn't wanted, and it hurts, Gordy, it hurts!' Knitting her fingers, she clamped them between her thighs to stop them trembling, as her mother's words filled her mind: *For fuck's sake, why don't you go and help Luna with supper . . .*

'I'm not your parents, Nora. I am not those people. Yet you always treated me as if I was going to run out at any second. I didn't deserve it.'

'Oh, the irony!' She let a small laugh escape her mouth. 'Did you forget you want a divorce?'

He ran his hands through his hair and jumped up to grab a log from the basket, hurling it on to the glowing embers to keep the fire going, as much, she suspected, as a distraction as out of necessity. 'Okay, Nora. If you want to talk openly, let's do it.' He pulled the small chair that had been placed by the wall and positioned it in front of her. 'Come on, let's do this. It's long overdue. So, you suspect you don't love me enough, what else?' His tone was direct, targeted and cold, and she understood, recognising it as one of her tactics when it came to self-preservation.

'I didn't say that. I said I wondered if I loved you enough.'

'And that's different how?' he fired.

'*Enough*,' she repeated, 'loving you enough, like . . . like nothing could ever feel wrong or irritating because I loved you so much that everything bad, everything negative would fall at the gate, loving you like a fortress, like a superpower!'

He actually laughed, a sharp snort of laughter, like the one she had heard before when it had tainted her love, her belief that he supported her no matter what.

'I fear, Nora, that what you want is the love they show in the movies, literature love, fiction love, fairy-tale love. But here's a newsflash, it doesn't exist. This is real life and real love!'

'I know that. I—'

'No, you don't know that!' He cut her short. 'You have never seen real love because your only example is your messed-up parents who, it seems, had infinite love for each other and yet very little spare for you. That's not how it is for most people. It's unhealthy, skewed.'

'I know that much,' she huffed, embarrassed to hear her crappy childhood spelled out in so many words.

'And you talk of wanting to escape. Don't think you haven't irritated the shit out of me at times, or that I haven't thought about buying a big fuck-off yacht, telling the army to stick their job and sailing off into the sunset with a locker full of cold beer and the promise of casual sex with a willing deck hand who lives in a bikini?

You think I don't have dreams, doubts, fantasies, moments when the responsibilities I have both at home and at work threaten to bloody drown me? Because I do! I fucking do!'

She looked towards the door, waiting to see if Ted had heard or was coming down the stairs. His words left her a little winded. Gordy took the hint and when he next spoke, he was quieter, more contained.

'Our love *was* good enough. Our love *was* strong enough. For me, at least. I loved you, I desired you, I wanted to be with you. But if it isn't enough for you, I honestly don't know what else I could have done. And that's why divorce should not be off the table and that's why I found the courage to use the word, rather than limp on with you resenting me, blaming me and watching bitterness set in.'

That word again that made her heart miss a beat. 'But that's just it, there's lots you could have done.'

'Like what? Tell me, *help* me!' he pleaded.

He looked like he might be close to tears and this she hated but knew, while they had the momentum they needed, to keep talking; this was her one opportunity, and what did they have to lose? They were already, it seemed, at the end of the rope. And oh, how she wished she'd had a chance to say things to her parents, to remind them as he was reminding her that the way they loved her was just not good enough. She would have no such regrets when it came to Gordy. 'You . . . you suffocate me sometimes, Gordy.'

'How do I suffocate you?' He stared at her.

'Checking on me, organising me. Like telling Jasmine Leech I'd go for a drink at her house when I'd already told you I wanted to go to bed. You make choices on my behalf; you steer me sometimes in directions I don't want to go. You take control.'

'Oh well, pardon me for caring!' he snorted. 'For trying to make your life easier, for thinking of what's best for you every single second of every single fucking day!'

She could tell he was riled from his swearing, which was rare, and impactful because of it.

'There's a world of difference between caring for someone and clipping their wings.' She swallowed.

'Jesus Christ, you think I clip your wings?' His expression was one of hurt. But this was the time to say it as it was.

'In some ways, yes. I follow you. I follow you everywhere. I'm never in one place long enough to plant a garden and watch it grow – that is one of the most important things to me, you know that.'

He jumped up, pacing now in front of the fire, his voice more forceful, louder. 'So this is about a *garden*?'

'I love flowers, I love gardening! I wanted that to be my business.'

'I know you did, and you are brilliant at it, but . . .' He licked his lips.

'But what, Gordy?' she barked.

'You've never chased it, never made it a priority, never stated this is what I want to do and got on with it, as if . . .'

'As if what?' She was curious.

'As if it felt safer not to try, not to put yourself out there because if you don't try, you can't fail, as if you are still so scared of failure or rejection, as if still trying to win your parents' approval . . .'

His words landed like a punch to her throat. It was true. He was right. Her voice, when she found it, came out quietly and she felt unable to look him in the eye.

'It takes confidence to put yourself out there, Gordy, confidence I don't have. And I know that it's down to me, but every time I pick up a pot or plant a seed or draw a garden, you smile as if it's a sweet hobby or a distraction. Can you imagine what that feels like? It diminishes my efforts and it stifles my creativity because I think everything I'm about to do is going to be crap.'

'But that's you, that's not me!' he fired.

194

'I remember what you said to the Brigadier's wife that time.'

'Oh God, not that again!' He rubbed his brow. 'I've told you, not only was I nervous and possibly a little sloshed, but back then I carried the outdated view that being an officer's wife was a full-time job. And actually, it still feels a bit like that – there's always some commitment required from you, something to attend or support, and that's before we get to the constant moving. But honestly, Nora, I never wanted you to feel like that, never. I say go for it, do it! Get out there! Build a garden! Start the business! Do your thing! Just don't expect too much from it, and then you won't be disappointed.'

'Jesus, talk about proving my point! You always quote "It always seems impossible till it's done!" so why don't you say that about my gardening? About me having a career as a gardener and garden designer?'

He seemed to ponder this. 'Why don't I?' he asked aloud, but she got the impression he addressed himself. 'Because as usual I'm trying to second-guess all the reasons why you might not see it through and I'm trying to mitigate them for you, not overplay anything to avoid you feeling like a failure; the one thing you try your best to avoid!' He rubbed his brow. 'I feel like I can't win.'

Again, his words cut her to the quick and she felt her tears pool.

'I have loved you, Nora, maybe too much, but certainly enough. I wanted to keep all disappointment from your door because I think you've had enough of it in your life. I wanted all bad things to fall at the gate, like I was your fortress, your super-power, because I do, I love you too much.' He nodded at this truth.

'Gordy, I . . .' She didn't know how to respond, his words were as moving as they were maddening. And knowing that they were just about done as a couple made it even harder to hear.

He wasn't done. 'And I want to add, Nora, that you say you follow me here, there and everywhere, suggesting you do so blindly, but there have been many aspects of our life where you have taken a decision and I've followed . . . accepted it blindly.'

'Children,' she mouthed. 'You're talking about me not wanting children.' The words were no more than a hoarse whisper, so hard were they to say.

'I am.' He walked over from the chair and dropped down on to the carpet, his arms across her knees, as if he knew that to broach this topic would need physical support, and it took all of her resolve not to fall into him. 'We discussed it a little, but I remember you resolutely telling me when we first met that it was non-negotiable, that it was your body and your decision and that if I wanted you then that was a sacrifice I had to make, and honestly' – he took a breath – 'it's been a bloody big one.' His bottom lip trembled as if it contained more than he was able to voice, and it cut her to the core.

How could I have a child, Gordy? How could I bring a baby into a world where people die, and people leave you and you feel as if you are sitting on the edge of a volcano, and you can't decide whether to run down the outside and escape it or sit tight and wait to get drenched in boiling lava . . . How could I bring a child into a world like that? How could I love a child when no one loved me? I don't know how! I had no one to learn from! No one showed me the ropes, took me to split kindling – my parents were disinterested, bored by me, so what kind of mother would I have made? And then Nana Dilly, her words, her face . . . shouting at me that I was just like my mother, and she was right, because I was responsible for Kiki, and she could have so easily been killed!

'There's not a lot I can say about that, is there? That ship has sailed and here we are.' It was that old direct, targeted and cold thing. Self-preservation. But right now, she hated the clipped sound of her words, hated the shape of them in her mouth, the bitter taste of them on her tongue, and hated even more that they were directed at Gordy, the man who loved her too much.

He stood and reached for her hand, pulling her upright and into him, nuzzling her face gently and cradling her against him in a long, warm hold. It was conciliatory, it was healing. She inhaled the scent of him, doing her best to keep her tears at bay. She kept very still, wanting to stay like this, feeling the physical and emotional support of the man she had relied on. It was bittersweet. A reminder of the difference he could make, his ability to help her cope, and yet a prompt of what was about to be taken away.

'I love you, Gordy.' Turning her face into his chest she closed her eyes against his thick, checked cotton shirt and gripped the fabric at the back. 'I do, I love you.' It took all of her strength to say the words, to allow her thoughts, unfiltered and uninhibited, to flow from her mouth, something that was alien to her. No matter what came next, it felt important to say it and it took all of her bravery.

'I know.' He rocked her gently and the motion reminded her that when she let him, Gordy could take her to a happy place, where she felt loved and not as if the ground was going to fall away at any moment. The thought that this was how Ted lived too was the worst feeling. 'I just can't help but wonder what our life would have been like if you'd let us explore parenthood. I think we'd be different. I see how wonderful you are with Ted and it . . .' He paused. 'It's like a glimpse into what we might have had, what I would have loved.'

She nodded against him, feeling the wretched realisation that she had denied him so much.

'Loving you is not and never has been easy, Leonora. You're like a prickly pear.'

She sprayed her nerves with a titter. 'Charming!' It broke the rhythm of their sadness, helped them reset and they both breathed deeply, clearly glad of the change of direction.

'Yes, you are. You're a prickly pear.'

'How so?' She placed her hand tentatively on his neck and he kissed her scalp. The touch of his lips on her head sent firecrackers of joy to explode in the base of her gut. She liked the warmth of it. His kiss breaking through her reserve, softening her. To be held was one thing, but to be kissed quite another. How she had missed the feel of his skin, the human contact. It was a shock to feel this level of attraction to the man who was leaving her behind. It felt sorrowful, futile and yet almost a rite of passage, a wonderful goodbye that in the moment made her forget the ache of loneliness . . .

'Have you ever tried handling one? They're prickly.'

'Yes, I rather gathered as much by the name.'

He ignored her comment. 'And yet they are sweet and uncommon and so you do it, you handle them, and you tolerate the prickles because the reward is great. They are cacti, growing and flowering in the harshest of environments and are all the more incredible because of the beauty they provide in that place where other fruits would only wither. And those that stumble across them or harvest them are grateful for their presence, their colour and the sweet treat of their fruit. You beat the odds, Nora, you are incredible in spite of your less than perfect upbringing, in spite of all the things that would break lesser mortals, that deep level of rejection – you're wonderful. Yes, you are a prickly pear. But you have always been *my* prickly pear.'

He reached for her fingers and kissed the palm of her hand. She felt a warm twist of longing in her gut coupled with the bloom of strength in her core; he was right, she had beaten the odds, she had not let herself get broken . . . With one of his hands rubbing her back she slipped further against him and kissed the man who loved her and the man she loved in return.

'I don't,' she breathed, 'I don't want to lose you, Gordy. I don't want to lose us.' She gulped back the tears as without preamble or further discussion and with an urgency on both their parts, they tore at buttons and pulled at zips until skin to skin they sank down in front of the fireplace, quite lost to the moment and the deep, powerful, all-consuming, reunifying nature of the act, which was somehow more intense because of the infrequency of it.

And in the dying embers of the fire, with their bodies entwined and their breathing in sync, it certainly felt like enough even for a prickly pear . . .

CASA PINO

'Mateo! Mateo!' His papá's call was loud and urgent. Mateo practically dropped his coffee cup into the sink, caring little if it shattered or if the dark brew splashed the pale wooden cabinetry or doused the floor. This was what he was on hand for, shouts such as this, each and every emergency! His heart raced as he fled the room on high alert, skidding around the corner of the corridor and into the study, breathless with concern and anticipation.

He was, however, stunned to see his papá sitting in the chair by his desk, with his head lolling back, laughing.

'What's . . . what's wrong?' he asked, the words having hammered his tongue from the moment he heard the shout. He did his best to control his breathing.

'Nothing's wrong!' Santiago beamed, as if not entirely unaware of the effect his holler might have had. 'In fact, it's something good, very good, very good indeed!' He brandished a small square of card in his hand, waving it back and forth. 'Look! Look what I have found!'

Mateo swallowed and exhaled deeply as his pulse calmed. He took the card from his papá's hand and read aloud. 'Magda Farraday, 22 Clove Court, Maida Vale, London. Who's Magda Farraday?'

'Who is Magda Farraday?' Santiago boomed, slapping the arm of the chair as laughter fled from him. 'She is the next part of the jigsaw, *hijo*! The next part of the jigsaw! Dilly Brown was a dead end but Magda! I knew I had this somewhere. She was Nessa's mother and quite a woman, let me tell you. Formidable! Everyone was scared of her, including Guy. Everyone! She never thought he was good enough for her daughter, and she was probably right, but what she failed to understand is that it was only because he was so very happy, content with his lot in life, that he was able to create such breathtaking art!'

'Fire.' Mateo remembered his father's words. They had stuck with him, ignited something within him, the wonderful concept that when you were paired with the right person you could create something extraordinary, an extraordinary life!

'Yes. Fire.' Santiago looked thoughtful. 'Not that Magda saw it like that; she would have preferred Nessa to be with someone more conventional, but I am sure she would have died from boredom.'

'Instead of dying in a car accident with Guy drunk at the wheel?'

Santiago stopped laughing. 'You dismiss him so easily. His addictions were his flaw, but show me a human who isn't flawed, and I'll tell you it's an angel. There is none so pure who walks the earth. And Guy was only human, and Nessa was only human, and they were of the same spirit.'

Mateo felt duly reprimanded. This was his papá's way, when words or comments felt disparaging or dismissive of a subject he felt strongly about – it invoked something close to wrath. He decided to change the subject.

'But Magda will also be long deceased, Papá, *si*?' He hated being the stoical pragmatist, but someone needed to be. Santiago's flights of fancy were legendary.

I want a sculpture in the garden, bigger than any other in the country!

I need a new lemon grove, not a tennis court, dig it up and get one planted, make it happen!

I'm going to New York! Right now, today, this very minute! If your Mamá wants baked New York cheesecake, she shall jolly well have it!

'Of course, *hijo*.' Santiago smiled, and just like that his spirit and tone were restored. 'But at least it's an avenue to explore! It's something! I will write to the address immediately. Where's the paper? I need to write to Magda's old address! Clove Court, Maida Vale.' He banged the desk.

Mateo reached into the drawer for the paper and his papá's favoured pen and left him to it.

CHAPTER SEVEN

Nora watched Ted wander into the playground and stood with a smile on her face. She carried a feeling in her gut of peace, despite all that was going on with Kiki and the uncertainty and worry. Gordy had made no promise, offered no commitment, and their marriage still very much teetered on the brink, yet she felt a contentment line her stomach that she knew was the result of wonderful, wonderful sex with her husband. It had been healing, unifying and spoke of hope. Snippets of their evening kept flitting into her mind: the gentle bite of his mouth on her shoulder, the feel of his strong arms holding her . . . This overriding the words exchanged that spoke of love and connection but had not entirely diminished the threat of divorce.

'Well, look at you with a spring in your step and a wide grin on a damp Monday morning. Good weekend, Nora?' Mina winked at her.

'It was, thank you.' She felt her cheeks redden and was at a loss as to how to respond, unused to this kind of ribbing. 'It was . . .' What was it? *Complicated? Confusing?* 'It was nice.'

'Nice? Nice is when you nab a good parking space in the Tesco car park, nice is when you see someone who has driven past you like an arsehole broken down in a layby farther up the road. You don't look like your weekend was nice. You look flushed, zingy, hot.'

'Thank you.' She coughed, embarrassed and simultaneously chuffed. Did she look different? Mina certainly seemed to think so.

'Morning, ladies!' Fi ushered Rafe and his big sister into the playground, waving at him as he looked back a little cautiously. 'He doesn't want to go in today.'

The little boy walked slowly with his Fortnite backpack sitting low on his back. He cut a sorry figure. It was in stark contrast to the way the boys usually raced to get inside once their feet hit the tarmac.

'Why not?' Mina asked.

'No reason I can fathom, just one of those days when he'd rather stay in bed.' Fi shrugged, clearly not perturbed or overthinking it. It was a lesson to her that little ones, like adults, sometimes had off days and not to over-worry when and if it happened to Ted.

'God, I know how he feels.' Mina sighed.

'You know how *God* feels?' Fi pulled her head back and looked at her friend quizzically.

'Oh, don't start that again. I've told you, I can't help it, Fi! Every time I talk to you, I say God! Jesus! Bloody hell! Like, the moment I see you!'

'I know you do.' Fi twisted her mouth in a smile.

Mina used her hands as if signing while she spoke. 'It's like I have this fear of saying something about God or Jesus or church or nuns and I tell myself not to say it, not to mention those things, but then the second I see you they pop out of my mouth! I've always been like that.'

Fi laughed. 'It's nerves, Mina, but maybe we should talk about why my job makes you nervous. Is there some aspect of God, Jesus, hell, church or nuns you would like to explore?'

'Oh God, no, fuck off! See, you're vicaring me! This is what I'm talking about!' Mina shivered.

'Mina, you're my friend, I'm loving you, not vicaring you.' Fi winked at Nora. It was a wink, no more, but to Nora it was inclusive, it was sharing a joke, it made her part of the gang. She thought of Jasmine and her 'girls' gathered on the terrace that night, talking about their kids, school and life in general; had she tried to join in? No, she had sat quietly with her mind on other things and her eye on the clock, wanting to slope off at the first opportunity. So would she do things differently now?

Mina stared at them both. 'See, I'm not sure if you're vicaring me now . . .'

'Morning all!' Sheila appeared with her red curls bouncing around her pretty face. 'How was Ted this weekend?'

'Fine. He liked being out and about, helping Gordy chop wood and whatnot, but there were a couple of moments when he wanted his mum.' It felt easy to open up a little to these women who opened up to her, who doused her with love and humour when she most needed it. She didn't want to be the mistrustful woman Gordy had so accurately described.

'Any news on when Kristina might be up for visitors or when she could come home?' Sheila, as ever, kind and caring.

Nora shook her head. 'Not really. I'm in touch with the hospital, but things seem to be grinding slowly and I don't know enough about the process to understand what should be happening. The ball is in her court and I don't want to rush her or push her. It's a case of going with the flow and planning for all eventualities. I just want to see her.' She cursed the crack to her voice.

'Well, you know where we are for whatever you need.' Fi took a step towards her and wrapped her in a warm hug. Nora didn't fight it, didn't shrug her off or grimace. This the second hold in the last couple of days that had felt welcome. Her thoughts again flew to Gordy.

'I do, thank you.'

'Anyway, Miss Sheila, would you care to elaborate on the rather flirty exchange I heard you share with a certain Year Two teacher at Friday pick-up?' Mina sucked in her cheeks and gazed at Sheila who threw her head back and laughed.

'It was a joke! I think we all know Jason well enough to be able to muck around like that. Anyway, he's gay, isn't he?' Sheila posed the question.

'Is he?' Mina asked.

'We're lucky to have him.' Fi looked towards the school. 'I know Rafe is a bit wobbly today, but it feels good to know Jason will be there for him.'

'We are lucky,' Sheila agreed.

'Right.' Mina clapped. 'Off to get my lady garden tended to – a landing strip I'm thinking, not too adventurous, but just neat enough to say I have standards.'

'Do we need to know this?' Sheila rolled her eyes. 'You'll put me off my breakfast.'

'Jesus, calm down, it's only a fanny!' Mina tutted.

'Did you hear that, Jesus?' Fi looked skyward. 'You need to calm down, it's only a fanny.'

'I did it again, Fi, didn't I?'

'You did.'

'God, what's wrong with me?' Before Fi had a chance to comment, Mina slapped her hand over her mouth and walked backwards until she reached her car. Nora couldn't help but laugh; they were funny women, funny and kind.

'See you later, Nora. Have a fab day.' Sheila fastened her scarf around her neck.

'He's not.' Nora shook her head, glad the others were out of earshot.

'Who's not what?' Sheila looked a little perplexed.

'Not gay. Jason. He's not.'

'Oh.' Sheila seemed to consider this. 'I see.' There was no mistaking the huge smile that split her face.

As Nora walked back to the flat, treading the familiar route she ambled four times a day, her phone rang.

'Good morning.' She kept her voice low in pitch and volume, a semi-flirtatious voice she had used a lot when she and Gordy first met, a voice that had been shelved, replaced by a sometimes shrill voice of discontent or a whiney voice of complaint or a quiet, nasal voice that would rather not be talking at all . . .

'Good morning.' He sounded bright. 'I don't know about you, but I can't stop thinking about the weekend,' he whispered, as if aware of the proximity of others.

'Yes, the bacon and eggs were to die for.'

'Yes, that.' He laughed. 'That was good too. Don't know where it came from, Nora, but I reckon we need to fight more often . . .'

'It wasn't the fighting, Gordy.' She took her time. 'It was being honest, being heard, paying attention, that's what led to Friday night.' *And Saturday night* . . . She felt a little coy, aware of how she had relinquished control and the joy it had brought them both.

'I was thinking that maybe you and Ted should come back again on Friday, don't you? We have more talking to do.' The slight edge to his voice told her that this was in part metaphorical, and her heart sang at the thought of it. It wasn't a reprieve, anything but, but it was a surge of hope that things were not entirely lost between them.

'I suppose we could come back on Friday,' she said softly.

'You seem . . .' He paused.

'I seem what?' She stopped on the pavement, looking into the entrance of the park towards the bench where she and Ted had sat on that first day.

'You seem to have shed some of your prickles.'

'Gosh, are you saying I'm turning full pear?'

'Gotta go, meeting starting in five, have a good day, Nora.'

'I will.' This she knew to be true, based on no more than the thought of returning to Westbury this weekend and more of that talking.

Folding her phone into her pocket she considered her husband's words. Was she less prickly? The bench came into focus and she remembered the awkwardness she had felt at having to address the little boy, the nerves surrounding her conversation and how ill at ease she had felt in his company. In a short time, she now ran his bath, cooked his supper, collected his coat from the floor where he shrugged it off, sat close to him on the sofa, brushed his hair . . . Yes, she had lost some of her prickles, or rather Ted had knocked them off.

With her phone in her hand, she again saw the message icon and knew that Jasmine had tried to make contact. It felt like as good a time as any to make that call. She closed her eyes and slowed her pace as Jasmine answered the phone.

'Nora!' Her enthusiasm was still apparent.

'Morning, Jasmine, hope this isn't a bad time?' She half hoped it might be so she could postpone the call, as her confidence to chat to the woman dwindled.

'No, no, it's a good time. I'm just back from the supermarket and it's already too hot outside, you know what it's like.'

'I do.' Nora scanned the autumnal golds, russets and yellows that flecked the trees and hedges and already found it hard to imagine the warmth of the sun on her skin that she had so recently given up. 'Sorry I haven't got back to you sooner, things have been a bit . . .'

'No need to apologise, I more than understand,' she boomed. 'I was, we all were, very sorry to hear about your sister.'

The woman's tone was a little quieter now than Nora was used to, and she was glad of it.

'Thank you, yes it's been . . .' Again words were hard to find.

'Hang on a mo, Nora!'

She rolled her eyes. Bloody typical, the woman was multitasking, probably whipping up a quiche with her left hand and organising a Halloween ball while she chit-chatted . . . it bothered Nora, diminished any kind sentiment when the words were sandwiched between other activities, Jasmine's attention diverted.

'That's better, sorry. Just wanted to make sure the kitchen door was closed and no one was lurking in the hallway.'

'Right.' Her thoughts felt mean when it became apparent that Jasmine had just been ensuring privacy.

'I know that you and I . . .' Jasmine began, and Nora screwed her face up; it sounded horribly like she was going to rake over their relationship – if you could call it a relationship. 'Well, we weren't close, were we?'

'Don't take it personally, Jasmine, I'm not close to many people.' She pictured Mina, Sheila and Fi and their banter that very morning.

'I got that.' She laughed and Nora smiled. It was natural speech, relaxed and honest. 'I know I can be a lot.'

'You have always been kind to me.' This was the truth, and a good diversion, she figured, from Jasmine's admission, which had made her cringe.

'I . . . I only have two settings, you see: very happy, positive and on it! Or low, very low. I find it hard to reach the middle ground and sometimes, it's, erm, sometimes it's an effort to lift my head up off the pillow.'

'Jasmine . . .' She didn't know what to say, but again felt the familiar creep of guilt that she hadn't bothered to get to know Jasmine, hadn't dug deeper. And why? Too preoccupied with her own thoughts and reflections; it was at best naive and at worst selfish. She wondered how many others lived a life like Kiki's, a life where kindness would make all the difference.

'No, it's okay, I'm not saying it to get a reaction.' Nora heard her swallow. 'But I did want to say that I know what it's like to carry depression, poor mental health. I know what it feels like to have it bookend every thought, every action and what it's like to have to make a super-effort every day just to get up and get out and make life happen. It's exhausting.'

'I had no idea, I . . .'

'No, I'm good at masking it. Medication helps, and Benedict is just wonderful.' Nora could tell she was smiling and pictured the couple, always active, always laughing . . . What was the phrase? You never can tell anyone's story just by looking. *Ain't that the truth.* 'And the girls here, in fact wherever we're posted, I seek out friends, and it makes all the difference, you know? When you have those women who love you and who will hold you up and lift you high until the storm has passed. That's what my friends do.'

'Yes.' Nora felt a flash of envy that this had not been her experience, tinged with shame that she had not put herself forward, not helped to lift Jasmine high.

'I tried to take my own life when we were first married.'

The news stopped her in her tracks. *Just like Kiki . . .*

'Oh Jasmine, I am so sad to hear that, I had no idea.' She felt shame slide over all the preconceived assumptions she had had about the woman who dressed in a rainbow of tunics, the life and soul . . .

'I don't tell many people. And it came out of nowhere, like a tsunami. I woke one day and was overwhelmed. The point is, I got a lot better, it passed, and it can and probably will for your sister and that's what I wanted to say really; that it can and usually does get better. So tell her to hang in there and you too, be strong, be there and know that things will not always feel so bleak, so hopeless.'

'I feel . . .' *How did she feel?* 'I feel honoured that you have shared this with me, and I feel happy that you're well. It gives me hope that I've seen you living such a full life, makes me think that it might be like this for Kiki, that she can come back from this.'

'She can. And yes, for now I'm well, and probably will be tomorrow, but with mental illness, it's like walking a tightrope and you never really know when you might lose your balance.'

'That sounds scary.' She meant it and considered the ropes of support she would have to put in place to keep her sister anchored.

'It is. Scary for me, for Benedict, for the kids, my parents, my sister. It is scary and that's why I wanted to talk to you, to tell you that I understand what you're going through, what you're *all* going through, and my thoughts are with you and, what's your sister's name?'

'Kiki,' she whispered from vocal cords pulled taut with emotion.

'Kiki. Scariest of all for Kiki.'

'I'd no idea what she was going through, what you were going through . . . it makes me feel terrible.' She hated the thinness of her words.

'Don't feel terrible, there's no point. Just look forward. And remember, Nora, you have my number, you know where I am and I am on the end of this phone day or night if you want to chat, if you want advice or if you just want to let off steam.'

'Thank you, Jasmine.' She meant it. 'We should keep in touch.'

'I'd like that.'

Nora felt the slip of tears down the back of her throat. 'Me too.' It felt odd to consider that this woman had been offering her the hand of love and friendship, which she had not so much wiggled free from but had dodged altogether.

'Oh, I can see Jennifer and Sophie coming up the path, hello there, you two!' Jasmine boomed with such energy it spoke of pure joy. 'Gotta go, Nora! Speak soon!' she gushed and just like that she was gone.

'Yes' – Nora popped her phone in her pocket – 'it must be exhausting.'

Speeding up her pace, she neared the flat, keen to call the hospital again, determined this time to push to see Kiki, and wanting to get a message directly to her, a direct request asking to visit. She was taking action.

Slowing a little, she noticed the sporty car parked half on the pavement and half on the road. It was a low, boxy, fancy Audi with shiny black paint and red leather seats. Its ostentatiousness quite incongruent to the red-brick cottages and family run-arounds that dotted the street.

'R8,' she read on the back of the car as she went through the gate, which was already open. Her thoughts jumped; she was sure she had shut it as she always did, confident, in fact. There was a tendency to double-check each door, each lock, each window as the place was under her watch. She looked up to the front door and saw it was ajar. Her heart leaped into her mouth as her fingers trembled with fear. Had someone broken in? What was going on? It was as she reached for her phone from her pocket that the front door swung fully open and there stood Richie Morris, the flash Harry.

'Hello, Nora!' he enthused as if they had bumped into each other at a cocktail party.

'How did you get in?' She felt the thump of anger and irritation in her veins. All prickles fully restored.

'I have a magic little stick made of metal; we call it "a key".' He over-enunciated and grinned to show blueish-white teeth that were straight and much bigger than the ones that had inhabited his mouth the last time they had met. His jeans were neat, his pink shirt immaculately pressed, his beard close-trimmed and his skin buffed, polished and preened. She wondered if he, like Mina, had a landing strip, just to show he had standards.

Dickhead . . .

'How did *you* get a key?' She couldn't disguise her disapproval at the fact.

'The mother of my son gave it to me. Anyway, why wouldn't I? It's my flat!' He dropped the enthusiasm and now sounded like he meant business. 'More to the point, how did *you* get a key? I mean, you've hardly set foot here for years.' He knew how to hit the spot. *Touché.*

'My sister gave it to me, mother of my nephew.'

This wasn't, of course, strictly true, but the lie felt entirely necessary.

The two stared at each other and her breathing and pulse slowed a little. This was not how she wanted to behave. There was so much going on, bigger and more important things – like Kiki's mental decline and Ted's well-being – to make it about her dislike for the man who had cut and run on her little sister. Besides there was truth in his words that left her feeling cloaked in shame.

'Would . . . would you like a cup of tea, Richie?'

'I would, yes please.' He came out of the house and waited for her to pass. It was a conciliatory gesture and one she noted with a softening of her expression.

She filled the kettle, watching as he scanned the walls and windows. 'The place looks tidy, clean and nice. I'm glad, better for Ted. Last time I dropped in it was a shithole.'

She bit her lip, wanting to comment on how if this was indeed the case why he hadn't pitched in and done something about it, or how he felt qualified to comment when her sister, alone, was clearly struggling, but again his words came into focus – she hadn't set foot in here in years.

'I think Kiki has been under a lot of pressure, clearly more than any of us understood or realised.'

'How's she doing?' She noted the tension in his jaw.

'I think it's going to be a long, slow process. I spoke to her and she was a little foggy, upset, as you might expect.'

'Truth is, Nora, I don't know what to expect. I never expected her to try and top herself in the home she shares with Ted!' He wiped his chin and mouth with his cupped palm.

'You sound angry.' It bothered her, because what Kiki needed was kindness, the same kindness Gordy had showed her.

'I am bloody angry! How could she? It's the most selfish, selfish thing I can think of. Imagine if she'd been successful, the nightmare we'd be living, and even though she wasn't successful look what shit we're having to deal with now!'

His lack of empathy threatened to derail her plan to remain pleasant as angry defence of her sibling flared in her veins.

'Well, in fairness we've been dealing with the shit quite well, Ted and I.' She splashed milk into the tea and handed him a mug. Without the offer or inclination to sit, they rested against the sink and work surface respectively, facing each other. She felt at once responsible for Kiki and wanted to be her voice, but was also aware that she was an imposter of sorts, newly turned up and a relative stranger.

'It was hard for me to get away.' He took the hint and a sip of his tea. 'My wife's not too keen on me coming down to spend time with my ex, as you can imagine.' He raised his eyebrows, like the topic was in some way comedic, fodder for his mates at the bar, regaled in laddish tones with a pint in his manicured hand.

'And is your wife equally unkeen on you spending time with your little boy?'

'More so.' He held her eyeline, unflinching and unapologetic. 'Nearly as unkeen as Kristina, who told me, in so many words, to disappear and never come back after my last visit. And so those are the forces I battle with: the wife who explodes if I so much as mention Stroudly Green, and the ex-wife who told me if I so much as knocked on the door she'd go grab the bread knife.'

'You poor thing.' Her sarcasm slipped out.

He ignored her. 'And add to that the fact that Kristina is clearly nuts and I worried that if I pitched up, there's no telling what she might do – it might have sent her over the edge again.'

Nora placed her mug on the countertop and folded her arms across her chest to stop them from shaking. 'She's not nuts. She's ill. Big difference.'

'She cut her bloody wrists in the bath! You are telling me that's an act of sanity?'

She ignored the comment. 'Whatever the situation between you and Kiki, there is Ted. A lovely, kind, sweet little boy who might just have needed all the support he could get.' She cursed the crack to her voice at the mention of her nephew.

'But as you say, Aunty Nora, you've had it all under control.' His sarcasm wasn't lost on her.

'I don't want to argue with you, Richie. And I don't have to like you and you don't have to like me, so let's just cut to the chase: why are you here right now, what is it you want or hope to achieve?'

'I don't know.'

She wondered if this was where Ted had got his stock phrase from.

'I know what you think of me, Nora.'

Doubt it . . .

'But stuff has gone on you're unaware of.' He paused and looked towards the window. 'Stuff you don't know about me and Kristina.'

'What stuff?' She spoke softly to encourage him to speak freely.

215

He put his cup down and shoved his hands into the tight front pockets of his jeans. 'She was really hard to live with. She blew hot and cold and when she was good, she was very, very good but when she was bad' – he blew out from his cheeks – 'let's just say it was tough, hard, too hard. Her mood swings, her sadness, her taking to her bed and showing no interest in Ted at all.' He shook his head. 'And as for me, I didn't even figure. She only had room for her depression and Ted. I was just an afterthought.'

The image he painted was desperate and a whole world away from the image of her sunny sister that she had carried until recently. Jasmine's words and her explanation of the mask she wore and the effort it took just to remain upright came to mind.

'So you knew she was ill?'

'Yeah, she used to say she'd kill herself one day, that she'd never make old bones, that she dreamed about the rest she'd have when she didn't have to think any more, and she used to tell Ted that if ever she couldn't be with him, she'd come back as an eagle to watch over him.' He winced and she felt the smallest flicker of pity, knowing how hard it had been to hear her nephew talking about just this only a couple of days ago. Richie shifted from foot to foot. 'Have you ever heard anything so fucked up? It used to scare the shit out of me. I knew she wasn't joking. I got in the habit of calling out when I came home at night, worrying what I might find. I knew she'd do it eventually and so when I got the message from the doctor I wasn't at all surprised. I still think she'll do it one day. I'm sorry, Nora, but I do. I feel like it's inevitable.'

She held her gentle tone, which belied the fact that her insides churned at his succinct admission, as she silently prayed he was wrong.

'First, I don't think anything is inevitable. It's like a balancing act, walking a tightrope and so *if* and *when* she falls, we need to make sure we are around to catch her.' She borrowed this from

Jasmine. 'Second, I will do all in my power to stop that being how my sister's story ends, and finally, you may be right, there's probably "stuff" I don't know about you, but I do know this: you're a disgrace of a man, of a human. You abandoned her and you abandoned Ted and you made no provision to ensure she or your son were safe, and you did so knowing that she was unwell. And as for your current wife being so horribly possessive, I understand why: how can she trust you when she knows how easily you gave up on wife number one and your little boy? She probably thinks it's only a matter of time until you are on the hunt again.'

'Anything else?' He tilted his chin upwards and looked at her down his aquiline nose.

'Yes, I understand why Kiki didn't want you near Ted. You're not reliable, not steadfast or loyal – all the things that help make a little boy feel secure.'

'Go back to sleep!' came the fuzzy, wine-infused voice of her mother. 'Daddy and I are busy, this is grown-up time, go back to sleep . . .'

Richie nodded, his bottom lip out over his top and a slight smile around his eyes. 'Well, now you've had your say, I guess I get to have one last word?'

'Fire away.' She pushed her feet down on to the laminate flooring, knowing she might have sounded strong, but her head swam with the exertion of it all.

'You can give your crazy, fucked-up sister a message from me: tell her I'm selling the flat.'

'Isn't it her flat, or at least half her flat?' Her voice had gone up an octave or two.

'Nope.' He smiled. 'It's all mine. She's got six weeks to clear her shit out.'

Nora felt her mouth fall open. 'You can't do that! Not now! Not to Ted. How can you do that? She has rights!'

'She's a tenant who hasn't paid rent despite a legal agreement signed by her. As I say, tell her she's got six weeks.'

He walked past her and threw his car keys in the air, catching them as they dropped. He turned at the gate, as the lights on his car flashed, like a beast roaring on the savanna. 'I could take him, you know, if I wanted. I got a big house, plenty of cash, great schools in the area. And he wouldn't have to worry that he might come home and find me dead.'

Nora cursed the flash of emotion that crept up the back of her nose and made her throat sting – she didn't want to cry, not in front of him. Managing, just, to control her rage, her utter horror at the prospect, there was a single thought that turned her blood to ice: was this her fault? Had she provoked him into this? She kept a steady pose even though her voice warbled.

'But you don't want him, do you? And neither does number two.'

He sucked his teeth and bit his cheek before seemingly deciding not to respond and sliding on to the vulgar red leather seats of his motorcar, before roaring out of sight.

With a shaking hand and trying to control her desire to be sick, she texted Gordy, wanting to hear his reassurance, his thoughts. He called as soon as he stepped out of his meeting, and she relayed word for word what Richie Morris had done and said and how.

'What do you think?' she asked, stirring brown sugar into her coffee with her free hand, a treat for much needed energy. The whole encounter had left her feeling zapped.

'I need to do some digging; he has no right to turn up, let himself in with a key, landlord or not, he has to give notice, I believe. But as to whether she has any rights to remain in a property where she's in default on the rent, I just don't know. I mean, you and Kiki probably have more of an idea than me, you own the London flat that's tenanted.'

'But she's ill! Ted is his son!'

'Nora, I know. It's not me that's doing this, it's that nasty little shit Kiki hooked up with.'

'I know, and what you've said echoes my understanding. I'm just mad and worried on her behalf. And the London flat has thankfully always run like clockwork. It's been with the same agent for decades and new tenants are vetted and whatnot; this all feels a lot more personal.'

'I can see that. Don't worry, though. If the worst comes to the worst, there's plenty of room here in Westbury. Nora, look, I'm so sorry, but I have to go to my next meeting, call me later.'

'I will.'

The coffee was hot and restorative and she closed her eyes, trying to control her breathing, still flustered by Richie's manner. Gordy was right, he was a little shit. He had, however, offered insight: the fact that Kiki had spoken openly about suicide, had, in his words '*been on the edge . . .*' It did nothing to allay her deep-seated fear that her sister might try again. And again, the twin lances of guilt and worry pierced her spirit. On the upside, Gordy had offered Kiki and Ted a place to stay and that implied that he might just be thinking of them in terms of family, not just now, but in the future too.

Picking up her phone, determined not to be fobbed off and to be a little more forceful in her desire to see her sister, she put a call in to St Margaret's and after waiting with the sound of tinny lift music in her ear, interrupted only by a robotic-sounding voice telling her how much they valued her call and would get to her as soon as possible, a woman answered. Nora identified herself and asked if there was any chance she might be able to visit her sister.

'Kristina Morris . . .' The woman sounded as if she were running her finger down a list or looking her up on a computer screen. Nora felt the seconds tick by.

'Yes, yes you can visit.'

'I can?' She thought she might have misheard. 'Really?'

'Yes, this afternoon between three and five. Ms Morris had specifically asked for no visitors, but that's changed as of today.'

'Thank you. Thank you! Oh, that's wonderful!' The relief was sweet and fierce.

It was only when she ended the call and her heart raced at the prospect of seeing Kiki that she realised Ted's pick-up time was three fifteen. Taking them up on their offer, she decided to ask for help from one of the trio who had befriended her – the school-gate mums.

'Fi, it's Nora.'

'Hey, how's it going?'

'Okay, good.' She would not tell a soul about Richie and his nasty intentions. 'I was just wondering, I have the chance to go and visit Kiki, but it's when I should be collecting Ted.'

'I'll stop you right there, I can of course fetch him when I get Rafe and bring them back here.'

'Thank you, Fi. I considered waiting and taking Ted with me, but I thought it best I see how Kiki is and what she wants before pitching up with him, thought it might be a bit too much for them both.'

'I think that's wise and there's no rush at all. There's an after-school club that Rafe, Zac and Afsar go to, they do craft and build stuff out of old loo roll tubes, they love it! Ted used to go, but, erm . . .'

'Why did he stop going?' Fi's hesitant tone had made her curious.

'I think Kristina found it hard to meet the extra expense. I offered to pay for Ted, Mina did too, but she was adamant.'

Shit. She pictured Richie's very expensive car and very expensive teeth and disliked him even more.

'Can I re-enrol him? I'm more than happy to pay for him to go.' She hated the thought of him not being with his little gang of mates doing something he loved and knew that if she and Kiki had been closer, this was the type of situation that with simple communication could have been headed off at the pass.

'Leave it with me. I'll call Jason and text you and then I'll bring him back to mine and feed him and you can collect him whenever, no rush!'

'Thank you, Fi.'

'No thanks needed, that's what friends are for, right?'

She held the phone against her cheek. *Friends.* She pictured the booming Jasmine and wished things had been different, never guessing for a second that the woman she had done her best to avoid, who seemingly took everything in her stride, might have struggled to get out of bed on any given day and might just have benefited from having a friend like her . . . Nora looked around the kitchen and recalled the state of the place on that first day: the bare fridge, the empty cupboards, the lack of shampoo and laundry soap. She had assumed it was because of her sister's mental state that things had so declined, but what if it was financial too? It can't have helped the situation.

'Oh Kiki . . .' Nora closed her eyes and felt a wave of anxiety about what she might find at St Margaret's. 'We are going to make a plan. We are going to make sure that you have what you need in place to thrive, we going to be a proper family. You need to be able to rely on me. And I need to be able to rely on you.'

SANTIAGO AGOSTÍ'S SECOND LETTER

The pain in Santiago's chest was intensifying and despite often wishing for death so he could once again look upon the face of his beautiful wife, he felt a flicker of regret; there was still one thing he wanted to achieve – well, two in fact. To return the art of Guy Brown to its rightful owner and to see Mateo as happy with a partner as he and Sofia had been. Girls had come and gone but none that Mateo wanted to be with for life. It bothered him, knowing what it felt like when loneliness was the demon in your ear.

Taking a moment, he steadied his arm on the desk, breathing slowly with his eyes closed until it passed. Had they been within reach, he would certainly have popped one of the little pills under his tongue that Dr Garcia had prescribed, but they were on his nightstand, and he was in his study and the trek up the stairs with his unwieldy catheter stand was more than he could contemplate. Mateo was in the pool, he had heard him dive in and pictured him now, pulling through the water with his muscled arms. A fine swimmer, a fine man, his boy. He was proud of him. Had he told him this enough? Possibly not, but there was still time. For proud of him he was, admiring the fact that Mateo seemed to be without his own tempestuous tendencies and was far more like his mother, with a contented, calm nature that was its own reward.

Santiago drew a sharp breath. It was as if a vice were tightening across his ribcage, and it frightened him. He felt the drip of sweat over his nose and sniffed and swiped at it with his fingers. He wasn't afraid of death, not a bit. But he would be lying if he said he wasn't afraid of dying: the act, the discomfort, the pain and the unpredictable nature and timing of the event. He was a man who thrived on order, who liked things to be contained, and death, it seemed, was so very disordered. With the pain easing, passing as quickly as it had arrived, and his breathing a little more regular, he took his trusty pen into his hand, and taking time to let his hand steady, he wrote.

> *To whomever is opening this letter,*
> *My name is Santiago Agostí, and I am writing*
> *to you today because I am an old man in need of*
> *your help . . .*

After much consideration, he folded the letter and placed it with the previous correspondence sent to Maggie Yates along with her reply and put the bundle in a large manila envelope, addressing it in his spidery hand to 'Magda Farraday, or to whomever it may concern', at the address in Clove Court, Maida Vale, London.

CHAPTER EIGHT

Nora rode the bus with a grumbling sense of foreboding in her stomach. She was worried about Ted, despite the text from Fi assuring her that he had a place in the 'make it, stick it club' and that she would whisk him back to hers for hot dogs and a jump on the trampoline – the combined effect of which she could only guess at. Of course, it wasn't only that she was worried about Ted.

Psychiatric patient, suicide risk, mental breakdown. The words alone were enough to fill her with fear. And yet it was Kiki she was going to see, her pretty little sister, how bad could it be?

Stepping off the bus she cursed the swirl of nausea, not wanting Kiki in any way to pick up on her fear or doubt her competency that things weren't absolutely under control. She had made the decision not to pass on Richie's message, not when her sister had other more pressing things to worry about. But Gordy was right, he was a nasty piece of work and it irked her that he was Ted's father, when there were so many other lovely men around who Kiki could have chosen.

The security in the hospital was lax, very different to what she was used to, living on an army base where visitors handed over their ID for scrutiny by stony-faced operatives who carried over-inflated ideas of their importance. This was nothing like that. The lady behind the desk gave her no more than a cursory nod and smile, before pointing a finger in the direction she had to travel. The nurse who greeted her as she entered the psych ward was smiley, broad and with tired eyes.

'How can I help you?' he asked casually, as if she might be visiting any ward, any patient, which of course for him was exactly the case. She hitched her handbag on to her shoulder and buttoned up the soft camel cardigan she wore over a white shirt, suddenly feeling a chill despite the heating in the hospital being cranked up to a little higher than was comfortable.

'I'm here to see my sister, Kristina Morris?' Her voice a little clipped as she was wont to do when putting up a shield of defence.

'Kristina yes, she's having a good day, much better. Yesterday was tough, she was very emotional. But today is better.'

'Good.' She breathed with relief. 'That's good.'

'And great that she feels ready for visitors.'

Nora nodded as nerves began to bite. She couldn't seem to make her face relax: her smile was forced, her eye twitched and her mouth was fixed unnaturally. This she recognised as the agitated face she had worn in the years following her parents' death and one she had quite forgotten about, but the feeling that she didn't know how to let her face be, couldn't relax her expression, yes, with this feeling, it all came flooding back.

'Let me show you where to find her.'

He stood and Nora walked behind him. She looked ahead, straight down the corridor towards double doors, lest she should inadvertently stare at a patient or their relatives in one of the ante-rooms that led off the main corridor. Fearful of what? Staring, catching the eye of someone and seeing the same anxiety as her own etched in the expression of those also visiting? All of the above. It felt easier to keep her head down and listen to the clip-clop of the wooden block heel of her boot on the floor, following the stocky nurse who walked with purpose.

225

They stopped abruptly outside an open door, and it was a relief to find the environment was not as she had dreaded, it was indeed just like any other ward with nothing specific for someone with issues like Kiki's; no clanking metallic door, no wailing, no wall link and chain, just a regular hospital room with bland, shiny magnolia-painted walls, a blue linoleum floor and very little by way of furniture. The bed was in a corner and the mattress looked a little thin with a pale blue coverlet pulled taut across it. Everything was clean, neat, mundane and Nora was glad of it.

And just like that, there she was! Her sister sat propped against the headboard with a pillow folded in the small of her back and her legs bent up to meet her chest. Nora thought she looked small, shrunken, diminished in the face of her illness, and all the more pathetic because of it. Her heart flexed at the sight of her and her throat tightened with all it tried to contain.

It was Kiki, of course she knew it was Kiki – the mane of glorious hair, the wide eyes of their father, the hesitant smile with a lift to one side of her mouth, the good teeth – but despite knowing these things, there was very little about the woman sitting quietly on the bed that reminded her of her sister. That vivacious, glossy, laughing girl who had twirled barefoot in the courtyard as Blondie played and they stabbed fat olives and drank wine, bringing the Mediterranean to the small courtyard of her flat in Stroudly Green – correction, Richie's flat in Stroudly Green – well she was nowhere to be seen. In her place sat this husk of Kiki with an expression that was vacant, a demeanour that was bent and a spirit that seemed broken. Dressed in white surgical stockings and a green hospital gown, which swamped her slender frame, she reminded Nora of a broken bird perched on the pillows who with every fibre of her coiled being seemed to be wishing she could take flight. Not so much eagle as sparrow, and one with a broken wing.

With her shoulders rounded and her arms clasped around her shins it was impossible not to notice the wide white bandages that bound her wrists. They had been tied with tiny, neat bows that looked almost artfully decorative, like fancy accessories, which somehow made them more grotesque. The sight of them was jarring and filled her with a sorrow that threatened to choke her.

You did that to yourself, darling . . . little Kiki . . . you cut your arms . . . I can't bear it . . .

'You have a visitor, Kristina.' The nurse spoke kindly, respectfully, to her sister and Nora warmed to him. 'I'll be in and around the corridor if you need anything. We don't want you tired out, do we?' He paused and smiled at his patient, before turning to Nora. 'Not too long.'

Kiki glanced at her and then away again, as if wary of taking anything other than glimpses. It was like she feared her sister might be judging her, or worse, not there at all. And Nora understood, remembering looking at her parents in the same way, knowing they were unreliable and that one day they might just disappear. Until one day, they just disappeared.

She put the brakes on the avalanche of words that tumbled into her throat, knowing that to overwhelm her sister would not be helpful, so she stayed quiet, hoping her presence and smile would be enough to get Kiki talking and that she could then follow her lead, go at her pace. After pulling a chair from the wall to the side of the bed, the nurse left them alone.

'I don't . . . I don't really want you to see me in here, like this.' Kiki's voice was steady, normal, and Nora was relieved. What had she expected? Ranting, wailing, the wild, uncontrolled eruptions and violent accusations she had seen in movies? This was nothing like it. The atmosphere was calm, a salient reminder that her sister was ill, sick, no more, no less. It just happened to be a malaise of her mind and not her body, although the wide bandaging on her wrists somewhat contradicted this.

'I'm just happy to see you anywhere.' It was the truth.

'When did you come back from Cyprus?'

'A little while ago.' It felt smart not to detail how she had been summoned.

'Is . . . is Gordy with you?' Her voice was flat, her words scratchy. Nora felt the threat of tears at this reminder that everyone, Kiki included, saw them as a matching pair, a couple.

'No. Just me at your flat, looking after Ted who misses you so much.' Nora didn't know if it was the right thing to mention him but was also aware that this visit was on a timer, and it therefore felt prudent to say everything of importance.

Kiki let her head rest on her forearms and her shoulders shook.

'Don't cry, Kiki, it's all going to be okay.' Anxiety flared at the fact that she had caused her sister's tears; the whole situation felt precarious, but it was down to her to remain collected, to try to set the tone. She cooed and scooted the chair forward so she could run her hand over Kiki's arm, and her leg. Little hairs spiked her shins where a razor would, in different circumstances and with different priorities, have swirled.

'I almost' – Kiki lifted her head – 'I almost can't talk about him. I miss him so much! It hurts me here.' She touched her fingers to her chest.

Despite her sister's obvious distress, Nora took comfort from it and her words *I miss him* meant she was feeling something, and the only way to stop missing something was to see it, touch it, engage with it and that meant action, planning and, crucially, it meant the future. And someone who was picturing a future, even if it was only a day, a week, a month ahead, was not thinking, at that precise moment, of leaving the earth.

228

Nora spoke steadily, mimicking the way she had heard Gordy speak in a crisis, but making it her own, reaching out to her sister and discovering that she could, with her words, make a difference. It turned out she knew exactly what to say.

'I should also say that even though he misses you, he's doing great, seeing his friends, helping me out with directions and shopping lists. You've done a great job with him, Kiki, he's a credit to you.'

'What . . . what did you tell him?'

'That you were feeling a bit down in the dumps and that you were in hospital for a rest and a good old sleep.'

Her sister's eyes crinkled as if more tears might be forthcoming, but they weren't, it was instead an expression of despair on a face where tears were in short supply. 'How do I face him, Nora? How do I do that?'

'He has no idea what's happened, and there's no reason for that to change, not while he's so little. And all he wants is to see you, be with you, nothing else will matter. I know and you know that certain illnesses can allow for the most out-of-character decisions. You can't blame yourself.'

'I'm not crazy,' Kiki snapped.

'I know that too and no one has suggested it. It's severe depression, Kiki, isn't that it?'

Her sister nodded. Confirmation of this did nothing to remove the dagger of guilt from Nora's breast. She was starting to see how being closed off, contained and aloof damaged people. It damaged Gordy and it hurt Kiki. She had let her sister down and was unsure if her own marriage was going to survive.

'And you say I can't blame myself, but who else am I going to blame? I might not have meant to do it, not really, but I did it, nonetheless. I'm ill. I know that. I was on medication for a couple of years, but it made me foggy and tired, so I stopped taking it and then everything just seemed to . . .' She outstretched her fingers and made a downward motion like a plane plummeting. Nora pictured the collection of mouldy coffee cups on the bedside table, the greasy bedsheets in need of a hot wash and the thin layer of dust and hair that had stuck to the laminate flooring.

'You should have told me.'

'Should have told you what?' Kiki held her eyeline.

'That you were struggling.'

Her sister laughed, and that one small act seemed to leave her exhausted, her words were laboured. 'I've been struggling my whole life, Nora. My whole life. And when? When do you think it would have been good to mention? During the Christmas morning phone chat with Ted opening his gifts or your visit a few years ago when you breezed in?'

Nora nodded and looked away. This, too, she more than understood. She felt a fresh surge of guilt at all she had kept from Gordy, bottled up, swallowed, so as not to let the genie out of the bottle. Why had she not told him of her fears, her loneliness, her dread that one day he would, just like her parents, see she was not worthy of love and leave?

'You sound angry, Kiki, and you have every right to be.' She faced it head on. 'I didn't mean to abandon you, it was more like . . .' She paused. 'More like I was dealing with my own problems, and you seemed so together, so happy!'

Kiki let out a laugh of derision. 'Yeah, that's me, living the dream! It's all lollipops and rainbows.'

Nora rubbed her eyes and took a moment to let her pulse steady, before wiping the slick of sweat from her palms to her jeans.

'I honestly thought it was only me who was messed up by Mum and Dad, I thought you were too little to have any recollection and therefore your memories wouldn't be . . .' – she searched for the right word – 'sullied. I thought you'd only think of Nana

Dilly and baking cakes and walking to school in Yorkshire, going home to a tea in front of the fire at Midland Road.'

'Are you kidding me?' Kiki raised her tone, rallying a little. Nora looked towards the door, aware of where they were and her sister's volume, but Kiki wasn't done. 'And how were you messed up by Mum and Dad? At least you *had* Mum and Dad! At least you can picture them, know what their voices were like, had them read to you!' Her expression was one of anguish with two high spots of colour on her pale, pale face.

'Read to me?' Nora drew breath. 'I spent my time hiding in corners, trying to keep out of the way; they weren't interested in me and when they told me they were having another child, I couldn't believe it! They didn't want the one they'd got! And Nana Dilly was my safety net, but she cut me loose, she picked you!'

Nora stopped talking and closed her mouth to stop any more truths that might prove incendiary popping out of her mouth. Kiki stared at her, horrified.

'How are we doing in here?' The nurse poked his head inside the door as if alerted by Kiki's rise in tone and language.

'We're fine,' Nora answered on their behalf.

'Not too much longer, we don't want your sister to get over-tired and visitors can be quite draining when you have been used to your own company for a while.' He gave them both a rather stern look before leaving.

Nora felt suitably admonished and more than a little embarrassed at the fact that he'd felt it necessary to pop his head into the room at all.

'We have a lot to talk about, but today I came to tell you that you don't need to worry, Kiki, that you're not alone. That your friends love you so much and wanted me to tell you that they are there for you, as am I, and the flat is cosy and Ted is good, and I wanted to put your mind at rest.' She calmly and sincerely spoke all

231

the thoughts and words she had been mentally firing in her direction before she fell asleep at night and during any lull in her day.

Kiki nodded her acknowledgment and stared at her wrists and Nora wondered what it might feel like to have the permanent reminder of why and how she had ended up in this room.

'I saw a new doctor today.' Kiki sniffed.

'How did you get on?'

'Yeah, she was nice, they're all nice, but they're also busy and it's a bit like a conveyer belt in here. They take you in, put you on one end, make sure you're stable and while you're coming round there's another person knocking on the door and they're processing you ready to push you off the other end and send you back out into the real world. I get it, they have to give attention where it's most needed and I'm on the mend, apparently.' Kiki's tone and expression didn't fill Nora with hope that this was the case, or rather, that her sister believed this might be the case.

'Do you *feel* on the mend?' She was unsure if it was okay to ask, but it was a little too late for that, apprehension at what the immediate future might look like had urged the question. She wanted to know what it might be like when Kiki was released. Would she be able to look after Ted? Might she try again to take her life?

Kiki took her time in answering. 'A little bit, I guess. And if it means I get to come home then yes, I'm on the mend!' She again raised her voice and angled her head towards the door where the nurse might or might not have been lurking.

'That's good.' Nora hoped her words masked the doubt she felt.

'I just want to see Ted. Well, I do and I don't. You say he's good but I'm his mum and I need the detail; I won't settle until I can see him for myself. God, I miss him!' Her tears came in loud gulping sobs, in part, Nora suspected, because Kiki, like her, was thinking of how much he must be missing her and how close he had come to losing her entirely. And this was all the reminder she needed that

232

her sister's struggle was in no way over. It was a daunting prospect and she was unsure of how she could keep placating Ted when all he wanted was to see his mum, be with his mum. They were lucky in so many ways, Kiki and her boy . . . *For fuck's sake, why don't you go and help Luna with supper?*

'He is good, honestly. He's sleeping and eating well and playing with Afsar and his little gang, cleaning his teeth. He makes me laugh, Kiki, he's so matter-of-fact and calm, a wise little head.'

'And . . . and clever,' her sister stuttered through her tears. 'He's so clever!'

'Takes after his mum.'

'Does Richie know what happened?' It was as if this was the first time she had thought about her ex, her voice subdued and her blink rate high.

'Yes, he was contacted when I was.' She decided to say no more, to change the topic rather than inadvertently slip in the uncomfortable details about his visit.

'I was thinking that it might be good for Ted to see his dad; it's not been easy between us, but I was thinking that it might be good for him to know that his dad is around, no matter what happens . . .'

Nora hated the ominous inference. 'He's got me and he's looking forward to having you back.'

'I know.' Her sister held her gaze. 'And thank you for everything.' She smiled. 'But Richie's his dad. And you can never have too many people.'

The image of him throwing his car keys in the air and sneering at her made Nora's bowel spasm.

'If you think it's best.' She let this trail. 'Sheila has filled me in on just how much of an arsehole he is.'

Kiki gave a weak laugh. 'That's funny, hearing you say arsehole. You hardly ever swear and to hear you talk about Sheila – she's a great mate and it's weird for me that you guys have met without me being there.'

'That must be strange,' Nora acknowledged.

There was a moment of silence and she wondered if Kiki, like her, was thinking of how Sheila found her, saved her. And again, she felt the pull of tears at how close they had come to losing her.

'It is strange, but then this whole thing is a bit strange, right?'

'Right.' Nora again reached for her sister's hand and marvelled at the daintiness of it, not letting her eyes stray to the neatly tied bandages with the bows. 'I like her – I like all your friends.' Saying it aloud focused her on the truth of it: she did like them, very much.

'So, tell me again, what does Ted know?' Her voice cracked as her thumb moved over the back of Nora's hand. It was the first time Nora could recall them holding hands, touching each other, since that day when Nora took Kiki in her arms and held on to her tightly on the wet tarmac of the road.

'She's crying! She's crying, love!' Mrs Deveraux, Nana Dilly's neighbour, shouted above the din. *'And if she's crying, she's good. It's when they're quiet you really have to worry.'* Nora realised that the way she felt on that day – a sick emptiness in her gut, her whole being wrapped in desolate failure – was how she had felt every time she saw Kiki; the sibling she loved was a reminder of all she had lost and all she had never had. Not that it was her sister's fault. Of course it wasn't.

'Nora, what does Ted know?' Kiki repeated, drawing her back to the moment.

'Erm, very little, other than you've been poorly and are in hospital and that you miss him. I tell him every day that you miss him and that you send your love, and you can't wait to come home.'

The high-pitched squeak of her sister's distress was unpleasant to hear, painful in that it was the sound of suffering and this, Nora knew, Kiki did not deserve.

'Thank you, Nora. Thank you.' Her sister yawned involuntarily and her eyes drooped with fatigue.

'No need to thank me. He'll see you soon. I'm going to go now and let you rest. Try and sleep. And I know it's a ridiculous phrase but try not to worry.'

Her sister painted on a brief wide smile that didn't quite reach her eyes.

'Bye, Kiki.' She bent low and held her sister in a hug that was unfamiliar. Nora was sure this was because without the touch of their parents to normalise such behaviour, she felt reticent, a little shy about contact. It felt nice to feel her younger sibling in her arms, strangely comforting.

'Thank you, Leonoranoodle.' And again, this word, created on the lips of her father and mimicked by Nana Dilly, had the power to melt her heart.

It was as the bus trundled along the lane with Nora deep in thought, that her phone buzzed with a text from Jason.

Nothing to worry about.

These words guaranteed to fire a bolt of worry through her gut as her mind conjured images of something terrible befalling Ted . . .

Ted has had a great day and is all booked up for after-school club and then heading home with Zac, but is there any chance you could pop in later? I'll be here until sixish?

She replied immediately.

Of course. Be there in about 40 minutes.

'God, what now?' she muttered, twisting her neck to relieve some of the tension and wondering how soon she could climb on to the blow-up mattress. It had been hard to see Kiki, but also quite wonderful too. There had been an unmistakable connection that boded well for their future. She was determined to be there for her and for Ted, to get to know them better, to be a bigger part of their lives. They would, to coin one of her most loved phrases, figure it out. But one thing was for sure, there was no quick fix. And this was as scary as it was motivating. Not only did she fear losing Kiki but was also wary of what that might mean for a sweet and trusting little boy like Ted. This relationship was not going to come without responsibilities. She hoped she was up to the task.

The bus stopped a little way along from the school and Nora walked briskly to make sure she didn't miss Jason. It had been quite the day and fresh from sitting with Kiki, adrenaline now provided a buffer to the fatigue that pawed at her senses.

She pressed the entry buzzer and Jason himself answered. 'Come on through, Nora!'

At the sound and sight of the gate whirring, she stepped across the tarmac and into the school, thinking of when she had arrived with her heavy suitcase in tow and nerves that rendered speech almost impossible as she set foot in the alien environment.

The main door swung open and there was the smiling face of Ted's teacher.

'How was your day, Nora?' He spoke to her as if she were one of his charges.

'Oh, you know, so-so.' It felt easier than going into detail – too harrowing to recall the two encounters that had shaped her day and which would keep her from sleeping tonight.

'Thanks for coming in. Ted has gone home with Fi and Zac. The boys were in quite high spirits, so I hope Fi has gin to hand.' She smiled, liking his natural ability to draw tension from the air. 'Come through.' He pulled the only other grown-up-sized chair next to his at the desk and sat down and she followed suit.

'I've been worried since I got your text; is everything okay with Ted?'

He took his time, speaking with his hands in a prayer pose clamped between his thighs that made him look quite childlike.

'It's not unusual when kids are going through trauma or upset for them to have little upsets and Ted has a lot to deal with right now.'

Her face fell. He did, he did have a lot to deal with and what little upsets was this man talking about?

'Not that you aren't doing a fantastic job, Nora, you really are!'

'Thank you.' Her tone was curt; she wished he'd get to the point.

'Ted didn't quite make it to the loo today and had a little accident. We dealt with it calmly and with absolute respect. None of his classmates were aware and we asked all the children in the class to get into their joggers for gym early, so it wasn't odd for him, and no one was any the wiser, but it's not like him.'

Her heart flexed at the thought of the little boy being embarrassed or uncomfortable in any way.

Jason continued, 'These things happen, and there could be a whole bunch of reasons for it: he may have drunk more than usual, been distracted and forgotten to go to the bathroom, it happens. So don't worry, but I wanted to check in and give you his stuff.' He reached down and handed her a plastic bag with his wet clothes in. 'Shelley, our TA, rinsed them for you.'

'Thank you.' She placed the bag on her lap. 'He . . .' She worried about making the admission, concerned it might bring greater enquiry into Ted's life that she knew he could do without. She wasn't sure how it all worked. 'He's wet the bed a couple of times at home.'

Jason nodded. 'As I say, there could be a bunch of reasons, but sometimes with upheaval, change or upset, any situation in fact that they might find stressful or hard to express, this can happen. We'll keep an eye on it, and I'm sure it's just a phase, a blip. It usually stops of its own accord, but if it doesn't then there are measures we can take, things we can do to help Ted talk about anything that might be bothering him, worrying him.'

'What measures?' She was curious.

'Like speaking to a child therapist, someone trained in just this thing.'

'*A therapist?*' She heard Gordy's words on her last day in Cyprus. '*I don't go and talk to therapists – some nosey busybody who's done an online course and has a framed certificate above their desk . . .*'

'As you say, probably just a blip,' she reasoned, unsure whether it should be her call to put Ted in front of a therapist.

'Yes.'

'I went to see Kiki today.'

'Oh.' He leaned on the desk, as if keen to hear. 'How's she doing?'

'She looked . . .' Nora paused as the sight of her sister perched on the bed as if waiting to take flight filled her mind. 'Frail, I guess.'

'I think the sooner she gets home and can start to put this behind her the better.' He looked at the floor and she suspected that he, like her, knew it was not quite that simple.

'I hope so.'

'Parenting is not easy, Nora, it's not easy even when things are plain sailing.'

'You think so?' She settled back on to the chair. 'I worry about getting it right. It's not as if I've had practice. This is all new – I've been thrown in at the deep end and all that.' She felt the weight of her nephew's damp clothes on her lap and wondered how she was to 'fix' this.

'Just by showing up you are getting it right.'

'Really?'

'Yes.' He held her eyeline, unflinching, as if what he had to say was law, and she felt emboldened by it. 'It's true. You're here for Ted, you're concerned for his well-being and when it comes to parenting, these are two huge requisites. You'd be surprised how many don't turn up for their kids and don't care that much.'

She pictured Richie, the gum-chewing chancer.

'I never saw myself as a mum, just didn't feel it was for me.'

'Never?'

'No, never.' She smiled at this aspect that set her apart from most of the women she had met. 'But I see the attraction of it a little now I'm more in Ted's life. I get it, and all the things that go with it: the camaraderie of the other parents, the busyness of it, I can see how it becomes your whole life. But I'm willing to learn. I want to learn! If for nothing else than to help Kiki shoulder the responsibility. To see them more, be there more.' *Know them better* . . .

'So, do I detect a hint of regret? If that's not too personal, are you saying you wouldn't mind becoming a parent?'

Her laugh was natural and instant. 'Oh, I'll never become a mother. That ship has definitely sailed.' She shook her head as if her words might not be enough to convey the finality and certainty of her statement and to try and disguise the fact that having seen Gordy interact with Ted so marvellously, her heart had torn a little at the path she had set them on as a couple. Picturing Gordy's trembling bottom lip, his expression laden with all he contained, she felt such sadness that her decision, denying him fatherhood, was the cause, and he had gone along with it because he loved her.

'There are many ways to become a mother, Nora,' he paused trying, she knew, to offer a glimmer of hope on the assumption that the reason for her words was that she found the situation unlikely or improbable.

'I guess there are.' She shifted in the chair. 'But you know for much of my adult life, I've heard it from other army wives, old school friends and even strangers, each feeling confident to comment and every one of them telling me how sad that is and how I *might* change my mind and how their kids are the greatest thing ever to happen to them, while all being terribly excited about any time away from them and drinking gin at the first whiff of dusk just to get through the day! People find my decision to remain childless unfathomable, I guess, because it's so far from their lives. I've heard them call it a shame, selfish, odd . . . and so yes, I know there are many ways to become a mother and I know that they are probably not for me. But now I have a bigger role in Ted's life, one that I hope will continue, I will work on being the best aunty I can, and that's mothering, right?'

'Right.' He spoke slowly, not in the least bit flustered despite her breathless rant. 'Being the best aunty you can be really is mothering.'

The bag of damp clothes was a good prop and she jostled it on her legs. 'So what about you, Jason? Any deep-seated longing to father offspring? To have a little sproglet of your own? I mean, I know a few single mums who might be interested – one with curly red hair in particular . . .'

'God, I wish I'd never told you!' He shook his head, and just like that they were chatting as friends and it felt nice. 'And besides, how do you know I don't already have offspring?' He had borrowed the word and smiled as he said it.

'Have you?' she asked directly; he had after all felt at ease asking her something along similar lines.

'Not that I know of.' He smiled again. 'But unlike you I am open to the idea. Trouble is, I'm very fussy and want it to be right, with the right person. I find it hard enough organising care for Wilf, I don't think I could parent alone.'

'Very wise. But here's the thing, Jason, if you don't tell the person how you feel, they might slip through your fingers, and wouldn't that be a waste?' She thought of how she had resisted talking openly to Gordy and how easy it was to give the advice she too should follow. Her thoughts again turned to Kiki going it alone for all these years and how she had chosen the wrong person – Richie, the little shit – and her heart jumped in her ribcage. How on earth was she going to tell her frail sister she was being turfed out of the flat? 'I'd better go fetch Ted. Don't want Fi turning him out on to the streets because I'm late.'

Jason laughed. 'Nice talk, Nora.'

'Yes.' She stood and popped her handbag over her shoulder. 'Nice talk.'

Ted skipped along by her side, darting around her like a minnow as they trod the pavement home and night pulled its blind on the day.

'You had a nice time at Rafe's house?'

'We had ice cream and he's got a PlayStation 5!'

This he stated with such emphasis, suggesting that it would have been hard not to have a nice time with such a thing at his fingertips and a tum full of ice cream.

'Wowsers! Not sure what that is.'

241

He laughed and looked at her over his shoulder with the closest thing to disdain a little boy could muster. It made her smile. The ease with which they now chatted was a thing of joy to her. Jason was right, she was doing well, and the thought gave her confidence. Gone were the awkward silences, the second-guessing every suggestion and action, and the removal of tension meant life was better for them both.

'I watched Rafe and his sister play, and they let me have a go.'

'Cool.' She picked up her pace to match his, having planned what and how she would tell him of her visit to Kiki. The words had been so rehearsed they were slick on her tongue. 'And I have some news – today was a good one for me too.'

'It's my dad!' His yell cut through the autumn air, halting her words mid-sentence and slicing right through her joy. 'Look, Aunty Pickle! It's my dad!' *What on earth?*

Shrugging off his anorak, Ted hared along the pavement towards the black sports car that, parked beneath the street lamp, gleamed like a bauble even in the darkness. Picking up his coat where it had dropped, she placed it over her shaking hands. Richie stood with his arms open and bent low to scoop up Ted who careered into him. With his son against his body, Richie twirled on the pavement and transferred the boy to his hip, where he sat comfortably, pointing as he called out to her, 'Aunty Pickle! Look who's here!' He was breathless with joy.

'Hello, Aunty Pickle.' Richie winked at her.

Nora felt an icy rage deep in her gut; it was an odd sensation and one she had not experienced before. Never had she been so furious and yet so aware that to give in to that fury would not be the right thing to do. It was vital she kept things civil and didn't scare Ted. It was also important she didn't show Richie how scared she was; his very presence, in light of their earlier exchange, was confrontational and challenging enough to make her legs quake.

'*I could take him, you know, if I wanted.*' This thought was more frightening than any other – to lose Ted while Kiki wasn't here to fight her corner was unthinkable.

'Hi.' She managed to keep the warble from her voice. 'Well, this is a surprise.'

'I wanted to see my boy!' Richie jogged him up and down and Ted giggled as he wobbled. Nora half willed him to bring up all that ice cream . . .

'Is that your car, Dad?' Ted asked in astonishment as Richie swung him down on to the pavement.

'It's one of them.' He beamed and pressed a button on a key fob that made the lights come on.

'It's a racing car!' Eyes wide, his son was impressed. 'Can we go out in it?'

'Sure!' Richie took a step towards the car.

'Ted, I don't want to be a spoilsport but it's your bedtime and you have school tomorrow. I think it's a bit late to go for a ride.' There was so much that bothered her about the situation it would have been hard to pick one reason, but getting into a fast car, getting into a fast car in the dark, getting into a fast car in the dark with Richie the shit driving . . .

Earlier that day, Kiki had spoken about her ex with the suggestion that it might be good for Ted to know that his dad was around, an extra person. But in Nora's opinion, his dad was the kind of person she'd rather keep him away from, understanding more than most that the same blood running through your veins and an arbitrary title meant little when it came to loving someone, being there for them. Her instinct and earlier encounter with him told her he was reckless, impulsive – neither trait did anything, in her opinion, to recommend him as father of the year. Her suspicions were that he was hanging around to prove a point, score points, sabre-rattling at best, or at least that was what she hoped.

'What about tomorrow after school? Can we go for a ride then?' Ted looked up at the man who would willingly make him move to a new home in the midst of all else he had to deal with. His skinny legs jumped, and his fingers flexed: he was ecstatic, excited, hyped-up. And it tore at her heart. Not only to see this little boy investing in this man who didn't deserve it, but also, and it was hard to admit, she felt the bitter bile of jealousy that Ted was so enamoured with him.

Richie shot her a look. 'Sure, we can do that.'

'Yes!' Ted did a mini fist pump of victory and threw his arms around Richie's waist.

Nora felt backed into a corner; she wanted to refuse, rail against it, tell Richie to go far away and to place Ted safely in his cosy corner on the sofa with a pizza and a cartoon . . . but she was merely minding him and Kiki had expressed her view that this man, like it or not, was his father.

'We'll be back from school by four.' She shot him a look over the top of Ted's head, hoping it conveyed her contempt but wasn't overly hostile, lest Ted should see.

'I'll be here.' He gave his white-toothed smile and chewed gum, which must have been lodged in his cheek.

'See you tomorrow, Dad!' Ted reluctantly let go his grip and watched as Richie climbed into the slick automobile and roared off.

Nora heard the window of the flat above rise and Mr Appleton stuck his head out. 'What a bloody racket!' He shook his head.

'That's my dad! He's got a racing car!' Ted beamed as he danced on the spot.

'I always think a small man who needs a car like that must be trying to compensate for something! And racing car or not, it's still a bloody racket!'

Ted smiled, oblivious and wrapped in a bubble of excitement that no crotchety adult could burst. The old man let the window clatter shut and Nora chuckled. Taking a sudden liking to Mr Appleton.

CLOVE COURT, MAIDA VALE, LONDON

Austin Davenport closed the wide front door of Clove Court that led to the shared vestibule of the mansion block in Maida Vale that he called home. He shook the rain from his umbrella. It was an atrocious day with rain falling so hard and fast it formed rivers in the roads, all the street and car lights strobed and every wheel that passed him kicked up London dirt to splatter his slacks. His father had insisted he take the item, grabbing it from the closet under the stairs.

'Just pop it in your case! No man goes to London and does not take an umbrella. That would be foolish. It rains, it rains a lot.' He had pushed the navy-blue brolly into his hands.

'It rains a lot here, and surely I could buy one there, Dad, if it rains as much as you say, they must sell them there too?'

'They do, I even recall a shop – James Smith and Sons – who are umbrella specialists. A fancy shop with an ornate facia; I took a photograph of it, I'll see if I can find it and send it to you.'

'That's okay, I'll go find the shop and take a photo myself.' He smiled and pushed his glasses back up on to the bridge of his nose from where they had slid.

'You don't want my umbrella, you don't want my photo . . . What's going on, Austin? Next you'll be telling me you don't want me to make you a bag lunch for your journey?'

'Okay, Dad, you win, I'll take the umbrella!'

His dad pulled him into his arms and held him uncomfortably tight.

'Can't . . . breathe . . .' Austin managed.

'I don't care, I'm going to miss you so much!'

'Put him down, Wendell!' His mum waved a duster from the stairs as she descended. 'You'll flatten him and he's skinny enough as he is!'

He smiled now at the memory; how he missed them. Their noise, their bickering, their limitless affection, and their fussy concern for every aspect of his well-being. Not that he wasn't having a great time here in London, he was. He liked the newness of everything and loved the fact that the sights and scenes he had read about and seen in movies were right here in real life! It made him feel as if *he* were in a movie! But there was also something about being so far away from the two people who loved him most on the whole planet that made him feel a little adrift. Like he'd lost his safety net. It was both thrilling and terrifying.

He liked his new job. The pay wasn't great, but working in the British Library he got to be around books all day and so what was not to love? Plus, he had lucked out in the rental market. His mother's cousin Pam had married a Brit and their son had a flat . . . yada yada . . . and here he was, sharing with Pam's grandson, Lorne, a confident, twenty-four-year-old fitness freak who did chin-ups while waiting for the kettle to boil, existed on chicken, broccoli and protein shakes and had the worst gas of any living thing Austin had ever encountered – and he had once worked in a zoo. Lorne's farts aside, he enjoyed this new pace of life. His father was fond of saying about his own trip to London some three decades since, 'I had a feeling I wasn't in Kansas any more!' The joke being that they were from Kansas, Arkansas to be precise.

'Hi.' He heard the soft voice as the front door closed. He looked up and felt his face blush red. It was her. The girl from the flat below. Just the sight of her enough to send a bolt of longing right through his core. He folded with lust for her, thought about her before he fell asleep and then woke in the night tortured with the thought that she lay only feet below him . . . the mousy girl who favoured turtlenecks in mustard and green, wore woolly tights on her skinny legs, had heavy bangs that sat on the top of glasses and who carried a 'Books Are My Bag' bag that made him believe they were kindred spirits, because books were his bag too! He had never, ever felt such a surge of longing for another and now here they were, standing only feet apart, both reaching for mail from the communal table.

'Hi,' he replied, remembering to keep calm, and concentrating on *not* saying, '*You are in my mind all day! I once put my ear to the bathroom floor because I thought I might be able to hear you in your kitchen! I like to walk behind you and inhale the scent of you so that any lingering breath in the air that had once been in your lungs, inside your body, will now be in mine! I love books and I think I love you!*'

'Terrible weather. Even my socks are soaking wet.' She wiggled her drenched suede pixie boots and he wanted so badly to offer her a warm towel or to sit in front of the electric fire with a cup of tea.

'You . . . you need an umbrella,' he stuttered.

'I do!' She nodded, before squeezing excess rainwater from her limp hair. 'I need an umbrella!'

'There's an umbrella shop, umm' – he swallowed as nerves ravaged his eloquence – 'James . . . James Smith and Sons. It's umm, it's pretty specialist . . .' He let this trail.

'Pretty specialist? Wow! In that case I shall seek it out.' She smiled and he knew she was being sarcastic, but also that it was done affectionately, and he liked it. It was that British sense of humour thing.

He watched as she lifted the pile of mail and sifted through.

'Nicholas Ward, is that you?' She held out a brown envelope.

'No.' He watched her fingers deftly sorting through.

'Henry Thompson by any chance?' She held out a flat box, a delivery of some sort.

'No.'

'Ruby Martin?' She made to hand him a pink flyer offering a discount on a make-up brand.

He shook his head.

'God, help me out here, I'm trying to find out your name!' She put the pile of mail down and her hands on her hips.

'Oh!' He laughed, feeling flattered and overcome all at once. 'I'm . . .' He paused.

'You're . . . ?' She rolled her hand.

'Austin, I'm Austin.'

'Hi Austin.' She smiled at him. 'I'm Leah. Leah Richards.'

'Leah.'

'Yep.' She pulled a face and they both laughed. 'Austin, I hope you don't mind me saying this . . .'

'What?' He felt the beat of nerves as his heart raced.

'You need to up your game.'

'Up my game? I don't . . . what?' He was confused.

'We've seen each other before and please tell me if I've got the wrong end of the stick here, but we shared a look, right?'

'Right.' He blushed. 'We did.'

'And that look, if I'm not very much mistaken, had promise, don't you think?' She held his gaze.

'I-I do! Yes! Yes, absolutely!' Was this conversation really happening? It was the stuff of dreams, the possibility that she might have been thinking about him too . . .

'Okay.' Leah turned. 'So I'm going to go outside and come in again, and we're going to start over, and you need to think about what you might like to say or how you might like to act and that's how we get out of the blocks. It's been three months of silence and lingering looks and I think it's time we moved things forward, don't you?'

'I do. I really, really do.' He felt something rise inside him like a ball of happiness that was hard to keep down. It made him want to leap up and shout out!

'Okay, so I'm going now.' She pointed towards the front door.

'Out into the rain?' he quizzed.

'Yes, Austin, out into the rain.'

He watched as she walked back outside, the sight enough to make him laugh: she was crazy! Good crazy! Putting her key once again in the door, closing it behind her and shaking the fresh droplets from her bangs, he listened to her squelching pixie boots make their way across the tiled floor and walk up to him.

'Hi Austin, nice to see you. So how was your day?' She stood close to him and he liked the way she looked like she might fit under his chin were he to hold her.

'My day was good, damp but good and I think we should go out for a drink or dinner or just a drink, whatever.' He swallowed the nerves that wrapped his chat.

'Well, what a lovely idea!' She smiled at him over her shoulder as she continued to sort the mail. 'Yes, let's do that. A drink, then dinner, then a drink, then whatever . . . This Thursday, meet you here at seven?' He saw the smallest flicker of nerves in her eyes, as if this level of bravado might have taken a lot.

'I shall really look forward to it, Leah.' He exhaled, feeling a little as if a weight had been lifted from his chest. He felt tall! Muscular! Invincible!

'Me too.' She flicked through the last of the envelopes. 'Magda Farraday – I don't know that name. Not seen it before.' She squeezed the bulky envelope.

'It might be someone from the management company, or an owner who rents out a flat?'

'Possibly, but my landlady is Leonora Brightwell, so it's not her. I'll pop it in the miscellaneous pigeonhole.'

'It's like a black hole that little cubby on the end, once things go into it, they really never leave . . .' He tried to relax, tried to think about how he'd chat to one of his friends or his dad.

'Sounds like my job.' She pulled a face.

'What do you do?' He wanted to know so he could picture her during the day.

She sucked her teeth. 'Well, that's the tricky thing' – she lowered her voice and leaned closer to him so he could smell her and she smelled like flowers – 'I don't really know what I do.'

His laugh came easy. 'You don't know what you do?'

'Uh-uh.' She pulled a face.

'So how does that work?' He was curious.

'Well, I turn up at a government department.'

'So, you're a civil servant?'

'Kind of. I sit behind a computer, and I prioritise incoming emails for a minister, and I weed snail mail for that minister, and I occasionally make bookings.'

'So, like a personal assistant?'

'Not really, they have one of those. I'm on a fast-track programme that involves a lot of admin and various tasks.'

'Fast track to what?' He was none the wiser.

'I'm not entirely sure.' She giggled.

'And they pay you for this?'

'Yes, rather handsomely, and the best thing is I get to sneak read when no one is around!'

'What do you like to read?' This was crucial, and he felt his heart skip at the prospect of her response – suppose she named a genre or subject so niche he would have nothing to say on it?

'I read any good book. Any good story.' She smiled and he nodded, *yes yes!* 'Fiction, non-fiction, memoir, graphic novels, translations, poetry . . . I have an eclectic taste, but if it grips me, it grips me and if it doesn't, I ditch it.'

'That's a smart philosophy.'

'I think so. Anyway' – she lifted the packet – 'I'm shoving this in the black hole cubby of doom and I'm going to dry off, nap and think about our conversation and I might plan what I'll wear on Thursday. I like to plan.'

'Me too.'

She wedged the fat envelope sideways into the wire racking along with the bank card of a tenant long since left, a padlock key retrieved from behind the bins, a voting card for one Yitzhak Josef and a laminated card detailing the fire exits in the building.

He watched as she gathered her bag and made her way up the stairs.

'See you Thursday!' he called up after her, fascinated by the twist of her calf as she climbed and the way her skirt kicked out over the curve of her bottom.

'Yes, see you Thursday, Austin!' She turned on the stairway and smiled at him and he felt something a lot like happiness enveloping him with its promise and holding him fast.

Leah . . . Leah . . . Leah . . .

CHAPTER NINE

Nora stood at the school gate, early and in position, waiting to grab Ted so she could at least give him some advice on . . . what? She was hardly going to fill him in on the reality of his shit of a father. In fact, she didn't know what she wanted to say, but knew it felt paramount to settle him, be near him, reassure him that she'd be at home waiting when he returned from their trip, and to continue the conversation they had started about Kiki, where she had told him how great his mum was doing and he had responded with, 'How fast do you think Dad's car goes?' He was distracted by the expensive toy. As much as she disliked Richie, she had to admit it was good to see her nephew so excited, so happy. The little worried crease that regularly sat at the top of his nose was nowhere to be seen. She had called earlier and left a message for Kiki, asking if it was okay for Ted to go out with his dad after school? The one-word answer had been texted back from Kiki's phone.

Sure X

Did this mean Kiki was in no fit state to consider it or was she confident that Ted could and should see his dad? Either way, it bothered her.

'Penny for them?' Afsar's mum, early for once, drew her from her thoughts.

'Hey, Mina. I was miles away.'

'I could see. Hope it was somewhere nice? With a beach and a strawberry daiquiri close to hand?'

'Not quite.' She pushed her hands into her pockets and looked at her feet.

'You know, Nora, sometimes sharing what's bothering you, especially with someone who has no vested interest in advising you either way, can help clarify things. At least it does for me. My parents are full of guidance, my brother the king of advice! They all drive me mad, but the women here at the school gate, they walk in my shoes, they get it. And even if they don't get it, sometimes it just feels good to share things.'

Nora looked up and ordered her thoughts, then she took a deep breath. 'Ted's dad arrived last night and has promised to take him out after school. I'm a mess. I know it's his dad, but the thought of waving him off with someone who's been less than reliable . . .'

'Welcome to the world of single parenting. It's not easy. That back and forth is hardest and it's almost impossible not to let your feelings influence every interaction. It's a skill, smiling widely, waving them off and trying to convince the kid that everything is great! Before going back inside, sinking down on the sofa and bawling your heart out. I don't know a parent in the same situation who hasn't done just that. Even the ones who are keen to tell you what great mates they are with their exes. I don't buy it.'

'Thank you, Mina.' She meant it, not only grateful for the advice but also the acknowledgment that she was parenting Ted. It meant the world that Kiki had chosen her, and she seemed to be doing a good job. The woman was right, she did feel better for sharing it. 'Fi and Sheila running late?'

'No, Rafe and Zac have got chess club.'

'Chess club?'

'Yes, and don't worry about Ted missing it, it's invite only, very exclusive, and Ted and Afsar didn't get invited. I was going to complain, but . . .'

The rest of her sentence was drowned out by the loud, bassy thrum of an engine that reverberated inside her chest. The women, and everyone else present, turned to see the shiny black R8 parking outside the school gates.

'What the fuck?' Mina spoke for them both.

Nora felt her face blush red and her pulse increase, embarrassed to be even remotely associated with this elaborate display and the man behind the wheel.

Richie jumped out and waved as he strode over.

'Well, well, well.' Mina sighed. 'The ego has landed. God, I hate him.'

Nora had never liked her more. It felt nice, like she wasn't facing Richie alone, but was doing so with a friend by her side.

'Good afternoon, ladies!' He gave a small bow.

'I thought you were coming to the house. That's what we agreed!' She cut straight to it, barely able to disguise her frustration.

'Did we?' He looked up towards the sky and shook his head. 'Oh well, here I am!' He threw his arms wide.

The school door opened and out traipsed the little ones; all of them gasped, pointed, and gawped at the car. Nora felt her face continue to flame with embarrassment at no more than the slightest connection with Richie and his 'racing car'.

Parents and carers alike all gave the vehicle a wide berth, an alien thing landed among the routine of their day. She cringed. Ostentatious displays had never and would never be her thing. Next, she saw Jason corralling Ted's class along. Spotting her nephew's dark hair and his blue puffer coat, her heart sang at the sight of him. Recognising that to refuse access to Ted, even if it were in her remit, would only cause a ruckus, she turned to Richie. 'He needs to eat, and please make sure he's back by six thirty. He'll have reading to do for homework and needs to have his bath.' It wasn't yet four o'clock, which meant a good couple of hours to roar around the streets or whatever it was he had planned.

'No problem.' He looked straight past her, waving to Ted who now pogoed up and down on the spot. Jason nodded at her and released Ted who ran as fast as he could into Richie's arms.

'See, Jonah!' he called over his shoulder. 'I *have* got a dad! And this is his racing car!'

Nora's heart threatened to burst at the little boy's words. And she understood: Richie had all but disappeared from his life, then Kiki, but Richie had come back, which no doubt gave Ted hope that his mum would too. It was clear the man held power over Ted, dangling the carrot of fatherhood, all wrapped in a shiny sports car. Who wouldn't be tempted?

Ted bundled his school bag and PE bag into her arms and shrugged free of his coat, which dropped to the floor. Nora bent and scooped it into her arms, loaded up like Buckaroo as she watched the excited boy, whose grin was wide, buckle up, before the roaring engine spirited him away and out of sight.

'You okay, hun?' Mina put her arm around her waist and Nora could only nod. Her stomach churned with anxiety, knowing she wouldn't rest until it was six thirty and Ted was home safe and sound, back in her care.

The flat gleamed. The floors were swept, the kitchen sparkled and the fridge had been cleaned. The French windows shone and with a scented candle burning on the counter, the place looked homey and welcoming. A quick glance at the clock told her there was only thirty minutes to go before Ted came home. Taking a deep breath, she sat at the breakfast bar and thought about Gordy. The memory of their wonderful union had faded in the face of the week's events, replaced with something that left her feeling a little grubby. Was it tawdry to have slept with the man as they stared into the abyss of divorce? Was it really a rung on a ladder that might see them reach safety or was it no more than two lonely souls hooking up for old time's sake? She hoped not, but these thoughts made the prospect of heading back to Westbury this weekend a nerve-wracking one. That feeling, the frisson of desire in itself a novelty, now coated her with something that felt a lot like shame.

Having wiped the shiny sink one more time and refolded the towels in the bathroom, she stared in the mirror. 'You need to calm down, Nora.'

The words, however, were easy. Living with a military man and often at the mercy of his schedule, timings were adhered to, and she understood how they gave a day order, routine. Yet six thirty came and went. The tick of the kitchen clock grew louder and louder, her heart raced as she paced the laminate floor, watching, waiting, coiled and at a loss as to the correct course of action. Her temptation was to call the police – and say what? Ted was a little late coming home from a trip out with his father? Even she could see how this would most probably be brushed off. But at what point should she panic? Seven. Seven thirty . . . These milestones passed, and Nora was agitated, highly so. She felt wired and out of step. Like she'd had too much caffeine or was unable to sleep. Standing at the end of the path in the cool night air, she stared up and down the road, gripping the front gate, her breath blowing smoke into the dusk, as she glanced repeatedly at her phone, first to check the time, with every minute that passed seeming to tighten the bolt in her gut, and second to see if the police had called . . . To her mind, both were entirely plausible as dark images threatened. *Supposing they've* come off the road? Richie going too fast, that flashy car, showing off in front of Ted. It happens . . . Lord above, she knew it could happen!

'This way, Leonora, quick, quick! Don't keep Matron waiting . . .'

Every time a car came into view or she heard the chatter of people nearby, her heart skipped with relief, only for that relief to be replaced with a new level of fear as it was revealed to be imposters with no clue of how their presence toyed with her emotions. Why had she let him take Ted? What in God's name was she going to say to Kiki if something happened to him?

'Where are you?' she muttered under her breath – this book-ended with the cold, icy dread of a new thought: that Richie might not bring him home at all! He might at that moment be hotfooting it up the motorway to Cheshire or anywhere else on the planet, and what would she do then? Her knees felt a little soft and she held on to that gate even tighter, knowing that she needed to get a grip for when he came home or in case he didn't. She needed to be calm and unflustered.

'Oh, please God! Please let him come home!'

Her fingers were cold, her feet numb, and the feeling of help-lessness knitted around her insides and pulled her down.

I'm going to have to call Kiki. Why didn't I get Richie's number? Why didn't I give him mine? A rookie error . . . but it all happened so fast and not as planned, him turning up . . . Ted so excited . . . what on earth am I going to say to my sister who trusted me? Why didn't you get his number you idiot? Basics, Nora. Basics . . .

It was at ten to eight that Nora closed the gate and walked inside. Scooped out, she was a husk of the feisty woman who had felt she could take on Richie Morris; she was weakened, quiet and riven with a dark tangle of invasive thoughts of all that might have befallen her nephew. Standing in the kitchen, she fired off a text to the WhatsApp group that contained Mina, Sheila and Fi. She needed their words of reassurance, reaching out, asking for the arms of friendship to hold her fast, to keep her upright.

Ted not back. Over an hour late. At what point do I panic?

She tried to keep it light, not wanting to reveal her state of utter helplessness that one glimpse of her ashen face in the oven door confirmed.

Probably just lost track of time. Let us know when he's home safe! X

Fi's response was reassuring, dampening the sharp edge of all she feared.

Zac and Zoey's dad does this all the time, doesn't understand how disruptive a late night or a missed appointment can be. Or maybe they're just having too much fun?

It was typical of Sheila to not only relate but share this optimistic slant.

God, I hate the prick!

Mina's message actually made her laugh out loud. It defused a little of her tension – that and the fact that these experienced mothers weren't yelling down the line for her to CALL THE POLICE! SEARCH AND RESCUE! DO IT NOW! GO! GO! GO!

Nora put her phone down and filled the kettle. Tea. It always helped. It was as she flicked the switch that she heard the knock on the front door. And it was a sound she recognised. Ted's knock: sloppy and accompanied by a little kick on the wood as he reached

259

up to move the knocker. Fighting to control the tears of relief, she took a second to compose herself before walking briskly to the door and painting on a smile.

'Hello, Ted! Have you had a lovely time?' She addressed the boy who stood in front of her with a chocolate-smeared mouth and holding a large box.

'I got a PlayStation!' His eyes were bright, whether in delight or overdosed on sugar it was hard to tell. 'My dad bought me a PlayStation!'

'Goodness me!' She touched her hand to his shoulder, confirming that he was real, giving her heart permission to slow down.

Richie stood behind him. His smile she would best describe as triumphant. Nora wasn't a violent woman, but as the man's white, white teeth glowed in the dark, she momentarily fantasised about punching him.

Ted rushed past her, and Richie went to step inside. Her stance clearly made him hesitate and she was glad.

'I promised I'd help him set it up, unless you fancy trying your hand?' Again he chewed that infernal gum.

'You're late,' she spat, realising that much of her anger had been bound in fear, which she could now relegate.

'Late? I only see the kid once a year, who's going to begrudge me an extra hour or so?'

His expression told her that he spoke without irony. Mina was right, he was a prick. Frustration, felt on behalf of her sister and nephew, flared. 'Sure, come in and set up the PlayStation.' The thought of Ted not being able to use the darn thing because of her technical ineptitude was not something she could consider. She was not going to be the one to take the gloss off his moments of joy.

Nora watched from the breakfast bar, sipping the hot tea and smiling when Ted looked up, as his dad fiddled with wires and leads and pressed buttons on a little black, curved remote control with blue and red buttons.

'There.' Richie ruffled Ted's hair. 'All done.'

'Thanks, Dad!' There was no mistaking her nephew's delight at the trip and its lucrative outcome. The thought that this man might be filling some of the gaps left inside Ted at his mother's absence was galling. Determined now, she would explain to Kiki tomorrow that it wasn't enough to send love or weep over how she missed the boy; he needed to see her, to touch *her* shoulder and confirm she was real, so that he could give *his* heart permission to slow down . . .

'Will you come to my football match next week, Dad? I'm in goal!'

She watched the little boy's face fall as Richie stood and brushed off his neat jeans. ''Fraid I can't next week, mate, but maybe the week after that?'

'Okay, Dad.' His faltering voice broke her heart. This kid loved saying the word *Dad . . . Dad . . . Dad . . .* and she understood, having similarly courted such love and approval. But unlike her, Ted was smart enough, had experienced enough to know that it was likely his dad would not be in attendance the week after that or the week after that or the week after that. She wanted to pull him into her arms and hold him close, to tell him that he was good enough, more than! That he was a special boy who was so loved by everyone.

Instead, however, she called out, 'Right Ted, bath time then bed. You have school tomorrow.'

He ran to Richie and again clung to the man with his arms locked around his waist.

'See you soon.' Richie looked more than a little uncomfortable.

'Promise?' Ted looked up, seeming to understand that the truth could be found in his dad's eyes.

'Do as Aunty Pickle says, go jump in your bath!'

It was the first time she felt even a flash of respect for the man who made no attempt to lie.

'Thank you for my PlayStation,' Ted managed as he slowly released his dad from his grip.

'I'd better run that bath,' she added with as much enthusiasm as she could muster. Richie took the hint and left, quietly and without the key-throwing antagonism he had displayed on his last visit. She heard the roar and thrum of the engine as he made his way back to his family.

With his PJs on the loo, she placed a big towel on the radiator to warm and was about to leave him to his bath when her nephew spoke quietly. 'I've got a brother and a sister.'

'You have?' This she knew but thought he might like to be the bearer of news.

'They're called Kiera and Logan.'

'Have you ever met them?'

'No.' He shook his head. 'They're littler than me.'

'Well, I'm sure you'll see them one day and won't that be exciting?'

Ted shrugged, as if he wasn't so sure and she wondered if this was what it had felt like for Kiki; knowing her sister was out there but rarely seeing her. She could now see how not being part of each other's lives as they grew up had cut them adrift when all they really needed was something to cling to, driftwood, an anchor point for when things got rough.

'When's my mum coming home?' His voice quavered in the way that she now recognised as the forerunner to tears.

'I don't know exactly, but I know that she wants to be home and won't stay in hospital any longer than she absolutely has to.'

'I miss her,' he whispered as his tears finally broke their banks and tumbled down his cheeks.

'I know, darling. And she misses you. And I promise you, Ted, I am going to do my very best to make sure you see her soon. I know that would make everything feel better. I'll start work on it tomorrow. I know you want to see her so leave it with me. Do you trust me?'

He nodded and her heart lifted.

'You can talk to me about anything, Ted. Anything that's worrying you and you can ask any questions that you might have, because I'm sure that your head is very busy right now what with seeing your dad and with Mum being away. You must feel as if the whole world is a bit wobbly.'

He nodded.

'But remember, anything, at any time, I'm right here, okay?'

'Okay.' He stared at her, his chest heaving inside his little vest.

'How . . . how would you say you were feeling, if you had to describe it?'

'I don't know.'

'No, of course you don't, it's a very hard thing to get your head around. But remember, everything is going to be okay. Mummy will come home soon, and she will be here to cook your tea and take you to school, just like she always does, and I will do my very best to make sure you see her.'

'I'm going to . . .' He sniffed. 'I'm going to get in my bath now.' He stared at the bubble-filled water.

This was her cue to leave and she went and flopped on to the sofa.

Her phone rang.

Gordy.

'Nora, this is the first chance I've had to call all day, been up to my eyes. Everything okay?'

Holding the phone close to her face she took her time.

'Are you crying?' he asked tenderly.

'Uh-huh.' She nodded, finding it hard to explain how her tears were of relief that Ted was home, but also of sadness at all the ways parents were able to mess up their kids. Her own included. 'I'm nervous about seeing you, Gordy.'

'Don't be.'

'It's easy to say, but what was that last weekend? What's happening with us? I saw Ted so confused tonight, laughing one minute, crying the next, and I get it. I need to know if we are reconnecting or saying goodbye. Because when I know what's happening, I can start to mentally plan, to prepare, but this feels a lot like limbo and it's not good for me, Gordy. In fact, it feels cruel.'

'It's ironic, Nora, because that's how I've felt for the last couple of years. Like the ride broke down and we were left hanging like one of those flimsy buckets on a Ferris wheel that's swinging at the very top with some poor unfortunates stuck in it; we might have had a nice view, but it was cold and scary.'

She shivered, yes, it was cold and scary. She knew he hated Ferris wheels.

'Yes, that's what it's felt like, you and me, Nora. Left swinging with no idea of how or when we might get going again.'

'Unfinished business,' she whispered.

'Exactly, either way. Unfinished business,' he repeated. 'So what's the answer, Nora?'

With tears clogging her nose and throat, speech was tricky. 'I don't know,' she squeaked. 'I don't know what the answer is. But I know I don't want to lose you.'

◆ ◆ ◆

Nora had tried twice to speak directly to Kiki, only to have her calls fielded by different nurses.

'She's with her doctor right now. But I will take a message.'

And: 'Yes, we have a note you've called,' a different impatient voice had sighed two hours later. 'We'll pass it on to your sister and she has her phone if she wants to return your call.'

'But it's just that . . .' she began, knowing if she let her frustration be directed at the very people who were doing their best to help Kiki, no good would come of that. 'Thank you. And yes, please ask her to call. Her son is desperate to see her.'

'Will do.' The line went dead.

'We don't have to go to Westbury if you'd rather stay here,' Nora reassured as they drove out of Stroudly Green after school pick-up.

'I want to go.' He peered out of the window, a little quiet, a little preoccupied. 'I like playing with Gordy.'

She smiled. They were fast becoming friends, he and Gordy, and she liked the fact, knowing that no matter what, he was a man Ted could count on.

'Are you going to eat your snacks?' She spoke into the rear-view mirror. Ted sat in the back with his snacks in Ziplock bags on his lap.

'In a minute.'

'Remember what I said? That we can talk about anything, any time and you can ask me anything. I meant it.'

He nodded. 'Do you think my dad will go and watch Logan play football?' Staring now at the mirror, their eyes met, and she saw her own younger face reflected. She understood, knowing what it felt like not be chosen, to be supplanted, to feel like you just weren't good enough.

'He might,' she levelled. 'But that's okay. He will go and see Logan play and he'll think about you in goal, and he'll probably miss you a bit. And it's okay to feel angry that he'll see Logan play and not you and it's okay to feel sad about it too. But the important thing to remember is that you are wonderful, Ted.' She meant it.

'You are a wonderful little boy and I feel so lucky to spend time with you, to get to know you better, and if your dad doesn't see you in goal that's his loss.' There was no disguising the crack to her voice.

'Do you think they tried to look for him?'

'Who?' She had lost the thread.

'Norman's mum and dad?'

'Oh, I'm sure they did.' She remembered their chat on their previous journey.

She watched as her nephew, seemingly satisfied, tucked into his cheese sandwiches cut into squares, his quartered apple and his stinky bag of crisps, his smile restored.

Gordy was in the garden, leaning on the wide rake with his jeans tucked into his boots and wearing the moth-eaten jersey that had once been a favourite. She liked the way he looked and smiled as she parked behind his Landy.

'That's a good thing to do, rake up all the leaves and stop the rot, better to let the grass breathe.' She admired the large pile of russet leaves heaped on the edge of the drive.

'I remembered.' He smiled, holding her gaze for a second longer than someone who was looking to cut and run. It warmed her. 'Hey, Ted!'

'Do you need me to come and cut some wood?' the boy asked, clearly remembering Gordy's previous instructions, as he shrugged off his coat and let it drop to the floor, knowing with certainty his Aunty Pickle would be there to pick it up.

'I do indeed. We're running low.' He watched as Ted ran to retrieve his wellington boots from the back of the car. Turning to face her, he let the rake drop and walked over until they were almost touching. 'I've got it.' He reached out and touched a wisp of hair that had worked its way loose from her ponytail.

'You've got what?'

'The answer!' He pulled her to him, holding her fast against the rough wool of his jersey, which smelled of moss and woodsmoke. 'We need to keep our promises, Nora. All the things we ever said and all the things we planned. To love each other, to make a future, to get a dog . . . we made promises and we have to go back to that. That's the answer.'

'Is it that simple?' She closed her eyes, not wanting to be the one who threw another grenade into this moment of rekindling.

He held the tops of her arms and pulled away, addressing her directly. 'It is that simple, but not necessarily easy. And I reckon it's a bloody good place to start! We remember all that we planned and all that we loved about each other, and we talk, Nora, we talk until we figure out how to get back to that time when we weren't stuck, when the Ferris wheel went round and round, and we laughed and enjoyed the ride.'

'You don't like the Ferris wheel,' she reminded him as he bent forward to kiss her gently on the mouth.

'I don't, but I love you, Leonora Brightwell. I really love you.'

Nora clung to him, feeling for the first time since she'd left Cyprus that the ground beneath her feet was solid.

'I love you too.'

'Come on, Gordy!' Ted called impatiently from the garden path.

'I'll see you in a bit.' He leaned in and kissed her once more with such promise it sent flutters of joy down into her gut.

'I guess I'll go make supper.' Watching the twosome lope off to chop wood, she considered all the promises they had made; promises that over the last few weeks had felt unattainable: to always communicate, to spend time together, to support each other and to listen . . . Gordy was right, they needed to get back to that. Her heart swelled at the thought that for now, the D word was erased from their vocabulary. She walked into the house with a spring in

267

her step, this lovely old house with a fireplace that needed disguising, and a place for her plants to flourish, her new home . . .

◆ ◆ ◆

'Drive safely!' It was raining on Monday morning when Gordy kissed her on the cheek and closed the driver's door of the once shiny hire car, where the mud from the tracks around their semi-rural Wiltshire home now clung in licks to the wheel arches and grille.

'Always do.' Nora smiled at him as the rain hit the side window, blurring him into a khaki smudge. She pressed the button and it whirred down a little, the droplets finding their way in and landing on the dashboard. She stared at the man who had again given Ted, now sitting in the back of the car in his school uniform, the most memorable weekend. They had, according to the excited debrief over supper, scrambled across the forest floor with full camo cream smeared over their faces, just in case the enemy were hiding behind the saplings or the baddies were littering the path on which squaddies, who often shared rooms and were in want of a little privacy, liked to loiter with their partners. Ted had returned to the house bouncing with energy and enthusiasm for the mission, having crawled over mud and twigs with a yellow wooden rifle. Despite still being mightily impressed with his PlayStation, it was good to know that he got just as much out of crawling around in nature. It was a week since Jason had called her into school for a chat and there had been no more little accidents of a bathroom nature. She was glad. All she needed to figure out now was how to get him in front of his mum; they had spoken on the phone, but a promise was a promise.

'See you on Friday, Gordy!' Ted called out. Gordy bent low and pushed his face to the gap in the window.

'See you then, soldier!' His stiff salute was met by a sound imitation from their nephew.

She couldn't deny the surge of attraction she felt at this softening of the man. The way he took time, invested patiently in Ted, giving the child the very best weekend as a balm to the tricky weekdays at home without his mum. They had again had sex, which was urgent, intense and satisfying, and the joy of it lingered still in her veins, tingled in her toes and she knew would make her smile on those mornings when she woke on the blow-up mattress with a stiff back, wishing she were in Westbury and within reaching distance of her husband. It felt a lot like a beginning for them. There was no doubt Gordy had been right when he'd said something needed to shift, and this felt like a new dawn, a rewind where if they got it right, they could only emerge stronger as a couple. It was a glorious, warming thought.

'Call me.' He held her gaze in a knowing look and she giggled.

'I'll call you.'

'I mean it, call me!' He folded down his three middle fingers and with his thumb and pinkie outstretched blinked and held his fist up to his ear, doing his best to imitate a teen on the pick-up. She laughed again. What *was* this? This flirtation, this harmony, this desire? As a couple, the old adage that 'absence makes the heart grow fonder' had been tested with regularity when Gordy was posted to hot and dusty places, while she languished on borrowed army-issue furniture and dreaded and longed for his return in equal measure. But this was different, entirely different. They were apart, yes, but it was more than that, they had changed – she had changed. Her self-reliance, the taking on of responsibility and seeming to do a good job was a factor. Who knew? Maybe she had shed a few prickles, maybe caring for Ted and letting her guard down was the key. As the car pulled out of the lane, she waved goodbye and honked the horn with a certain melancholy in her heart at the thought of five whole days until she could reach for him again.

'How you doing back there, Ted?'

He yawned. 'I'm okay.'

'You can sleep if you want to, we have an hour or so journey ahead, and I've got your breakfast right here when you fancy it.'

It was Monday morning, and the plan was to head straight to school. A spur of the moment decision, but one that gave them an extra day and night with Gordy and therefore welcomed by them both. Kiki had finally chatted to Ted on the phone yesterday and he had come alive! His little legs jumping in joy, as he curled on to the sofa. She had left them alone to talk, overhearing him download his news to his mummy. '. . . and then Gordy and me jumped down and it was really far and mud splashed up and went all over my jeans and I told him about my PlayStation and FIFA, which I'm going to get really good at, I'm going to beat Rafe's sister!' He barely took a breath. There was no denying the chat with Kiki had settled him like nothing else. The memory of it warmed this early, rainy start.

'I won't sleep. I'm not tired . . .' His last words before his head flopped to the padded side of his car seat and he closed his eyes, snoring soon after.

She smiled at the sight of him in her rear-view mirror, feeling less fearful now of travelling with a little one in tow, still aware of the responsibility of him, but it wasn't something that scared her, not any more. It was as if by spending time in Kiki's life and having started to heal her relationship with Gordy, she realised that she didn't need permission to show love, to feel love. She might be a prickly pear, but what was it he had said? '*You beat the odds, Nora, you are incredible in spite of your less than perfect upbringing, in spite of all the things that would break lesser mortals, that deep level of rejection – you're wonderful . . .*' Just the memory of this was enough to calm her, make her feel warmer. It was now about how she could made Kiki and Ted feel the same.

With her nephew fed and having seen him happily run into school with Afsar, Zac and Rafe, she dropped the car at the hire garage across town and apologised for the mud to the nice young chap with whom she was on quite friendly terms. Taking a slow walk back to the flat on the route she knew well, and having purloined a fat almond croissant for her lunch, Nora sipped on a double espresso in its paper cup. She felt . . . happy. Content in a way that had, prior to coming back from Akrotiri, been a dim and distant memory.

As she drew closer, with the brown paper bag containing a croissant dangling from her teeth and her coffee in one hand, fishing in her bag for the front door keys, she saw a person inside the gate. It took a second to place the face, as was often the case when you didn't expect to see someone, or you saw them in an unexpected place and your brain was forced to recalculate, trying to match the location and identity.

Running now, she shoved the croissant in her bag and reached out.

'Kiki! Oh! Oh Kiki!' Stopping abruptly, she ran her fingers over her sister's wan face, her touch light, overly aware of her physical frailty, her fragility. She looked so pale and so thin inside the grey jogging bottoms and sweatshirt that swamped her; her eyes, however, were huge and searching. Nora worried that she might fall, as if a strong gust might knock her down. 'How are you here? What's happening? I don't know whether to be delighted or petrified!' As ever her truth slipped from her lips.

'I didn't want to be there any more. I couldn't stand it. I missed Ted so much. I couldn't sleep, I just wanted to come home. And when I spoke to him yesterday . . . I just had to see him!'

'Oh darling, come in, come in, he will be so happy! You have no idea how much he's missed you!' With the keys in her fingers, she forged ahead to the front door; it felt odd to be inviting her sister into her own home.

Kiki shuffled forward, her head bowed, her hair, in need of a wash, falling over her eyes and her feet moving as if they were clad in concrete. Her step was hesitant and Nora understood why. Her eyes darted to the closed bathroom door and Nora guessed that, like her, she was picturing herself in her waterlogged underwear, the red bath, the splats on the tiles . . .

'I can't believe they didn't tell me you were coming home! I'd have come and picked you up! I had the hire car until an hour ago.'

'I discharged myself. Got a cab.'

This information was enough to send a watery wave of worry around her gut – was her sister ready to be home? How was it best to care for her? Broken bones, bugs and physical ailments Nora could take in her stride, but a broken head? That was a whole other story.

'It smells really nice in here.' Kiki stood in the lounge and gave the first flicker of a smile. Able to look her sister squarely in the face for the first time, Nora took in the dark bruises of fatigue and ill-health that sat beneath her eyes like purple moons.

'You look so tired.'

Kiki nodded and closed her eyes briefly. 'I am. I really am.'

Nora felt the sharp nudge of anxiety, unsure how best to care for this woman who might right now need more than she could give. She would have felt different if the hospital had discharged her, but the fact that she had done a runner . . . 'Kiki.' Reaching out, Nora placed her hands on the tops of her sister's arms as her sibling fell against her, resting her head on her chest, with her arms dangling down by her sides and her full weight supported by Nora.

'Did . . . did Mum smell like you, I wonder? I often think things like that. Did she look more like you or me? And did she smell like you? I imagine she did.'

Nora closed her eyes, knowing this was where they started to lay the foundations for their future, by her answering questions just like this, by having these discussions, by facing them head on. Just as she had told Ted that it was okay to be sad, validating his fears and worries, she needed to do the same for her sister who had her own sad legacy that needed exploring. Nora spoke into her sister's scalp, which carried a rather medicinal scent mixed with sweat. It was unpleasant but of small consequence in the face of having her sister home.

'I do look like her a bit; I'm tall like her and Granny Magda, and as for her smell . . .' *What do I remember: wine, cigarillos, gin, garlic . . . nothing pleasant, unlike Luna, who always smelled of almonds . . .* 'I don't think I smell like her.'

Kiki pulled away and slumped down on to the sofa as if the effort of standing was too much.

'Would you like me to make you a cup of tea?'

Her sister nodded, her eyes sweeping the place. Nora felt a bloom of unease at the fact that she had tidied, cleaned and polished every surface to within an inch of its life. It was, she knew, invasive, assumptive, almost accusatory, as if Kiki's domestic ability, or lack of, was being highlighted, and yet it had felt like the best use of her time during the hours in which she waited for Ted.

'Ted's had a lovely weekend – we've been in Westbury, as you know. The house is great, in a forest with lots of random logs for den-building, a ready supply of army paraphernalia and Gordy, who I actually think might like playing at soldiers in the undergrowth as much, if not more, than Ted does!' she gabbled. 'We stayed over last night and watched a Ninja Turtle movie with a bowl of popcorn. I dropped him at school this morning and he had breakfast en route.' She felt her face colour. Was that overstepping the mark, taking her nephew away from his home, making decisions about his food, his travel, his viewing material? It was odd how quickly her confidence in her right and ability to make these decisions diminished in the face of his mother's return.

'Is he okay, do you think?' Kiki bit her lip.

'Yes, he is.' She decided not to mention the bed-wetting, not just yet, wanting to let Kiki get her bearings, settle in. 'He's missed you so much and has asked me every day, *twice* a day if he could visit you, and he'll be so happy you're home!' She placed two mugs on the countertop.

'But . . . Is he okay?' She elaborated on the wider question. 'How much does he know?'

It seemed Kiki didn't remember too much about their conversation in her hospital room when similar ground had been covered, or at least she needed it reiterating. Nora abandoned the tea-making and sat on the stool in front of the sofa, assuming the position Sheila had taken on that first day, which simultaneously felt like minutes and years ago. Her eyes were drawn to the tight bindings that remained around Kiki's wrists. Fresh white bandages that were again pristine and tied neatly. And again, she hated the sight of them.

'He knows you're poorly – he asked if you'd been shot. I told him you were getting better and that you would never ever have wanted to leave him, even just to go to hospital.'

It was at this statement that Kiki's face contorted, her mouth twisted and she made a sound that was part wail, part howl. It was, Nora guessed, drawn from a place where her deepest sadness lay. She matched her sweet sister tear for tear, not only at the sorrowful situation, the horror at what might have been, but also at her lack of awareness, lack of love and involvement that she felt had allowed it to escalate.

'But I *did* want to leave him, Nora, I did!' she gulped, swallowing tears and snot that snaked over her top lip and into her mouth. 'And one day he will know that. I don't know what to say to him or how to explain it!' Her eyes were instantly red, inflamed, and Nora's heart twisted to see such agony.

'You're ill, Kiki, and he will understand when he has to. He's a smart, kind boy. You have done a wonderful job of raising him. He's so proud of you.'

Her sister shook her head. 'I'm scared.'

'Me too,' Nora admitted. 'Me too.' Of what, it would have been hard to voice, but certainly fear of the unknown path that lay ahead, fear of losing her sister.

The two sat quietly as the air settled around them.

'I don't know what to ask,' Nora began, this being the truth, overly aware of her sister's mental state and wary of doing or saying anything that might not be healing. 'I don't know what's appropriate, but . . .' She took her time, wanting so badly to get the words right, words without pressure or judgement. 'Are you feeling better?'

Kiki sniffed and wiped her nose on her sleeve. 'A little bit.'

'Well, I guess that's good. A little bit better every day.' It was a tone she borrowed from Jason. Lovely Jason.

'I didn't plan it.' And just like that her sister was talking about the day, the moment, the incident, the unravelling that had led to this point in time and the subject that had up until that point been firmly off limits. It was a relief and felt a lot like progress.

'No?'

Kiki shook her head. 'I mean, don't get me wrong, I'd thought about it a few times, but more as a kind of "what if . . .". Sometimes it felt like a solution to all my problems.'

'It's not.' Nora spoke firmly, her tone wrapped in cold fear at the prospect.

'I know that now.' Her sister gave a smile, designed, Nora was certain, to reassure her. 'Or rather, I know that for now.' This admission, followed by a sharp intake of breath, was as sobering as it was honest. Nora was both shocked by and appreciative of it.

Kiki continued, 'I dropped him at school and chatted to the girls, we spoke about the fact that Ted was going in goal for the first time, which was kind of a big deal.'

Nora nodded, choosing not to divulge how marvellous it had been to see him in goal, and yes, it had been a big deal.

'I walked home quite slowly and my head was' – she picked at her cuticle – 'my head was busy, but probably no more than usual. I felt quite anxious without being able to pinpoint why. Mr Appleton waved to me out of the window, and I remember thinking that he might be the last person to see me alive and I don't know where that thought came from, but it got louder and that was when I realised that I was thinking about checking out, because of that single thought.' She sniffed her tears, Nora reached for her sister's hands and held them gently in her own. 'I came inside and the idea got bigger, and I was actually quite comforted by it, excited by it. The thought of not being here, of just going to sleep . . . it made me feel better to know that all my problems would just go away, and I could sleep.'

Nora shook her head at the sorrow of it, not only at how unaware she had been, but also the potential waste of Kiki's wonderful, wonderful life: her son, her friends, the chance for them to connect as sisters . . . and how much she was loved!

'What problems, Kiki? Tell me about them.'

Her sister exhaled and looked at their conjoined hands. 'That's just the thing, nothing big. It's not like I have one giant issue. I see people who are physically ill coping, coping well! Fi wrestles with matters of the universe and takes it in her stride, Sheila has her hands full with two kids and lives in a grotty place, Mina and her family have been through a lot, and then there's me. What problems do I really have? But no matter how much I tell myself this, life feels . . .' She paused. 'Life often feels like it's all too much.'

Nora pictured herself alone on the beach or watching reruns of *Midsomer Murders* alone, doing her level best to avoid the likes of Jasmine Leech.

'I understand that.'

'And that morning, I walked in, looked around the flat, which was in a state, and the thought of washing the dishes or changing the bed linen or doing the laundry . . . none of it insurmountable, but at that moment it was overwhelming, all of it, and I wanted my thoughts to stop. I wanted everything to stop. I wrote a note, a couple of notes, I got the legal stuff and left it on the side. I just wanted to go to sleep and not' – her tears came thick and fast – 'I wanted to go to sleep and not wake up . . .'

'You poor love, I hate, hate to think of you on that morning, hate to think of you that sad.' Nora knew she had had off days, sad days, but had never ever come close to thinking that to check out might be an option.

'I wasn't sad,' her sister interjected, her gaze now steady. 'I wasn't sad, Nora, I was numb. Sad would have been an upgrade; I was numb, and I'd had enough.'

Nora swallowed. 'You didn't think about Ted or—'

'I told you, I didn't think about anyone or anything, I was numb. There were no consequences, no concern, no plan. It was like I was already dead, frozen. Nothing.'

'You are not nothing, Kiki, you are not nothing. You're Ted's mum, you're Sheila, Fi and Mina's friend and you're my little sister.' She couldn't help the crack to her voice. 'You're my sister.'

'You don't . . . you don't feel like my sister.'

'I . . .' Kiki's words were like a slap. 'I don't?'

'No, not really. I feel like I'm on my own.'

'But you're not.'

Her sister shrugged as if Nora's words were of little interest.

'You're not on your own. I know it has felt that way and it's felt that way for me too for much of my life, but things are going to be different. I'm going to be here for you. I want you to feel like I'm your sister!' She held Kiki's gaze. 'I can do better. I will do better,' Nora whispered.

'It'll take time, I guess, and being here, times like this. You just being here, it's nice.' Kiki tucked her hair behind her ear and tried out a smile.

'Okay.' Nora sniffed. 'Shall I make that tea?'

'Please.' Kiki nodded and took a deep breath.

Nora was glad of the chance to go to the kitchen area to mentally regroup; this kind of open exchange was rare and important in equal measure. She needed to try to stop her hands from trembling. Working in silence, she felt the presence of Kiki in her own home almost like an unwelcome thing, which simultaneously made her feel guilty and wretched. It was she who had no right to be there, an interloper in this borrowed life, and it flew in the face of all she had promised, but it was the truth: it had felt easier to 'be' in her sister's home alone, finding her feet. To be starting over with Kiki observing felt a little like taking a couple of steps backwards.

'It's weird for me,' Kiki began, 'you being here, in the kitchen, knowing where everything is.'

'For me too, although not as weird as when I first turned up.'

'We've never been those people, have we? Never been sisters who are in and out of each other's homes, calling each other to catch up on nothing much, friends.'

'I guess not. I've always lived far away from you. But it's been more than that for me. You reminded me of some bad times, Kiki, feelings that seem to have been locked in since I was a teenager.' It was, she knew, vital to speak the truth, to rip off the Band-Aid beneath which years of hurt and denial had been festering. 'But now I think that avoiding you or adopting an "out of sight, out of mind" policy, has done me more harm, done *us* more harm. I want to be in your life, and I want you in mine. We can make up for it. I hope we can.'

'I hope we can.' Kiki sat up a little straighter. 'I guess our age gap didn't help when we were younger, different generations almost, but now we're older . . .'

'Yes. I only ever saw you as a baby in my mind, until you weren't and by then' – she put the milk back in the fridge and spoke to its confines, far easier than addressing Kiki – 'we were already miles apart in every sense.'

'You disappeared after I ran into the road. Hardly came up to see us.'

Nora closed her eyes briefly before taking the tea and handing a mug to her sister, who coiled her legs beneath her on the sofa in the way Ted did.

She pictured herself sitting wordlessly sobbing with Kiki in her arms. '*She hit the car . . . I saw it . . . she hit the car . . . I heard the sound . . .*'

'That day . . .' She heard again the sound of the car screeching to a halt, Kiki crying and Mrs Deveraux repeating, '*She'll be bruised, lass, but ain't nothing broken! She's fine! She's crying! She's crying, love!*' as though it was a good thing. 'It changed lots of things for me. I knew I couldn't be trusted to look after a little one, and Nana Dilly confirmed that because not only did she pick you over me, but she said that I was just like my mother, who she blamed for Dad's life, Dad's death.'

'She was grieving.'

'Yes, we both were.' Nora sipped her tea.

Then the image of Nana Dilly running up the road with her shopping bag in her hand and her face . . . her face was thunder.

Nora had felt something inside her snap. Nana Dilly had been her haven, until that moment when she knew nothing would be 'fine' again.

'Nana Dilly was the last connection to my old life, a family life, an odd family, but the only one I'd got. The way she looked at me, spoke to me . . .'

'She was afraid.'

'Yes, we both were,' Nora echoed, taking her time. 'But she was an adult and I was a little girl who had been through a lot. It was a deep and hurtful rejection and I kept everyone at arm's length after that, knowing how their affections could turn. It felt safer to put up walls, build barriers with people who wanted to be my friend, with my husband to a degree and even with you. I couldn't cope with anyone else cutting me loose.'

'That's so sad.'

'It is.' Nora smiled weakly.

'I remember that day. And it's weird, I was only afraid because everyone else seemed freaked out. I don't fear death, Nora. I mean I can see that the ripples it would cause for those left are hard, but I don't fear it.'

'In all honesty, I wish you did.' She took a sip of the tea.

'I could have been in that car. I think about that a lot.' Kiki blinked.

Nora knew she referred to her parents and the fateful day they skittered down the mountainside. And just like that she heard the knock on the classroom door, remembered the older girl marching her along the corridor to Matron's office where Sister Edwina, head of school, a police officer and the matron herself were all waiting . . .

'But you weren't.' She focused back on the conversation. 'You weren't in that car.'

'But I could've been, and I wouldn't have known any different, wouldn't have known a life, and I sometimes think that might have been easier.'

This admission was like a knife to Nora's gut, the thought that her little sister, who she thought was too young to be as scarred by events as she was, carried her own heavy damage. 'You wouldn't have got Ted, wouldn't have got to be his mum, so surely it's worth it for that alone.'

Kiki closed her eyes as more tears found their way through her lashes and on to her cheek.

'You weren't in that car, Kiki. You were given a glorious shot at life, saved!'

'I was with Luna, we were in the house. "Luna" is just another name. I don't remember anything about her.'

'I do, she was lovely.'

'Did she have kids?'

'Yes, older than me, than us, and I guess she went home to them at night, but that didn't occur to me when I was little; she was so vital to me, so intrinsic to my daily life that I figured it must be reciprocated. It was only years later that I considered the fact that looking after me and then looking after you, cleaning the house, preparing supper and whatnot, was just her job and at the end of the day she got to go home and tell her family all about the crazy goings-on at La Fosca.'

'Why was it crazy?' Kiki used the word sharply, a reminder of where she had come from and how recently.

'Mum and Dad were . . .' – she wanted to phrase it accurately – '. . . preoccupied. He was considered this great artist, a visionary – in our house, at least.' She was aware of the hurtful nature of her words, but when she was hurting over the facts, it somehow felt justified. 'And it was as if Mum thought that gave him some kind of magic, she revered him and it was all about their wants, their social life, their parties, their guests. Their appetites. I was just a pain.' She cursed the thickening of her throat; it was hard to say, even now, despite her attempt at bravado.

'Why do you think that?' Her sister sat forward, interested.

'Because they only gave me a tiny bit of their attention and their energy and there were times when I could have been in danger.' *Like roaming the corridors in the dead of night, being left alone to bump into Señor Agostí who thankfully was kind, but could so easily not have been.* 'Dad never painted me, never. I mean, why not? He painted complete strangers but not me! I guess he didn't want to spend time with me. And they'd get drunk or high and if the place burned to the ground and I was in bed unable to get out, they wouldn't have known or been able to do anything about it. I felt kind of scared most of the time, but never really knew why. It was only as I aged that I realised how lucky I was that something terrible didn't befall me.'

'Like rolling off the track in a car and being smashed to pieces.' Kiki reminded her what could so easily have been her ending.

'Yes, something like that.' She pulled a face, aware again of what her sister had carried. And whether this conversation was timely, considering she'd only just arrived home.

'Do you have anything of theirs, of Mum and Dad's?' Kiki asked with a note of hope that was heartbreaking.

'No, I think everything was left in the villa or got rid of – all dad's work. I think the furniture and things belonged to the house, but their personal effects . . .' She tried to picture what they did own. 'I guess they were given away. I do have Granny Magda's kimono that I borrowed to take to school, still wear it, but no, nothing of our parents.'

'That's a shame.' Kiki picked at her nails.

'What would you like of theirs?' Nora was curious.

Kiki shrugged. 'I don't know, anything, something . . . just something. I'd like to see his art.' She yawned, as if events were catching up with her.

'Are you sure you want to talk, darling? Would you like a nap or—'

'No.' Kiki shook her head. 'I've had too much time to nap, to think. I want to talk. I need to talk. Tell me more about how you feel, about Mum and Dad.'

'I still worry about so many things, feel anxious, and hate how easily so many bad things *could* have happened. There were always dangers dotted around the place and Mum and Dad were often less than attentive.' She pictured the honey-coloured glow of the candles in Moroccan lanterns around the inner courtyard, while her parents lay sprawled and inebriated on the tiles, but rather than dwell on it, she said, 'I've started to realise that it was nothing to do with me. It wasn't my fault. I was just a little girl who needed more, needed better, but Mum and Dad's choices were just that. I need to let it go, look forward, find the good, *appreciate* the good. And Ted will do the same.'

'He'll know about my bad choices . . .' Kiki bit her fingernail and ripped it with her teeth.

'He will. But he will know they were made under the fog of illness, and he will know that he is loved. Loved by you. Big difference. In fact, to me that would have made all the difference. If I'd thought they loved me but just didn't show it in a conventional way or were too preoccupied, but just to know I was in their thoughts, it would have been everything.'

'You don't think they loved you?' Kiki asked with her face screwed up, as if this had not occurred to her.

'It was as if the message was, "*We don't care if we live or die or what happens next or how it might affect Leonora* . . ." Selfish, and that's not love.' She cursed the warble to her voice, aware also of her judgement on her parents who seemed to dice so casually with her safety when Kiki had done that very thing to Ted, but it was different: Kiki was ill, her parents just lax.

'So do you think they loved *me*?' Kiki's expression was so hopeful, so innocent, it could have been Ted asking and it folded Nora with distress. How she wanted to plug these gaps of sadness for her sister, to fill her up and show her that she was worthy of love, his love, no matter her start in life, just as Gordy had done for her.

Nora wiped her eyes on her sleeve, her distress was visceral – it wasn't easy to revisit this time, to share this with Kiki. 'I distinctly remember when you were born, coming home for the holidays and the way Dad spoke to you and the way Mum and Luna looked at you and I would say they loved you, Kiki. They did. I'm sure of it.'

'Because I was still too little to be a nuisance?'

'Possibly.' Nora pictured her six-year-old self, wandering the halls of the villa in the dark, wondering where her mummy was as the cicadas chirped their night song, so desperate for a pee she would do it in a closet.

Her sister shrugged. 'It makes no difference to me really. Nana Dilly was my whole world and then when she died, I started to unravel.'

'You did?' Kiki's cool response was troubling to say the least.

'Uh-huh. I started to have dark thoughts and started to want to disappear. That's when it started. I was seventeen and had a lot going on.'

'Why didn't you tell me?' she asked softly.

Kiki looked her in the eye. 'Do you know you say things like that all the time: *why didn't you tell me? Why didn't you let me know? Why didn't you say something?*' Kiki tucked her hair behind her ears. 'Well, why didn't you *ask*, Nora? Why didn't you *find* out? Why didn't you *say* something? Why didn't you *ask* your little sister how

284

she was faring? Whether she had ever stood on a bridge over the motorway and felt the attraction of plummeting down and down.'

'Kiki . . .' Guilt lapped at her heels and hammered in her chest. She remembered when Dilly died and feeling so sad that the final link to her parents had gone, and so had the chance to rebuild a relationship with her nana, but she had also felt a little relieved: never would she have to face the woman again and see the disappointment tinged with fury in her eyes, as if she, Nora, were in some way responsible for her beloved son's death.

'You seem to think you were hard done by, losing your parents at twelve, but I was only seventeen when I lost Nana Dilly and had to move from Midland Road; I didn't realise for many years that it was only rented, ex-local authority, and the landlord wanted to sell. She was all I had, all I knew, and if I hadn't met Richie . . .' She shook her head. 'It was easy for everyone to tell me how much they disliked him, but he was the one who scooped me up, gave me shelter for all those wonderful years before I got pregnant and then we had Ted and he was the icing on the cake for me.' This admission caused tears anew. 'But after Nana's funeral, you just painted a new life and stepped into it and that was it – you were gone! Mrs Gordy Brightwell!'

'I told you to come and visit any time!'

'Yes, but people say lots of things. It didn't feel like you meant it, you didn't follow it up, make a plan.'

Kiki was right and her words cloaked Nora in shame. 'I guess it felt easier to put it all behind me and follow Gordy like a bird chasing summer, never looking back.'

'Yes, that's exactly what it felt like. And with your husband's big old title and fancy houses in great places, you just went, Nora – it was like you disappeared! And communication was sporadic. Sending me the odd card that hinted of a life I couldn't begin to imagine. And I didn't begrudge you it, not a minute of it, I was happy for you! But I can't pretend it made things any easier for me, knowing you were racing ahead in life, even further out of reach. And all while I was figuring out how to stay upright.'

'I'm sorry. I am. I'm so sorry.' Her voice was low from the sadness that swamped her.

Kiki sucked her teeth. 'And the odd time you came here, I was so paranoid about living in a rubbish flat, not like the flat in Maida Vale, which even though we share it has never felt like mine. I mean I have absolutely zero recollection of Granny Magda.'

The woman had passed away soon after her daughter and had only met Kiki once, and with Nana Dilly and Granny Magda fiercely blaming the other's child for the death of their own, relations had been, to put it mildly, strained. They were opposing camps and each sister had unwittingly picked a side.

'It never occurred to me. I always think of the flat as ours, the rent is split fifty–fifty and we discuss any arrangements or new tenants or—'

'It's not that.' Kiki shook her head, her tone adamant. 'I just never knew Magda, just like I never knew Mum and Dad, that's the point.'

'So how can I fix it?' Nora's question and interest was genuine.

'How can you fix it?' Kiki laughed briefly. 'Do you mind if we go outside so I can smoke?'

'Sure.'

They stood and Kiki opened the French doors wide to let the chill of the blue autumnal sky whip around the room. She lit a cigarette and drew on it like it was nectar. 'You can't fix it. It's done. But it's hard for me that Magda never thought of me as part of the family, never saw me as her granddaughter, not part of their lives – Nana Dilly told me that.'

'I don't know if that's true. I mean, that might only be Dilly's take on it.'

'They rowed and Magda said I was just a blip, an afterthought.' Kiki drew on the cigarette again. 'And she was right in a way; I arrived too late and was too little to count, and that's kind of how I viewed myself too, but I am here, Nora! I *am* part of this family!' She jostled the cigarette between her fingers, which Nora suspected was part prop. Her sister's words focused her. It was astounding that Kiki, too, felt adrift, both of them in their own way longing for the comfort and security of a family.

'You are. And we are a tiny family. That much I've learned over the last few weeks. And that's why we need to support each other, help each other, pick up the slack and provide shelter. We need to encourage each other and help carve something beautiful out of the ashes that Guy, Nessa, Dilly and Magda left behind.'

'That's what I wish for, Nora, what I've always wished for. For me and for Ted.'

'It's not too late.' She scooted closer to her sister along the step. 'I've loved being part of Ted's life and I want to be part of yours if you let me.'

The two sat with chests heaving and tears falling, as their words settled like dust around them. Silence was their balm until eventually Kiki rested her head on Nora's shoulder. It was an act so intimate and trusting, it moved her.

'I'll let you. I need you. Ted needs you.'

Nora placed her arm around her sister's narrow shoulders, knowing they had a lifetime of catching up to do. It brought peace, her thoughts calmed and her breathing slowed. It felt a lot like coming up for air without ever realising that she'd been drowning.

'Thank you for looking after my boy, I can never thank you enough.'

Nora knew she would lock away her sister's words for the longest time, letting them warm her gently and helping to thaw the cold kernel of rejection that had sat in her gut for the longest time.

She had cared for her nephew, and she had done a good job, she knew it!

'He's wonderful.' She sniffed. 'You've raised a great little human.'

'So far.' Kiki sat back and looked up at her.

'So far,' she conceded.

'I'm glad you're here, Nora.'

'There's something I have to tell you, Kiki.' She coughed to clear her throat.

'Sounds ominous.' Her sister sat up straight and flashed the megawatt smile that she was famed for.

'When Richie came here, he said he wants to sell the flat.' It was as much detail as she thought appropriate to share on her sister's first day out of hospital.

'He wants to sell the flat?' Kiki looked around the walled garden where Nora was certain all her memories echoed, as they did anywhere when the prospect of leaving loomed.

'Yes. That's what he said.'

'His timing is perfect.' She flicked ominously at the little white bow on the bandage that swaddled her wrist. 'I've . . . I've got a bit behind on the rent.'

'I can help you out.'

Kiki cut her short. 'The rent money from Magda's and what I earned in my little jobs was always more than enough to cover my bills, but the more ill I felt, the less I could work and then bills built up and it just all . . .' She shook her head.

'We'll figure something out.' There it was again, that stock phrase. 'We could . . . we could sell Magda's flat? Then you'd have the cash to buy this one?'

'You'd do that for us?'

'I would.' She meant it. 'I'll do whatever it takes, apart from sit on this step a moment longer. I'm bloody freezing!'

The two laughed as they rose. Kiki stubbed out her cigarette and tossed the butt into a wintering hydrangea, before shutting the doors. They made their way to the sofa.

'I'm scared, Nora.' Her sister slipped from the cushions, and sinking down on to the floor, she fell against her sister's shins and lay her troubled head on Nora's lap.

Reaching out, Nora smoothed the hair from Kiki's face. 'What are you scared of?' She hardly dared ask.

'I'm scared that I might feel like that again, like the world is too much and like I just want to go to sleep, want to take flight, want to disappear . . .'

'Well, we shall have to work very hard to make sure this is not the case. You have a lot to live for, Kiki.' *We both do.*

Her sister looked up at her with so much hope in her eyes it was almost painful to witness. 'I hope so, I really hope so. And Nora?'

'Yes?' She braced herself for more revelations.

'I don't want to see anyone. I want to see Ted, but I don't want visitors, I'm not ready . . . I know it was Sheila who—' She swallowed. 'But I'm not ready.'

'That's okay.' She ran her hand over her sister's scalp. 'You don't have to see anyone. Not until you're ready. But when you are, you have those women who love you and who will hold you up and lift you high until the storm has passed. That's what friends do.'

CASA PINO

Mateo trod the wide marble stairs to the upper floor of the villa. Since a small boy, he had liked to place his foot in the slight well in the centre of each tread, to feel the comforting smoothed edge worn by generations before him. It helped him feel closer to his heritage and all the Agostí men and women who had gone before, rushing up or climbing down this very staircase for a million different reasons.

Yes, it helped him feel closer to his family, but also it made him feel less alone, as he sometimes did in this big old house where ghosts waited around every corner, his mother's laughter lurked behind closed doors and the scent of previous celebrations wafted from still and silent kitchens . . . It bothered him that he would likely never father a future Agostí who might also one day set their foot in the same place his shoe now trod. Never share this life.

Confident enough to know he wasn't unpleasant to look at and that he had a smart enough head on his shoulders, he had still not found the person he wanted to settle down with. And now in his forties, it all felt a bit futile, and his enthusiasm for dating had waned. It was all so predictable: the bland and clichéd conversation over glasses of wine at social events, the mixed doubles with women who either let him win trying to curry favour or played fiercely to beat him as if trying to prove their worth – neither was appealing to him. He had wined and dined many eligible, pretty things who would show what he perceived to be flaws so deep that he would be planning his exit strategy before they had reached dessert. And these flaws were to him non-negotiable: vanity, self-absorption, a sense of entitlement . . .

There had been some relationships that had lasted a short while. Savannah, for example, who had been a fun companion and the sex had been fantastic, but then on her very first visit to Casa Pino had detailed how she would, given the chance, redecorate the rooms, pointing at the vine-clad stone columns that lined the lemon grove and suggesting they could be removed for a deck with a bar. He had stuttered, unable to find the words that might relay his utter abhorrence at her lack of empathy for such a classical home. No, Savannah had not been the one. And then there had been Emilia who had sipped wine, danced until dawn and made him roar with laughter, until he realised she didn't eat, didn't, in fact, like eating or cooking or food! He couldn't imagine a life lived without great food and the celebration of food at the heart of all he did. No, Emilia with her fantastic laugh and dancing feet had not been the one.

Not that his single status was something that overly consumed him, it was more a background hum of frustration in an otherwise charmed life. And today, he had more pressing things to worry about, like the fact that his father needed to be ferried into town for his hospital appointment. And the frustration that he was still no closer to returning his beloved artwork to Guy's children made his papá an irritable and preoccupied companion.

So, what's new? He smiled to himself.

With his mind concerned with bringing the car around to the front, and the slow descent down the stairs where he would support his papá in the way that worked for them both and which they had figured out over time – a keen lean to the left with their arms crooked, preserving dignity while providing safety – Mateo didn't enter the bedroom with caution or trepidation as was his usual way. Instead, he strolled in, a small smile playing on his mouth, a positive stance required he knew to cajole his father through what needed to happen that morning.

It was therefore heart-stoppingly jolting to find his beloved papá slumped forward at his mother's dressing table. His wide bottom sat squarely on the padded footstool, his catheter stand had toppled and his arms formed a cradle that supported his large head. A bottle of his mother's scent had been knocked over, spilled, the smell of it strong. As if her presence was never more obvious.

'Papá!'

Racing forward he lifted the man into an upright position, before gently lowering him to the floor and placing a soft, silk pillow under his head. He was alive, his father's guttering breath told him he was not too late, and this alone was enough to calm his naked fear.

'*Quédate quieto,* Papá. Just stay still and I'll call an ambulance!' He reached for his phone while his papá reached up and took his hand, rendering him unable to dial. His pulse raced with urgency.

'No, *hijo*, no time . . .'

'Don't say that! You're going to be fine.' He found a false smile and kept it in position. 'I'll call the doctor and we'll get you into hospital, and—'

Santiago slowly shook his head and stared at him. It was only in hindsight that Mateo would consider how even now, in these, his papá's final moments, he was still trying to placate, to bolster, to paint the positive, wanting to be the best he could be for this lion of a man, to make him proud. Santiago gripped his hand as tightly as he was able, and Mateo bent low to properly hear his whispers.

It took Santiago every last drop of effort to form words, to communicate with the final breaths that filled his failing lungs.

'Two things . . . two things, *hijo* . . . The painting, the painting has to go back to them . . . and the second—' He stopped speaking and screwed his eyes shut as the pain of departure knocked on his earthly door and invited him in.

'Papá? Papá?' Mateo couldn't stop the tears that ran down his face and landed on his papá's shirt front.

'I want you to . . . I want you to find . . .'

'You want me to find what?' Mateo held his breath as if this might better help him hear the old man's final words.

His papá did not speak. Instead, he reached past his son and gazed over his shoulder with a lift to his fingers and his arm out-stretched, as his face broke into a smile; the lines of pain criss-crossing his brow had gone, his mouth full, his eyes almost bright as he settled back on the pillow. The scent of his mother again filled the room most powerfully, and as Santiago Agostí took his last breath on earth, his muscles seemed to soften and he slumped backward, relaxed, resigned and happy as he travelled home . . .

CHAPTER TEN

Rushing to make sure she got to the school gates on time, Nora sped along the pavement. Fi and Mina waved from their usual spots.

'Nora!' Mina yelled, holding up her hand. 'Stay right where you are! Don't move an inch!' Nora, more than a little alarmed, slowed and came to a standstill, wondering what was going on.

'Why?' she called out, looking awkwardly towards the group of parents on the other side of the street who heard her yell, as her heartbeat increased, fearful of what Mina had seen or had to tell.

'Because,' Mina hollered back, 'you're nearly late and for the first time in as long as I can remember it won't be me! It'll be you, Miss Cool Knickers, who hasn't quite judged the journey time right. Please, Nora, just stay there! Just for a minute. I need this win!'

Nora laughed and walked briskly towards the women she'd been eager to see, to catch up with and to share her news that Kiki was home, because sometimes it was good to talk to the women who walked in her shoes, the women who got it. She looked at her watch. 'Not today, Mina, your tardy crown is still intact.'

'How was your day?' Fi asked while eating a bar of chocolate. 'Don't mind me, I missed lunch!'

'Fi, if you missed lunch, you should be eating a sandwich, not chocolate,' Mina tutted.

'Give me a break!' Fi shoved the bar into her mouth.

'Ted and I drove back from Westbury, and when I got home, Kiki was there.'

'What?' Fi stopped chewing and Mina stared at her.

'Oh my God! How is she?' Mina asked, wide-eyed with concern.

'She's . . .' *How was she?* 'Thoughtful, reflective, glad to be home.'

'Stable, is she stable?' Fi screwed the chocolate wrapper and shoved it in her pocket.

Nora nodded, hoping this was accurate.

'And she's home for good?' Mina clarified.

'Yes.'

'What does she need? Can we pop in?' Mina asked.

'She's not up to visitors, but I promise to tell you when she is. I think what she needs is time, space and rest.'

'Of course.' Mina reached out and was there again with the arm stroke.

'That's so wonderful!' Fi clasped her hands and looked skyward.

'It is.' She gave a tight-lipped smile.

'Is it wonderful?' Fi placed a hand on her arm, which Nora covered with her own, taking warmth and strength from the contact. 'Are you worried, Nora, about her being home? Do you think she's still in danger?' Fi asked so matter-of-factly it almost winded her.

'I don't honestly know.' She borrowed the standard response that seemed popular in her family. 'But we're talking openly, about everything, and I think that's how we build the foundation, right? To try and get her on a solid footing?'

'Absolutely,' Mina encouraged. 'And you know where we are.'

'I do, thank you, Mina.'

'No worries, that's what friends are for.'

Nora nodded, knowing that this was exactly what they were – friends.

'Go gently, that's the answer, just go gently and things will seem a little bit better every day.' The vicar's words were slowly delivered and gratefully received.

The main door of school opened and out trawled the lower years with their teacher at the helm, just as Sheila arrived.

'I know one little boy who's going to be mighty glad to see his mummy.' Fi beamed.

'Who's going to be mighty glad to see his mummy?' Sheila asked casually, craning her neck to look out for Zoey and Zac.

'Ted.' Mina nodded and smiled.

'Oh my God, is she home?' And the woman who was the reason Kiki was able to come home at all, the person who pulled her back from the brink so Ted did not have to look to the sky, trying to spot his mum, an eagle flying overhead, placed her hand over her mouth, trying to contain the emotion.

'She is. She's home.'

'Oh Nora! Nora!' Sheila fell into her arms and the two women stood in a warm embrace while Fi placed her hand on Nora's back and Mina hugged Sheila. She stood for a while, gratefully accepting the love and friendship that enveloped her and from which she had no intention of trying to wiggle free.

With Ted's bag in her hand, she walked briskly as the little boy skipped ahead, running his hand over the neat hedging and low brick walls of front gardens. She knew she didn't have to stop him or remind him that sharp objects like twigs or broken bottles might be lurking in the hedge. Confident he already knew these things, her smart, smart nephew.

'I have a surprise for you, Ted. A big surprise!' She cursed the lump that gathered in her throat, a lump of emotion at how things were going to change, how she was once again, in time, going to be relegated to the role of aunty and how her life would, she knew, be less rich without living at the beck and call of this little boy; a life of glancing at the kitchen clock, working out how long until she had to leave for pick-up, how long the chicken nuggets had been in the oven and whether or not it was bedtime.

'What's my surprise? Is it a new game for my PlayStation?' He stopped to stare at her with the dark-brown liquid eyes of his mother and grandfather and the inquisitive crease at the top of his nose, *family* . . .

'No, better than that. Mummy's home.'

She watched his eyes scan her face, as if waiting for the punchline.

'She's not in the hospital?'

'No. She's feeling much better, and they've let her come home.' She bent down until their faces were level and in one swift move-ment and without hesitation she pulled him to her, holding him fast against her and feeling the beat of his young heart fluttering against her chest as his small face nestled next to hers.

'She's home right now?' he whispered in her ear.

'She's home right now, and she's waiting for you.'

He lifted his arms and held his hands around her neck, and that's how they sat on the pavement, cheek to cheek. Nora thought her own heart might burst, overwhelmed by the contact, the feel of him in her arms.

'I love you, Aunty Pickle.' His words were the sweetest ever to float into her ears and she knew she would treasure them always. Maybe this, this was what it felt like to be a mother and, in that

297

moment, she more than understood the intoxication of it. The sweet exclamation of love was tinged with sorrow that Gordy – that Gordy and she – would never hear such words from the mouth of their own child and the realisation that it was she who had denied them this one wonderful thing.

'And I love you, Ted.' She spoke the truth, sticking her tongue on her top lip to catch those darned tears; she had never been one for public crying and was not about to start now.

'I'm a bit scared,' he quietly confessed.

'I know, darling, we all are, but you know what? Whatever happens, everything is going to be okay.'

'Promise?' He pulled away and stared into her face.

'I promise.'

14 MIDLAND ROAD

'What are you doing in the dark?'

Maggie looked up at the sound of her son, Jordan, as he walked into the kitchen, his hair mussed from sleep, his face creased with the indent of a pillow on his cheek and his eyes a little hazy.

'Just having a think.' She stared at her boy who had drawn her from her thoughts.

'In the dark?'

'Since when do you need light to think? I do some of my best thinking with my eyes closed.' She looped her fingers through the wide mug handle to draw warmth from the hot cocoa into her palm and smiled at her boy. 'Anyway, it's not that dark when your eyes get used to it. I've got the light of the moon and I can see you.'

'If you say so, Mother!' He lumbered to the fridge and pulled out a plate, before peeling away the foil to reveal a heap of cold chicken wings.

'I don't know how you can eat that in the middle of the night.' She pulled a face.

'I don't know how you can sit at the table on your own in the dark in the middle of the night. But here we are!' He bit into a piece of chicken and closed his eyes as if the taste was blissful.

'My body doesn't know if it's morning or bedtime; I thought coming off nights would be easy and yet, here I am!' she echoed.

'I like you being here at night.' He spoke with his mouth full.

'You do? I'm glad, I like it too. Did you not sleep well without me here, love?' It had always been a concern.

'Not because I was scared or owt, but I used to worry about you getting the bus on your own and I didn't like the fact it was you who was in charge of that place if a fire broke out or anything.'

'Well, now I'm in charge of it during the day – just the same but with more sunshine! And what are you saying – that you don't think I'm capable?' There was the hint of jest in her tone, but she got his lovely sentiment.

'No, I'm just saying that when we're all here at night, I kind of think that me and Robbie could take care of *you* if anything bad happened. But when you're there, I don't know who'll be looking out for you.'

'You know, lovey, that is the sweetest thing to say, but it's *my* job to look after *you*. I'm the mum!' It was and always had been her role, looking out for and looking after her children, making sure they were fed, warm, safe and comfortable. She considered it the greatest privilege.

He stopped chewing. 'I think it's all of our job to look after each other, actually.'

'I think you're right, love.'

With the plate of chicken wings in his hand, he made for the stairs, his overly long pyjama bottoms grazing the cold linoleum.

'Night.'

'Night.'

She smiled after her sweet, sweet boy.

The swell of emotion came from nowhere; maybe it was because her period was due or because of Jordan being so kind, maybe it was tiredness catching up, her body clock out of sync with the shift pattern change, or maybe it was the fact that the boy's dad was having a baby . . . something he was yet to tell the kids about.

Not that she was jealous, not at all, in fact she was happy for him, truly, and his girlfriend, Keeley, seemed great and had made the boys welcome when they visited.

No, it was something more fundamental and less easy to justify. How could she begin to tell her son that she was lonely, and it was this loneliness that poked her in the chest when she woke in the morning and lay across her pillow as she slept. Loneliness that saw her creep around the aisles of the supermarket looking at a ton of fantastic produce but knowing that even if her food budget hadn't been miniscule and she *could* indulge in all the wonderful, succulent, flavoursome and generously portioned recipes that rattled around in her mind, cooking for one, as the boys kept their own hours and dived in and out of the fridge for leftovers, was just not the same.

Not having someone to cook for was, she felt, indicative of a much bigger hole in her life. She had no one to cook for, which meant no one to eat with or to hold her hand when she might need a little support, no one to take her into their arms when the night felt long, no one to think about when work was hard, no one to picture on the rainy commute home when just the thought of them was enough to lift even the most flagging spirit. It was wearing thin, all of it, and this feeling of desolation seemed to come along just as her forties were fast approaching.

This wasn't the life she had planned! Marriages broke down, people fell in and out of love, she got all that and knew that she had been blessed in so many ways: two fantastic, healthy sons, a lovely little home and a soft mattress to cocoon her aching bones at the end of a long shift, but the truth was, Maggie wanted more. Her boys would fly the nest soon enough and were such wonderful citizens of the planet, she knew they would soar! But what would that mean for her? Quieter nights and longer days. *Loneliness.*

'What *do* you want?' she whispered into the confines of the quiet little kitchen, where the clock ticked out its rhythm and the hands raced towards the wee small hours. 'I want love.' She sighed at the rarely voiced truth, running her fingertips over the faint crow's feet that were appearing at her temples. 'But where the hell are you going to find that, Maggie? Certainly not sat here in the kitchen talking to yourself!' She laughed, before downing the remains of her cocoa and washing up her mug at the sink, with a view of the garden and the rolling hills beyond, all lit by that big old beautiful moon.

CHAPTER ELEVEN

Nora didn't know what to expect for the mother and son reunion, but if she'd had to guess she would have plumped for a running through the door with open arms and a tight, long-lasting hold where words of reconnection were sincerely exchanged. But no, this was nothing like that. Initially, it was, if anything, stilted and a little awkward.

'We're home!' she called as she put the key in the door, giving Kiki as much notice as was possible to sit up, take a breath, paint on a smile, dry her tears, pull down the sleeves of her sweatshirt, whatever might be required to present the most positive face she could to the little boy who had missed her day and night.

Ted ran in and stopped short of the sofa on which his mother was curled. He shrugged his arms from his navy coat and let it drop to the floor. Nora picked it up and popped it on the peg in the hall-way. Going slowly, taking her time, she did her best to allow them the privacy of reunion. When she returned to the sitting room, she was surprised to find him still standing on the rug, staring at Kiki as if she were an exhibit and Kiki staring back, her eyes wide, crying and with her thick hair falling over one side of her face.

Nora's mouth went a little dry and she felt a surge of discomfort in her gut, realising that she needed to be the glue, the catalyst of reintroduction. Locking eyes with Kiki, there flowed a current of understanding, an awareness that this was how it would be: she would be there for her, help her and pick up the slack when needed. And it was needed now.

'Ted, Mummy is still a little under the weather, and you know how when you don't feel one hundred per cent and it makes you feel a bit, blurgh? A bit teary?'

He nodded, his chest rose and fell with the deep breaths of uncertainty and it tore at her. 'Well, it's like that, but I know what would make her feel a bit better – why don't you sit with her and pop your cartoon on while I make the supper? What do you say, Kiki, would that be a good thing, do you think?'

Kiki smiled through her obvious anguish, a smile that was both forced and fleeting as she wiped her face with her hands.

'I . . . I do.'

Ted looked away from Kiki and up at Nora, his expression a little confused, as if he had momentarily forgotten she was there.

Kiki patted the space on the sofa beside her, a new hopeful expression replaced instantly with one of gratitude as her son sank down beside her and reached for the remote control. She and Kiki exchanged a knowing look and Nora crinkled her eyes in a smile, doing her best to encourage and support without patronising.

With the cartoon burbling in the background, Kiki coughed to clear her throat and used a soft voice of reassurance, as if trying to let Ted know that she might seem a little changed, a little unfamiliar, but was in fact just the same old Mumma.

'A little bird told me you saved a goal.' Her voice was gravelly and packed with emotion, no doubt tamping down all that she tried to keep at bay and her body folded towards him, making a hollow in her shape, a space around her stomach where he used to fit so perfectly. Nora looked away, feeling a throb of loss that she would never know what that felt like.

'It wasn't a little bird who told you that, it was Aunty Pickle,' he mumbled.

'You're right, but the point is, you saved a goal!' She spoke with an enthusiasm that Nora could see took every ounce of her strength and her heart ached for them both. Ted's voice echoed with the familiar ring of anger, common to those who felt abandoned, no matter how temporarily. She recognised it as her own MO, even in recent times. Picturing the clipped latently aggressive way she had addressed Gordy, she resolved to not speak like that to him again. He deserved better. They both did. Looking at Ted, she guessed that the questions likely to be cued up on his tongue were not necessarily ones her sister wanted to hear or would be able to answer.

'It was a good save. Mr Ormond gave me house points because it was my first time in goal. Jonah said it wasn't fair because it was at football and not in school and Mr Ormond said he could give them whenever he liked, and Jonah kicked the table and had to take a time out in the reading corner.'

'Wow! Sounds like it's all been going on, but house points for goal-saving, that's really well done, Ted. And I see your tooth is still missing; any more wobblers?'

He nodded and ran his tongue over one of his bottom teeth that rocked back and forth in his young gums. It made Nora feel queasy.

'I don't want to go to the dentist though, Mum. Aunty Pickle went and the dentist stood on her chest and all her blood came out!' He spoke quickly.

'What a terrible thing!' Kiki looked at her quizzically. 'Is that what happened, Pickle?'

'Not quite.' Nora felt her blush at having been busted by her nephew.

'And how's your reading?' Kiki sounded eager to catch up.

'Good.'

'And how are Afsar and the boys doing?'

'Good.' His voice was low, barely a whisper.

Nora took her time in the kitchen, preparing supper, slowly washing mugs and refilling the tea caddy, performing any task she could think of that meant her sister and nephew had as much space as was possible in the open-plan environment, while being on hand to fill in any gaps, help build the bridge that time apart had weakened a little.

The two sat in silence as the minutes ticked by and one cartoon rolled in to another, as if her sister could think of nothing more to try and engage him, and her little boy sat next to her with a stiff spine and fixed eyes, glad of it. Kiki ran her fingers over his hair, like she was relearning the shape of her son, and no doubt replaying scenarios where she might never have got the chance to do so . . . It was beautiful and Nora looked away, feeling it invasive to watch.

'Dinner is served! Who's hungry?' Nora called with energy. 'We have fishfingers, chips and peas.'

'I'm not hungry.' Ted stared at her and seemed to have resumed the wide-eyed, caught-in-the-headlights look of alarm that had painted his face when she had first arrived.

'You say that, but when I put the scrumptious grub in front of you, you won't be able to resist!' She laughed, trying like a clown to joke her way out of the awkward atmosphere, trying to lighten the mood. 'Especially when you get to bathe everything in a sheep dip of tomato ketchup. What is it with him and ketchup, Kiki? He has it on everything!'

'Yep,' her sister whispered.

'And what about you, Kiki, fishfingers?'

'That'd be lovely, thank you,' she replied with more enthusiasm than her eyes suggested was genuine. Her movements from the sofa to the kitchen area were slow, lumbering, and anyone looking on might be excused for thinking her ailment was purely physical. 'Hospital food wasn't great.'

Ted blinked and his eye twitched, as if the reminder, the mention of the place they were all tiptoeing around was almost more than he could stand.

'Well, good news is' – Nora clapped – 'you have my cordon bleu efforts to sample from now on!'

With supper on the breakfast bar and three places set, Nora sat opposite Ted and Kiki, tucking into the food for which she had no real desire, wanting not only to fill the quiet void, but to encourage Ted to eat too.

'You're doing great,' she mouthed at her sister who gave an almost imperceptible nod in response.

Kiki held the knife and fork in her hands and toyed with a chip, but didn't eat, eventually putting the cutlery down as if even the weight of them was too much. Her words when they came were spoken from a mouth that was twisted with nerves.

'I've missed you so much, Ted. I've dreamed about being here and eating fishfingers with you.'

'What happened to your arms?' he responded, the question blurted with such urgency it had seemingly been something he had wanted to ask the moment he had arrived. This was the kind of question she had worried over earlier.

'My arms.' Kiki ran the palm of her right hand over the wide-wrapped wrist of her left, the bandage visible beneath the cuff of her sweatshirt. 'They got hurt.'

'How did they get hurt? Did you fall over?' He teased the peas with the tines of his fork, pushing until they dropped off the edge of the plate and rolled across the breakfast bar.

'Yes.' Kiki smiled briefly, unconvincingly. 'I fell over.'

'Like when Mr Appleton fell over and had to have an operation on his foot?'

'Yes, just like that.'

Nora and Kiki exchanged a look, her sister's eyes searching. Nora gave a warm smile of encouragement.

He nodded. The anxious crinkle at the top of his nose was fixed as he seemed to consider his mother's response. The air was suddenly a little sluggish as a dust of discomfort settled over them all.

'When . . . when Mr Appleton went into hospital he couldn't walk.'

'That's right,' Kiki encouraged, no doubt glad to be conversing at all. 'And we went to visit him.'

'But when he came out of hospital, he could walk, because the doctors fixed him.' He scratched his nose.

These were the succinct words from a little boy who had clearly expected his mother to come home 'fixed' and to now be jumping around the flat with joy, or at the very least tapping her foot to music like Mr Appleton had. It was hard enough for Nora to comprehend just what her little sister was going through, and she could easily understand how much harder it was for Ted. That feeling in her gut of helplessness, of being carried along by events without the power to fix anything. Her parents were dead. Kiki was going to Nana Dilly's, and she was to stay at school. All decisions made and rubber-stamped without anyone thinking to ask her opinion or offer options. It had made her feel rootless. It had made her feel stupid, as if her thoughts on the matter, on any matter, just didn't count.

'I'm not completely fixed, Ted, that's true, but I'm feeling so much better than I did and I'll feel much, much better soon. I'm sure of it.' Kiki reached out and placed her hand over the back of her son's. The bandages were wide and obvious and seemed to grow larger and brighter when being discussed.

'Do you think' – he took a stuttering breath that belied his tender years – 'do you think you might fall over again?'

Kiki's tears were instant and desperate. 'I hope not, darling.' She sniffed. 'I really, really hope not.'

When Nora spoke, her optimism bounced off the ceiling and ricocheted around them, lifting their mood. 'And the good news, Ted, is that if your mum falls over again, we shall pick her up, brush her off and stand her upright. Because that's what families do. So you don't have to worry.' She and her sister locked eyes knowingly. 'Now, I don't know about you folks but I'm ravenous!' Nora forked a lump of fishfinger into her mouth and Ted followed suit. Kiki picked up her cutlery, nibbled the chip and swallowed a couple of peas but clearly her appetite was non-existent.

'Are you going home now, Aunty Pickle?'

'No, I'm just going to clear the plates and wash the dishes—'

'I mean,' he interrupted, 'are you going back to Gordy's house now Mummy is home?'

'Oh!' She looked at Kiki, the fine details of her support and her possible withdrawal back to her own life yet to be discussed. 'Not right away and even when I do go back to Gordy's house' – she smiled at the little boy's view – 'I'm only an hour away. You and Kiki aren't going to get rid of me that easily!'

'Can I have my bath now?' Seemingly satisfied, Ted hopped down from the stool.

'I'll go run it.' Kiki walked hesitantly to the bathroom door, pausing for a second with her hand on the door frame, as if recalling the last time she had been within its confines, the horror of it . . .

'Do you want me to get his bath ready?' Nora offered brightly.

'No.' Her sister's response was considered. 'I've got it.'

Kiki's strength and determination was a reminder that this was not her life, not her home or her child and that prior to moving in to look after Ted, she was no more than an occasional visitor. She watched with something heavy lodged in her heart as Kiki and Ted disappeared behind the bathroom door, into the room that she had scrubbed and fretted over, knowing that she would be going home when the time was right, and oh how she would miss this little boy . . .

♦ ♦ ♦

With Ted splashing in bubbles, Kiki now stood next to her in the kitchen, resting in the spot where Jason had stood while they drank wine.

'I'm proud of you, Kiki, you really are doing great. Everything is an adjustment, I'm guessing, and I'm quite sure you could do without me lumbering around the place, force-feeding you fishfingers.'

'I love you being here force-feeding me fishfingers.' She pulled her sleeves over her wrists. 'I feel like I should be able to slot into where I left off and do all the things I did before, like get supper, run baths. But getting back to normal is hard.'

'I'll stay for as long as you need me to, but I don't want to overstep or outstay my welcome, or worse, stop you finding your feet.' She spoke quickly.

Kiki rubbed her brow. 'I'm glad you're here. It'd be hard with *anyone* here, but harder still if I was on my own. I mean, I love my girls but I'm dreading seeing Sheila, Fi and Mina, having to rerun what happened, and the day Sheila came in and what happened next . . .' She shook her head as if even the prospect of these wearying interactions was more than she could cope with. 'How do we go back to talking about wine and the weather after this?'

Nora sighed. 'Time will help.'

'Thing is, Nora, I'm kind of torn. I want to get back to normal, whatever that is, but I'm also scared of picking up where I left off as that was a very dark time. But *not* snapping back into shape feels like failure. Ted's right, Mr Appleton came back fixed.'

'You're not Mr Appleton. And it's not failure, it's illness and you need to get well. You need to take the time to get well. That needs to be your priority for as long as it needs to be.'

'If words of encouragement, quirky cards with mottos of self-belief and "you got this, girl!" hashtags were the cure, I'd be the happiest chick in the world right now. You don't know what it's like to come that close.' Kiki bit her trembling lip as her eyes once again brimmed.

'So, tell me.' She held her ground.

'It's like . . . it's like . . .' Kiki began, taking her time. 'Every sigh over something I've forgotten, every comment from Richie, every eye-roll from strangers when I don't have the correct change for the bus, every face-twitch when I ask for details again because my fuddled brain has stopped me getting all the information first time, all of that, all of it, all those tiny paper cuts of unkindness and impatience, they have chipped away a little bit of me and now I'm this shell, this skinny, faint thing, a shadow . . . Everyone talks about being kind, but impatience and lack of understanding are the opposite of kindness. I just need some kindness.'

'You do need kindness, and for the record I don't see you as a faint thing, a shadow. Sure, you look like you need a little bit of help, but you're still Ted's brilliant, beautiful mum.'

'Do you think so?'

'I do. Hashtag you got this girl!'

They both laughed and it eased the atmosphere. She and Kiki both looked at the floor; for all their words and efforts, this was a hard conversation to have.

'Ted's looking at me as if I'm home but I'm not really home and he's right, because that's exactly how it feels.'

'But you are home! You are, and he'll rest easier because of it.'

'God, I hope so.' Kiki looked towards the bathroom door.

311

'You have to find the fight, Kiki, and I will be right here, with Fi and Sheila, Mina, Jason, all of us cheering you on, helping you stay upright. I mean it.'

'I can do this!' Kiki gripped the countertop, her arms braced and her head hanging forward.

'You can! You can do this! You will do this!'

And I can too: one family, in it together.

They turned to see Ted wrapped in a towel in the hallway.

'You all right, mate?' Nora asked.

'I . . . I just wanted to tell you, I did a wee in my trousers at school, Mum.' He spoke so matter-of-factly, as embarrassment sent his face puce. 'They put my wet pants in a plastic bag.'

'Oh well, we've all done that, darling!' Kiki smiled. 'I've lost count of the times I've had to lob my wet pants into a plastic bag! How about you, Nora?'

'All the time. I once weed in a closet, if you can believe that!'

Her sister laughed and just like that showed a glimpse of the old Kiki, the one who believed in herself, who had such a capacity for joy and who had the whole wide world at her feet.

Ted rushed over and held his mum close. Nora looked away, feeling a heady combination of joy and envy, knowing that no matter how many big old titles her husband might have, or fancy houses in great places she might live, no matter how far her life might feel out of the reach of her sister, it was Kiki, little Kiki, who in these four walls with her son by her side did indeed have the whole wide world at her feet . . . the whole wide world.

CLOVE COURT, MAIDA VALE, LONDON

It had been eight months since Nora had packed up her small bag of belongings and left Kiki and Ted in their flat, leaving them to *figure out* life one step at a time. Eight months since she had made her way down the motorway and properly moved into their home in Westbury, Wiltshire, a county famed for its White Horses, Stonehenge and ham. That first drive away from Stroudly Green had been tricky, what with tears clouding her vision and a heart that felt like it might burst through her ribs with all it tried to contain. She missed Ted the moment she had said goodbye to him, watching him in the rear-view mirror as he hung over the gate of the front path, waving furiously, until he was no more than a dark dot. The thought of not lying on the floor next to him, lulled to sleep by the dulcet whistle of his gentle snore, the thought of not walking him to school, feeling his hand inside hers whenever they crossed a road, not preparing trays of beige, breaded food for him to douse in ketchup before getting lost in a noisy cartoon, the thought of not having to retrieve his little blue padded coat from the floor where he let it drop, the thought of missing all of it was almost more than she could bear. It was, of course, right that Kiki took the reins, right that Nora left her sister to figure out how to stay upright, to be mistress of her own home, her own life. Of course it was right, and yet on that afternoon before she hopped into the hire car for the last time and her sister came to rest in her arms in a long, lingering and reluctant goodbye, Nora felt like an axe had been placed in her chest, so acute was her loss.

'I'm going to miss you, Aunty Pickle.' Ted's bottom lip had wobbled.

'Now, I won't hear any talk like that. I shall collect you the weekend after next and I'm quite sure you can manage two weeks, can't you?'

This was what she and Kiki had settled on. A weekend or two a month where Ted would come to Westbury, run in the forest, play soldiers with Gordy, build fires and dens, and sleep in the big room with the sink, the one with his nameplate on the door. And on those weekends Kiki could rest, sleep, think, walk, enjoy time to herself or go out with the girls. Nora knew she was lucky to have this opportunity, this role in his life, but boy, how she missed him on all the days in between.

As she left, he had nodded unconvincingly, fat tears dripping from his chin.

'Good. Me too! See you in two weeks!' she had added brightly before putting the key in the ignition . . . *Paint on a happy face and soldier on, darling!*

Her garden, no matter only hers to borrow, took up much of her time, and with her nails full of dirt, mud on her boots and her planting progressing nicely, to spend time in it made her so happy. She also now volunteered at a sensory garden that had opened a short drive away. As a guide, she took children and young adults around the plants and flowers, letting them feel the puff-headed tickle of a blousy bloom against their cheek or to inhale the potent scent of lavender, rosemary and thyme. When a child placed their hand in hers, allowing her to show them the wonders of nature, she felt her heart lift at the gift she had of being able to connect with them; for yes, it was a gift.

'You're so good with the kids, a natural!' Penny, the head gardener, had commented.

'I am rather.' She'd smiled back, loving the confidence Ted had given her.

◆ ◆ ◆

Things between her and Gordy were good, steady with moments of pure joy. They revelled in their shared love of nature, of horticulture, hiking, good food, a well-mixed G&T. And their frequent sex was a revelation, often powerful, all-consuming and somehow more intense because of the surprise of it.

Today she had left Gordy and made her way into London, a treat and all the more exciting for it. How she loved to be trotting over the cobbles of the capital, to feel the echo of her youth and the days when she and Gordy were courting all around her.

'So, what's the deal with your trip to the big smoke, you've got new tenants moving into your flat?' Jasmine had asked, her voice clear as she called from Edinburgh where Benedict was newly posted. With a new openness, and after the false start of their time in Akrotiri, the two had built their friendship from the ground up, texting, calling, and meeting up when schedules allowed. True to her word, she and Gordy had bought Kiki out of her half of the flat and just as they had planned, Kiki now owned her home in Stroudly Green. Because that's what families did: supported each other, helped each other and provided shelter. Neither Kiki nor Ted had heard from Richie since the ink on the contract to sell had dried. His loss.

Nora jostled the phone against her ear. 'Yes, I'm furious. Well, actually that's not true. I'm furious because of the inconvenience, but delighted for Leah who has rented from us for a couple of years – a lovely girl. She's having a baby and she and her fiancé are moving. So yes, a big inconvenience for me, but so great that she's found love! It's the usual – she now wants a garden, more space, less traffic, so I can't really blame her. Anyway, he's American so they're relocating to where he's from in Kansas.'

'Should make moving easy, can't they just click their heels?'

'Yes. I'll let them know that.' She laughed. 'Save a fortune on the airfare.'

'So, what are you doing at the flat, giving it a good old clean? Can't you get someone to do that for you? I mean, come on you are the colonel's wife, no one expects you to shove on your Marigolds and grab a loo brush!' Jasmine sounded horrified by the idea. It made her laugh.

'Actually, I quite like shoving on my Marigolds. I like to give the place a once-over before anyone new moves in.'

'Well, if I wasn't in Scotland, I'd grab my bucket and sponge and come and give you a hand.'

Nora smiled, knowing her friend meant it. *Her friend* . . .

'Oh, bless you, but actually I really like being here alone.' She took her time phrasing things, not wanting to sound overly sentimental or gaga. 'It's more than just giving the place a good clean. I can't exactly visit when it's occupied and so I take the opportunity whenever I can to just come and stand in the kitchen, run my fingers over the walls of what was my parents' room and let my hand rest on the balustrade of the lovely old wooden staircase, knowing my dad's hand has rested here too.'

She heard her dad's voice as surely as if he was standing in front of her. '*Don't dawdle Leonoranoodle* . . .'

'It makes me feel a little closer to him, and I know that sounds nuts.' She gave a short burst of nervous laughter. 'We were never really close, but . . .'

316

Nora found it hard to explain how she had one or two memories of being at Clove Court when she was little, before La Fosca, a time when she was unaware of how neglectful they were, and was yet to wake up afraid and alone in that big old creaky bed at the end of the long, dark corridor . . .

'No, it doesn't sound nuts. It sounds sweet. How's Kiki getting on?'

How was Kiki getting on?

'As someone wise once said to me, it's scary, like walking a tightrope and you never really know when she might lose her balance. But she has many more good days than bad. She's training to be a teacher and loving that. I'm so proud of her. We laugh, Jasmine, laugh so hard at all the little things we remember and our shared love of Ted. It's lovely.'

'That's so great!'

'It really is.' She smiled with pride at all Kiki had put in place. 'She's going to be a great teacher and has a lot of support. I know that helps. Ted comes to stay with us often and I try to spend a couple of days a month in Stroudly Green with them when I can, just enough to keep a hand on the tiller, but without taking over entirely, and her friends are amazing. *Our* friends are amazing.' She smiled, knowing that some of her very best times were spent in that little flat, laughing with the girls over a glass of plonk. Mina ribbing Fi, Sheila crying as soon as the booze hit her system . . .

'And how is Ted?'

Nora felt her face break into a smile at the thought of him. 'He's eight – don't know where the time goes – and he's supersmart, loves football, and his artwork is incredible.'

'He sounds great.'

'Oh, he is! A very special little boy.'

She heard Jasmine chuckle.

'And I hear on the grapevine that you and Gordy have been posted, where are you off to?'

'Yep, all very sudden, but goodbye Wiltshire, hello Devon!'

'Devon, ooh lovely!'

'I hope so.' It was inevitable, only a short time in Westbury and she was once again packing up boxes and preparing to be marched out by a woman with a clipboard. Gordy was excited for his new post, and she had made enquiries and was waiting to hear about a job with a coastal project that tended the plants and trees along the walkways and clifftops. They were planning great things for the boy in Devon and Kiki had already called dibs on a little attic bedroom with a view. She had overheard Ted and Gordy plotting to buy a little boat. The thought made her smile.

And as for their marriage. Well, they had enrolled to take up line dancing in Barnstaple and with hats, boots and fringed shirts at the ready, they were all set. Nora was certain she'd be rubbish at it, but as long as they laughed and did it together, it would be fine. She was still a prickly pear, but had finally, as her fifties came knocking, learned how to love and be loved. The good times, the moments of glorious connection, eating bacon and eggs in the kitchen and great sex, were once again their glue. They liked nothing better than to sit in front of the fire with the Sunday papers, Gordy chortling as he read an article he found amusing, laughing, tittering, and reading out snippets to bring her up to speed so she could laugh too.

Nora knew what it felt like to be held closely and to feel safe, knew what it felt like to be held in such a way that the rest of the world seemed to disappear, as her face melted into happiness . . . Yes, she was still a prickly pear, but she was his and he was hers. And it was enough.

'Right, Jasmine, I'd better crack on, this flat isn't going to clean itself. Speak soon.'

'Yes, darling, speak soon! Benedict and I will await our invite to Devon! We'll pack our cowboy boots!'

'I'll look forward to it!' Laughing, she ended the call and looked around the vestibule that had been home to two generations of women before her. Women like her who were more celery than marshmallow.

Nora pulled the mail from the little cubby and balled it, junk mail all of it. Handfuls of taxi cards, pizza flyers and advertisements for everything from double-glazing to tarot readers went straight into the bin. It was as she rummaged in her bag for her key to the flat that a rather overstuffed corner of the pigeonhole rack caught her eye. Closing her bag, she walked along and pulled the wedge of mail from within its confines. None of it was interesting and some was postmarked some two years since: voting cards for one Yitzhak Josef and what looked to be an old padlock key. She twisted the junk and placed that too in the bin by the door, figuring that if it had lain untouched for this long, no one was going to claim it any time soon.

The cream envelope she yanked out of its hidey hole was bulky and a little dusty with dirty grey smudges on its once pristine surface. Spider poo littered it in tiny brown dots. She felt her nose wrinkle. Turning it over, however, the breath caught in her throat.

'What on earth? Magda Farraday!' she read aloud.

To read her gran's name, to see it in print on a letter had the oddest and most unexpected effect. She felt a rush of memories, could see her gran, tall and elegant, her waspish tone, sharp tongue, red, red lipstick, and her cigarette in a long holder that made her look like a starlet of yesteryear. 'Magda Farraday!' She shook her head. It was a strange sensation, knowing she was now the custodian of the flat and that only she and Kiki had a vague right to this mail. She glanced over her shoulder, as if expecting to see her gran standing there with her hand out saying, '*I believe that's for me!*

Nora climbed the stairs with excitement, not only keen to rip open the envelope and satisfy her curiosity, but also delighted to be in the flat where her only real memories of home lived. Sure, La Fosca had been a wonderful place to visit and some images of it were vivid, but this flat, before La Fosca, before Kiki, before she lost her parents for good, was where she had lived with her mummy and daddy.

It might have only been for a few years and her memories were patchy, but some were almost snapshots that lived in her mind with clarity: her father's hand on the banister for one, and her very own bedroom, the smaller of the two, where she would lie on a narrow bed with a pink counterpane and a walnut headboard, watching the headlights of cars motoring up and down the main road, throwing wide arcs of light across her ceiling that were at times things of wonder and yet also quite fearful. And she remembered the smell of something savoury cooking and could picture her mittened hand in her mother's as they counted up and down the stairs from their front door to the main door of the building. It wasn't much, but when the rest of your life had been shaped by the neglect and then the absence of your parents, it was actually everything. Nora was now able to revisit these memories and think about her upbringing without pain. She and Gordy enjoyed a full life and a glorious closeness that suggested an equally glorious future. The fact that her parents had been less than marvellous, well, there was very little she could do about it and to let it cloud the life she now loved seemed like a great shame, a waste. Plus, they might not have known how to care for her, but they had given her Kiki and she really was the most marvellous gift.

Turning the key in the lock, she stepped over the threshold. No matter that Leah had no doubt cooked many meals and lived in its confines for a couple of years, one step over the brass strip of the front door and Nora could smell her mother. Her particular scent that reminded her of black pepper. Of course, it wasn't possible that her mother's scent lingered in the hallway, but so strong was her recollection of such a thing that it filled her nostrils just the same.

Granny Magda's leather club lounge chair with creases and cracks along the arms still sat by the side of the fireplace. Nora sank into it and let her body settle in the spot where her gran, mother and a dozen or so tenants had done the same. She studied the stamp of the rather bulky envelope.

'España!' The plot thickened. To her surprise, there wasn't one but three letters that lay in her palm.

'To whom it may concern . . .' she read aloud. Her breathing growing deeper and her heart jumping at the mention of her gran, her nana and then finally the original letter from Santiago Agostí. These people all dead, long gone, made real by the names her eyes danced over and the images they conjured in her head. 'Oh!' Nora paused from her reading and took a moment, letting her pulse settle as she read and reread the paragraph which she knew would stay with her, live with her!

> . . . I have a large room in my house, a gallery if you will, and in it hangs a piece of his magnificent work. It is entitled, My Own Sweet Darlings. I came across it quite by chance among the artefacts and detritus of life that was left behind after the sad death of the Browns.
> . . . I wish to return the painting to Guy's daughters, Leonora and Kiki. It feels only right that it finds a home with them . . .

'Oh, my goodness!' she exclaimed aloud to no one who could answer, as tears fell down her cheeks and her gut bunched with all it tried to contain. It was a poignant reminder that no matter all the failings that lived sharply in her memory, he was still her father; the artist, Guy Brown. She pictured Ted's face when Richie buckled him into the fancy racing car – is that what he would remember of his childhood? The man scooping him up, taking him for a spin and treating him to a PlayStation? It was a reminder that we choose what and how to remember those we have loved and lost. It was also possible that Luna's husband in the town thought only of her as his beloved wife, the mother of his children, and yet she had seen the look on Luna's face when she had stood, slumped in the arms of the burro man . . .

And now Santiago Agostí, who had shown Nora such kindness when she was no more than six years old, was doing so again by returning to her and Kiki one of their father's paintings. He had told her that you never knew when something wonderful might happen and something wonderful *was* happening! Something wonderful that *he* was making happen! She held the bundle of correspondence to her chest and cried happy tears.

Nora sat for some time, an hour or more, and read and reread the letters; they were golden, the most extraordinary gift. She sipped tea, letting the honey-coloured brew calm her before scrabbling in her bag for her phone, desperate to tell the person she most wanted to share the news with, the person who would know more than any other exactly what it would mean.

'Gordy?' She held the phone close to her face.

'Hello darling, how's it going, you arrived safely?' he whispered almost, as if the call was illicit or she'd called at a bad time.

'Gordy—' Her voice broke away, as emotion overtook her.

'Nora, are you okay, where are you, do you need help? You're scaring me! Speak to me!' His tone was a little fraught, rare for this military man.

She laughed, an open-mouthed laugh of relief and pure, pure joy. 'I'm fine. Good, in fact. Better than I've felt in an age!'

'Well, that's good. Have you been drinking?'

This she found terribly funny, but understood the question as she did indeed feel a little heady. 'No, but I have two things to tell you.'

'Fire away!' He joined her in her moment of jollity.

'One of my father's paintings has turned up. And it's going to be returned to us, can you believe it?' She couldn't wait to tell Kiki.

'That's wonderful!' he enthused. 'Absolutely wonderful!' It was typical of Gordy: no asking how or questioning why, just an expression of unreserved support, and her heart flexed with love for the man. 'And what's the second thing, Nora?'

'The second thing?'

'Yes, you said there were two things.'

'The second thing is that I love you.'

'Well, thank you, I love you too.'

'I know, Gordy,' she interrupted. 'But I need to say it. I need to say this: you to me are perfect and golden; my steadfast thing, a rock in the fast-flowing river of my life. You pulled me ashore, Gordy, you held me tight. You make me feel safe. I'm looking forward to our next move, but I want us to have a permanent house, not an army quarter. Somewhere we can make memories. And it'll be home because you'll be there and you to me are glittery and shiny. And I love you. I love you.'

She could hear the banging of palms on wood, the shrieks and hollers of loud voices.

'I'm not crying!' he shouted out, slightly away from the phone. 'I have something in my eye, dammit!'

'Gordy? Gordy where are you?'

'It's my dine-out. I'm in the mess, a formal lunch before we ship off to Devon, and we were just getting to the speeches.'

'God!' She put her hand over her mouth and laughed, trying to picture him, the CO sitting at the head of the table, surrounded by regimental silverware, sparkling crystal and the room chock-full of soldiers, with tears streaming down his face. 'I'd better let you go.'

'Oh, what the hell!' he boomed. 'I love my wife!' he yelled and the roar of appreciation in the background only got louder. 'I bloody love my wife!'

MATEO'S LETTER

Maggie ran through the front door, keen to get out of the rain. She stood in the narrow hallway, shaking droplets from her hair and face.

'It's bucketing down! Look at me, I'm soaked!'

'What's for tea?' Robbie called from the chair in front of the TV.

'Oh hello, Mum, how was your day? Nice to see you home, would you like a cuppa as you've been rushing around without a break?' She spoke sarcastically.

He looked up and grinned. 'Hello, Mum, how was your day? Nice to see you home. And what's for tea?'

'Sausage and mash with onion gravy.'

She pulled off her boots and hung her damp coat on the hook by the door before heading to the kitchen. It caught her eye instantly, the cream envelope propped up by the toaster. Sitting down, she dried her hands on the tea towel that someone had lobbed on to the table and picked up the letter. The postmark was now familiar, 'Correa, España,' she read with excitement before carefully tearing the envelope and extracting one very crisp sheet of paper.

Dear Maggie,

My name is Mateo Agostí, and I know you com-
municated with my father, Santiago Agostí, via let-
ter. It is with sadness that I write to inform you that
he passed away a while ago now. I was today packing
up the painting by Guy Brown that he was so very
keen to return to his daughters, when it occurred to
me that if it wasn't for your reply, your encourage-
ment, this may not be happening at all. You are a
part of this story and maybe you have not given it
a second thought, but I thought you would like to
know that the painting is, at this very moment, mak-
ing its way to England and to Guy's children.

Thank you for your kindness to my father, your
words, and your involvement, it made all the differ-
ence to a man at the end of his life on a quest.

Sinceramente,

Mateo.

I am enclosing my telephone number – should
you want to call; +34 93 . . .

Maggie was ordinarily cautious – her sons teased her about
it – but in that moment, it felt like the most natural thing in the
world to grab her phone from her pocket and dial the number.
Her heart hammered at the prospect of talking to the family of the
man whom she had given so much *more* than a second of thought!
She had pondered in the dead of night whether Leonora and Kiki
got their picture and whether Senor Agostí had made it home . . .

It was only when it was quickly answered that she felt the
churn of nerves in her stomach and almost instantly regretted being
so rash. What on earth did she have to say to the son of Santiago
Agostí?

'*Hola?*'

'Oh gosh.' She swallowed. 'I don't, erm . . . I don't speak Spanish, but it's me. It's . . . it's Maggie.' She closed her eyes, sorely tempted to press the little red button, end the call and let him think it was dialled in error.

'Maggie!' Bizarrely, he sounded pleased to hear her and she laughed.

'Yes.'

'You called!'

'Apparently so.' She opened her eyes and sat up straight. 'I just wanted to say . . .' *What did she want to say?* 'I was sad to hear about your dad.'

'You got my letter?'

'Of course, that's how I got your number!'

It was his turn to laugh out loud. 'Oh yes!'

'How have you been? Losing a parent isn't easy.'

'It's not easy.' He sighed. 'No one has said that to me really, I think because I'm in my forties, a grown-up, I'm expected to keep going, to be fine . . .'

'Well, I'm about the same age and I'm often not fine.' She sat back in the chair.

'Because you lost someone?' he asked softly.

'Because I lost myself.' She shook her head, why was she telling a stranger this?

'Hold on, Maggie, I call you back.'

'Oh!' And just like that he was gone. She put the phone on the table, a little embarrassed by the whole short, bizarre exchange.

'What time's tea?' Robbie called out.

'Twenty minutes!' she yelled, the standard response. Eyeing the fridge, she tried to summon the energy to get cooking, when her phone rang. It was a FaceTime call from . . . *Oh shit!* Wishing she had put make-up on or at the very least brushed her damp hair, she answered the phone, staring into the screen.

And there he was. Her heart sang at the sight of him.

A striking man, handsome, with an aquiline nose and a feminine mouth, the collar of his open-necked white shirt sat crisply against a blue linen blazer. Tucking her hair behind her ears, she smiled. His attractiveness wiped out any earlier bullishness, leaving her feeling coy.

'There you are.' He stared at her.

'Here I am.' She smiled nervously.

'Tell me how you lost yourself,' he asked quietly and sincerely, making it easy to reply, as if they had been chatting for hours or forever.

'I just' – she looked up and took a breath, cursing the tears that threatened – 'I let life pass me by, I guess. One minute I was excited with everything ahead of me and the next . . .' She looked around the room where damp bloomed in the corner and two of the cupboard doors listed to the left, in need of replacing. 'I was running so fast just to stand still and now I'm knocking forty. It happened in a blink.'

He nodded. 'But that's the beautiful thing about life, it begins when we let it, when we take the chance, when we leap . . .'

'I guess so.'

'Don't cry, Maggie.'

'I hadn't realised I was!' Mortified, she wiped her cheeks with her fingertips.

He showed her a white linen handkerchief. 'I would give you this, but . . .'

He made her laugh again, and she grabbed a square of kitchen roll which would have to suffice.

'It's embroidered with the initials S&S.' He held it up to the screen.

'I can see that, it's beautiful.'

'Sofia and Santiago, my parents,' he explained. She liked the sound of his voice, his accent, his soft, kind manner. 'And before them my grandparents: Francisco and Fidella. And before them Esteban and Elvera. And before them Vicente and Valentina. It's become a tradition, if not an expectation. The joining of the same initials, the symmetry.'

'That's a nice thing.' She took in the opulence of the light fitting behind him and wondered at the marvel of living in a house like that.

Mateo drew breath. 'What was it you said in your letter to my papá?' He looked skyward and then back at her as if to remove his eyes from her face was unacceptable. He clicked his fingers. 'I've got it. You said, "*I know I have never been loved like that and I know I have never loved like that and even though it's so sad that your wife is no longer with you, how wonderful it is to have experienced such a thing.*"'

'I did say that.'

'It stayed with me. I thought it was so sad and so beautiful.'

'And the truth.' She held his eyeline.

'We should get some coffee, do you like coffee?'

'Yes, but I usually have tea at this time of day, if I have it too close to bedtime—'

'No, no!' He interrupted her. 'Not virtually, I will come to you, and we shall have coffee and maybe cake.'

'You'll come to me? How? I mean, great, but it's a long way away . . .'

'Not really. Papá once went all the way to New York to get my mother some cheesecake.'

'Jeez, it must have been bloody good cheesecake!' she laughed.

'I'll come soon, this week.'

Maggie felt her pulse race; was he *really* going to come and find her, take her for coffee?

'I'd like that.' She meant it.

'Mum! When's tea ready? I'm starving!'

'I'd better go, Mateo, I need to cook supper for my son.'

'You like to cook?'

'I do. Maybe I'll cook for you one day?' She held the phone close and studied the face of the man.

'I would like that very much. I'll see you soon.'

'I'll see you soon.' She put the phone down, feeling the giddy thrill of teenage joy that had been missing for the longest time. Surely he was not going to come all the way over to Yorkshire for a cup of coffee and a slice of cake?

Smiling, she reached into the fridge for the sausages and laughed, quite unsure what to make of the whole exchange, thinking how remarkable it would be if Santiago's quest to return Guy Brown's art might also be the thing that brought two lonely people together.

Mateo and Maggie . . . now wouldn't that be something?

CHAPTER TWELVE

It was a sunny day – Nora's favourite kind. One where the sky stretched clearly for miles ahead, and the breeze bathed whomsoever it touched in sunshine. Colours, which had been sharpened by the caressing hand of a kind summer, made the grass the very greenest and the sky most blue. It was a day where joy lifted the spirits of all who breathed the sweet air and tomorrow hung like a promise with all it might possibly bring.

She looked up and smiled at the light streaming in through the wide bow window, warming her face and flooding the desk with intricate shadow. High in the sky, an eagle circled, arching her magnificent wings as she rose higher and higher, seemingly to let the sun kiss her feathers as she rode the current, heading for the golden horizon that called to her. Nora watched her in all her glory and felt her heart swell at the privileged sight. Gordy was right, they really were the most majestic of birds.

Her view was captivating and distracting: sun danced on the sea and fishing boats bobbed on the waves as the salt-tinged air floated up from the harbour of their Ilfracombe home. Gordy's new post at Chivenor was to be his last, and this place, this place was where they had decided they would retire. The waterfront cottage with its listing floors, wonky walls and breathtaking view was their own. A place with a sun trap terraced rear garden with plenty of rooms for pots, which she planted and tended with joy.

The first thing she had done was paint a wall blue and fit fancy, luxurious lampshades from Carbon Velvet on to all the ceiling pendants and wall lights, just because she could. The new sofas were squishy and linen coloured, the wooden floors waxed and the pillows pale and cotton. The whole décor felt part seaside, part Nordic minimalist. And with everything done to her taste, without an army-issue item in sight, this was how she spent her days, sitting here in her study, looking out over the sea or working four days a week in her new role, where she walked the cliff paths with buckets of soil and her trusty secateurs.

It felt good to have such a feeling of purpose; the day stretching ahead, her fingers limber, her thoughts ordered, and a soft blanket of contentment thrown over her knees, as she lifted her pencil and began to sketch out her idea for the renovation of a garden overlooking Hele Bay. Her first proper commission.

'Can I get you anything?' Gordy popped his head around the study door.

'No, just getting started, but I'm happy.' The two held each other's gaze and she stared at her man, her love. 'I am, Gordy. I'm happy.'

Amber, their golden Labrador pup, barked and settled down on her soft dog bed by her feet.

'Me too, my love, me too.' He winked and quietly closed the door behind him.

Nora let out a long and satisfied breath as her fingers moved across the stiff white sheet of cartridge paper. Again, the study door opened, and Gordy popped his head in.

'Sorry to disturb you, darling, but a van has just pulled up – it's arrived!'

'Oh Gordy!' She put her hand over her mouth and closed her eyes. This was it. Abandoning her pencils, she raced down the stairs, with her husband and Amber following in hot pursuit.

The burly couriers hefted the wide box into the boatshed/workshop that sat alongside their home and removed the outer wooden frame before departing. Nora, egged on by her husband, set to immediately, using her sharp craft knife to remove the sheets of paper and bubble wrap in which it had travelled from Catalonia.

As agreed, she called Kiki on FaceTime.

'Are you in position?' she laughed.

'I am. I've got coffee and two jam tarts, all prepared!' Kiki smiled that megawatt smile that warmed her sister's heart. She looked good.

'I wish Ted was with you.'

'I know, but I could hardly keep him off school just so he could FaceTime his aunty!'

'I don't see why not. If Jason was still his teacher he'd have said yes.'

Kiki laughed. 'You're probably right, although Jason's a bit busy right now.'

'Of course, when's Sheila due?'

'Another ten weeks, but she's ready!' Kiki pulled up her shoulders in excitement. 'They've all moved into Jason's place and the last I heard were painting the nursery!'

Nora had found it hard to contain the flare of tears that took her by surprise when she found out Sheila and Jason were pregnant. It was a combination of the emotion at such a glorious event but also a visceral acceptance of the envy that bunched her womb: this would never be her and she knew in that moment that it would have been wonderful. To have a child like Ted reach for her hand, to know the pulse of another heartbeat inside her, to leave a legacy, just like Guy and Nessa, to see a little human running around that was part her and part Gordy.

'Hey Aunty Pickle! Hey Gordy!' Her nephew's sweet face loomed on to the screen.

'Ted! You *are* there! I'm so happy!'

'You don't think I'd let him miss it, please woman,' Kiki tutted and pulled a face. 'Less waffle, get on with it!'

'Hold this, Gordy.'

'Hey Kiki!' He took the phone and angled it to give her the best view. She waved. Her mouth full of jam tart.

Lifting the knife, Nora removed the last of the wrapping to reveal the picture that had hung on Santiago Agostí's wall for decades. She had never seen it before, and it took her breath away. The size of the work was impressive, but it was more than that. She took a step backwards and Gordy followed suit, then one more, and suddenly the lines, streaks and shadows formed a beautiful scene: two young children on the beach she knew well, their faces with an angled frailty to them. The older girl, with trousers unevenly rolled, holding a net and a jar as she waded barefoot in the rockpool. Nora recognised herself in her straw hat. Next to her, a toddler sat on the sand; it was chubby, gorgeous Kiki, her expression one of obvious delight as she watched her sister. She, too, was in a straw hat, tied with a ribbon under her chin. The sun warmed the composition, shading the sky with golden hues that suggested mid-morning.

'Is that us?' Kiki expressed what Nora was thinking.

'Yes.' Her voice came from a throat that was a little overwhelmed.

'That never happened, did it? The ages are wrong – I was only a tiny baby when they died.'

'It never happened,' Nora confirmed as her tears gathered at the back of her nose. 'But how wonderful that it happened in his mind and that he captured it, captured it for us.'

'Where's Mum, do you think?' Kiki leaned forward.

'I think . . .' she managed, 'I think she's just out of sight. She's sitting by his side as he paints and she's drinking wine and calling out to us to be careful as we paddle and fish, and shouting not to remove our bonnets, protecting us from the sun.'

'And we're all happy. And all together. A little family. There on the beach.' Kiki's voice faltered at the beauty of it.

Nora nodded, the thickening in her throat making speech impossible.

She recalled how her mother had told her that when her world fell apart, she had two choices: she either collapsed and sank into the ground, as if she were never really there at all, too broken to be, disintegrated, back to the earth. Or she could pick up all the little pieces and rebuild herself.

And she had. She had picked up every last piece and here she was. On FaceTime to her beloved sister, in her forever home with the man she loved, staring at the picture her daddy had painted.

My Own Sweet Darlings. The title.

'Yes, Kiki, that's it. All happy. And all together, a little family, there on the beach . . .'

ABOUT THE AUTHOR

Photo © 2012 Paul Smith
www.paulsmithphotography.info

Amanda Prowse is an international bestselling author of twenty-eight novels published in dozens of languages. Her chart-topping titles *What Have I Done?*, *Perfect Daughter*, *My Husband's Wife*, *The Coordinates of Loss*, *The Girl in the Corner* and *The Things I Know* have sold millions of copies around the world. Other novels by Amanda Prowse include *A Mother's Story*, which won the coveted Sainsbury's eBook of the Year Award. *Perfect Daughter* was selected as a World Book Night title in 2016, and *The Boy Between* (a memoir written with her son, Josiah Hartley) was selected in 2022. She has been described by the *Daily Mail* as 'the queen of family drama'.

Amanda is the most prolific writer of bestselling contemporary fiction in the UK today. Her titles consistently score the highest online review approval ratings across several genres.

A popular TV and radio personality, Amanda is a regular panellist on Channel 5's *Jeremy Vine* show, as well as featuring on numerous daytime ITV programmes. She also makes countless guest appearances on national and independent radio stations, including LBC and talkRADIO, where she is well known for her insightful observations and infectious humour.

Amanda's ambition is to create stories that keep people from turning off the bedside lamp at night, that ensure you walk every step with her great characters, and tales that fill your head so you can't possibly read another book until the memory fades . . .